Mary Shelley's
FRANKENSTEIN

INTRODUCTION TO MARY SHELLEY

In the introduction to the 1831 edition of *Franken-stein*, Mary Shelley presents herself as "the daughter of two persons of distinguished literary celebrity." She was also the lover and wife of one of the most prominent poets of the second generation of Romantics and the author of the most disturbing novel of the period. In her time, Mary Wollstonecraft Godwin Shelley was, and continues to be, a subject of enormous interest and fascination. Her life and literary career give insight into a period of radical transformations, many of them generated by the two major revolutions of the period: the Industrial Revolution (1780–1830) and the French Revolution (1789–93). Mary Shelley's turbulent life and prolific literary career reflect the hopes and disillusions of a complex time of transition. They also reflect the ambiguities inherent in any period—issues that fundamentally question the old order of things and, at the same time, envision revolutionary ways of inaugurating a new social, economic, and political order.

As her own words reveal, Mary Shelley's exquisite parental heritage played an important role in her life and literary career. The revolutionary works and radical ideas of her parents, and the contradictions between these ideas and their personal lives, significantly influenced Mary. *Frankenstein* is dedicated to her father, and many of the ideas in the novel engage in a very precise and often critical dialogue with Godwin's *Political Justice* (including his ideas on rationalism, happiness, technological progress, and moral evil). Between 1814 and 1816, Mary read almost all her mother's books, and *Frankenstein* also engages in a profound conversation with Wollstonecraft's *Vindication* of the Rights of Woman (on such issues as domestic affection, education, and the dynamics between rational and emotional). Grasping all the implications of Mary Shelley's novel is difficult without having a sense of her parents' social, political, and philosophical ideas.

Mary Shelley's Mother, Mary Wollstonecraft

A rebellious but sensitive child, Mary Wollstonecraft grew into a daring and independent young woman. At 21 years of age, she declared herself against marriage because she perceived it as nothing more than legalized slavery for women. After her mother's death, Mary Wollstonecraft left her home and worked as a governess.

With the help of Fanny Blood, a close and dear friend, Wollstonecraft set up a school for girls, and in 1786, she wrote her first book, *Thoughts on the Education of Daughters*, advocating for an educational system to free women intellectually and economically. At age 28, she went to London to become a writer. She wrote a largely autobiographical novel titled *Mary: A Fiction* (1788) and met the famous liberal publisher Joseph Johnson, who hired her as an editor and introduced her to London's radical intellectuals.

The French Revolution began when Wollstonecraft was 30, and its initial ideals of a new order based on justice, equality, and freedom, made her one of the most ardent supporters of the revolution. In 1790, she wrote *Vindication of the Rights of Men* in response to a conservative attack on the revolution's ideology. In the work, she argues for equality and

Mary Wollstonecraft.
© *Bettmann/CORBIS*

justice and for the supremacy of reason. Her second political tract, *Vindication of the Rights of Woman* (1792), is a passionate defense of the rights of women to equal education. The book expresses Mary's fundamental belief that all human beings ar e equal in their capacity to reason. She insists that female inferiority is simply a way for men to justify an abusiv ely secured position of superiority; b y perpetuating a female image of w eakness and fragility, they could exclude women from higher understanding. The book quickly became one of the most widely r ead texts of the day and established Wollstonecraft as the prominent feminist thinker of her time.

In 1792, Mary Wollstonecraft traveled to France, where she fell madly in lo ve with G ilbert I mlay, a handsome American businessman, and later, in 1794, she gave birth to an illegitimate child, a girl—F anny Imlay. Abandoned by her lover, she attempted suicide but was saved by him, and then she was sent to Scandinavia for business. In September 1795, she returned

to England, but finding Imlay living with an another woman, she again attempted suicide, this time jumping into the Thames River. Saved by boatmen, Wollstonecraft remained in a state of depression for several months. Her scandalous affair with Imlay, her out-of-wedlock birth to Fanny, and her suicide attempts all seriously damaged her reputation and her image in the popular press of the time.

In April 1796, Mary Wollstonecraft met the radical philosopher William Godwin. They soon became lovers, but being notoriously against the institution of marriage (Godwin often described the affair as one of "property—and the worst of pr operties."), lived separately for about a y ear. Only when M ary became pregnant with their child did they agree to become a family for the child's sake. Mary and William wed at St. Pancras church in March 1797. The new family then settled at 29, The Polygon, in Somers Town.

After Mary died giving birth to their daughter, Mary Wollstonecraft Godwin, in 1797, her husband published all her private love letters to Gilbert Imlay and to Henry Fuseli, an eccentric Swiss painter with whom she had a complicated affair in 1792. In the introduction, he writes that the collection of letters "may possibly be found to contain the finest example of the language of sentiment and passion ev er presented to the world." G odwin thought that he was paying tribute to her enormous literary talent. However, many readers disagreed; Robert Southey, another poet of the time, rightly obser ved that the collection "stripp[ed] his dead wife naked." Godwin's well-meant but irresponsible gesture amplified the already strong public per ception of M ary Wollstonecraft as a depraved woman and an inveterate atheist created by the scandal with Imlay and the two suicide attempts. Her reputation as a serious feminist writer, which was established by the publication of her *Vindication* in 1792, was significantly injured.

Shelley's

Frankenstein

Edited by Dr. Stephen C. Behrendt

George Holmes Distinguished Professor of English

University of Nebraska-Lincoln

Complete Text + Commentary + Glossary

Commentary by Anca Munteanu, Ph.D.

WILEY

Wiley Publishing, Inc.

About the Author
Anca Munteanu earned her Ph.D. from the University of Nebraska–Lincoln and teaches at Morningside College in Sioux City, Iowa. Her expertise is in nineteenth century British literature, with an emphasis on Romanticism.

Publisher's Acknowledgments
Editorial
Project Editor: Kathleen A. Dobie
Acquisitions Editor: Gregory W. Tubach
Copy Editor: Mary Fales
Illustrator: DD Dowden
Editorial Manager: Christine Meloy Beck
Special Help: Jennifer Young
Production
Wiley Indianapolis Composition Services'

CliffsComplete™ Shelley's *Frankenstein*
Published by:
Wiley Publishing, Inc.
111 River Street
Hoboken, NJ 07030
www.wiley.com

Somers Town.

Mary Shelley's Father, William Godwin

Educated to serve as a minister, William Godwin renounced the ministry and became the most influential political thinker of his time. His famous book, *Enquiry Concerning Political Justice* (1793), shocked England and won him the enthusiastic approval of nearly all radical intellectuals of the period.

The book's central argument is that if people were instructed to reject emotion and social sentiments and center their lives on reason, equality, and perfectibility, they would be able to govern themselves. As a result, institutional authorities—nations, organized religions, and customs—would be unnecessary, and any form of government would be superfluous. He maintained that education was a central factor in training men and women to be useful, happy, and virtuous, and in helping them to become independent and self-sufficient individuals.

Godwin hated monarchy but opposed revolution as well, regarding it as degrading and antirational. He

rejected certain values and dispositions, such as charity and guilt, but encouraged equality, justice and generosity. He also declared that individuals have no inviolable rights, that private property is evil, and that contractual arrangements (such as marriage) are harmful. Individuals should not be selfishly interested in their own benefit and pleasure, but in the general good of the community. He maintained that community— a community based on egalitarian principles, discernment, and equity—is the only source of authentic happiness and moral virtue.

True to his philosophical principles, Godwin owned no property; he supported his family largely on money gained from his published work and lived discreetly in the cheap suburb of Somers Town. He was often visited by many loyal disciples, including William Wordsworth, Robert Southey, Samuel Taylor Coleridge, and his future son-in-law, Percy Shelley, who claimed that he became "a wiser and better man" after reading Godwin's book.

After his wife's death, however, Godwin's popularity, impact, and visibility declined considerably. His exaggerated optimism in man's perfectibility exposed him to serious personal disappointments, and the publication of his unpopular wife's love letters damaged not only her reputation—for which he felt inconsolably guilty—but also his book sales and his o wn public image. With the exception of a few loyal friends, he lived in solitude and became increasingly conservative.

Four y ears after M ary Wollstonecraft's death, Godwin married Mary Jane Clairmont, but the marriage was somewhat turbulent, largely due to constant financial hardship. Following his new wife's advice to publish literature for children, Godwin opened the Juvenile Library in 1805, but despite the second Mrs. Godwin's keen practical sense, money was always insufficient for a large family of sev en. Godwin continued to publish no vels (some of them v ery well received), biographies, and political writings, but the family was never financially secure.

Mary Shelley's Early Years (1797–1812)

Mary Shelley was born on August 30, 1797, in Somers Town. Her mother died eleven days after Mary was born from complications of childbirth. Mary and her older half sister, Fanny Imlay, were raised by William Godwin, with the help of Louisa Jones, a governess intensely devoted to the family. The girls were educated by a French tutor. The first four years of Mary's life were, almost without exception, happy and serene ones. She adored Louisa J ones, whom she came to consider a surr ogate mother, and she dev eloped a strong attachment to her demanding but affectionate father. At the same time, she learned about her illustrious mother and took tr emendous pride in her heredity, something that helped her understand her father's unusually high expectations of her.

Godwin was obsessively interested in Mary's education—he kept meticulous records of her activities, readings, and general dev elopment—and adopted many of M ary Wollstonecraft's educational ideas for his young daughter's daily routine. He encouraged her

early passion for reading as a necessary condition for the development of imagination—a faculty that Godwin insisted must be cultivated as early as possible in a child. "Without imagination," he explained, "there can be no genuine ardour in any pursuit, or any acquisition, and without imagination there can be no genuine morality, no pr ofound feeling of other men 's sorrow." To excite Mary's imagination and to reveal to her the magical universe of literature, Godwin advised his daughter to read books that he consider ed essential for all childr en's early education. These books included *Mother Goose, Robinson Crusoe, Arabian Nights, and Aesop's Fables.*

In 1801, when Mary was four years old, Godwin dismissed Louisa Jones and married Mary Jane Clairmont, a widow and mother of two children. To Mary, who resented her stepmother from the very beginning,

Poet John Milton.
© Bettmann/CORBIS

the delightful days of her first years were clearly over. Godwin's new wife, though a relatively clever and well-educated woman, could not escape the haunting memory of her glamorous predecessor and regarded Mary as a constant reminder of her mother. Moreover, Mrs. Godwin had to contend with managing a chaotic, blended family—with sons and daughters from multiple relationships—in the midst of increasing financial problems.

These years were hard and confusing for Mary, who felt rejected, unloved, and neglected. Her stepmother's difficult character and open favoritism of her own children, combined with Mary's complex relationship with an eminent but complicated father, created a difficult environment for the young Mary. She learned early in life about disappointment, suffering, and loss. Unusually intelligent, highly perceptive, and amazingly well-read for her age, Mary started to write at a young age.

In 1808, at the age of ten, she published her first book, *Mounseer Nongtongpaw*, an expanded version of a popular comic song from Charles Dibdin's musical comedy, *The General Election*. Godwin, who proudly acknowledged his daughter's precocious talent, continued to encourage her love for literature by recommending that she read Latin and Greek classics and works by Shakespeare and Milton. He regarded these works as first-rate literary models, capable of refining, ennobling, and edifying the character of his favorite daughter.

And yet, these years (1806-1812) also coincided with Godwin's total engagement with the opening of a publishing firm and children's library. At the suggestion of his second wife, Godwin, in 1805, had created the Juvenile Library, an enterprise that completely absorbed him and greatly reduced the time he spent with Mary. At the same time, the family moved to London, and Mary lost not only her father's attention but also the familiar surroundings of the countryside, which reminded her of the blissful days of her early years.

Mary loved the intellectual energy disseminated by her father's fascinating friends, especially the insight

Mary Shelley.
© Bettmann/CORBIS

of Samuel Coleridge, whose famous lectures on Shakespeare and Milton she attended in 1811. She was endlessly captivated by discussions of her father's philosophical ideas. However, the long hours spent in the presence of her stepmother intensified an already tense relationship. To alleviate the conflict between his rebellious daughter and his wife, Godwin sent Mary to live in Dundee, Scotland, in June 1812. Mary stayed with the family of William Baxter, a wealthy manufacturer and fervent admirer of Godwin. The painful separation from a father, whom she adored, intensified the feeling of abandonment created at her mother's death.

Nonetheless, the time she spent in Scotland was relaxed and enjoyable, and the Baxter family was welcoming and extremely kind to Mary. In November, Mary returned to London accompanied by Baxter's youngest daughter, Isabel. She met the twenty-year-old anarchist and poet, Percy Bysshe Shelley, and his young bride, Harriet Westbrook. Shelley was a young admirer of Godwin's radical philosophy as w ell as Wollstonecraft's feminist ideas. After a short visit, the two girls returned to Dundee, where Mary remained for ten more months. During this time, she toured Scotland and discovered places of spectacular beauty, many of them later evoked in her novel, *Frankenstein*.

When Mary returned to England in 1814, Godwin was impressed with his beautiful sixteen-year-old daughter. Mary was growing into a distinguished and beautiful y oung woman, r esembling her eminent mother in many ways. In London, Mary found everybody passionately debating the political issues of the day: Napoleon's defeat; the restoration of the divine right of kings in France; the tensions between Princess Charlotte and her father, Prince Regent; and, especially, the end of two agonizing decades of war with France.

The war at home, ho wever, was not o ver. The conflict between Mary and her stepmother was still active, and M ary spent most of her time at her mother's grave in St. Pancras, fantasizing ambitiously about her future as a writer and dreaming about fame, love, and independence.

Family Life (1814–1822)

One day in early spring, Percy Shelley, now separated from his wife and their infant daughter, visited Godwin to discuss the disastrous financial situation of the Godwins' book business. Mary and Percy fell immediately and violently in love. During the long hours the lovers spent near M ary Wollstonecraft's tomb, Percy confessed to Mary that his marriage had been a disaster, "a heartless union" that deprived him of intellectual companionship, joy, and lo ve. On July 28, 1814, they eloped to the Continent, accompanied by Jane (later Clair e) Clairmont, M ary's stepsister . Mary was almost 17 years old and Percy not quite 22. They returned in less than two months, in September 1814, forced by serious financial troubles.

Meanwhile, Shelley's wife, Harriet, was pregnant with her second child, and Mary's father was furious: "I cannot conceive of an event of more accumulated horror," he wrote to a friend in August 1814. Within months, Mary gave birth prematurely to a baby girl, baptized Claire, who died less than two w eeks later. Life was difficult for the young couple; they had only a few friends nearby, and they were poverty-stricken and constantly pursued by creditors. Life was especially difficult for Mary. She had just lost her first child and was violently rejected by her father. And although Mary was a sincere advocate of free love, she was seriously concerned about her husband's interest in her stepsister, Jane.

In January 1815, Shelley's grandfather died, leaving Shelley a yearly allowance of 1,000 pounds, which permitted Mary and him to liv e comfortably for a while and gave him time to r ead, write, and study Greek. Pregnant again, M ary gave birth to her son William on January 24, 1816. During the summer, the Shelleys returned to the Continent, following Jane

Percy Bysshe Shelley.
© Bettmann/CORBIS

Clairmont, who was pregnant, and her new lover, the flamboyant Lord Byron, to Geneva.

Byron's reputation as a poet was huge in England. After the publication in 1812 of the first parts (Cantos I and II) of his poem *Childe Harold*, Byron became instantly famous. But his personal life was a scandal. He married a woman of exceptional intellectual abilities—an accomplished mathematician who, after the birth of their daughter, left him and made public his promiscuous relationships with other women, especially his incestuous relationship with his half sister Augusta Leigh. Cast out by the same society that had adored him, Byron exiled himself on the Continent. In the summer of 1816, he rented Villa Diodati on the shore of Lake Geneva in Switzerland.

In her introduction to *Frankenstein*, Mary Shelley recalls that the summer of 1816 was capricious with its beautiful days "and pleasant hours on the lake" as well as torrential rains and lightning storms, which "often confined [them] for days to the house." On one stormy night, the group—including the Shelleys, Jane, and John Polidori, Byron's physician and close friend—decided to read German ghost stories to entertain themselves. Out of a "playful desire of imitation," Byron suggested a literary contest: Each person would write a story involving supernatural elements, awe-inspiring instances, or terrifying events. Most of the other participants abandoned the idea, but the project continued to intrigue Mary, who found the intense literary and philosophical discussions that followed fascinating. These discussions, as well as the debates among Byron, Polidori, and Shelley, on current scientific theories and on "the nature of the principle of life" contributed substantially to the birth of what was to become the famous story of Frankenstein.

Unlike his wife, Shelley completely abandoned the idea of writing a ghost story. Inspired by the majestic landscape of the Alps, he instead worked on two of his most celebrated poems, "Mont Blanc: Lines Written in the Vale of Chamouni" and "Hymn to Intellectual Beauty."

Lord Byron.
©Bettmann/CORBIS

A series of tragic events accompanied the Shelleys' return to England. In October, Fanny Imlay, Mary's half sister, was found dead of an overdose of laudanum; in December, Harriet Shelley, Percy's estranged wife, pregnant with her third child, drowned herself in the Serpentine River in London's Hyde Park.

Eager to regain Godwin's acceptance, Mary and Percy were married within a month of Harriet's death, and on September 1, 1817, Mary gave birth to her third child, Clara Everina. In the same year, she published her travel notes from Europe under the title *History of a Six Weeks' Tour*. In 1818, after the publication of *Frankenstein* and after Shelley lost custody of his two children by Harriet, the Shelleys, accompanied by Claire and her daughter Allegra, moved near Pisa, Italy.

Percy Shelley never saw England again. Mary started work immediately on her next novel, *Valperga*,

Villa Diodati.

but Percy, exhausted by the long custody battle and insurmountable financial difficulties, found little comfort in the beautiful landscape of Italy.

The death of Mary's children—Clara in September 1818 in Venice and William in Rome the following summer—devastated Mary, though she was already severely depressed by her husband's periodic sexual escapades, negligence, and indifference. She wrote to a friend in Rome, "Everything on earth has lost its interest to me." During this sullen time, Mary wrote the dark short story, *Mathilda*. Narrating a father's incestuous love for his daughter, the story shows disturbing signs of Mary's disfigured soul. Although Mary gave birth on November 12, 1819, to Percy Florence, their only child who survived to adulthood, Mary and

Shelly's marriage suffered substantially. Percy's accentuated depression and failing health put added strain on their deteriorating relationship.

After Mary had finished *Valperga* in 1821, the family moved to the Casa Magni near Pisa, where Edward and Jane Williams, two new friends the Shelleys met the previous year, came for a short visit. Early in June, Mary suffered a near fatal miscarriage, and she was miraculously saved by Percy, who packed her in ice in order to stop the bleeding. Three weeks later, on July 8, 1822, Percy and Edward were drowned when their boat went down in a storm in the Bay of La Spezia. Mary Shelley was 25 years old. The two widows returned to London and lived together for the next five years.

Later Years (1823–1851)

Mary Shelley's last 28 years were dedicated to meticulously collecting and editing Shelley's work, to educating her only surviving child, and to working on her own writing. In 1839, Mary Shelley published four volumes of *The Poetical Works of Percy Bysshe Shelley*, as well as Shelley's *Essays* and *Letters*. After Shelley's death, she wrote four more novels—*The Last Man* (1826), *The Adventures of Perkin Warbeck* (1830), *Lodore* (1835), and *Falkner* (1837)—in addition to numerous stories, essays, and reviews. After 1840, she traveled with her son to Italy and Germany and later published her melancholy reflections and travel notes as *Rambles in Germany and Italy*. She never even considered a second marriage, and she lived alone in Harrow and London, surrounded by a small circle of friends. Her son graduated from Cambridge University. He inherited Field Place, his grandfather's estate in Sussex, and in June 1848, he married Jane St. John, an intelligent and affectionate widow whom Mary strongly liked. After a difficult winter and suffering from frequent nervous attacks and partial paralysis, Mary Shelley died at home on February 1, 1851. She was buried near her parents in St. Peter's churchyard.

INTRODUCTION TO *FRANKENSTEIN*

Mary Shelley began the story of *Frankenstein* in the summer of 1816, probably between June 10 and June 16. Originally intended as a short narrative of only "a few pages," Mary developed the story into a full-length novel at Percy Shelley's suggestion. Her expedition to Chamonix and the Mer de Glace at the end of July inspired her creation of the majestic scenery of the end of Chapter 9 and the beginning of Chapter 10. She worked regularly on her story until December 1816, when a number of personal tragedies interrupted her writing. She resumed writing early in 1817, and in April, she completed the first draft of the book. At the end of April, she gave a revised version to her husband, Percy, whose editing drastically altered the book's original style. On March 11, 1818, *Frankenstein; or, The Modern Prometheus* was published anonymously in three volumes and accompanied by a preface written by Percy Shelley.

Walter Scott, whose novels were a great popular success, wrote a fairly laudatory review praising the author's "uncommon powers of poetic imagination." He also observed that the "ideas are always clearly as well as forcibly expressed" and that "the descriptions of landscape have in them the choice of requisites of truth, freshness, precision, and beauty." Other reviews were a mixture of positive and negative comments, but whatever their criticisms, most reviewers recognized the book's unusual intensity and power.

Republished in 1831, the novel was heavily revised and incorporated Mary Shelley's own preface, the "Author's Introduction." The surviving sections of the original manuscript of *Frankenstein* are kept in the Abinger Shelley Collection in the Bodleian Library at Oxford University. If William Wordsworth was indeed right in his claim, "Enough if something from our hands have power / To live, and act, and serve the future hour," Mary Shelley's novel proved beyond any doubt that the life and work of this truly remarkable woman contributed essentially to the edification of future generations.

The Novel

Frankenstein is certainly Mary Shelley's greatest literary achievement and one of the most complex literary works of all times. The novel is also an important document of the period. It addresses the issues—including the nature of knowledge, the power of imagination, the function of the artist and of the artistic act, and the relationship with nature—that obsessed all the major Romantic writers. But more importantly, the novel articulates a vision that significantly contradicts the idealistic Romantic perspective on these issues. Unlike most Romantic writers, Mary Shelley seems interested in the dark, self-destructive side of human reality and the human soul. The 1831 edition of *Frankenstein*, the one that this book presents, articulates an even darker perspective and, consequently, a more powerful critique of the optimistic, uplifting Romantic ideology than the original, 1818 version.

Romantic artists invested imagination with an almost religious function and attributed poets, and artists in general, to not only a political role (Percy Shelley) as well as an educative role (Coleridge and Wordsworth) but also to a prophetic one. Mary Shelley responded to this glorification of imagination with some skepticism. In her novel, Victor Frankenstein's creation seriously questions the role of imagination in our lives and the consequences of divorcing imagination from all ethical implications. I f, as F rancesco Goya suggests in his disturbing painting, " The sleep of reason creates monsters," Mary Shelley may very well have used her pr otagonist and his cr eation to demonstrate that an imagination ungoverned by moral values creates not only monsters but also existential nightmares. M any R omantics believ ed in the supremacy of knowledge and revered the ability of the human mind to decipher the secrets of nature. Moreover, they celebrated any act of transgression (such as the violation of laws, the r ebellion against rules, and the rejection of established order) as an act of human excellence. This passion for the forbidden knowledge conjoined with a strong attachment for the sublime essentially translates into an obsessive fascination with power and with the idea of dominance in general. Mary Shelley not only declares these obsessions ignoble and destructive, but supports a philosophy based mainly on love, beauty, and humanistic values.

The Romantic faith in nature, as well as in man's blissful relationship with nature, represents another Romantic myth that Mary Shelley demystifies in her novel. In the final edition of *Frankenstein*, natur e ceases to be the benevolent, nurturing, gentle force that the poetr y of Wordsworth, Coleridge, and so many other Romantic artists invoked and celebrated. Instead, nature appears as a mighty machine acting blindly and capriciously in a universe emptied of love, beauty, and compassion. Victor is undoubtedly the victim of a selfish desire to transgress the limits of his condition and to obtain unlimited power and understanding, but he is also, if not mor e so, the victim of forces beyond his contr ol. Victor and most of the other characters of the novel live in a mechanistic and arbitrary world wher e ev erything is, as E lizabeth Lavenza recognizes, "regulated by the same immutable laws." To these laws, Justine advises Elizabeth as well as r eaders that individuals need "   to submit in patience."

Frankenstein is clearly a novel that not only repudiates or problematizes most of the doctrines established by Romantic ideology, but anticipates the grave existential questions about human natur e and human existence that characteriz e M odernism. Thus, the Monster's ambiguous nature is especially effective and conveys the disturbing message that each creature and each creative act possesses the potential for both good and evil. I magination, mind, and cr eativity—categories that formed the foundation of R omanticism's firm conviction in man's superiority and perfectibility and in human beings' ability to change themselves and the world—can all be associated with the M onster and, as a result, can all be distrusted.

Equally modern is the manner in which M ary Shelley positions her audience. S he does not allo w readers to remain passive, intellectually inert observers, but instead, she invites them to become active participants in the creation of meaning. In fact, readers are somehow coerced to actively engage with the situations, characters, and philosophical ideas of the novel because the familiar and r eliable narrator—who knows, explains, and decodes everything for the readers—is simply eliminated. The French critic Roland Barthes offers a useful distinction between traditional texts presenting a world that can be comprehended with a minimum or even no effort from the readers and modern texts testing the readers' interpretative abilities and encouraging them to cooperate with the writer in unveiling the complexity of the text and the world. The first category of traditional texts he calls "readerly texts," and the second category, the modern ones, he considers " writerly texts." M ary S helley's novel is obviously a text that constantly requires readers' participation, judgment, and insight. Therefore, *Frankenstein* constitutes a writerly text and, consequently, a modern one.

The novel's original narrative structure and use of different narrators and different points of view are all strikingly modern as well. Critics almost unanimously notice that the novel's structure is similar to a set of Chinese boxes, each of which fits into the next larger box. The frame of *Frankenstein*—the biggest box of all—is constituted by the letters that Captain Robert Walton, the explorer of the North Pole, sends to his sister, Mrs. Saville, in England. These letters (the epistolary box) open and close the novel. Within these letters, the reader, together with Walton's sister, reads the bizarre narrative of Victor Frankenstein and, within Victor's narrative, the narrative of the Monster. Interestingly, the narrative of the Monster consists of two different perspectives: Victor's account of the Monster and the Monster's direct confession to Walton. Consequently, what Mrs. Saville reads is Victor's doubly mediated story (first Victor's version and then Walton's account of Victor's story) and the Monster's triply mediated story (first Victor's version, next the Monster's direct account, and then Walton's narration of the Monster's story).

To complicate this situation even further, whether the letters Margaret receives are in fact the complete letters or simply large fragments of them is not clear. By the time Victor tells Walton his story, he is almost recovered from his illness. But Victor is still in a state of exhaustion: He speaks in "broken accents" and is "weakened" by the "paroxysm of grief that had seized" him. Furthermore, Walton is clearly biased and seems blinded by his enthusiasm, a rather strange combination of exhilaration, uncritical devotion, and agitation. "Will you smile at the enthusiasm I express concerning the divine wanderer?" he timidly asks his sister and, implicitly, the readers, but Walton surely knows that, by calling Victor divine and by insisting that Victor possesses a certain quality "that elevates him so immeasurably above any other person," a smile and a

certain type of distrust may indeed be the natural reactions to his strange attachment.

And yet, the one who essentially weakens any illusory trust in the narrator's reliability and forces readers to pay special attention to the novel's seductive but difficult-to-pinpoint story is Mary Shelley herself. Toward the end of her introduction to the 1831 version of the novel, Mary Shelley writes, "I have an affection for [my hideous progeny], for it was the offspring of happy days, when death and grief were but words," and in the final paragraph, she writes, "I have changed no portion of the story nor introduced any new ideas or circumstances . . . leaving the core and the substance untouched." However, the informed reader realizes that she does not tell the truth. The days she invokes may be declared the happy days of her life, but death and grief are, without question, not simply words, but almost permanent companions of her young and troubled existence. (See the "Introduction to Mary Shelley," earlier in this book.)

In the second version of the story, the novel was heavily revised in ways that fundamentally altered the "the core and the substance" of the book. The revisions added a note of profound pessimism, even desperation, regarding man's tragic condition. Mary Shelley knows now "the horror, the horror" of being a creature, but like Marlow in Conrad's novella, she decides not to tell the whole truth. *Frankenstein* is, in fact, compared to Conrad's *Heart of Darkness*, which, again, attests to its modernity. The book is also compared to Coleridge's *Rime of the Ancient Mariner*. These stories present disturbing events in which a direct participant relates the story to an audience. However, Mary Shelley is not simply a participant in a story; she is the creator of one. Her fertile imagination, conceived and expanded "upon so very hideous an idea," created a story that does indeed speak "to the mysterious fears of [human] nature" and makes readers "dread to look around, to curdle the blood, and quicken the beatings of the heart."

But what was initially intended to test the author's power of invention and confirm her as a gifted writer became a dangerous and terrifying experiment. She discovered that imagination was no longer a source of invention and freedom, or the "Sanity of True Genius" as Charles Lamb wrote in 1826, or "the poetry of life" as defined by her husband, Percy Shelley. But instead, imagination became a *monstrous* faculty, one that, like Pandora's box, could open secret doors into unknown territories of darkness. Instead of liberating or enchanting her, imagination "possessed" and "haunted" her. Too late to go back to the controllable and predictable reality, Mary Shelley had to write her "unlucky ghost story" and let what "terrified" her "terrify others." And as a result, the disturbing story of Mary Shelley's monster possesses and haunts everyone's lives, constantly and inescapably reminding everyone that the world is a beautiful but perilous place.

Today, Mary Shelley's novel remains profoundly relevant not only because of the previous reasons but also because it addresses issues of general interest in any time period—education and the importance of knowledge; alienation and loss of friendship or love; rejection and abandonment; and responsibility and ethical conduct. Contemporary audiences can immediately recognize that the questions raised by the novel are questions of tremendous importance for intellectual and emotional development as are the questions about identity, freedom, the nature of evil, love, knowledge, suffering, death, and faith. And the fact that Mary Shelley's novel has achieved such visibility and prominence in popular culture—because of its adaptations to stage, film, music, and television—testifies to its enduring ability to provoke and intrigue readers. Despite the novel's inconsistencies, obscurities, complicated syntax, difficult diction, and exotic references, it certainly constitutes one of the most powerful literary works of the English Romantic period.

The Summer of 1816

Mary Shelley spent the greater part of the summer of 1816 in Geneva, Switzerland, with her son William (born in January of the same year), Percy Shelley (her lover), and Claire Clairmont (her stepsister). It was her second visit to the Continent after her elopement with Shelley in 1814.

In 1816, Mary Shelley was still seriously depressed from the death of Clara, her first child, a year earlier. She was exhausted by her second pregnancy and from nurturing her second child, and she was deeply saddened by her father's inexorable decision to never see her again. The discipline of a strict and intense program of reading designed by Percy for both of them and, for a while, the daily study of Greek contributed significantly to the family's slow return to a quasi-normal life. Also, constantly encouraged by Shelley, who expected a lot from the daughter of two famous literary figures, Mary had produced a substantial amount of good writing based on her observations and reflections from their first trip. Her notes, together with some journal entries and a number of letters, were later published as a book titled *History of a Six Weeks' Tour*. This book reveals an intelligent and sensitive writer with an authentic talent for natural descriptions and with solid readings in the latest aesthetic theories of the time, including Burke's ideas on the beautiful and the sublime and Gilpin's speculations on the picturesque. Equally profitable for Mary's physical and emotional rehabilitation was Claire's decision to finally free the Shelleys from her presence. (Mary was constantly irritated by Claire's constant presence in their life and by Percy's declared attachment to her.) Her recovery was also aided by their move alone to a village near Lynmouth. Moreover, the financial tension that overwhelmed the family was considerably eased in 1815, when Shelley's grandfather died and left Shelly with a substantial annual allowance and the prospect of a more secure life.

At Claire's suggestion, the Shelleys came to Switzerland to meet her new lover, the famous poet and infamous outcast from British society, Lord Byron. That summer, Byron, accompanied by his personal physician, John Polidori, rented a beautiful mansion called Villa Diodati on the shore of Lake Geneva and relatively close to the Shelleys' residence, chalet Chappuis. Byron and Shelley liked each other immediately;

they became good friends, sailing often on the lake and spending almost all their evenings together at Byron's villa, a place that soon became the stage of some of the most fascinating literary and philosophical conversation that Mary ever witnessed. As Mary describes in her introduction to the novel, this particular summer

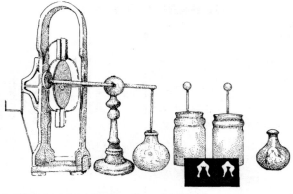
Luigi Galvani experimented with frogs' legs and electricity.

proved an unusually capricious one with the "incessant rain" that "often confined [them] for days to the house." One such rainy and stormy night, when they were reading from volumes of ghost stories, Byron challenged the entire group to create their own tales of horror. Mary was the only one who took Byron's provocation seriously and "busied" herself to come up with an idea for a story. Anxiously, she waited in vain several days for a spark to ignite her imagination, but the only response to her "invocations" was the greatest agony of authorship—"a dull Nothing." The following evenings, the group continued the discussions, and one of the long conversations between Byron and Shelley concerned galvanism, Darwin's experiments, "the nature of the principle of life," and whether creating life via electricity was possible. When Mary went to bed, she had a nightmare of a creature brought into existence by such means, and the creature terrified its creator and made him rush away "from his odious handywork." The next morning, Mary announced to everybody that she had found an idea for her story. She then wrote the famous words that open Chapter 5 of *Frankenstein*: "It was on a dreary day in November."

Context

Understanding the events of Mary Shelley's life as well as some of the philosophical, political, and aesthetic ideas that shaped and informed her literary creation is

indeed vital for decoding *Frankenstein's* complexity. This complexity explains the amazing abundance of interpretations generated by Mary Shelley's narrative, many of them as intriguing and as provocative as the novel itself. Some read the book as a metaphor of the writing/creative process and its ethical implications; for example, the novel questions whether artistic creations can be monstrous. Others read the story as an allegory of the reading act; interpretation centers on the function of the "excellent" Margaret Saville, the ideal reader whose act of reading makes the novel possible. Some discuss the novel as a version of the Promethean myth, and others consider the novel a variant of the Faustian myth. Some equate Victor's laboratory with an artificial womb, reading Mary Shelley's narrative as a critique of the attempt to deprive women of their power, as a "maker of children"; others read the novel as a warning against the usurpation of God. Some believe that the novel is a critique of a society based exclusively on reason (a model supported by Mary Shelley's parents and by her husband), whereas others argue that the story is a critique of the masculine model of knowledge. Some read it as an allegory of the colonial master-slave relationship; others, as an allegory of revolution. Some interpret the novel in connection with Edmund Burke's reflections on the nature of the sublime; others, in connection with the scientific theories of the time, especially the experiments with galvanic electricity. No matter what interpretation is placed on it, *Frankenstein* remains a powerful and provocative novel.

CHARACTER MAP

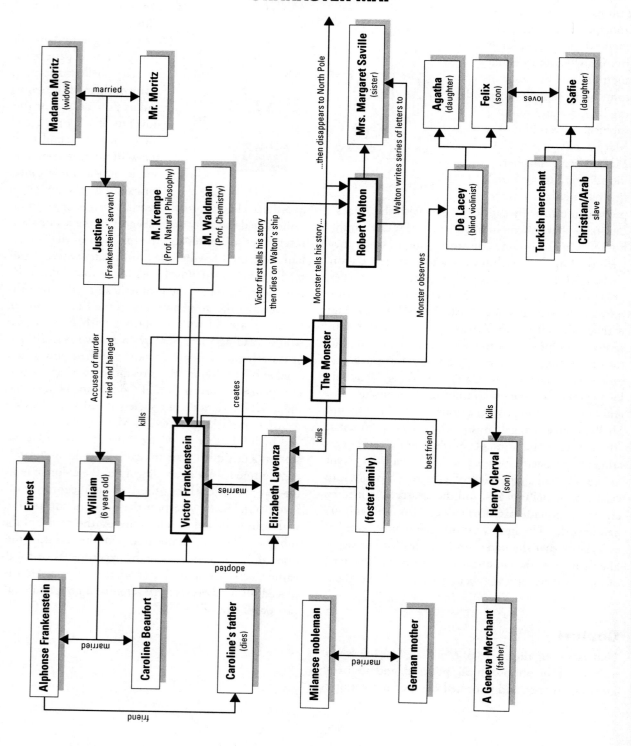

CLIFFSCOMPLETE

MARY SHELLEY'S FRANKENSTEIN

Letter 1

The first letter contains information regarding Walton's projected voyage to the North Pole. It also reflects on Walton's early years and on his passionate desire to become a famous navigator.

LETTER I

To Mrs. Saville, England

St. Petersburgh, Dec. 11th, 17—.

You will rejoice to hear that no disaster has accompanied the commencement of an enterprise which you have regarded with such evil forebodings. I arrived here yesterday, and my first task is to assure my dear sister of my welfare and increasing confidence in the success of my undertaking.

I am already far north of London, and as I walk in the streets of Petersburgh, I feel a cold northern breeze play upon my cheeks, which braces my nerves, and fills me with delight. Do you understand this feeling? This breeze, which has travelled from the regions towards which I am advancing, gives me a foretaste of those icy climes. Inspirited by this wind of promise, my day dreams become more fervent and vivid. I try in vain to be persuaded that the pole is the seat of frost and desolation; it ever presents itself to my imagination as the region of beauty and delight. There, Margaret, the sun is forever visible, its broad disk just skirting the horizon and diffusing a perpetual splendour. There—for with your leave, my sister, I will put some trust in preceding navigators—there snow and frost are banished; and, sailing over a calm sea, we may be wafted to a land surpassing in wonders and in beauty every region hitherto discovered on the habitable globe. Its productions and features may be without example, as the phenomena of the heavenly bodies undoubtedly are in those undiscovered solitudes. What may not be expected in a country of eternal light? I may there discover the wondrous power which attracts the needle; and may regulate a thousand celestial observations, that require only this voyage to render their seeming eccentricities consistent for ever. I shall satiate my ardent curiosity with the sight of a part of the world never before visited, and may tread a land never before imprinted by the foot of man. These are my enticements, and they are sufficient to conquer all fear of danger or death, and to induce me to commence this laborious voyage with the joy a child feels when he embarks in a little boat, with his holiday mates, on an expedition of discovery up his native river. But, supposing all these conjectures to be false, you cannot contest the inestimable benefit which I shall confer on all mankind to the last generation, by discovering a passage near the pole to those countries, to reach which at present so many months are requisite; or by ascertaining the secret of the magnet, which, if at all possible, can only be effected by an undertaking such as mine.

NOTES

St. Petersburgh: Russian city in the eastern end of the Gulf of Finland.

These reflections have dispelled the agitation with which I began my letter, and I feel my heart glow with an **enthusiasm** which elevates me to heaven; for nothing contributes so much to tranquillise the mind as a steady purpose,—a point on which the soul may fix its intellectual eye. This expedition has been the favourite dream of my early years. I have read with ardour the accounts of the various voyages which have been made in the prospect of arriving at the North Pacific Ocean through the seas which surround the pole. You may remember, that a history of all the voyages made for purposes of discovery composed the whole of our good Uncle Thomas's library. My education was neglected, yet I was passionately fond of reading. These volumes were my study day and night, and my familiarity with them increased that regret which I had felt, as a child, on learning that my father's dying injunction had forbidden my uncle to allow me to embark in a seafaring life.

These visions faded when I perused, for the first time, those poets whose effusions entranced my soul, and lifted it to heaven. I also became a poet, and for one year lived in a Paradise of my own creation; I imagined that I also might obtain a niche in the temple where the names of Homer and Shakespeare are consecrated. You are well acquainted with my failure, and how heavily I bore the disappointment. But just at that time I inherited the fortune of my cousin, and my thoughts were turned into the channel of their earlier bent.

Six years have passed since I resolved on my present undertaking. I can, even now, remember the hour from which I dedicated myself to this great enterprise. I commenced by inuring my body to hardship. I accompanied the whale-fishers on several expeditions to the **North Sea**; I voluntarily endured cold, famine, thirst, and want of sleep; I often worked harder than the common sailors during the day, and devoted my nights to the study of mathematics, the theory of medicine, and those branches of physical science from which a naval adventurer might derive the greatest practical advantage. Twice I actually hired myself as an under-mate in a Greenland whaler, and acquitted myself to admiration. I must own I felt a little proud, when my captain offered me the second dignity in the vessel and entreated me to remain with the greatest earnestness; so valuable did he consider my services.

And now, dear Margaret, do I not deserve to accomplish some great purpose? My life might have been passed in ease and luxury; but I preferred glory to every enticement that wealth placed in my path. Oh, that some encouraging voice would answer in the affirmative! My courage and my resolution is firm; but my hopes fluctuate, and my spirits are often depressed. I am about to proceed on a long and difficult voyage, the emergencies of which will demand all my fortitude: I am required not only to raise the spirits of others, but sometimes to sustain my own, when theirs are failing.

This is the most favourable period for travelling in Russia. They fly quickly over the snow in their sledges; the motion is pleasant, and, in my opinion, far more agreeable than that of an English stage-coach. The cold

enthusiasm: frenzy; literally means to be inspired by a divine force.

North Sea: body of water between England, Scandinavia, and Northern Europe.

is not excessive, if you are wrapped in furs,—a dress which I have already adopted; for there is a great difference between walking the deck and remaining seated motionless for hours, when no exercise prevents the blood from actually freezing in your veins. I have no ambition to lose my life on the **post-road** between St. Petersburgh and **Archangel**.

I shall depart for the latter town in a fortnight or three weeks; and my intention is to hire a ship there, which can easily be done by paying the insurance for the owner, and to engage as many sailors as I think necessary among those who are accustomed to the whale-fishing. I do not intend to sail until the month of June; and when shall I return? Ah, dear sister, how can I answer this question? If I succeed, many, many months, perhaps years, will pass before you and I may meet. If I fail, you will see me again soon, or never.

Farewell, my dear, excellent Margaret. Heaven shower down blessings on you, and save me, that I may again and again testify my gratitude for all your love and kindness.

Your affectionate brother,
R. Walton

post-road: a road on which mail was carried.

Archangel: A port on the White Sea coast in Northern Russia.

COMMENTARY

The story of Frankenstein is narrated in a series of four letters written by Robert Walton, a twenty-eight-year-old British explorer, to his sister, Margaret Saville, in England. Following a long-held dream to become a distinguished navigator, Walton has left and his sister as well as despite her declared anxiety about the enterprise and her presentiments of danger. The first letter is written in December, when Walton arrives in St. Petersburg, Russia, to embark on an expedition to the North Pole.

Robert Walton's Relationship with his Sister

The first sentence of the letter highlights the tension between Walton and his sister. Walton's ironic tone clearly emphasizes his "increasing confidence" in the success of the expedition and, at the same time, arrogantly minimizes Margaret's justified fears.

Walton not only mildly ridicules his sister's fears, but he also questions her ability to understand the importance of his dream and the elevated feeling such a dream generates. Walton is already convinced that his sister cannot possibly comprehend the intensity and depth of his emotions. Isolated in a region of absolute purity that only men can hope to reach, Walton is not only far north of London, he is even farther from everything that normal family life and family relationships represent. Written by

a man who has lost any real connection with the world, this letter chronicles nothing else but the beginning and the evolution of an obsession.

Robert Walton

Robert is a young and passionate scientist whose entire life focuses on one dream—to navigate through the seas surrounding the North Pole to the North Pacific Ocean. He wants to satisfy his obsessive "curiosity" by discovering "a part of the world never before visited" and by stepping on a land "never before imprinted by the foot of man." Despite the people who try to convince Walton that the pole is nothing more than a cold, barren place, he continues to believe that the region is beautiful and delightful. But more importantly, the pole represents for Walton the promise for great discoveries in the field of magnetism and astrology and the possibility of finding a terrestrial paradise in the very heart of the North Pole. Walton passionately maintains that these advantages are worth any sacrifice, even death, because the whole of humankind will benefit.

In his youth, Walton's imagination was excited by the fascinating accounts of famous voyages that he read in his uncle's library. Reading the books collected by Uncle Thomas was, in fact, the only instruction he ever received, and his knowledge comes almost exclusively from his endless passion for reading those inspiring volumes. Mary Shelley may be reflecting on her own educational experiences. Like Walton, whose surrogate father (his uncle) didn't offer him a conventional education, Mary Shelley was deprived of a formal education at the suggestion of Mrs. Clairmont (her surrogate mother).

The young Walton's passion for discovery somewhat paled when, for the first time, he was captivated by poets. The dream to gain access into the paradise of science was briefly replaced by the longing for the paradise of poetry, for a "niche in the temple where the names of Homer and Shakespeare are consecrated." Unfortunately, he had to accept that his passion for reading poetry did not translate into the ability to produce poetry. Failing as a poet, Walton returned to his initial and never entirely forgotten passion. A timely inheritance provided him with the means necessary to finance his expedition, and after six years of harsh training, intense study, and several apprenticeships, he was ready to transform his dream into reality. Now, Walton informs his sister that in two or three weeks he plans to leave for Archangel, hire a ship and crew, and in June, begin his greatest adventure.

Themes

The smoldering conflict between Walton and Margaret constitutes one of the novel's major themes: the difficult, tensioned relationship between men and women. These two spheres, the masculine sphere and the feminine one, remain completely separated throughout the novel. Although Margaret never speaks, readers sense the serious disagreement between Walton and his sister. She intuitively knows that the North Pole is not a terrestrial paradise, and that Walton's ambitious expedition is based on a distorted sense of reality. Yet Walton not only ignores but ridicules Margaret's feminine perspective, and he relies exclusively on men—the navigators. Moreover, the first important image of the book, a young man isolated in the sterile world of the North Pole, anticipates Victor Frankenstein's essential incompatibility with women. It also mirrors the disagreements between Mary

Shelley and her husband. In a letter dated June 1822, Percy Shelley writes, "I only feel the want of those who can feel, and understand me . . . Mary does not." Percy's sentiment sounds suspiciously similar to Walton's rhetorical question to his sister: "Do you understand this feeling?"

Despite its emotional tone and delicate language, the letter introduces an aggressively masculine perspective, one that overlooks and silences the feminine perspective. Margaret remains quiet; she reads the letters but never answers them. By positing Walton as a scientist who, on the one hand, wants to conquer nature and, on the other, wants to silence Margaret, Mary Shelley exposes the dangers inherent in the masculine paradigm of existence. Instead of absorbing and trusting Margaret's intuitive qualities, an inflexible Walton indulges in a tenacious and rigid pursuit of a goal. Again, Walton anticipates Victor Frankenstein, whose intellectual eye remains firmly attached to an obsessive purpose.

Note that Walton's dreams have recurrent themes: prominence and fame; conquering and dominating nature; an almost unbalanced, insane dedication to an idea; and an unhealthy, selfish separation from the world. These obsessive dreams forecast the most frightful dream of all—Victor Frankenstein's fixation to create life.

Mary Shelley's pessimistic beliefs in a mechanical universe and in a blindly determined destiny for human beings play an essential role in the way she constructs Walton and Victor Frankenstein as characters. Walton and Frankenstein are fascinated with greatness and with forbidden knowledge, and they want to transgress the limits of their human condition. Thus, the nature of knowledge and the moral implications of acquiring knowledge constitute two other major themes of the novel. Related to these two themes is the theme of the scientist who manipulates the forces of nature to acquire power over it. Critics observe that Mary Shelley makes a clear distinction between scientists whose goal is understanding nature and scientists whose goal is to control and dominate it.

Letters 2–3

The second letter expresses Walton's sorrow at not having a friend to share in his success, to comfort him in moments of sadness, and to help him overcome the deficiencies of an inadequate and incomplete education. Despite his frustration, however, Walton remains determined to continue his voyage exploring the mysterious ocean.
In the third letter, Walton informs his sister that, although the ship advances slowly, they have already reached a high latitude. He is absolutely convinced that he must finish the journey.

LETTER II

To Mrs. Saville, England

Archangel, 28th March, 17—.

How slowly the time passes here, encompassed as I am by frost and snow! yet a second step is taken towards my enterprise. I have hired a vessel, and am occupied in collecting my sailors; those whom I have already engaged appear to be men on whom I can depend, and are certainly possessed of dauntless courage.

But I have one want which I have never yet been able to satisfy; and the absence of the object of which I now feel as a most severe evil. I have no friend, Margaret: when I am glowing with the enthusiasm of success, there will be none to participate my joy; if I am assailed by disappointment, no one will endeavour to sustain me in dejection. I shall commit my thoughts to paper, it is true; but that is a poor medium for the communication of feeling. I desire the company of a man who could **sympathise** with me; whose eyes would reply to mine. You may deem me romantic, my dear sister, but I bitterly feel the want of a friend. I have no one near me, gentle yet courageous, possessed of a cultivated as well as of a capacious mind, whose tastes are like my own, to approve or amend my plans. How would such a friend repair the faults of your poor brother! I am too ardent in execution, and too impatient of difficulties. But it is a still greater evil to me that I am self-educated: for the first fourteen years of my life I ran wild on a common, and read nothing but our Uncle Thomas's books of voyages. At that age I became acquainted with the celebrated poets of our own country; but it was only when it had ceased to be in my power to derive its most important benefits from such a conviction, that I perceived the necessity of becoming acquainted with more languages than that of my native country. Now I am twenty-eight, and am in reality more illiterate than many schoolboys of fifteen. It is true that I have thought more, and that my day dreams are more extended and magnificent; but they want (as the painters call it) *keeping*; and I greatly need a friend who would have sense enough not to despise me as romantic, and affection enough for me to endeavour to regulate my mind.

Well, these are useless complaints; I shall certainly find no friend on the wide ocean, nor even here in Archangel, among merchants and seamen.

NOTES

sympathise: an important word in the vocabulary and literature of Romanticism. In the late eighteenth and early nineteenth centuries, sympathy and sensibility were regarded as marks of true virtue, and men and women capable of identifying with other people and their emotions were considered models of moral excellence. For a long time, this type of character was the popular hero of novels and plays.

keeping: perspective.

Yet some feelings, unallied to the dross of human nature, beat even in these rugged bosoms. My lieutenant, for instance, is a man of wonderful courage and enterprise; he is madly desirous of glory: or rather, to word my phrase more characteristically, of advancement in his profession. He is an Englishman, and in the midst of national and professional prejudices, unsoftened by cultivation, retains some of the noblest endowments of humanity. I first became acquainted with him on board a whale vessel: finding that he was unemployed in this city, I easily engaged him to assist in my enterprise.

The master is a person of an excellent disposition and is remarkable in the ship for his gentleness and the mildness of his discipline. This circumstance, added to his well-known integrity and dauntless courage, made me very desirous to engage him. A youth passed in solitude, my best years spent under your gentle and feminine fosterage, has so refined the groundwork of my character, that I cannot overcome an intense distaste to the usual brutality exercised on board ship: I have never believed it to be necessary; and when I heard of a mariner equally noted for his kindliness of heart, and the respect and obedience paid to him by his crew, I felt myself peculiarly fortunate in being able to secure his services. I heard of him first in rather a romantic manner, from a lady who owes to him the happiness of her life. This, briefly, is his story. Some years ago, he loved a young Russian lady, of moderate fortune, and having amassed a considerable sum in prize-money, the father of the girl consented to the match. He saw his mistress once before the destined ceremony; but she was bathed in tears, and throwing herself at his feet, entreated him to spare her, confessing at the same time that she loved another, but that he was poor, and that her father would never consent to the union. My generous friend reassured the suppliant, and on being informed of the name of her lover, instantly abandoned his pursuit. He had already bought a farm with his money, on which he had designed to pass the remainder of his life; but he bestowed the whole on his rival, together with the remains of his prize-money to purchase **stock**, and then himself solicited the young woman's father to consent to her marriage with her lover. But the old man decidedly refused, thinking himself bound in honour to my friend, who, when he found the father inexorable, quitted his country, nor returned until he heard that his former mistress was married according to her inclinations. "What a noble fellow!" you will exclaim. He is so; but then he is wholly uneducated: he is as silent as a Turk, and a kind of ignorant carelessness attends him, which, while it renders his conduct the more astonishing, detracts from the interest and sympathy which otherwise he would command.

stock: livestock.

Yet do not suppose, because I complain a little, or because I can conceive a consolation for my toils which I may never know, that I am wavering in my resolutions. Those are as fixed as fate; and my voyage is only now delayed until the weather shall permit my embarkation. The winter has been dreadfully severe; but the spring promises well, and it is considered as a remarkably early season; so that perhaps I may sail sooner than I expected. I shall do nothing rashly: you know me sufficiently to confide in my prudence and considerateness, whenever the safety of others is committed to my care.

I cannot describe to you my sensations on the near prospect of my undertaking. It is impossible to communicate to you a conception of the trembling sensation, half pleasurable and half fearful, with which I am preparing to depart. I am going to unexplored regions, to "**the land of mist and snow**;" but I shall kill no albatross, therefore do not be alarmed for my safety, or if I should come back to you as worn and woeful as the "Ancient Mariner?" You will smile at my allusion; but I will disclose a secret. I have often attributed my attachment to, my passionate enthusiasm for, the dangerous mysteries of ocean, to that production of the most imaginative of modern poets. There is something at work in my soul, which I do not understand. I am practically industrious—painstaking;— a workman to execute with perseverance and labour:—but besides this, there is a love for the marvellous, a belief in the marvellous, intertwined in all my projects, which hurries me out of the common pathways of men, even to the wild sea and unvisited regions I am about to explore.

But to return to dearer considerations. Shall I meet you again, after having traversed immense seas, and returned by the most southern cape of Africa or America? I dare not expect such success, yet I cannot bear to look on the reverse of the picture. Continue for the present to write to me by every opportunity: I may receive your letters on some occasions when I need them most to support my spirits. I love you very tenderly. Remember me with affection, should you never hear from me again.

Your affectionate brother,

Robert Walton

LETTER III

To Mrs. Saville, England

July 7th, 17—.

My dear Sister,

I write a few lines in haste to say that I am safe, and well advanced on my voyage. This letter will reach England by a merchantman now on its homeward voyage from Archangel; more fortunate than I, who may not see my native land, perhaps, for many years. I am, however, in good spirits; my men are bold, and apparently firm of purpose; nor do the floating sheets of ice that continually pass us, indicating the dangers of the region towards which we are advancing, appear to dismay them. We have already reached a very high latitude; but it is the height of summer, and although not so warm as in England, the southern gales, which blow us speedily towards those shores which I so ardently desire to attain, breathe a degree of renovating warmth which I had not expected.

the land of mist and snow: a line from Coleridge's haunting poem, "The Rime of the Ancient Mariner," first published in 1798 in the *Lyrical Ballads.* The Mariner, on a voyage in the south polar seas, kills an *albatross,* a bird sailors consider a sign of good fortune. The dead albatross is hung on the Mariner's neck, and its death brings a terrible curse upon his ship. The curse vanishes when the Mariner blesses the beauty of strange sea creatures and realizes that he must respect all creatures, large and small.

No incidents have hitherto befallen us that would **make a figure** in a letter. One or two stiff gales, and the springing of a leak, are accidents which experienced navigators scarcely remember to record; and I shall be well content if nothing worse happen to us during our voyage.

make a figure: be significant.

Adieu, my dear Margaret. Be assured that for my own sake, as well as yours, I will not rashly encounter danger. I will be cool, persevering, and prudent.

But success *shall* crown my endeavours. Wherefore not? Thus far I have gone, tracing a secure way over the pathless seas: the very stars themselves being witnesses and testimonies of my triumph. Why not still proceed over the untamed yet obedient element? What can stop the determined heart and resolved will of man?

My swelling heart involuntarily pours itself out thus. But I must finish. Heaven bless my beloved sister!

R.W.

COMMENTARY

Written four months after the first letter, the second letter informs Margaret that a vessel has been hired and that Walton is now preoccupied with hiring sailors. Considering Walton's conceptions exposed in his first letter, one should not be surprised to read that the sailors he employs for the voyage are "certainly possessed of dauntless courage." The word "possessed" is especially significant in connection with "certainly," which makes the impression even more inescapable. These sailors are all men who love isolation and who probably share with Walton a passion for "undiscovered solitudes." Like Walton, they are indisputably animated by the spirit of adventure and by a desire to conquer and control nature. "Possessed" by courage or "madly desirous of glory" like the English lieutenant, these men understand Walton and his obsession, and consequently, they can completely depend on him.

Education and Friendship

Mary Shelley's emphasis on education, and on the suffering produced by the absence of education, is reintroduced in the second letter alongside the theme of male friendship. Knowing how imperfect his education is, Walton longs for a well-educated friend who can correct and guide him when his own knowledge proves insufficient. He also looks for a companion with whom he can share moments of achievement and joy and in whom he can find comfort and encouragement in times of depression.

Clearly, this friend must be a man. Margaret is a patient and engaged listener, and Walton will continue to relate his thoughts through letters, but such a friend (a woman) cannot satisfy Walton, and such a medium (letters) remains simply inadequate.

Some critics identify homosexual overtones in Walton's extended discussion regarding the advantages of having a male friend present on the ship. These overtones become even clearer in Walton's comments prefacing the story of the Russian sailor. Moreover, trying to explain his profound contempt for ruthless behavior on the ship, he parenthetically mentions his early years: They were "passed in solitude" or under his sister's "gentle and feminine fosterage" that "so refined the groundwork of my character." Undoubtedly, an effeminate Walton emerges.

But his description of an ideal male friend also has narcissistic overtones: Walton asserts that the friendship of a man, in whose image he can recognize himself, is simply a better friendship. Walton suggests that only a man can completely understand another man and can appropriately communicate with him; he specifically asks for a man who can sympathize with him and in whose eyes he can find an honest response to his own questions. This man should be generous, compassionate, extremely cultivated, and knowledgeable. Walton imagines that, along with the gaps in his education, such a friend will "repair" other faults too—his inability to control himself under pressure or difficult situations and, especially, to control his impatience. The end of his letter demonstrates that he knows how to be prudent and considerate when others are involved, but in his own affairs, he is too impetuous or too anxious.

At 28 years old, Walton considers himself illiterate, but he sees value in his ability to reflect on his own life and in his imaginative powers. However, his reflections and his dreams lack perspective, depth, and discipline. Like Percy Shelley who looked to William Godwin (Mary Shelley's father) for a man to temper his passions, Walton wants a friend to "regulate" his mind.

The Russian's Story

Walton tells Margaret the story of his master, a person who is gentle, tolerant, and of great integrity. He shares with the rest of the crew the same fearlessness, but compared to most of them, he is a "romantic character." His story comes straight out of chivalry. Years before, the Russian loved a young lady of modest fortune whose father consented to the marriage due to the Russian's wealth. Shortly before the marriage ceremony, however, the tearful young woman confessed her love for another man, whom she could not marry due to his poverty. The noble Russian not only abandoned his pursuit immediately, but, he offered almost all his possessions to the lady's lover. He left the country and returned only after the lady's father allowed her to marry according to her desire.

The Russian's story is another frame story, which Walton knows, not directly from the sailor himself, but indirectly from "a lady who owes to him the happiness of her life." Mary Shelley may have wanted to mark the difference between a potential friend (the Russian) and a real one (Victor) and the difference between direct and mediated contact. Although he is noble, generous, and honorable, the Russian cannot be Walton's friend, because he is uneducated and uncommunicative. The story also serves two other purposes: It reemphasizes how much Walton values and admires nobility, generosity, and honor, and it makes the differences between the sexes even more obvious.

Walton closes the letter by informing Margaret that, despite all his frustrations, he is more determined than ever to continue his voyage. But he asks her not to worry, because he will not kill the albatross. The albatross is a direct reference to Coleridge and his famous Ancient Mariner, the eternal wanderer who is rejected by society for killing an innocent creature. Walton clearly knows that, like the Mariner's journey, his voyage is an unusual one on which strange things may happen. However, he cannot stop, because he is compelled by a force that he cannot understand, he hopes not to repeat the Mariner's mistake and kill an innocent being. In other words, he hopes he will not disturb the order and beauty of the universe.

But his first two letters—especially the second one—are Coleridgean in a different sense. Walton's plan is evidently utopian, and he seems fully aware of the contradiction of his dream: to search for a warm and luxuriant place in the heart of the Arctic world.

Critics suggest that this paradoxical desire explains why Walton emphatically invokes Coleridge. Indeed, Coleridge often discussed the synthesis between opposing elements—for example, cold and hot, emotion and intellect, and spirit and matter. In his famous poem, "Kubla Khan" (alternatively titled "A Vision in a Dream"), the dome of pleasure is indeed a miracle: "A sunny pleasure-dome with caves of ice." However, unlike Coleridge, Walton struggles with separating his dreams from reality.

Letter 4

This letter narrates a strange occurrence from the previous week. While the ship was held fast in the polar ice, Walton and some of the sailors observed a dog-driven sledge with an unusually huge driver. In the morning, a big fragment of ice carried to the ship another sledge and a nearly frozen man. Slowly, the stranger's health improves, and he tells Walton his incredible story.

LETTER IV

To Mrs. Saville, England

August 5th, 17—.

So strange an accident has happened to us, that I cannot forbear recording it, although it is very probable that you will see me before these papers can come into your possession.

Last Monday (July 31st), we were nearly surrounded by ice, which closed in the ship on all sides, scarcely leaving her the sea-room in which she floated. Our situation was somewhat dangerous, especially as we were compassed round by a very thick fog. We accordingly lay to, hoping that some change would take place in the atmosphere and weather.

About two o'clock the mist cleared away, and we beheld, stretched out in every direction, vast and irregular plains of ice, which seemed to have no end. Some of my comrades groaned, and my own mind began to grow watchful with anxious thoughts, when a strange sight suddenly attracted our attention, and diverted our solicitude from our own situation. We perceived a low carriage, fixed on a sledge and drawn by dogs, pass on towards the north, at the distance of half a mile: a being which had the shape of a man, but apparently of gigantic stature, sat in the sledge, and guided the dogs. We watched the rapid progress of the traveller with our **telescopes**, until he was lost among the distant inequalities of the ice.

This appearance excited our unqualified wonder. We were, as we believed, many hundred miles from any land; but this apparition seemed to denote that it was not, in reality, so distant as we had supposed. Shut in, however, by ice, it was impossible to follow his track, which we had observed with the greatest attention.

About two hours after this occurrence, we heard the **ground sea**; and before night the ice broke, and freed our ship. We, however, lay to until the morning, fearing to encounter in the dark those large loose masses which float about after the breaking up of the ice. I profited of this time to rest for a few hours.

In the morning, however, as soon as it was light, I went upon deck, and found all the sailors busy on one side of the vessel, apparently talking to some one in the sea. It was, in fact, a sledge, like that we had seen before, which had drifted towards us in the night, on a large fragment of ice. Only one dog remained alive; but there was a human being within it, whom the sailors were persuading to enter the vessel. He was not, as the

NOTES

telescopes: optical instruments that render an upright, nonreversed, enlarged image of faraway objects or celestial bodies.

ground sea: a swell of the sea, breaking on the shore in heavy waves.

other traveller seemed to be, a savage inhabitant of some undiscovered island, but an European. When I appeared on deck, the master said, "Here is our captain, and he will not allow you to perish on the open sea."

On perceiving me, the stranger addressed me in English, although with a foreign accent. "Before I come on board your vessel," said he, "will you have the kindness to inform me whither you are bound?"

You may conceive my astonishment on hearing such a question addressed to me from a man on the brink of destruction, and to whom I should have supposed that my vessel would have been a resource which he would not have exchanged for the most precious wealth the earth can afford. I replied, however, that we were on a voyage of discovery towards the northern pole.

Upon hearing this he appeared satisfied, and consented to come on board. Good God! Margaret, if you had seen the man who thus capitulated for his safety, your surprise would have been boundless. His limbs were nearly frozen, and his body dreadfully emaciated by fatigue and suffering. I never saw a man in so wretched a condition. We attempted to carry him into the cabin; but as soon as he had quitted the fresh air, he fainted. We accordingly brought him back to the deck, and restored him to animation by rubbing him with brandy, and forcing him to swallow a small quantity. As soon as he showed signs of life we wrapped him up in blankets, and placed him near the chimney of the kitchen stove. By slow degrees he recovered, and ate a little soup, which restored him wonderfully.

Two days passed in this manner before he was able to speak; and I often feared that his sufferings had deprived him of understanding. When he had in some measure recovered, I removed him to my own cabin, and attended on him as much as my duty would permit. I never saw a more interesting creature: his eyes have generally an expression of wildness, and even madness; but there are moments when, if anyone performs an act of kindness towards him, or does him the most trifling service, his whole countenance is lighted up, as it were, with a beam of benevolence and sweetness that I never saw equalled. But he is generally **melancholy** and despairing; and sometimes he gnashes his teeth, as if impatient of the weight of woes that oppresses him.

melancholy: a tendency to be sad, gloomy, or depressed. Romantic melancholy is a complex concept and acquires various functions in the art and literature of the time. In Mary Shelley's novel, for instance, characters exhibiting melancholy are clearly highly sensitive individuals, able to *sympathise* (see Letter 1 Notes) with others.

When my guest was a little recovered, I had great trouble to keep off the men, who wished to ask him a thousand questions; but I would not allow him to be tormented by their idle curiosity, in a state of body and mind whose restoration evidently depended upon entire repose. Once, however, the lieutenant asked, Why he had come so far upon the ice in so strange a vehicle?

His countenance instantly assumed an aspect of the deepest gloom, and he replied, "To seek one who fled from me."

"And did the man whom you pursued travel in the same fashion?"

"Yes."

"Then I fancy we have seen him; for the day before we picked you up, we saw some dogs drawing a sledge, with a man in it, across the ice."

This aroused the stranger's attention: and he asked a multitude of questions concerning the route which the **daemon**, as he called him, had pursued. Soon after, when he was alone with me, he said,—"I have, doubtless, excited your curiosity, as well as that of these good people; but you are too considerate to make inquiries."

daemon: usually, an evil spirit.

"Certainly; it would indeed be very impertinent and inhuman in me to trouble you with any inquisitiveness of mine."

"And yet you rescued me from a strange and perilous situation; you have benevolently restored me to life."

Soon after this he enquired if I thought that the breaking up of the ice had destroyed the other sledge? I replied, that I could not answer with any degree of certainty; for the ice had not broken until near midnight, and the traveller might have arrived at a place of safety before that time; but of this I could not judge.

From this time a new spirit of life animated the decaying frame of the stranger. He manifested the greatest eagerness to be upon deck, to watch for the sledge which had before appeared; but I have persuaded him to remain in the cabin, for he is far too weak to sustain the rawness of the atmosphere. I have promised that someone should watch for him, and give him instant notice if any new object should appear in sight.

Such is my journal of what relates to this strange occurrence up to the present day. The stranger has gradually improved in health, but is very silent, and appears uneasy when any one except myself enters his cabin. Yet his manners are so conciliating and gentle, that the sailors are all interested in him, although they have had very little communication with him. For my own part, I begin to love him as a brother; and his constant and deep grief fills me with sympathy and compassion. He must have been a noble creature in his better days, being even now in wreck so attractive and amiable.

I said in one of my letters, my dear Margaret, that I should find no friend on the wide ocean; yet I have found a man who, before his spirit had been broken by misery, I should have been happy to have possessed as the brother of my heart.

I shall continue my journal concerning the stranger at intervals, should I have any fresh incidents to record.

August 13th, 17——.

My affection for my guest increases every day. He excites at once my admiration and my pity to an astonishing degree. How can I see so noble a creature destroyed by misery, without feeling the most poignant grief? He is so gentle, yet so wise; his mind is so cultivated; and when he speaks, although his words are culled with the choicest art, yet they flow with rapidity and unparalleled **eloquence**.

eloquence: expressiveness; strong speaking ability.

He is now much recovered from his illness, and is continually on the deck, apparently watching for the sledge that preceded his own. Yet, although unhappy, he is not so utterly occupied by his own misery, but that he interests himself deeply in the projects of others. He has frequently conversed with me on mine, which I have communicated to him without disguise. He entered attentively into all my arguments in favour of my eventual success, and into every minute detail of the measures I had taken to secure it. I was easily led by the sympathy which he evinced, to use the language of my heart; to give utterance to the burning ardour of my soul; and to say, with all the fervour that warmed me, how gladly I would sacrifice my fortune, my existence, my every hope, to the furtherance of my enterprise. One man's life or death were but a small price to pay for the acquirement of the knowledge which I sought; for the dominion I should acquire and transmit over the elemental foes of our race. As I spoke, a dark gloom spread over my listener's countenance. At first I perceived that he tried to suppress his emotion; he placed his hands before his eyes; and my voice quivered and failed me, as I beheld tears trickle fast from between his fingers,–a groan burst from his heaving breast. I paused;—at length he spoke, in broken accents:—"Unhappy man! Do you share my madness? Have you drank also of the intoxicating draught? Hear me,—let me reveal my tale, and you will dash the cup from your lips!"

Such words, you may imagine, strongly excited my curiosity; but the **paroxysm** of grief that had seized the stranger overcame his weakened powers, and many hours of repose and tranquil conversation were necessary to restore his composure.

paroxysm: frenzy; excitement to the extreme.

Having conquered the violence of his feelings, he appeared to despise himself for being the slave of passion; and quelling the dark tyranny of despair, he led me again to converse concerning myself personally. He asked me the history of my earlier years. The tale was quickly told: but it awakened various trains of reflection. I spoke of my desire of finding a friend—of my thirst for a more intimate sympathy with a fellow mind than had ever fallen to my lot: and expressed my conviction that a man could boast of little happiness, who did not enjoy this blessing.

"I agree with you," replied the stranger; "we are unfashioned creatures, but half made up, if one wiser, better, dearer than ourselves—such a friend ought to be—do not lend his aid to perfectionate our weak and faulty natures. I once had a friend, the most noble of human creatures, and am entitled, therefore, to judge respecting friendship. You have hope, and **the world before you**, and have no cause for despair. But I—I have lost everything and cannot begin life anew."

the world before you: allusion to the final lines of *Paradise Lost*: "The World was all before them, where to choose / Their place of rest, and Providence their guide: / They hand in hand with wand'ring steps and slow, / Through Eden took their solitary way."

As he said this, his countenance became expressive of a calm settled grief, that touched me to the heart. But he was silent, and presently retired to his cabin.

Even broken in spirit as he is, no one can feel more deeply than he does the beauties of nature. The starry sky, the sea, and every sight afforded by these wonderful regions, seem still to have the power of elevating his soul from earth. Such a man has a double existence: he may suffer misery, and be overwhelmed by disappointments; yet, when he has retired into himself, he will be like a celestial spirit, that has a **halo** around him, within whose circle no grief or folly ventures.

halo: luminous radiance; nimbus; aura; ring of light.

Will you smile at the enthusiasm I express concerning this divine wanderer? You would not, if you saw him. You have been tutored and refined by books and retirement from the world, and you are, therefore, somewhat fastidious; but this only renders you the more fit to appreciate the extraordinary merits of this wonderful man. Sometimes I have endeavoured to discover what quality it is which he possesses, that elevates him so immeasurably above any other person I ever knew. I believe it to be an intuitive discernment; a quick but never-failing power of judgment; a penetration into the causes of things, unequalled for clearness and precision; add to this a facility of expression, and a voice whose varied intonations are soul-subduing music.

August 19, 17—.

Yesterday the stranger said to me, "You may easily perceive, Captain Walton, that I have suffered great and unparalleled misfortunes. I had determined, at one time, that the memory of these evils should die with me; but you have won me to alter my determination. You seek for knowledge and wisdom, as I once did; and I ardently hope that the gratification of your wishes may not be a serpent to sting you, as mine has been. I do not know that the relation of my disasters will be useful to you; yet, when I reflect that you are pursuing the same course, exposing yourself to the same dangers which have rendered me what I am, I imagine that you may deduce an apt moral from my tale; one that may direct you if you succeed in your undertaking, and console you in case of failure. Prepare to hear of occurrences which are usually deemed marvellous. Were we among the tamer scenes of nature, I might fear to encounter your unbelief, perhaps your ridicule; but many things will appear possible in these wild and mysterious regions, which would provoke the laughter of those unacquainted with the ever-varied powers of nature:—nor can I doubt but that my tale conveys in its series internal evidence of the truth of the events of which it is composed."

You may easily imagine that I was much gratified by the offered communication; yet I could not endure that he should renew his grief by a recital of his misfortunes. I felt the greatest eagerness to hear the promised narrative, partly from curiosity, and partly from a strong desire to ameliorate his fate, if it were in my power. I expressed these feelings in my answer.

"I thank you," he replied, "for your sympathy, but it is useless; my fate is nearly fulfilled. I wait but for one event, and then I shall repose in peace. I understand your feeling," continued he, perceiving that I wished to interrupt him; "but you are mistaken, my friend, if thus you will allow me to name you; nothing can alter my destiny: listen to my history, and you will perceive how irrevocably it is determined."

He then told me, that he would commence his narrative the next day when I should be at leisure. This promise drew from me the warmest thanks. I have resolved every night, when I am not imperatively occupied by my duties, to record, as nearly as possible in his own words, what he has related during the day. If I should be engaged, I will at least make notes. This manuscript will doubtless afford you the greatest pleasure: but to me, who know him, and who hear it from his own lips, with what interest and sympathy shall I read it in some future day! Even now, as I commence my task, his full-toned voice swells in my ears; his **lustrous** eyes dwell on me with all their melancholy sweetness; I see his thin hand raised in animation, while the lineaments of his face are irradiated by the soul within. Strange and harrowing must be his story; frightful the storm which embraced the gallant vessel on its course, and wrecked it—thus!

lustrous: radiant.

COMMENTARY

Walton and some of the sailors look out one night over the vast and empty sea of ice. Suddenly, about half a mile north, they observe a sledge drawn by dogs and guided by a huge man. Later that night, the ice breaks, and in the morning, a big fragment of ice carries another sledge and a nearly frozen man to the ship.

When the stranger begins to recover, Walton becomes intrigued by the "expression of wildness, and even madness" in the stranger's eyes, an expression that intensifies when the stranger hears about the other sledge sighted from the ship. Walton observes that the news has an unusually strong impact on the stranger, whose feeble body seems animated by "a new spirit of life."

Walton portrays Victor as an impressive man—noble, gentle, selfless, wise, and enormously cultivated. Victor, despite his condition, is also responsive to the sublime landscape surrounding them. Walton remarks that Victor has a special quality that makes him clearly superior to his fellow human beings and proclaims that this quality is, in fact, the power of his mind, his ability "to penetrate into the causes of things." Walton's ability to identify Victor's essential genius demonstrates a powerful connection between these two men.

Slowly, the stranger's health improves under Walton's patient care. Because of his unusually strong affection for this new friend, Walton confesses his obsessive dream to break through boundaries into an undiscovered paradise and, simultaneously, his determination to sacrifice everything, including his life, for this enterprise.

Walton's heartfelt confession is unquestionably precipitated by the principle of sympathy that allows individuals to evaluate and understand themselves by communicating and interacting with others. Mary Shelley shared with her husband and many other intellectuals of her time an interest in the virtues of sympathy. The concept of *sympathetic sensibility* derives from the theories disseminated by eighteenth-century philosophers (such as David Hume, Ashley Cooper, Third Earl of Shaftesbury, and Adam Smith) who associated sympathy with a human's natural tendency toward benevolence and kindness. They maintained that *sensibility* is a force capable of forming bonds of intimacy between people and that these bonds are always stronger than the bonds created by friendship.

In the frigid territories of the North Pole, Walton meets a man whose feelings and ideas about friendship are clearly similar to his own ideas. Like Walton, this man believes that friends complement and complete each other by fulfilling the yearning of two imperfect beings for perfection and wholeness—especially two beings motivated by the same ambition for adventure and notoriety.

Walton's sailors see the Monster.

The stranger decides to tell Walton his incredible story because he recognizes the same dangerous ambition that once animated his own dreams. He understands that they share the same madness—the destructive desire to transgress the allowed limits of knowledge. Walton has moved away from his world and his family; he has left St. Petersburg and Archangel (two allegorical names that may signify St. Peter and the archangel Michael). He wants to discover a perfect world and regain Eden, so he is eager to hear the story of a man who had the same aspirations and who lost not only his soul but also his terrestrial paradise.

<table>
<tr><td>**Chapter 1**</td><td>**The stranger, Victor Frankenstein, begins telling the story of his life. He was born and raised in a good family in Geneva, Switzerland. His father, Alphonse Frankenstein, a well-respected member of the local government, married Caroline Beaufort, a much younger woman. While in Italy, Victor's parents adopted a lovely little girl, Elizabeth Lavenza.**</td></tr>
</table>

CHAPTER I

I am by birth a **Genevese**; and my family is one of the most distinguished of that **republic**. My ancestors had been for many years counsellors and **syndics**; and my father had filled several public situations with honour and reputation. He was respected by all who knew him, for his integrity and indefatigable attention to public business. He passed his younger days perpetually occupied by the affairs of his country; a variety of circumstances had prevented his marrying early, nor was it until the decline of life that he became a husband and the father of a family.

As the circumstances of his marriage illustrate his character, I cannot refrain from relating them. One of his most intimate friends was a merchant, who, from a flourishing state, fell, through numerous mischances, into poverty. This man, whose name was Beaufort, was of a proud and unbending disposition, and could not bear to live in poverty and oblivion in the same country where he had formerly been distinguished for his rank and magnificence. Having paid his debts, therefore, in the most honourable manner, he retreated with his daughter to the town of Lucerne, where he lived unknown and in wretchedness. My father loved Beaufort with the truest friendship, and was deeply grieved by his retreat in these unfortunate circumstances. He bitterly deplored the false pride which led his friend to a conduct so little worthy of the affection that united them. He lost no time in endeavouring to seek him out, with the hope of persuading him to begin the world again through his credit and assistance.

Beaufort had taken effectual measures to conceal himself; and it was ten months before my father discovered his abode. Overjoyed at this discovery, he hastened to the house, which was situated in a mean street, near the Reuss. But when he entered, misery and despair alone welcomed him. Beaufort had saved but a very small sum of money from the wreck of his fortunes; but it was sufficient to provide him with sustenance for some months, and in the meantime he hoped to procure some respectable employment in a merchant's house. The interval was, consequently, spent in inaction; his grief only became more deep and rankling, when he had leisure for reflection; and at length it took so fast hold of his mind, that at the end of three months he lay on a bed of sickness, incapable of any exertion.

His daughter attended him with the greatest tenderness; but she saw with despair that their little fund was rapidly decreasing, and that there was no

NOTES

Genevese: a person from Geneva, Switzerland.

republic: a state in which the sovereign power is vested in the citizens, who govern themselves through elected representatives. In a more general sense. a republic is any nation governed, not by a hereditary ruler, but by a legislative body.

syndics: municipal magistrates.

other prospect of support. But Caroline Beaufort possessed a mind of an uncommon mould; and her courage rose to support her in her adversity. She procured **plain work**; she plaited straw; and by various means contrived to earn a pittance scarcely sufficient to support life.

plain work: sewing.

Several months passed in this manner. Her father grew worse; her time was more entirely occupied in attending him; her means of subsistence decreased; and in the tenth month her father died in her arms, leaving her an orphan and a beggar. This last blow overcame her, and she knelt by Beaufort's coffin, weeping bitterly, when my father entered the chamber. He came like a protecting spirit to the poor girl, who committed herself to his care; and after the interment of his friend, he conducted her to Geneva and placed her under the protection of a relation. Two years after this event Caroline became his wife.

There was a considerable difference between the ages of my parents, but this circumstance seemed to unite them only closer in bonds of devoted affection. There was a sense of justice in my father's upright mind, which rendered it necessary that he should approve highly to love strongly. Perhaps during former years he had suffered from the late-discovered unworthiness of one beloved, and so was disposed to set a greater value on tried worth. There was a show of gratitude and worship in his attachment to my mother, differing wholly from the doting fondness of age, for it was inspired by reverence for her virtues, and a desire to be the means of, in some degree, recompensing her for the sorrows she had endured, but which gave inexpressible grace to his behaviour to her. Every thing was made to yield to her wishes and her convenience. He strove to shelter her, as a fair exotic is sheltered by the gardener, from every rougher wind, and to surround her with all that could tend to excite pleasurable emotion in her soft and benevolent mind. Her health, and even the tranquillity of her hitherto constant spirit, had been shaken by what she had gone through. During the two years that had elapsed previous to their marriage my father had gradually relinquished all his public functions; and immediately after their union they sought the pleasant climate of Italy, and the change of scene and interest attendant on a tour through that land of wonders, as a restorative for her weakened frame.

From Italy they visited Germany and France. I, their eldest child, was born at **Naples**, and as an infant accompanied them in their rambles. I remained for several years their only child. Much as they were attached to each other, they seemed to draw inexhaustible stores of affection from a very mine of love to bestow them upon me. My mother's tender caresses, and my father's smile of benevolent pleasure while regarding me, are my first recollections. I was their plaything and their idol, and something better—their child, the innocent and helpless creature bestowed on them by Heaven, whom to bring up to good, and whose future lot it was in their hands to direct to happiness or misery, according as they fulfilled their duties towards me. With this deep consciousness of what they owed towards the being to which they had given life, added to the active spirit of tenderness that animated both, it may be imagined that while during

Naples: port in central Italy, located on the Bay of Naples.

every hour of my infant life I received a lesson of patience, of charity, and of self-control, I was so guided by a silken cord, that all seemed but one train of enjoyment to me.

For a long time I was their only care. My mother had much desired to have a daughter, but I continued their single offspring. When I was about five years old, while making an excursion beyond the frontiers of Italy, they passed a week on the shores of the **Lake of Como**. Their benevolent disposition often made them enter the cottages of the poor. This, to my mother, was more than a duty; it was a necessity, a passion,—remembering what she had suffered, and how she had been relieved,—for her to act in her turn the guardian angel to the afflicted. During one of their walks a poor cot in the foldings of a vale attracted their notice, as being singularly disconsolate, while the number of half-clothed children gathered about it, spoke of **penury** in its worst shape. One day, when my father had gone by himself to **Milan**, my mother, accompanied by me, visited this abode. She found a peasant and his wife, hard working, bent down by care and labour, distributing a scanty meal to five hungry babes. Among these there was one which attracted my mother far above all the rest. She appeared of a different stock. The four others were dark-eyed, hardy little vagrants; this child was thin, and very fair. Her hair was the brightest living gold, and despite the poverty of her clothing, seemed to set a crown of distinction on her head. Her brow was clear and ample, her blue eyes cloudless, and her lips and the moulding of her face so expressive of sensibility and sweetness, that none could behold her without looking on her as of a distinct species, a being heaven-sent, and bearing a celestial stamp in all her features.

The peasant woman, perceiving that my mother fixed eyes of wonder and admiration on this lovely girl, eagerly communicated her history. She was not her child, but the daughter of a Milanese nobleman. Her mother was a German, and had died on giving her birth. The infant had been placed with these good people to nurse: they were better off then. They had not been long married, and their eldest child was but just born. The father of their charge was one of those Italians nursed in the memory of the antique glory of Italy,—one among the ***schiavi ognor frementi***, who exerted himself to obtain the liberty of his country. He became the victim of its weakness. Whether he had died, or still lingered in the dungeons of Austria, was not known. His property was confiscated, his child became an orphan and a beggar. She continued with her foster parents, and bloomed in their rude abode, fairer than a garden rose among dark-leaved brambles.

When my father returned from Milan, he found playing with me in the hall of our villa, a child fairer than pictured cherub—a creature who seemed to shed radiance from her looks, and whose form and motions were lighter than the chamois of the hills. The apparition was soon explained. With his permission my mother prevailed on her rustic guardians to yield their charge to her. They were fond of the sweet orphan. Her presence had seemed a blessing to them; but it would be

Lake of Como: picturesque mountain lake in northern Italy.

penury: poverty, especially lacking cash at hand.

Milan: a city in Lombardy, a region in the northern part of Italy.

schiavi ognor frementi: slaves forever in a rage; a reference to many leading Milanese citizens and intellectuals exiled to Britain to escape persecution and imprisonment in the famous prison of Spielberg (in Austria).

unfair to her to keep her in poverty and want, when **Providence** afforded her such powerful protection. They consulted their village priest, and the result was, that Elizabeth Lavenza became the inmate of my parents' house—my more than sister—the beautiful and adored companion of all my occupations and my pleasures.

Every one loved Elizabeth. The passionate and almost reverential attachment with which all regarded her became, while I shared it, my pride and my delight. On the evening previous to her being brought to my home, my mother had said playfully,—"I have a pretty present for my Victor— tomorrow he shall have it." And when, on the morrow, she presented Elizabeth to me as her promised gift, I, with childish seriousness, interpreted her words literally, and looked upon Elizabeth as mine—mine to protect, love, and cherish. All praises bestowed on her, I received as made to a possession of my own. We called each other familiarly by the name of cousin. No word, no expression could body forth the kind of relation in which she stood to me—my more than sister, since till death she was to be mine only.

Providence: destiny, fate, fortune.

COMMENTARY

This chapter opens with the history of the stranger, Victor Frankenstein, and his family. He is the eldest son of a Genevan magistrate, Alphonse Frankenstein, a well-respected man in the community for his many years of dedicated public service, integrity, and virtue. Late in life, Alphonse Frankenstein married the daughter of an old and close friend. Once a prosperous merchant, Caroline Beaufort's father lost his important social status and retired with his only daughter to Lucerne, where they lived isolated and in terrible poverty. Saddened by his friend's misfortune and willing to assist him in his financial recovery, Alphonse Frankenstein spent ten months searching for his friend.

When he finally found the house, his friend had just died, leaving his young daughter, who had cared for her father with the greatest affection, an orphan. Impressed by this young woman's devotion and virtue, Alphonse took her under his protection and, after two years, married her. Determined to restore Caroline's deteriorated health, Alphonse abandoned all his public functions and traveled with his wife through Europe, hoping to reestablish her health and well-being through a change in climate and landscape.

Victor was born in Naples and was idolized by his parents, who considered raising and guiding him to be their sacred duty. His parents devoted their lives to showering Victor with love and constant care. They felt a deep sense of responsibility for Victor's entire existence and paid constant attention to the values they wanted to instill in him.

One day in Italy, Victor's mother, who felt passionately inclined to help and comfort poor people, visited a particularly needy family and noticed, among the five children, a girl who didn't seem to belong. The peasant woman explained that the little girl was an orphan of noble birth whose German mother died during childbirth and whose father, a revolutionary Milanese nobleman, had disappeared without a trace. Despite their attachment to the little girl, the foster parents agreed to place Elizabeth Lavenza under the Frankensteins' care. She became Victor's little sister and was the joy of the entire family.

However, this almost perfect portrait of family life portrays some disturbing shadows. Beaufort, a proud but stubborn man, selfishly forces his daughter to follow him into his self-imposed exile, depriving her of an adequate education and of any real contact with the world. Consequently, she has to abandon the privileges of her class

and become part of the working class to support their
household and protect her not-
so-protective father from a
humiliation that his ridiculous
pride could not have suffered.
In fact, Beaufort is not only an
inefficient businessman but
also an irresponsible father,
who exploits and silences his
daughter. His pride functions
well with his male colleagues,
and he honorably pays off his
debts, but the same pride
seems to dissolve when it
comes to letting his very young
daughter support him. Her
future obviously does not concern him, and the reader may
raise serious questions about
how such a man may have
treated his deceased wife
(who was fairly young, considering Caroline's age).

Geneva
© Historical Picture Archive/CORBIS

Alphonse   Frankenstein's
friendship for such a man is, to say the least, questionable. His motives are not simply for class solidarity or out
of pure benevolence to help a ruined friend. Alphonse
rescues Beaufort's daughter, Caroline, in the only way a
woman in her position can be rescued—through marriage. Alphonse never offers her any alternatives (such
as protection without marriage, education, or inheritance). He is so impressed by her obedience to her father
that he takes her as a gift for himself—in the same way
that, later, he will buy Elizabeth Lavenza as a gift for his
son, Victor Frankenstein. His kindness and constant
attention for Caroline is based more on a sense of justice,
reverence, and admiration for her virtues than on authentic and spontaneous love. He protects her "as a fair
exotic is sheltered by the gardener." Happy to have found
such a perfect creature, he wants to express his gratitude more than his affection.

When the family adopts Elizabeth, their motives, again,
are questionable. Do they adopt her out of pity for the
poor family or out of concern for one of their class? Does
Victor's mother really sympathize with all the children, or
attracted by Elizabeth's fairness, does she buy herself an
angelic daughter as well as a sister for Victor? Victor's
mother presents Elizabeth as a gift for Victor, reinforcing
a social conception that women are supposed to please
and satisfy men. Responding to the same social conven-
tion, Victor looks upon Elizabeth as a possession of his
own. Not everything is quite perfect in the Frankensteins'
paradisical universe.

Chapter 2 **Victor and his best friend, Henry Clerval, are voracious readers, but whereas Henry is interested in poetry, Victor's passion is natural philosophy. When Victor is fifteen years old, a family friend talks to him about the subject of electricity and galvanism. Fascinated, Victor abandons the study of natural philosophy and dedicates himself completely to mathematics and this newly discovered science.**

CHAPTER II

WE were brought up together; there was not quite a year difference in our ages. I need not say that we were strangers to any species of disunion or dispute. Harmony was the soul of our companionship, and the diversity and contrast that subsisted in our characters drew us nearer together. Elizabeth was of a calmer and more concentrated disposition; but, with all my ardour, I was capable of a more intense application and was more deeply smitten with the thirst for knowledge. She busied herself with following the aerial creations of the poets; and in the majestic and wondrous scenes which surrounded our Swiss home—the sublime shapes of the mountains; the changes of the seasons; tempest and calm; the silence of winter, and the life and turbulence of our Alpine summers,—she found ample scope for admiration and delight. While my companion contemplated with a serious and satisfied spirit the magnificent appearances of things, I delighted in investigating their causes. The world was to me a secret which I desired to divine. Curiosity, earnest research to learn the hidden laws of nature, gladness akin to rapture, as they were unfolded to me, are among the earliest sensations I can remember.

On the birth of a second son, my junior by seven years, my parents gave up entirely their wandering life, and fixed themselves in their native country. We possessed a house in Geneva, and a *campagne* on Belrive, the eastern shore of the lake, at the distance of rather more than a league from the city. We resided principally in the latter, and the lives of my parents were passed in considerable seclusion. It was my temper to avoid a crowd, and to attach myself fervently to a few. I was indifferent, therefore, to my school fellows in general; but I united myself in the bonds of the closest friendship to one among them. Henry Clerval was the son of a merchant of Geneva. He was a boy of singular talent and fancy. He loved enterprise, hardship, and even danger, for its own sake. He was deeply read in books of chivalry and romance. He composed heroic songs, and began to write many a tale of enchantment and knightly adventure. He tried to make us act plays, and to enter into **masquerades**, in which the characters were drawn from the heroes of **Roncesvalles**, of the **Round Table** of **King Arthur**, and the chivalrous train who shed their blood to redeem the **holy sepulchre** from the hands of the **infidels**.

No human being could have passed a happier childhood than myself. My parents were possessed by the very spirit of kindness and indulgence. We felt that they were not the tyrants to rule our lot according to their caprice, but the agents and creators of all the many delights which we enjoyed. When I mingled with other families, I distinctly discerned how peculiarly fortunate my lot was, and gratitude assisted the development of filial love.

My temper was sometimes violent, and my passions vehement; but by some law in my temperature they were turned, not towards childish pursuits, but to an eager desire to learn, and not to learn all things indiscriminately. I confess that neither the structure of languages, nor the code of governments, nor the politics of various states, possessed attractions for me. It was the secrets of heaven and earth that I desired to learn; and whether it was the outward substance of things, or the inner spirit of nature and the mysterious soul of man that occupied me, still my inquiries were directed to the metaphysical, or, in it highest sense, the physical secrets of the world.

Meanwhile Clerval occupied himself, so to speak, with the moral relations of things. The busy stage of life, the virtues of heroes, and the actions of men were his theme; and his hope and his dream was to become one among those whose names are recorded in story, as the gallant and adventurous benefactors of our species. The saintly soul of Elizabeth shone like a shrine-dedicated lamp in our peaceful home. Her sympathy was ours; her smile, her soft voice, the sweet glance of her celestial eyes, were ever there to bless and animate us. She was the living spirit of love to soften and attract: I might have become sullen in my study, rough through the ardour of my nature, but that she was there to subdue me to a semblance of her own gentleness. And Clerval—could aught ill entrench on the noble spirit of Clerval? yet he might not have been so perfectly humane, so thoughtful in his generosity—so full of kindness and tenderness amidst his passion for adventurous exploit, had she not unfolded to him the real loveliness of beneficence, and made the doing good the end and aim of his soaring ambition.

I feel exquisite pleasure in dwelling on the recollections of childhood, before misfortune had tainted my mind, and changed its bright visions of extensive usefulness into gloomy and narrow reflections upon self. Besides, in drawing the picture of my early days, I also record those events which led, by insensible steps, to my after tale of misery: for when I would account to myself for the birth of that passion, which afterwards ruled my destiny, I find it arise, like a mountain river, from ignoble and almost forgotten sources; but, swelling as it proceeded, it became the torrent which, in its course, has swept away all my hopes and joys.

Natural philosophy is the **genius** that has regulated my fate; I desire, therefore, in this narration, to state those facts which led to my predilection for that science. When I was thirteen years of age, we all went on a party of pleasure to the baths near Thonon; the inclemency of the weather obliged us to remain a day confined to the inn. In this house I chanced to find a volume of the works of **Cornelius Agrippa**. I opened it with **apathy**; the theory which he attempts to demonstrate, and the wonderful facts which he relates, soon changed this feeling into enthusiasm.

Natural philosophy: eighteenth century term for the study of nature. The main tenet says that everything in the universe is alive and is connected to everything else. Natural philosophy contributed considerably to the study of magnetism, galvanism, and electricity.

genius: attendant spirit.

Cornelius Agrippa: Heinrich Cornelius Agrippa (1486–1535), German physician and author of *De Occulta Philosophia* (1531) and *De Vanitate Scientiarum* (1530). In these works, Agrippa maintains that the study of magic allows one to know God and the universe.

apathy: lack of enthusiasm; indifference.

A new light seemed to dawn upon my mind; and, bounding with joy, I communicated my discovery to my father. My father looked carelessly at the titlepage of my book and said, "Ah! Cornelius Agrippa! My dear Victor, do not waste your time upon this; it is sad trash."

If, instead of this remark, my father had taken the pains to explain to me that the principles of Agrippa had been entirely exploded, and that a modern system of science had been introduced, which possessed much greater powers than the ancient, because the powers of the latter were **chimerical**, while those of the former were real and practical; under such circumstances, I should certainty have thrown Agrippa aside, and have contented my imagination, warmed as it was, by returning with greater ardour to my former studies. It is even possible, that the train of my ideas would never have received the fatal impulse that led to my ruin. But the cursory glance my father had taken of my volume by no means assured me that he was acquainted with its contents; and I continued to read with the greatest avidity.

When I returned home, my first care was to procure the whole works of this author, and afterwards of **Paracelsus** and **Albertus Magnus**. I read and studied the wild fancies of these writers with delight; they appeared to me treasures known to few besides myself. I have described myself as always having been embued with a fervent longing to penetrate the secrets of nature. In spite of the intense labour and wonderful discoveries of modern philosophers, I always came from my studies discontented and unsatisfied. **Sir Isaac Newton** is said to have avowed that he felt like a child picking up shells beside the great and unexplored ocean of truth. Those of his successors in each branch of natural philosophy with whom I was acquainted, appeared even to my boy's apprehensions, as tyros engaged in the same pursuit.

The untaught peasant beheld the elements around him, and was acquainted with their practical uses. The most learned philosopher knew little more. He had partially unveiled the face of Nature, but her immortal lineaments were still a wonder and a mystery. He might dissect, anatomise, and give names; but, not to speak of a final cause, causes in their secondary and tertiary grades were utterly unknown to him. I had gazed upon the fortifications and impediments that seemed to keep human beings from entering the citadel of nature, and rashly and ignorantly I had repined.

But here were books, and here were men who had penetrated deeper and knew more. I took their word for all that they averred, and I became their **disciple**. It may appear strange that such should arise in the eighteenth century; but while I followed the routine of education in the schools of Geneva, I was, to a great degree, self taught with regard to my favourite studies. My father was not scientific, and I was left to struggle with a child's blindness, added to a student's thirst for knowledge. Under the guidance of my new preceptors, I entered with the greatest diligence into the search of the **philosopher's stone** and the **elixir of life**; but the latter soon obtained my undivided attention. Wealth was an inferior

chimerical: elusive; appearing and disappearing.

Paracelsus: Theophrastus Bombastus von Hohenheim (1486–1541), a Swiss alchemist, physician, and magician.

Albertus Magnus: (1193–1280) German Dominican monk and theologian, one of Percy Shelley's favorite philosophers.

Sir Isaac Newton: Sir Isaac Newton (1642–1727), English physicist, mathematician, and astronomer.

disciple: follower; partisan of a theory, idea, or doctrine.

philosopher's stone: sought by medieval alchemists, the secret formula that would transform other metals into gold or silver.

elixir of life: a potion that alchemists believed would lengthen life indefinitely.

object; but what glory would attend the discovery, if I could banish disease from the human frame, and render man invulnerable to any but a violent death!

Nor were these my only visions. The raising of ghosts or devils was a promise liberally accorded by my favourite authors, the fulfillment of which I most eagerly sought; and if my incantations were always unsuccessful, I attributed the failure rather to my own inexperience and mistake, than to a want of skill or fidelity in my instructors. And thus for a time I was occupied by exploded systems, mingling, like an unadept, a thousand contradictory theories, and floundering desperately in a very slough of multifarious knowledge, guided by an ardent imagination and childish reasoning, till an accident again changed the current of my ideas.

When I was about fifteen years old we had retired to our house near Belrive, when we witnessed a most violent and terrible thunder-storm. It advanced from behind the mountains of Jura; and the thunder burst at once with frightful loudness from various quarters of the heavens. I remained, while the storm lasted, watching its progress with curiosity and delight. As I stood at the door, on a sudden I beheld a stream of fire issue from an old and beautiful oak, which stood about twenty yards from our house; and so soon as the dazzling light vanished, the oak had disappeared, and nothing remained but a blasted stump. When we visited it the next morning, we found the tree shattered in a singular manner. It was not splintered by the shock, but entirely reduced to thin ribbands of wood. I never beheld any thing so utterly destroyed.

Before this I was not unacquainted with the more obvious laws of **electricity**. On this occasion a man of great research in natural philosophy was with us, and, excited by this catastrophe, he entered on the explanation of a theory which he had formed on the subject of electricity and **galvanism**, which was at once new and astonishing to me. All that he said threw greatly into the shade Cornelius Agrippa, Albertus Magnus, and Paracelsus, the lords of my imagination; but by some fatality the overthrow of these men disinclined me to pursue my accustomed studies. It seemed to me as if nothing would or could ever be known. All that had so long engaged my attention suddenly grew despicable. By one of those caprices of the mind, which we are perhaps most subject to in early youth, I at once gave up my former occupations; set down natural history and all its progeny as a deformed and abortive creation; and entertained the greatest disdain for a would-be science, which could never even step within the threshold of real knowledge. In this mood of mind I betook myself to the mathematics, and the branches of study appertaining to that science, as being built upon secure foundations, and so worthy of my consideration.

Thus strangely are our souls constructed, and by such slight ligaments are we bound to prosperity or ruin. When I look back, it seems to me as if this almost miraculous change of inclination and will was the immediate suggestion of the guardian angel of my life—the last effort made by the spirit of preservation to avert the storm that was even then hanging in the

electricity: In the eighteenth century, many scientists defined life as a power, similar to electricity, permeating all living things in the form of a fluid that could not be measured or weighted. Romantic writers, such as Byron, Keats, Percy Shelley, and Mary Shelley, identified and exploited the parallels between electricity and the Promethean myth (*Frankenstein* is subtitled *The Modern Prometheus*).

galvanism: electricity having animal or biochemical origins.

stars, and ready to envelope me. Her victory was announced by an unusual tranquillity and gladness of soul, which followed the relinquishing of my ancient and latterly tormenting studies. It was thus that I was to be taught to associate evil with their prosecution, happiness with their disregard.

It was a strong effort of the spirit of good; but it was ineffectual. Destiny was too potent, and her immutable laws had decreed my utter and terrible destruction.

COMMENTARY

Despite the fundamental differences between Victor and Elizabeth, their childhood is presented as idyllic—full of harmony and camaraderie. According to Victor's version of events, Elizabeth is moderate and serene, whereas he is profound and is intensely preoccupied with improving his knowledge. Elizabeth, fascinated by poetry and inspired by beautiful images, spends considerable time absorbed in poetry or admiring the majestic surroundings of the Swiss landscape, but Victor, intrigued by the origins of things, spends time investigating physical phenomena. Elizabeth enjoys the world; Victor scrutinizes it. Elizabeth takes pleasure in admiring the world; Victor in analyzing and mentally dissecting it. To Elizabeth, the world is a "delight"; to Victor "a secret." Victor Frankenstein feels "exquisite pleasure" in recalling happy events from his blissful youth, as does William Wordsworth in his famous autobiographical poem, *The Prelude* (1805). Wordsworth, while depicting the recurrence of "spots of time" from his memories of childhood, remembers how he relates to nature: "[I]n Nature's presence stood, as now I stand, / A sensitive Being, a *creative* Soul." Victor, on the other hand, never remarks on his responsiveness to the natural world. Instead, he recalls the tenacity of his research and the "rapture" that accompanies his learning of the "hidden laws of nature."

Henry Clerval

When the Frankenstein family finally settles in a beautiful rural area of their native country, Victor, despite being a solitary child, befriends Henry Clerval, the son of a Genevan merchant, who becomes Victor's best and only friend. Like Elizabeth, Clerval is passionate about literature. His powerful imagination and his love for books of "chivalry and romance" translate into a strong interest in composing songs and stories abounding in heroic deeds and glorious adventures. He is an artist at heart, a person who lets the mysterious

power of fantasy infuse the dreams of his childhood with magical energies. In contrast to his friend Clerval, Victor allows his studies to separate him from the life, actions, and dreams of human beings; Victor has little interest in language, politics, or social and moral values. The young Frankenstein is obsessed with the study of *metaphysics*—the mysterious laws of nature and of the human soul. The only person who seems to be able to penetrate Victor's self-absorption is his "cousin" Elizabeth. Victor's description of Elizabeth echoes the vocabulary of medieval poets. He describes her as a Beatrice figure, the woman who inspired Dante's *Divine Comedy*. Like Beatrice, Elizabeth has a "saintly soul" and "celestial eyes," and she is the "spirit of love." She is the light that attracts and unites all energies in the Frankenstein household. Curiously enough, she not only softens Victor's "violent" temperament and gloomy disposition with her contagious sweetness, but even Clerval, who is clearly more congenial than Victor, becomes "perfectly human" under Elizabeth's benevolent agency. Clerval's passion for adventure and his aspiration to a life of distinction are infused not so much by ambition but by a desire to increase the goodness of the world.

Elizabeth is everything that nineteenth century society expects women to be: pleasant, delicate, sensitive to the beauties of nature and poetry, and, above all, capable of creating domestic harmony and improving the disposition and general conduct of the other sex. In a treatise written in 1797, *The Duties of the Female Sex*, Thomas Gisborne remarks that the cultivation of faculties able to "unbend the brow of the learned, to refresh the over-laboured faculties of the wise" represents one of women's fundamental duties, one from which the entire "mankind" benefits. And yet, Victor's description of Elizabeth's virtues and of the differences in terms of education and comportment among Elizabeth, Clerval, and himself reveals a number of disturbing tendencies in Victor's attitude and character.

Victor's excessive love for Elizabeth and incontestably strong friendship for Clerval do not prevent him from employing an almost imperceptible but nevertheless dismissive vocabulary while talking about their work. Victor perceives that his own work is the product of his will (or the object of his desire), whereas work is something that happens to Elizabeth and Clerval, instead of being something that they generate—for example, Elizabeth "[busies] herself," and Clerval "[occupies] himself." Evidently, Victor sees himself as more focused and disciplined than Clerval, whose pursuits are sometimes "childish" and "indiscriminate." Likewise, Elizabeth, in the absence of a formal education, simply fulfills her domestic obligations (not her *ideals*) and enjoys the transitory pleasures of poetry and nature. Victor, on the other hand, seriously advances toward a clear career goal. Although Clerval invests in a much more diversified education, his interests remain restricted to human concerns, and his ambitions are perfectly predictable. What Victor calls Clerval's "soaring ambition" becomes, in this context, a slightly sarcastic comment. Victor seems to suggest that his ambition, not Clerval's, is soaring because he aspires to decipher the ultimate secrets of nature. Unlike Victor, Clerval is incapable of having Promethean dreams. He cannot aspire higher than his condition allows; he remains indeed "perfectly human."

Victor's camouflaged attitude of superiority raises serious concerns about his capacity for love and friendship early in the novel. At the same time, his arrogance anticipates a number of disturbing developments. Elizabeth's literary studies are never again invoked. She gradually becomes completely absorbed in her domestic obligations. Clerval, though not totally transformed, becomes, under Victor's influence, less and less preoccupied with moral concerns and increasingly animated by dreams of ambition and fame. Moreover, when Victor remarks that Elizabeth's soul "shone like a shrine-dedicated lamp," his words introduce an ominous ambiguity. Undoubtedly, the word "shrine" in conjunction with such a young and vital woman should give the observant reader pause. Perhaps, in his constructed rather than real paradise, Victor, like Coleridge's powerful Kubla Khan, hears "voices prophesying war!"—his own voices warring against nature, against God, and against his creature.

Victor's Early Readings

Mary Shelley deftly uses Victor's readings of Agrippa, Paracelsus, and Albertus Magnus, as well as the violent storm at the end of the chapter, to contradict Victor's image of idyllic domesticity and also to prepare the reader for upcoming events. Victor's account of his early studies is prefaced by allusions to future misfortunes, and it also invites the reader to establish connections between Victor's education, his tense relationship with his father, and the birth of a passion that will prove as ruinous as the energy that destroys the majestic oak tree in front of the house. At the age of thirteen, Victor discovers a volume of Cornelius Agrippa's works in circumstances curiously similar to those invoked by Mary Shelley in her account regarding the creation of *Frankenstein*. Like Mary Shelley and her circle of friends (who, when forced to stay inside by incessant rains, precipitated the famous contest that generated *Frankenstein*), Victor, constrained by "the inclemency of the weather," remains in his room all day during a short family vacation. The book changes Victor's life as dramatically as *Frankenstein* changed Mary Shelley's literary destiny.

Fascinated by Agrippa's ideas, Victor tells his father about his newly discovered passion, but instead of talking to his son, Alphonse Frankenstein dismisses Agrippa's work as "sad trash." Convinced that his father's quick disparagement of Agrippa only proves Alphonse' s total ignorance of his works, Victor continues to read avidly works from Agrippa and other alchemists and philosophers, such as Paracelsus and Albertus Magnus. Victor's already passionate search for the ultimate cause of all things becomes inflamed by his readings on magic and alchemy. Victor's reading about the alchemists' quest to understand God and nature by discovering "the philosopher's stone" and "the elixir of life" give his own studies a precise direction—to free man from disease and natural death. Thus, instead of deflecting his son's interest from the study of natural philosophy, the elder Frankenstein's irresponsible reaction and cruel repression of his son's youthful imagination give Victor's rebellious tendencies a "fatal impulse." Victor not only isolates himself from God, but he wants to usurp him. Curiously, this chapter starts with the celebration of the domestic paradise of the Frankenstein household and ends with a father-son schism at the center of the family. Victor's Promethean impulses are revealed, and the unbridgeable distance between him, his father, and his God are exposed. The final segment of this chapter is a metaphor of this "utterly destroyed" connection. Ironically, Victor's eccentric love for alchemy is cured by a new passion for electricity and galvanism, introduced to him by a nameless man of "great research." But the mark of his "first disobedience" remains, like Cain's sign, forged on his soul forever; there is no way back for this prodigal son.

Chapter 3

When Victor is 17, Elizabeth catches scarlet fever. Victor's mother, who insists on nursing Elizabeth, contracts the illness and dies. Soon thereafter, Victor leaves for the University of Ingolstadt and meets his new professors, M. Krempe and M. Waldman. At M. Krempe's suggestion, he attends Professor Waldman's lectures on the latest discoveries in modern chemistry and immediately becomes his disciple.

CHAPTER III

WHEN I had attained the age of seventeen, my parents resolved that I should become a student at the university of **Ingolstadt**. I had hitherto attended the schools of Geneva; but my father thought it necessary, for the completion of my education, that I should be made acquainted with other customs than those of my native country. My departure was therefore fixed at an early date; but before the day resolved upon could arrive, the first misfortune of my life occurred—an omen, as it were, of my future misery.

Elizabeth had caught the scarlet fever; her illness was severe, and she was in the greatest danger. During her illness, many arguments had been urged to persuade my mother to refrain from attending upon her. She had, at first, yielded to our entreaties; but when she heard that the life of her favourite was menaced, she could no longer control her anxiety. She attended her sickbed,—her watchful attentions triumphed over the malignity of the distemper,—Elizabeth was saved, but the consequences of this imprudence were fatal to her preserver. On the third day my mother sickened; her fever was accompanied by the most alarming symptoms, and the looks of her medical attendants prognosticated the worst event. On her death-bed the fortitude and benignity of this best of women did not desert her. She joined the hands of Elizabeth and myself:—"My children," she said, "my firmest hopes of future happiness were placed on the prospect of your union. This expectation will now be the consolation of your father. Elizabeth, my love, you must supply my place to my younger children. Alas! I regret that I am taken from you; and, happy and beloved as I have been, is it not hard to quit you all? But these are not thoughts befitting me; I will endeavour to resign myself cheerfully to death, and will indulge a hope of meeting you in another world."

She died calmly; and her countenance expressed affection even in death. I need not describe the feelings of those whose dearest ties are rent by that most irreparable evil; the void that presents itself to the soul; and the despair that is exhibited on the countenance. It is so long before the mind can persuade itself that she, whom we saw every day, and whose very existence appeared a part of our own, can have departed for ever— that the brightness of a beloved eye can have been extinguished, and the sound of a voice so familiar, and dear to the ear, can be hushed, never more to be heard. These are the reflections of the first days; but when the

NOTES

Ingolstadt: Town on the Danube river, in Bavaria, Germany. The University of Ingolstadt was founded in 1472 and had a well-regarded medical school.

lapse of time proves the reality of the evil, then the actual bitterness of grief commences. Yet from whom has not that rude hand rent away some dear connection? and why should I describe a sorrow which all have felt, and must feel? The time at length arrives, when grief is rather an indulgence than a necessity; and the smile that plays upon the lips, although it may be deemed a **sacrilege**, is not banished. My mother was dead, but we had still duties which we ought to perform; we must continue our course with the rest, and learn to think ourselves fortunate, whilst one remains whom the spoiler has not seized.

sacrilege: impiety, irreverence.

My departure for Ingolstadt, which had been deferred by these events, was now again determined upon. I obtained from my father a respite of some weeks. It appeared to me sacrilege so soon to leave the repose, akin to death, of the house of mourning, and to rush into the thick of life. I was new to sorrow, but it did not the less alarm me. I was unwilling to quit the sight of those that remained to me; and above all, I desired to see my sweet Elizabeth in some degree consoled.

She indeed veiled her grief, and strove to act the comforter to us all. She looked steadily on life, and assumed its duties with courage and zeal. She devoted herself to those whom she had been taught to call her uncle and cousins. Never was she so enchanting as at this time, when she recalled the sunshine of her smiles and spent them upon us. She forgot even her own regret in her endeavours to make us forget.

The day of my departure at length arrived. Clerval spent the last evening with us. He had endeavoured to persuade his father to permit him to accompany me, and to become my fellow student; but in vain. His father was a narrow-minded trader, and saw idleness and ruin in the aspirations and ambition of his son. Henry deeply felt the misfortune of being debarred from a liberal education. He said little; but when he spoke, I read in his kindling eye and in his animated glance a restrained but firm resolve, not to be chained to the miserable details of commerce.

We sat late. We could not tear ourselves away from each other, nor persuade ourselves to say the word "Farewell!" It was said; and we retired under the pretence of seeking repose, each fancying that the other was deceived: but when at morning's dawn I descended to the carriage which was to convey me away, they were all there—my father again to bless me, Clerval to press my hand once more, my Elizabeth to renew her entreaties that I would write often, and to bestow the last feminine attentions on her playmate and friend.

I threw myself into the chaise that was to convey me away, and indulged in the most melancholy reflections. I, who had ever been surrounded by amiable companions, continually engaged in endeavouring to bestow mutual pleasure, I was now alone. In the university, whither I was going, I must form my own friends, and be my own protector. My life had hitherto been remarkably secluded and domestic; and this had given me invincible repugnance to new countenances. I loved my brothers, Elizabeth, and Clerval; these were "**old familiar faces**," but I believed myself

"The old familiar faces": the title and refrain of a poem by Charles Lamb (1775–1834): "Where are they gone, the old familiar faces? / I had a mother, but she died and left me, / Died prematurely in a day of horrors—/ All, all are done, the old familiar faces."

totally unfitted for the company of strangers. Such were my reflections as I commenced my journey; but as I proceeded, my spirits and hopes rose. I ardently desired the acquisition of knowledge. I had often, when at home, thought it hard to remain during my youth cooped up in one place, and had longed to enter the world, and take my station among other human beings. Now my desires were complied with, and it would, indeed, have been folly to repent.

I had sufficient leisure for these and many other reflections during my journey to Ingolstadt, which was long and fatiguing. At length the high white steeple of the town met my eyes. I alighted, and was conducted to my solitary apartment, to spend the evening as I pleased.

The next morning I delivered my letters of introduction, and paid a visit to some of the principal professors. Chance—or rather the evil influence, the Angel of Destruction, which asserted omnipotent sway over me from the moment I turned my reluctant steps from my father's door—led me first to M. Krempe, professor of natural philosophy. He was an uncouth man, but deeply embued in the secrets of his science. He asked me several questions concerning my progress in the different branches of science appertaining to natural philosophy. I replied carelessly; and, partly in contempt, mentioned the names of my alchymists as the principal authors I had studied. The professor stared: "Have you," he said, "really spent your time in studying such nonsense?"

I replied in the affirmative. "Every minute," continued M. Krempe with warmth, "every instant that you have wasted on those books is utterly and entirely lost. You have burdened your memory with exploded systems and useless names. Good God! in what desert land have you lived, where no one was kind enough to inform you that these fancies, which you have so greedily imbibed, are a thousand years old, and as musty as they are ancient? I little expected, in this enlightened and scientific age, to find a disciple of Albertus Magnus and Paracelsus. My dear sir, you must begin your studies entirely anew."

So saying, he stept aside, and wrote down a list of several books treating of natural philosophy, which he desired me to procure; and dismissed me, after mentioning that in the beginning of the following week he intended to commence a course of lectures upon natural philosophy in its general relations, and that M. Waldman, a fellow-professor, would lecture upon chemistry the alternate days that he omitted.

I returned home, not disappointed, for I have said that I had long considered those authors useless whom the professor reprobated; but I returned, not at all the more inclined to recur to these studies in any shape. M. Krempe was a little, squat man, with a gruff voice and a repulsive countenance; the teacher, therefore, did not prepossess me in favour of his pursuits. In rather too philosophical and connected a strain, perhaps, I have given an account of the conclusions I had come to concerning them in my early years. As a child, I had not been content with the results promised by the modern professors of natural science. With a confusion of ideas only to be accounted for by my extreme youth, and my want of a guide on such matters, I had retrod the steps of knowledge along the paths of time, and exchanged the discoveries of recent inquirers for the dreams of forgotten alchymists. Besides, I had a contempt for the uses of modern natural philosophy. It was very different, when the masters of the science sought immortality and power; such views, although futile, were grand: but now the scene was changed. The ambition of the inquirer seemed to limit itself to the annihilation of those visions on which my interest in science was chiefly founded. I was required to exchange chimeras of boundless grandeur for realities of little worth.

Such were my reflections during the first two or three days of my residence at Ingolstadt, which were chiefly spent in becoming acquainted with the localities, and the principal residents in my new abode. But as the ensuing week commenced, I thought of the information which M. Krempe had given me concerning the lectures. And although I could not consent to go and hear that little conceited fellow deliver sentences out of a pulpit, I recollected what he had said of M. Waldman, whom I had never seen, as he had hitherto been out of town.

Partly from curiosity, and partly from idleness, I went into the lecturing room, which M. Waldman entered shortly after. This professor was very unlike his colleague. He appeared about fifty years of age, but with an aspect expressive of the greatest benevolence; a few grey hairs covered his temples, but those at the back of his head were nearly black. His person was short, but remarkably erect; and his voice the sweetest I had ever heard. He began his lecture by a recapitulation of the history of chemistry, and the various improvements made by different men of learning, pronouncing with fervour the names of the most distinguished discoverers. He then took a cursory view of the present state of the science, and explained many of its elementary terms. After having made a few preparatory experiments, he concluded with a **panegyric** upon modern chemistry, the terms of which I shall never forget:—

panegyric: praise, compliment.

"The ancient teachers of this science," said he, "promised impossibilities, and performed nothing. The **modern masters** promise very little; they know that metals cannot be transmuted, and that the elixir of life is a chimera. But these philosophers, whose hands seem only made to dabble in dirt, and their eyes to pore over the microscope or crucible, have indeed performed miracles. They penetrate into the recesses of nature, and show how she works in her hiding places. They ascend into the heavens: they have discovered how the blood circulates, and the nature of the air we breathe. They have acquired new and almost unlimited powers; they can command the thunders of heaven, mimic the earthquake, and even mock the invisible world with its own shadows."

modern masters: renowned scientists of the time.

Such were the professor's words—rather let me say such the words of the fate, enounced to destroy me. As he went on, I felt as if my soul were grappling with a palpable enemy; one by one the various keys were touched which formed the mechanism of my being: chord after chord was sounded, and soon my mind was filled with one thought, one conception, one purpose. So much has been done, exclaimed the soul of

Frankenstein,—more, far more, will I achieve: treading in the steps already marked, I will pioneer a new way, explore unknown powers, and unfold to the world the deepest mysteries of creation.

I closed not my eyes that night. My internal being was in a state of **insurrection** and turmoil; I felt that order would thence arise, but I had no power to produce it. By degrees, after the morning's dawn, sleep came. I awoke, and my yesternight's thoughts were as a dream. There only remained a resolution to return to my ancient studies, and to devote myself to a science for which I believed myself to possess a natural talent. On the same day, I paid M. Waldman a visit. His manners in private were even more mild and attractive than in public; for there was a certain dignity in his mien during his lecture, which in his own house was replaced by the greatest affability and kindness. I gave him pretty nearly the same account of my former pursuits as I had given to his fellow-professor. He heard with attention the little narration concerning my studies, and smiled at the names of Cornelius Agrippa and Paracelsus, but without the contempt that M. Krempe had exhibited. He said, that "these were men to whose indefatigable zeal modern philosophers were indebted for most of the foundations of their knowledge. They had left to us, as an easier task, to give new names, and arrange in connected classifications, the facts which they in a great degree had been the instruments of bringing to light. The labours of men of genius, however erroneously directed, scarcely ever fail in ultimately turning to the solid advantage of mankind." I listened to his statement, which was delivered without any presumption or affectation; and then added, that his lecture had removed my prejudices against modern chemists; I expressed myself in measured terms, with the modesty and deference due from a youth to his instructor, without letting escape (inexperience in life would have made me ashamed) any of the enthusiasm which stimulated my intended labours. I requested his advice concerning the books I ought to procure.

"I am happy," said M. Waldman, "to have gained a disciple; and if your application equals your ability, I have no doubt of your success. Chemistry is that branch of natural philosophy in which the greatest improvements have been and may be made; it is on that account that I have made it my peculiar study; but at the same time, I have not neglected the other branches of science. A man would make but a very sorry chemist if he attended to that department of human knowledge alone. If your wish is to become really a man of science, and not merely a petty experimentalist, I should advise you to apply to every branch of natural philosophy, including mathematics."

He then took me into his laboratory, and explained to me the uses of his various machines; instructing me as to what I ought to procure, and promising me the use of his own when I should have advanced far enough in the science not to derange their mechanism. He also gave me the list of books which I had requested; and I took my leave.

Thus ended a day memorable to me: it decided my future destiny.

insurrection: rebellion, revolt

COMMENTARY

Victor's father wants his son to experience a different system of education and decides to send him to the University of Ingolstadt in Germany. The date for the departure has already been established when Elizabeth contracts scarlet fever, a highly contagious disease. At first, her family convinces Mrs. Frankenstein to abstain from caring for Elizabeth, but hearing that her daughter's condition is deteriorating and that her life is seriously threatened, Caroline can no longer stay away from Elizabeth's sickbed.

Her mother's devotion and vigilant care saves Elizabeth, but Mrs. Frankenstein contracts the disease and dies within a matter of days. On her deathbed, Mrs. Frankenstein asks Elizabeth to marry Victor and take care of the younger boys, Ernest and William. Her unexpected death devastates the family, but a sense of higher duty reminds them that they still have family obligations and social responsibilities. Wisely, they return to their normal lives.

In his account to Walton, Victor calls his mother's death the first "misfortune " of his life and "an omen" of the coming tribulations. Indeed, Caroline's death is the first tragic event to perturb what appears to be the Edenic life of the family, breaking its unity and marking the beginning of a series of calamities that dramatically affect every family member except Ernest.

Probably the most spectacular change is for Elizabeth. Her new role as a mother, lover, sibling, friend, and companion reveals the expectations for women in the Frankenstein household (as well as in society, in general) and subtly invites the reader to reevaluate Caroline Frankenstein's position and the image of perfect happiness portrayed by Victor in his first account. The fact that Elizabeth quickly and effortlessly steps into her mother's role reveals Caroline Frankenstein's dependent, subordinate position. After her marriage to Alphonse, Caroline clearly continued to behave more as a dutiful daughter than as a wife; she served her husband and children in the same way that she had served her father. At the same time, Victor's admiration for Elizabeth, a woman who can hide her grief and who strives to comfort the family, clearly indicates that female suffering is, if not totally disregarded, at least seriously minimized compared to male suffering, which is deliberately accentuated in the novel.

Elizabeth and Victor.
Everett Collection

Departure for Ingolstadt

Several weeks after his mother's death, Elizabeth completely adjusts to her new role, and Victor is finally ready to depart for the University of Ingolstadt. Despite his friend Henry Clerval's assiduous attempts to persuade his father to let him attend the university with Victor, Henry stays behind. A "narrow-minded trader," the senior Clerval remains adamant that a liberal education will ruin his son's already decided profession as a businessman. After spending a long and sad evening with Henry, Victor leaves Geneva, and his family and domestic lifestyle, for Ingolstadt. Only the promise of acquiring a superior knowledge diminishes his melancholy.

M. Clerval's unwillingness to allow Henry to pursue a liberal education and Victor's eagerness to learn more echo Walton's regret at his own incomplete education as well as his obsession with knowledge.

University Life

At the University of Ingolstadt, Victor meets his new professors, M. Krempe, professor of natural philosophy, and M. Waldman, chemistry professor. Abrupt and rather ill-mannered, M. Krempe sarcastically dismisses Victor's former studies and ridicules his interest in the philosophy of the old masters. He prepares a list of books with a modern perspective on natural philosophy and announces that Victor needs to begin his studies "entirely anew." This first encounter with M. Krempe neither surprises Victor nor motivates him, and he is convinced that modern science has lost its passion for grand ideas.

M. Waldman, whose chemistry lectures Victor attends at M. Krempe's recommendation, is the complete opposite of M. Krempe. Charismatic and gracious, M. Waldman impresses Victor from the beginning. His vibrant speech revitalizes Victor's enthusiasm for science and persuades him to return to his old studies. The speech, a masterpiece of rhetorical manipulation, recapitulates the entire history of chemistry, making the differences between the old masters and the new ones even more dramatic and adding substantially to the emotional impact of his words on the audience. Then he describes chemistry's present state in enthusiastic, fervent words and also suggests that chemistry is the foundation of all sciences.

The Novel's Scientific Background

Several critics document that M. Waldman's speech is based on the work of Humphry Davy, a prestigious scientist of the late eighteenth century, whose ideas had a critical impact on the development of modern science. At the newly founded Royal Institute on January 21, 1802, Davy presented a series of lectures, arguing that the new science of chemistry gives the contemporary chemist "powers which may be almost called creative; which have enabled him to modify and change the beings surrounding him." These lectures were later published under the title *A Discourse: Introductory to a Course of Lectures on Chemistry*, a book widely read and discussed in England. Based on Mary Shelley's journal entries from the same period, critics conjecture that she probably read Davy's famous treatise in October 1816 while working on *Frankenstein* and that she was strongly influenced by his personality and ideas in the creation of M. Waldman's character. She was also familiar with another important text of Davy's titled *Elements of Chemical Philosophy* (1812), ordered by Percy Shelley the same year.

Davy's emphasis on the chemist's creative powers, which can alter and transform beings around him, resonates with Victor's admiration for the old masters who frenetically searched for means of attaining immortality and with his own desire of discovering a new way that will fully reveal the powers and secrets of nature. Like Waldman and Davy, Victor appears to prefer the more predatory aspects of science, and therefore, he is immediately captivated by Waldman's portrait of the ideal scientist who "penetrate[s] into the recesses of nature and show[s] how she works in her hiding places." And of course, the professors and Victor echo the beliefs of Walton, who expects to discover all nature's secrets and to be empowered by its miraculous energies. Readers should remember how, from the first moments of their encounter, Walton sensed Victor's penetrative mind—his interest in the causes of things.

Mary Shelley's View of Science

Some critics even suggest that Mary Shelley associated science with rape, portraying scientific research as dangerous and reprehensible. However, many critics hypothesize that instead of discrediting science, Mary Shelley distinguishes between two very different types of scientists. The first type is the Promethean scientist who uses nature to gain power and abusively alter it, and the second type is the "good" scientist, who respects and celebrates nature and resists the temptation to fundamentally change the way it operates.

Mary Shelley's model for the good scientist was another famous scholar, Erasmus Darwin, who wrote extensively on the life of plants and whose work influenced many contemporary poets, including Percy Shelly, who compared *mimosa sensitiva*, the sensitive plant, with the delicate and sensitive poet. Percy Shelley confirms Darwin's influence on *Frankenstein* in the preface to the novel's first edition from 1818: "The event on which this fiction is founded has been supposed, by Dr. Darwin . . . as not of impossible occurrence." Mary Shelley reinforces this view in her own preface to the 1831 edition by alluding to Darwin's experiment with "a piece of vermicelli" preserved "in a glass case, till by some extraordinary means it began to move with voluntary motion." This experiment is most likely fictitious, but unquestionably, Mary Shelley knew of and probably used Darwin's well-known concept regarding the superiority of sexual reproduction over solitary paternal procreation. Victor Frankenstein is clearly inspired by Waldman's violent and manipulative concept of science (Davy's view), not by Darwin's ideal of the scientist who observes, describes, and draws conclusions from the progressive evolutionary process of nature. In the same way that Victor wanted to make Elizabeth a possession of his own (Chapter 1), he now wants "to penetrate" and transform nature. This chapter is critical to understanding Mary Shelley's position and the philosophy informing the novel. She obviously wants to alert readers that Waldman's idealistic, romanticized view of chemistry is, in fact, dangerous, violent, and destructive. According to this model, nature is raped and exposed.

Victor becomes M. Waldman's Disciple

Listening to his passionate lectures, Victor is entirely convinced by M. Waldman's ideas, and he becomes his disciple. In his account to Walton, Victor remarks that Waldman's lectures prophesied his own destruction and that, as the professor continued, he felt that his soul was wrestling with an evil force or energy. Victor affirms the inevitability of his death, reinforcing the idea that his destiny was, in his perception, "irrevocably . . . determined." At the end of M. Waldman's speech, Victor's mind was "filled with one thought, one conception, one purpose." Clearly, his passion for knowledge was transformed into a dangerous obsession.

Chapter 4 After learning everything that his mentors can teach him, Victor considers returning to Geneva, but instead, he absorbs himself in a new experiment and accidently discovers the terrible secret of creating life. Obsessed with the idea of creating a living body, Victor starts collecting bones and body parts, working frantically on his experiment. And yet, the closer he gets to completing his creation, the more anxious and nervous he becomes.

CHAPTER IV

FROM this day natural philosophy, and particularly chemistry, in the most comprehensive sense of the term, became nearly my sole occupation. I read with ardour those works, so full of genius and discrimination, which modern inquirers have written on these subjects. I attended the lectures, and cultivated the acquaintance, of the men of science of the university; and I found even in M. Krempe a great deal of sound sense and real information, combined, it is true, with a repulsive **physiognomy** and manners, but not on that account the less valuable. In M. Waldman I found a true friend. His gentleness was never tinged by **dogmatism**; and his instructions were given with an air of frankness and good nature, that banished every idea of **pedantry**. In a thousand ways he smoothed for me the path of knowledge, and made the most abstruse inquiries clear and facile to my apprehension. My application was at first fluctuating and uncertain; it gained strength as I proceeded, and soon became so ardent and eager, that the stars often disappeared in the light of morning whilst I was yet engaged in my laboratory.

As I applied so closely, it may be easily conceived that my progress was rapid. My ardour was indeed the astonishment of the students, and my proficiency that of the masters. Professor Krempe often asked me, with a sly smile, how Cornelius Agrippa went on? whilst M. Waldman expressed the most heartfelt exultation in my progress. Two years passed in this manner, during which I paid no visit to Geneva, but was engaged, heart and soul, in the pursuit of some discoveries, which I hoped to make. None but those who have experienced them can conceive of the entice-ments of science. In other studies you go as far as others have gone before you, and there is nothing more to know; but in a scientific pursuit there is continual food for discovery and wonder. A mind of moderate capacity, which closely pursues one study, must infallibly arrive at great proficiency in that study; and I, who continually sought the attainment of one object of pursuit, and was solely wrapped up in this, improved so rapidly, that, at the end of two years, I made some discoveries in the improvement of some chemical instruments, which procured me great esteem and admi-ration at the university. When I had arrived at this point and had become as well acquainted with the theory and practice of natural philos-ophy as depended on the lessons of any of the professors at Ingolstadt, my residence there being no longer conducive to my improvements, I thought of returning to my friends and my native town, when an inci-dent happened that protracted my stay.

NOTES

physiognomy: facial features and expres-sions, especially as indicative of character.

dogmatism: narrow-mindedness, intoler-ance, fanaticism.

pedantry: ostentatious display of knowl-edge and self-importance.

One of the phenomena which had peculiarly attracted my attention was the structure of the human frame, and, indeed, any animal endued with life. Whence, I often asked myself, did the **principle of life** proceed? It was a bold question, and one which has ever been considered as a mystery; yet with how many things are we upon the brink of becoming acquainted, if cowardice or carelessness did not restrain our inquiries. I revolved these circumstances in my mind, and determined thenceforth to apply myself more particularly to those branches of natural philosophy which relate to **physiology**. Unless I had been animated by an almost supernatural enthusiasm, my application to this study would have been irksome, and almost intolerable. To examine the causes of life, we must first have recourse to death. I became acquainted with the science of anatomy: but this was not sufficient; I must also observe the natural decay and corruption of the human body. In my education my father had taken the greatest precautions that my mind should be impressed with no supernatural horrors. I do not ever remember to have trembled at a tale of superstition, or to have feared the apparition of a spirit. Darkness had no effect upon my fancy; and a churchyard was to me merely the receptacle of bodies deprived of life, which, from being the seat of beauty and strength, had become food for the worm. Now I was led to examine the cause and progress of this decay, and forced to spend days and nights in vaults and **charnel-houses**. My attention was fixed upon every object the most insupportable to the delicacy of the human feelings. I saw how the fine form of man was degraded and wasted; I beheld the corruption of death succeed to the blooming cheek of life; I saw how the worm inherited the wonders of the eye and brain. I paused, examining and analysing all the minutiae of causation, as exemplified in the change from life to death, and death to life, until from the midst of this darkness a sudden light broke in upon me—a light so brilliant and wondrous, yet so simple, that while I became dizzy with the immensity of the prospect which it illustrated, I was surprised, that among so many men of genius who had directed their inquiries towards the same science, that I alone should be reserved to discover so astonishing a secret.

Remember, I am not recording the vision of a madman. The sun does not more certainly shine in the heavens, than that which I now affirm is true. Some miracle might have produced it, yet the stages of the discovery were distinct and probable. After days and nights of incredible labour and fatigue, I succeeded in discovering the cause of generation and life; nay, more, I became myself capable of bestowing animation upon lifeless matter.

The astonishment which I had at first experienced on this discovery soon gave place to delight and rapture. After so much time spent in painful labour, to arrive at once at the summit of my desires, was the most gratifying consummation of my toils. But this discovery was so great and overwhelming, that all the steps by which I had been progressively led to it were obliterated, and I beheld only the result. What had been the study

principle of life: the origin of life.

physiology: the science of living organisms.

charnel-houses: houses for dead bodies.

and desire of the wisest men since the creation of the world was now within my grasp. Not that, like a magic scene, it all opened upon me at once: the information I had obtained was of a nature rather to direct my endeavours so soon as I should point them towards the object of my search, than to exhibit that object already accomplished. I was like the **Arabian** who had been buried with the dead, and found a passage to life, aided only by one glimmering, and seemingly ineffectual, light.

I see by your eagerness, and the wonder and hope which your eyes express, my friend, that you expect to be informed of the secret with which I am acquainted; that cannot be: listen patiently until the end of my story, and you will easily perceive why I am reserved upon that subject. I will not lead you on, unguarded and ardent as I then was, to your destruction and infallible misery. Learn from me, if not by my precepts, at least by my example, how dangerous is the acquirement of knowledge, and how much happier that man is who believes his native town to be the world, than he who aspires to become greater than his nature will allow.

When I found so astonishing a power placed within my hands, I hesitated a long time concerning the manner in which I should employ it. Although I possessed the capacity of bestowing animation, yet to prepare a frame for the reception of it, with all its intricacies of fibres, muscles, and veins, still remained a work of inconceivable difficulty and labour. I doubted at first whether I should attempt the creation of a being like myself, or one of simpler organization; but my imagination was too much exalted by my first success to permit me to doubt of my ability to give life to an animal as complete and wonderful as man. The materials at present within my command hardly appeared adequate to so arduous an undertaking; but I doubted not that I should ultimately succeed. I prepared myself for a multitude of reverses; my operations might be incessantly baffled, and at last my work be imperfect; yet, when I considered the improvement which every day takes place in science and mechanics, I was encouraged to hope my present attempts would at least lay the foundations of future success. Nor could I consider the magnitude and complexity of my plan as any argument of its impracticability. It was with these feelings that I began the creation of a human being. As the minuteness of the parts formed a great hindrance to my speed, I resolved, contrary to my first intention, to make the being of a gigantic stature; that is to say, about eight feet in height, and proportionably large. After having formed this determination, and having spent some months in successfully collecting and arranging my materials, I began.

No one can conceive the variety of feelings which bore me onwards, like a hurricane, in the first enthusiasm of success. Life and death appeared to me ideal bounds, which I should first break through, and pour a torrent of light into our dark world. A new species would bless me as its creator and source; many happy and excellent natures would owe their being to me. No father could claim the gratitude of his child so completely as I should deserve theirs. Pursuing these reflections, I thought, that if I could bestow animation upon lifeless matter, I might in process of time

Arabian: an allusion to Sinbad the Sailor's fourth voyage from *Arabian Nights.*

(although I now found it impossible) renew life where death had apparently devoted the body to corruption.

These thoughts supported my spirits, while I pursued my undertaking with unremitting ardour. My cheek had grown pale with study, and my person had become emaciated with confinement. Sometimes, on the very brink of certainty, I failed; yet still I clung to the hope which the next day or the next hour might realise. One secret which I alone possessed was the hope to which I had dedicated myself; and the moon gazed on my midnight labours, while, with unrelaxed and breathless eagerness, I pursued nature to her hiding-places. Who shall conceive the horrors of my secret toil, as I dabbled among the unhallowed damps of the grave, or tortured the living animal to animate the lifeless clay? My limbs now tremble, and my eyes swim with the remembrance; but then a resistless, and almost frantic, impulse, urged me forward; I seemed to have lost all soul or sensation but for this one pursuit. It was indeed but a passing trance, that only made me feel with renewed acuteness so soon as, the unnatural stimulus ceasing to operate, I had returned to my old habits. I collected bones from charnel-houses; and disturbed, with **profane** fingers, the tremendous secrets of the human frame. In a solitary chamber, or rather cell, at the top of the house, and separated from all the other apartments by a gallery and staircase, I kept my workshop of filthy creation: my eye-balls were starting from their sockets in attending to the details of my employment. The dissecting room and the slaughter-house furnished many of my materials; and often did my human nature turn with loathing from my occupation, whilst, still urged on by an eagerness which perpetually increased, I brought my work near to a conclusion.

profane: blasphemous, godless.

The summer months passed while I was thus engaged, heart and soul, in one pursuit. It was a most beautiful season; never did the fields bestow a more plentiful harvest, or the vines yield a more luxuriant vintage: but my eyes were insensible to the charms of nature. And the same feelings which made me neglect the scenes around me caused me also to forget those friends who were so many miles absent, and whom I had not seen for so long a time. I knew my silence disquieted them; and I well remembered the words of my father: "I know that while you are pleased with yourself; you will think of us with affection, and we shall hear regularly from you. You must pardon me if I regard any interruption in your correspondence as a proof that your other duties are equally neglected."

I knew well therefore what would be my father's feelings; but I could not tear my thoughts from my employment, loathsome in itself, but which had taken an irresistible hold of my imagination. I wished, as it were, to procrastinate all that related to my feelings of affection until the great object, which swallowed up every habit of my nature, should be completed.

I then thought that my father would be unjust if he ascribed my neglect to vice, or faultiness on my part; but I am now convinced that he was justified in conceiving that I should not be altogether free from blame. A human being in perfection ought always to preserve a calm and peaceful mind, and never to allow passion or a transitory desire to disturb his tranquillity. I do not think that the pursuit of knowledge is an exception to this rule. If the study to which you apply yourself has a tendency to weaken your affections, and to destroy your taste for those simple pleasures in which no alloy can possibly mix, then that study is certainly unlawful, that is to say, not befitting the human mind. If this rule were always observed; if no man allowed any pursuit whatsoever to interfere with the tranquillity of his domestic affections, Greece had not been enslaved; Caesar would have spared his country; America would have been discovered more gradually; and the empires of Mexico and Peru had not been destroyed.

But I forget that I am moralizing in the most interesting part of my tale; and your looks remind me to proceed.

My father made no reproach in his letters, and only took notice of my silence by inquiring into my occupations more particularly than before. Winter, spring, and summer passed away during my labours; but I did not watch the blossom or the expanding leaves—sights which before always yielded me supreme delight—so deeply was I engrossed in my occupation. The leaves of that year had withered before my work drew near to a close; and now every day showed me more plainly how well I had succeeded. But my enthusiasm was checked by my anxiety, and I appeared rather like one doomed by slavery to toil in the mines, or any other unwholesome trade, than an artist occupied by his favourite employment. Every night I was oppressed by a slow fever, and I became nervous to a most painful degree; the fall of a leaf startled me, and I shunned my fellow-creatures as if I had been guilty of a crime. Sometimes I grew alarmed at the wreck I perceived that I had become; the energy of my purpose alone sustained me: my labours would soon end, and I believed that exercise and amusement would then drive away incipient disease; and I promised myself both of these when my creation should be complete.

COMMENTARY

For two years, Victor Frankenstein is completely absorbed in the study of natural science, especially chemistry, and spends most of his time reading modern works, attending lectures, meeting scientists at the university, and learning how to use the various machines in the laboratory. M. Waldman constantly guides Victor on "the path of knowledge," making clear the most complex concepts, and elatedly praises his progress.

Victor's progress is so extraordinary and his discoveries so outstanding that he quickly becomes one of the most respected researchers at the university as well as his professors' favorite student. Convinced that his instruction at Ingolstadt is complete and that his mentors cannot teach him anything else, Victor plans to return

Victor in his laboratory.
Everett Collection

home to his family and friends. By accident, he makes a terrible discovery—how to create life artificially.

Parallels between Victor and Walton

Victor's tenacious pursuit of a single study echoes Walton's praise of a mind focused on a "steady purpose" in his first letter to Margaret. Victor's two years at the university may also be a subtle allusion to the two years Mary Shelley spent writing the novel. Like Victor's achievement and Walton's expedition, Mary Shelley's novel is the direct product of a concentrated, obsessive study.

Like Walton, who abandoned his family for his research, Victor substitutes the laboratory for his domestic life. For two years, he isolates himself from the love, warmth, and friendship represented by Elizabeth and Clerval, and he allows the seed planted by professor Waldman to develop into a dangerous obsession. In short, he loses the Eden of Geneva to the temptation of Ingolstadt.

In this episode, Mary Shelley offers an interesting analogy of the biblical story in which Eve is tempted by the serpent to eat from the forbidden tree of knowledge— the knowledge of good and evil. In the biblical story, Eve falls into the temptation. Interestingly enough, in *Frankenstein*, Victor, who listens to Waldman's seductive words, is entrapped by an ardent desire to transgress the limits of human knowledge and explore "the deepest mysteries of creation."

And yet, Victor's intense study of science brings him fame and recognition, but not happiness and pleasure. Instead of being a successful and overjoyed scientist, Victor is a tormented and unhappy man, painfully confronted with the disgusting realities of death, decay, and disintegration. Like the biblical God, Victor's father "had taken the greatest precautions that [his] mind should [have been] impressed with no . . . horrors." But Victor's curiosity takes him

precisely into a territory of horror and darkness. The reader should remember that Walton's father had also forbidden his son "to embark on a seafaring life." The same ambition that possesses Victor animates Walton and violates a patriarchal law. After days and nights of hard work and fatigue, he suddenly discovers the ultimate secret, and Victor's disgust is, of course, replaced by euphoria. But soon, he will return to his filthy work, this time for a much darker and more terrifying project.

In his account to Walton, Victor explains how his initial elation became a nightmare that led to "destruction and infallible misery." Talking to Walton, Victor now knows something that he could not understand then— namely, that obtaining knowledge to surpass his limitations is dangerous and destructive. Walton, listening to Victor speaking about the exhilaration he experienced reaching "the summit of [his] desires" and finding "a passage to life," probably hopes that his new friend will share with him the results of his discoveries. But he comes to understand how determined Victor is to never reveal the terrible secret.

Victor's Laboratory

Having control now of an extraordinary power, Victor resolves to create "an animal as complex and wonderful as man." Blinded by the sudden light that gave him the

Teniers' The Alchemist.
© *Philadelphia Museum of Art/CORBIS*

idea, Victor chooses to ignore the extent and complexity of his project, although he does consider its "impracticability." The decision to assemble a being of gigantic proportions is justified by his enormous enthusiasm and his impatience to see his project completed.

The feelings accompanying Victor's work on his project reveal his state of mind, his character, and his profile as a scientist. He wants to abolish the natural separation between life and death and create a new species of perfect beings who, aware of owing their distinction to him, will bless and bring tribute to their creator. Moreover, Victor imagines that knowing how to create life will gradually lead to eradicating death and corruption. Ironically, while working on these grandiose projects, Victor's cheeks become paler and his body gaunt from confinement. Professor Waldman's satanic influence worked, and as advised by his mentor, Victor aggressively and incessantly follows nature "to her hiding-places." He ignores the famous advice given by the archangel Raphael to Adam in the seventh book of Milton's *Paradise Lost*: "Solicit not thy thoughts with matters hid."

Victor establishes his workshop in an isolated area of his house and begins searching for the pieces necessary for his "filthy creation" in charnel houses in cemeteries. For the first time, Victor, the lover of nature, becomes insensitive to its charms, and the summer months pass unobserved by him. He also forgets his friends and family and all his "other duties," confirming his father's principle that an interruption in communication with one's immediate world indicates a general negligence, and abandonment of responsibilities. Engaged "heart and soul" in his research, Victor works frantically on his experiment. However, the closer he gets to completing his creation, the more anxious and more nervous he becomes. His enthusiasm is increasingly replaced by uneasiness; his pleasure by disgust. Instead of becoming a creator playing freely with the material of his creation, Victor becomes fate's doomed slave.

Some critics suggest that the description of Victor's laboratory shows how little Mary Shelley knew about science. All Victor's experiments, they argue, are undertaken in a small attic room by the light of a candle. But an explanation may be that what she was really interested in were the moral implications of Victor's research. The room is hidden, pointing to the illegitimate nature of his work. Also, the mixing of human and animal parts used in the composition of the creature suggests the creation of an inferior being on the evolutionary scale. In his laboratory, Victor Frankenstein appears as a usurper of the traditional God and of the female function of reproduction.

It is also possible to argue that in constructing Victor's laboratory, Mary Shelley may have considered Cornelius Agrippa's ideas from the *Occult Philosophy*, probably the book that Victor accidentally stumbles upon when he is thirteen years old. Although he does not mention the title of Agrippa's work, the *Occult Philosophy* is the alchemist's most famous treatise, in which Agrippa affirms that reanimating dead bodies in a laboratory can be accomplished by men with a powerful imagination, but they need to work in absolute secrecy and silence.

In his confession to Walton, Victor again recalls an uncontrollable power taking possession of his entire life. Despite his terrible anxiety, he explains to Walton that an almost demonic impulse forced him to continue his work. He confesses to losing all connection with the real world. Victor thought that his duty was to sacrifice everything for his goals. But unlike Walton, he now knows that an elevated mind must discriminate between transitory desires and ardent passions and a good, healthy, wise attitude in life. He declares a thirst for knowledge that destroys the taste for simple pleasures as not only immoral but also "unlawful."

Chapter 5 **Victor animates a giant eight-foot body. Disturbed by his own creation, he abandons the Monster, runs home, and hides in his room. After awhile, he falls asleep, and when he awakes, the wretched Monster is hovering over his bed. Terrified, Victor rushes out again and spends the entire night thinking about the horror of his act. Clerval arrives from Geneva and nurses him through several months of nervous fever.**

CHAPTER V

NOTES

IT was on a dreary night of November, that I beheld the accomplishment of my toils. With an anxiety that almost amounted to agony, I collected the instruments of life around me, that I might infuse a spark of being into the lifeless thing that lay at my feet. It was already one in the morning; the rain pattered dismally against the panes, and my candle was nearly burnt out, when, by the glimmer of the half-extinguished light, I saw the dull yellow eye of the creature open; it breathed hard, and a convulsive motion agitated its limbs.

How can I describe my emotions at this catastrophe, or how delineate the wretch whom with such infinite pains and care I had endeavoured to form? His limbs were in proportion, and I had selected his features as beautiful. Beautiful!—Great God! His yellow skin scarcely covered the work of muscles and arteries beneath; his hair was of a lustrous black, and flowing; his teeth of a pearly whiteness; but these luxuriances only formed a more horrid contrast with his watery eyes, that seemed almost of the same colour as the dun white sockets in which they were set, his shrivelled complexion and straight black lips.

The different accidents of life are not so changeable as the feelings of human nature. I had worked hard for nearly two years, for the sole pur-pose of infusing life into an inanimate body. For this I had deprived myself of rest and health. I had desired it with an ardour that far exceeded moderation; but now that I had finished, the beauty of the dream vanished, and breathless horror and disgust filled my heart. Unable to endure the aspect of the being I had created, I rushed out of the room, and continued a long time traversing my bedchamber, unable to compose my mind to sleep. At length lassitude succeeded to the tumult I had before endured; and I threw myself on the bed in my clothes, endeavouring to seek a few moments of forgetfulness. But it was in vain; I slept, indeed, but I was disturbed by the wildest dreams. I thought I saw Elizabeth, in the bloom of health, walking in the streets of Ingolstadt. Delighted and surprised, I embraced her; but as I imprinted the first kiss on her lips, they became livid with the hue of death; her fea-tures appeared to change, and I thought that I held the corpse of my dead mother in my arms; a shroud enveloped her form, and I saw the graveworms crawling in the folds of the flannel. I started from my sleep with horror; a cold dew covered my forehead, my teeth chattered, and every limb became convulsed; when, by the dim and yellow light of the moon, as it forced its way through the window shutters, I beheld the wretch—the miserable monster whom I had created. He held up the curtain of the bed; and his eyes, if eyes they may be called, were fixed on me. His jaws opened, and he muttered some inarticulate sounds, while a grin wrinkled his cheeks. He might have spoken, but I did not hear; one hand was stretched out, seemingly to detain me, but I escaped, and rushed down stairs. I took refuge in the courtyard belonging to the house which I inhabited; where I remained during the rest of the night, walking up and down in the greatest agitation, listening attentively, catching and fearing each sound as if it were to announce the approach of the demoniacal corpse to which I had so miserably given life.

Oh! no mortal could support the horror of that countenance. A mummy again endued with animation could not be so hideous as that wretch. I had gazed on him while unfinished; he was ugly then; but when those muscles and joints were rendered capable of motion, it became a thing such as even **Dante** could not have conceived.

Dante: Dante Alighieri (1265–1321), Italian poet, born in Florence. His most famous poem is *Divina Commedia*, or *The Divine Comedy*.

I passed the night wretchedly. Sometimes my pulse beat so quickly and hardly, that I felt the palpitation of every artery; at others, I nearly sank to the ground through languor and extreme weakness. Mingled with this horror, I felt the bitterness of disappointment; dreams that had been my food and pleasant rest for so long a space were now become a hell to me; and the change was so rapid, the overthrow so complete!

Morning, dismal and wet, at length dawned, and discovered to my sleepless and aching eyes the church of Ingolstadt, its white steeple and clock, which indicated the sixth hour. The porter opened the gates of the court, which had that night been my asylum, and I issued into the streets, pacing them with quick steps, as if I sought to avoid the wretch whom I feared every turning of the street would present to my view. I did not dare return to the apartment which I inhabited, but felt impelled to hurry on, although drenched by the rain which poured from a black and comfortless sky.

I continued walking in this manner for some time, endeavouring, by bodily exercise, to ease the load that weighed upon my mind. I traversed the streets, without any clear conception of where I was, or what I was doing. My heart palpitated in the sickness of fear; and I hurried on with irregular steps, not daring to look about me:

> Like one who, on a lonely road,
>
> Doth walk in fear and dread,
>
> And, having once turned round, walks on,
>
> And turns no more his head;
>
> Because he knows a frightful fiend
>
> Doth close behind him tread.
>
> [Coleridge's "Ancient Mariner."]

Continuing thus, I came at length opposite to the inn at which the various **diligences** and carriages usually stopped. Here I paused, I knew not why; but I remained some minutes with my eyes fixed on a coach that was coming towards me from the other end of the street. As it drew nearer, I observed that it was the Swiss diligence: it stopped just where I was standing; and on the door being opened, I perceived Henry Clerval, who, on seeing me, instantly sprung out. "My dear Frankenstein," exclaimed he, "how glad I am to see you! How fortunate that you should be here at the very moment of my alighting!"

Nothing could equal my delight on seeing Clerval; his presence brought back to my thoughts my father, Elizabeth, and all those scenes of home so dear to my recollection. I grasped his hand, and in a moment forgot my horror and misfortune; I felt suddenly, and for the first time during many months, calm and serene joy. I welcomed my friend, therefore, in the most cordial manner, and we walked towards my college. Clerval continued talking for some time about our mutual friends, and his own good fortune in being permitted to come to Ingolstadt. "You may easily believe," said he, "how great was the difficulty to persuade my father that all necessary knowledge was not comprised in the noble art of book-keeping; and, indeed, I believe I left him incredulous to the last, for his constant answer to my unwearied entreaties was the same as that of the Dutch schoolmaster in **The Vicar of Wakefield**: 'I have ten thousand florins a year without Greek, I eat heartily without Greek.' But his affection for me at length overcame his dislike of learning, and he has permitted me to undertake a voyage of discovery to the land of knowledge."

"It gives me the greatest delight to see you; but tell me how you left my father, brothers, and Elizabeth."

"Very well, and very happy, only a little uneasy that they hear from you so seldom. By the by, I mean to lecture you a little upon their account myself.—But, my dear Frankenstein," continued he, stopping short, and gazing full in my face, "I did not before remark how very ill you appear; so thin and pale; you look as if you had been watching for several nights."

"You have guessed right; I have lately been so deeply engaged in one occupation, that I have not allowed myself sufficient rest, as you see; but I hope, I sincerely hope, that all these employments are now at an end, and that I am at length free."

I trembled excessively; I could not endure to think of, and far less to allude to, the occurrences of the preceding night. I walked with a quick pace, and we soon arrived at my college. I then reflected, and the thought made me shiver, that the creature whom I had left in my apartment might still be there, alive, and walking about. I dreaded to behold this monster; but I feared still more that Henry should see him. Entreating him, therefore, to remain a few minutes at the bottom of the stairs, I darted up towards my own room. My hand was already on the lock of the door before I recollected myself. I then paused; and a cold shivering

diligences: public stagecoaches.

The Vicar of Wakefield: novel by Oliver Goldsmith (1728–74), written in 1766. The hero of the book is Doctor Primrose, a benevolent country clergyman, who, despite the many misfortunes that fall upon him and his family, maintains a steadfast and hopeful composure.

came over me. I threw the door forcibly open, as children are accustomed to do when they expect a spectre to stand in waiting for them on the other side; but nothing appeared. I stepped fearfully in: the apartment was empty; and my bedroom was also freed from its hideous guest. I could hardly believe that so great a good fortune could have befallen me; but when I became assured that my enemy had indeed fled, I clapped my hands for joy, and ran down to Clerval.

We ascended into my room, and the servant presently brought breakfast; but I was unable to contain myself. It was not joy only that possessed me; I felt my flesh tingle with excess of sensitiveness, and my pulse beat rapidly. I was unable to remain for a single instant in the same place; I jumped over the chairs, clapped my hands, and laughed aloud. Clerval at first attributed my unusual spirits to joy on his arrival; but when he observed me more attentively, he saw a wildness in my eyes for which he could not account; and my loud, unrestrained, heartless laughter, frightened and astonished him.

"My dear Victor," cried he, "what, for God's sake, is the matter? Do not laugh in that manner. How ill you are! What is the cause of all this?"

"Do not ask me," cried I, putting my hands before my eyes, for I thought I saw the dreaded **spectre** glide into the room; "*he* can tell.—Oh, save me! save me!" I imagined that the monster seized me; I struggled furiously, and fell down in a fit.

spectre: specter, ghost, phantom.

Poor Clerval! what must have been his feelings? A meeting, which he anticipated with such joy, so strangely turned to bitterness. But I was not the witness of his grief, for I was lifeless, and did not recover my senses for a long, long time.

This was the commencement of a nervous fever, which confined me for several months. During all that time Henry was my only nurse. I afterwards learned that, knowing my father's advanced age, and unfitness for so long a journey, and how wretched my sickness would make Elizabeth, he spared them this grief by concealing the extent of my disorder. He knew that I could not have a more kind and attentive nurse than himself; and, firm in the hope he felt of my recovery, he did not doubt that, instead of doing harm, he performed the kindest action that he could towards them.

But I was in reality very ill; and surely nothing but the unbounded and unremitting attentions of my friend could have restored me to life. The form of the monster on whom I had bestowed existence was forever before my eyes, and I raved incessantly concerning him. Doubtless my words surprised Henry: he at first believed them to be the wanderings of my disturbed imagination, but the **pertinacity** with which I continually recurred to the same subject persuaded him that my disorder indeed owed its origin to some uncommon and terrible event.

pertinacity: perseverance, determination.

By very slow degrees, and with frequent relapses, that alarmed and grieved my friend, I recovered. I remember the first time I became capable of observing outward objects with any kind of pleasure, I perceived that the fallen leaves had disappeared, and that the young buds were shooting forth from the trees that shaded my window. It was a divine spring; and the season contributed greatly to my convalescence. I felt also sentiments of joy and affection revive in my bosom; my gloom disappeared, and in a short time I became as cheerful as before I was attacked by the fatal passion.

"Dearest Clerval," exclaimed I, "how kind, how very good you are to me. This whole winter, instead of being spent in study, as you promised yourself, has been consumed in my sick room. How shall I ever repay you? I feel the greatest remorse for the disappointment of which I have been the occasion; but you will forgive me."

"You will repay me entirely, if you do not discompose yourself, but get well as fast as you can; and since you appear in such good spirits, I may speak to you on one subject, may I not?"

I trembled. One subject! what could it be? Could he allude to an object on whom I dared not even think?

"Compose yourself," said Clerval, who observed my change of colour, "I will not mention it, if it agitates you; but your father and cousin would be very happy if they received a letter from you in your own handwriting. They hardly know how ill you have been, and are uneasy at your long silence."

"Is that all, my dear Henry? How could you suppose that my first thought would not fly towards those dear, dear friends whom I love, and who are so deserving of my love?"

"If this is your present temper, my friend, you will perhaps be glad to see a letter that has been lying here some days for you: it is from your cousin, I believe."

COMMENTARY

The Animation of the Monster

On a bleak November night, Victor Frankenstein, in a paradoxical state of frenzy and terror, gathers his "instruments of life" and animates the gigantic eight-foot body lying lifeless at his feet. But as soon as the creature opens a "dull yellow eye" and moves its huge limbs, Victor is frightened and appalled. The body parts, chosen with painful precision for nearly two years and the features, meticulously assembled and attentively proportioned to create a perfect body, result in a monstrous creation that destroys the beauty of Victor's dream and fills his heart with "horror and disgust."

Philosophies of the Time

Victor's creation episode, largely constructed on the subtle irony of assembling a perfect and beautiful man out of degenerating bodies, can also be read as a parody of perfectibility, a concept to which Mary's father, William Godwin, and her husband, Percy Shelley, enthusiastically adhered. The following basic concepts informed the revolutionary ideals of her generation:

* Reason: The principle that guides human action.
* Equality: Justice and generosity can assure social equality.
* Perfectibility: If not corrupted by society and its institutions, individuals can progress constantly towards perfection.
* Necessity: History will assist man in his quest for perfection.

Never a passionate radical like her parents, her husband, and most of the intellectuals in her circle, Mary Shelley further distanced herself from their radicalism

The Monster (and his creator).
Everett Collection

Magnus, one of Victor's intellectual models who creates a mechanical man in his laboratory, relates thematically to the legend of the Golem, a story describing the animation of a clay man by a Jewish rabbi in the sixteenth century. In 1815, Mary Shelley read the story of Pygmalion and Galatea: Pygmalion, the king of Cyprus and a famous sculptor, falls ardently in love with a statue he creates of a beautiful maiden. Aphrodite, the goddess of love, hearing his prayers, gives the statue life. Whether these sources played any role in the creation of the Monster's character, Mary Shelley, like so many Romantic writers, was certainly interested in the supernatural dimension of folklore, fairy tales, and balladry.

Satan and Prometheus as Literary Models for Victor

Victor, playing God, resembles Satan from Milton's *Paradise Lost*, in which Satan is an archangel punished for his vanity, arrogance, and thirst for forbidden knowledge. Like him, Victor attempts to appropriate God's legitimate role as creator and master of the universe. This achievement, Victor imagines, will be a superior one, and its exuberant and admirable beings will worship and honor him like a most deserving father.

The Romantics, especially Blake, Byron, and Percy Shelley, interpreted Milton's account of the biblical story of Genesis as a celebration of Satan—the rebellious hero who defies the power of God. They regarded Satan, not as the embodiment of evil, but as a victim of the tyrannical power of the establishment. Satan triumphs in the battle against oppression and sacrifices his privileged position in heaven for the noble cause of freedom. Byron, for instance wrote two verse dramas, *Manfred* (1816) and *Cain* (1821), both works expressions of this new reevaluation of the role of Satan in history.

The character of Victor also owes much to Prometheus in his double role as fire-bringer (Prometheus *pyrphoros*) and as creator of humanity (Prometheus *plasticator*). The myth of Prometheus as father/creator of the human race

after 1823. By 1831, when she heavily revised the 1818 version of the novel, her own faith in reason and perfectibility had diminished significantly. After years of suffering disappointments and loss, Mary Shelley became less and less convinced that humans, assisted by reason, could design a good life for themselves and their communities. She felt that reason could be used for both admirable and ignoble ends and, moreover, that "the immutable laws" governing the universe could make everyone victims of destiny.

Myth and Legends

The animation of the Monster may have been inspired by any number of stories and legends. The story of Albert appears in Ovid's *Metamorphoses*, a book that Mary Shelley read before *Frankenstein* was conceived. The character of Prometheus especially appealed to the Romantics because he was another divine rebel. Prometheus defies Jupiter, the omnipotent and inexorable god, by stealing fire from him and offering it as a gift to humans. Just as Satan is cast out from paradise, Jupiter punishes Prometheus by having his liver eaten by vultures.

Like Satan and Prometheus, Victor Frankenstein is a rebellious character who has faith in his own creative powers and has the courage to aspire higher than his limited human condition allows. However, Mary Shelly does not present Victor's acts as positive or meritorious. Victor's intellectual curiosity and ambition does not contribute to any scientific advancement or social progress. Instead, he destroys a family and, symbolically, populates the world with monstrous fantasies.

Victor Abandons his Creation

Scared, disgusted, and confused by the Monster, Victor immediately abandons his creation and runs to his room. After vain attempts to forget the abominable image, he falls asleep and has an enormously disturbing dream. In this dream, Victor views the young and beautiful Elizabeth walking through the streets of Ingolstadt, and pleasantly surprised by this unexpected event, he kisses her passionately on the lips. Suddenly, she dies, and Victor finds himself holding not Elizabeth's body, but the corpse of their mother enveloped in a shroud covered with grave worms. Terrified, Victor wakes and sees the Monster at his bedside. Victor again runs away.

Victor's rejection of his own creation is so complete that he refuses even to give the creature a name; a failure with important implications. Generally, naming has a ceremonial, symbolic dimension by which the named one achieves identity. (In Genesis, Adam names all living creatures, thus becoming God's partner in creation.) Also, the namer gains authority over the named. (Adam reigns over all other creatures.) By not giving his creature a name, Victor

refuses him an identity, making his ambiguous nature (an assembly of animal and human parts) and problematic existence even more undetermined and enigmatic. Indeed, he can now be called various names, all of them alluding in one way or another to his abnormality, but none giving him a sense of belonging, affiliation, connection, or stability. Interestingly, Mary Shelley subtly involves the reader in this disturbing situation, forcing the reader to call the Monster whatever Victor calls him. Victor usurps the traditional monotheistic authority as well as the female prerogative to procreate, and, by depriving the creature of a clear identity and avoiding his responsibilities as a creator, loses his authority and credibility.

Victor's Nightmare

Victor's nightmare represents another pivotal moment in the development of the narrative, revealing complex

Rubens' Prometheus Bound.
© *Philadelphia Museum of Art/CORBIS*

connections between the three major characters in the novel: the Monster, Victor, and Elizabeth. A significant point is that Victor's nightmare occurs immediately after he creates the Monster. The overlapping of death and life undoubtedly mirrors Mary Shelley's conflicting ideas about death and life, as well as her own anxieties and fears. A sense of guilt associated with her mother's death at her birth, the death of her first child and the birth of another one, and the multiple suicides in her family and her lover's family, all contributed to blurring the distinctions between life and death in her young mind. Also, her anxieties about motherhood (at only 19 years old) and the pressure of authorship (by her father and her husband) probably played a role in the construction of this episode.

Victor's dream of his mother and his lover, Elizabeth, is significant in its symbolic representation of Victor's declaration in Chapter 4 proclaiming that he wants to "renew life where death had apparently devoted the body to corruption." Paradoxically, the dream reveals that instead of aspiring to restore his mother's life, presumably the first life he would want to restore, Victor rejects his mother, and by killing Elizabeth, Caroline's substitute, he kills his mother twice. Victor's murderous kiss repudiates and dismisses the maternal presence—and the female presence in general. Thus, Victor's actions alert the reader that the gender issues raised by this chapter are essential in understanding the complex message of the novel.

What the dream reveals is difficult to understand. But one can speculate that the dream reveals Victor's rejection of Elizabeth for replacing his mother, of his mother for abandoning him, and of the union with Elizabeth that was decided for him by his parents. In any case, the reality and the dream are equally terrifying, and Victor feels trapped in an existential nightmare. Moreover, the dream unites himself, his mother, his lover, and his creation—all of whom Victor refuses to associate with. Not only is Victor's dream of greatness destroyed, but his own life is disfigured. The

Monster does not reflect his creator, but he mirrors his creator's fall—his disfigurement. Elizabeth and the Monster share strange similarities as well. Both are orphans, both are abandoned by their fathers, and both are adopted or created to serve somebody else's idea of perfection. Moreover, critics suggest that the beautiful and mild Elizabeth and the ugly and ultimately violent creature can be viewed as doubles. The creature and Elizabeth may also constitute the two conflicting parts of Victor's psyche: Elizabeth is Victor's good part, and the Monster is his evil one.

Victor's Despair

The horror of his act and the terrible nightmare keep Victor awake the entire night. Fearing another encounter with the Monster, Victor hides in the courtyard. In the morning, he is disoriented, exhausted, and confused, and he aimlessly walks the streets of Ingolstadt, fearing to meet the Monster. Nearly delirious, Victor arrives in front of an inn, where Henry Clerval unexpectedly descends from a carriage. Henry's presence, as well as his news from home, makes Victor forget for a moment his fear. Back at his apartment however, Victor behaves strangely; he has a spasm and loses consciousness. Patiently, Clerval nurses him through several months of nervous fever. When Victor recovers, he is unable to tell his friend about his terrible creation.

The chapter starts with a creative impulse and ends with a failed creator suffering. Mary Shelly's novel is a critique of the Romantic myth of the artist who puts his entire trust in the power of imagination. Imagination, she seems to warn, can isolate the individual from community and from normal human concerns. Also, the obsessive pursuit of a dream does not allow other dimensions of one's personality to develop adequately. Mary Shelley, herself an artist, writing in isolation, understands the benefits of solitude, but as her life and work demonstrate, she also pays attention to her roles as mother, lover, wife, and daughter.

Chapter 6   A letter from Elizabeth reminds Victor about their faithful family servant, Justine Moritz, who has returned to Geneva to live with the Frankensteins. At Ingolstadt, Victor introduced Clerval, who came there to study Oriental languages, to his mentors. Before he returned to Geneva, the two friends toured the beautiful surroundings of Ingolstadt and Victor rediscovered the splendor of nature and the pleasure of life beyond the laboratory.

CHAPTER VI

CLERVAL then put the following letter into my hands. It was from my own Elizabeth:—

"My dearest Cousin,

"You have been ill, very ill, and even the constant letters of dear kind Henry are not sufficient to reassure me on your account. You are forbidden to write—to hold a pen; yet one word from you, dear Victor, is necessary to calm our apprehensions. For a long time I have thought that each post would bring this line, and my persuasions have restrained my uncle from undertaking a journey to Ingolstadt. I have prevented his encountering the inconveniences and perhaps dangers of so long a journey; yet how often have I regretted not being able to perform it myself! I figure to myself that the task of attending on your sick bed has devolved on some mercenary old nurse, who could never guess your wishes, nor minister to them with the care and affection of your poor cousin. Yet that is over now: Clerval writes that indeed you are getting better. I eagerly hope that you will confirm this intelligence soon in your own handwriting.

"Get well—and return to us. You will find a happy, cheerful home, and friends who love you dearly. Your father's health is vigorous, and he asks but to see you,—but to be assured that you are well; and not a care will ever cloud his benevolent countenance. How pleased you would be to remark the improvement of our Ernest! He is now sixteen, and full of activity and spirit. He is desirous to be a true Swiss, and to enter into foreign service; but we cannot part with him, at least until his elder brother returns to us. My uncle is not pleased with the idea of a military career in a distant country; but Ernest never had your powers of application. He looks upon study as an odious fetter;—his time is spent in the open air, climbing the hills or rowing on the lake. I fear that he will become an idler, unless we yield the point, and permit him to enter on the profession which he has selected.

"Little alteration, except the growth of our dear children, has taken place since you left us. The blue lake, and snow-clad mountains, they never change;—and I think our placid home, and our contented hearts are regulated by the same immutable laws. My trifling occupations take up my time and amuse me, and I am rewarded for any exertions by seeing none but happy, kind faces around me. Since you left us, but one change has taken place in our little household. Do you remember on what occasion Justine Moritz entered our family? Probably you do not; I will relate her history, therefore, in a few words. Madame Moritz, her mother, was a widow with four children, of whom Justine was the third. This girl had always been the favourite of her father, but, through a strange perversity, her mother could not endure her, and, after the death of M. Moritz, treated her very ill. My aunt observed this; and, when Justine was twelve years of age, prevailed on her mother to allow her to live at our house. The republican institutions of our country have produced simpler and happier manners than those which prevail in the great monarchies that surround it. Hence there is less distinction between the several classes of its inhabitants; and the lower orders, being neither so poor nor so despised, their manners are more refined and moral. A servant in Geneva does not mean the same thing as a servant in France and England. Justine, thus received in our family, learned the duties of a servant; a condition which, in our fortunate country, does not include the idea of ignorance, and a sacrifice of the dignity of a human being.

"Justine, you may remember, was a great favourite of yours; and I recollect you once remarked, that if you were in an ill-humour, one glance from Justine could dissipate it, for the same reason that **Ariosto** gives concerning the beauty of **Angelica**—she looked so frank-hearted and happy. My aunt conceived a great attachment for her, by which she was induced to give her an education superior to that which she had at first intended. This benefit was fully repaid; Justine was the most grateful little creature in the world: I do not mean that she made any professions; I never heard one pass her lips; but you could see by her eyes that she almost adored her protectress. Although her disposition was gay, and in many respects inconsiderate, yet she paid the greatest attention to every gesture of my aunt. She thought her the model of all excellence, and endeavoured to imitate her phraseology and manners, so that even now she often reminds me of her.

"When my dearest aunt died, every one was too much occupied in their own grief to notice poor Justine, who had attended her during her illness with the most anxious affection. Poor Justine was very ill; but other trials were reserved for her.

"One by one, her brothers and sister died; and her mother, with the exception of her neglected daughter, was left childless. The conscience of the woman was troubled; she began to think that the deaths of her favourites was a judgment from heaven to chastise her partiality. She was a Roman Catholic; and I believe her confessor confirmed the idea which she had conceived. Accordingly, a few months after your departure for Ingolstadt, Justine was called home by her repentant mother. Poor girl! she wept when she quitted our house; she was much altered since the death of my aunt; grief had given softness and a winning mildness to her manners, which had before been remarkable for vivacity. Nor was her residence at her mother's house of a nature to restore

Ariosto: Ludovico Ariosto (1474–1533), one of the great Italian writers of the Renaissance.

Angelica: the heroine of Ariosto's *Orlando Furioso.*

her gaiety. The poor woman was very vacillating in her repentance. She sometimes begged Justine to forgive her unkindness, but much oftener accused her of having caused the deaths of her brothers and sister. Perpetual fretting at length threw Madame Moritz into a decline, which at first increased her irritability, but she is now at peace for ever. She died on the first approach of cold weather, at the beginning of this last winter. Justine has just returned to us; and I assure you I love her tenderly. She is very clever and gentle, and extremely pretty; as I mentioned before, her mien and her expressions continually remind me of my dear aunt.

"I must say also a few words to you, my dear cousin, of little darling William. I wish you could see him; he is very tall of his age, with sweet laughing blue eyes, dark eyelashes, and curling hair. When he smiles, two little dimples appear on each cheek, which are rosy with health. He has already had one or two little *wives*, but Louisa Biron is his favourite, a pretty little girl of five years of age.

"Now, dear Victor, I dare say you wish to be indulged in a little gossip concerning the good people of Geneva. The pretty Miss Mansfield has already received the congratulatory visits on her approaching marriage with a young Englishman, John Melbourne, Esq. Her ugly sister, Manon, married M. Duvillard, the rich banker, last autumn. Your favourite schoolfellow, Louis Manoir, has suffered several misfortunes since the departure of Clerval from Geneva. But he has already recovered his spirits, and is reported to be on the point of marrying a lively pretty Frenchwoman, Madame Tavernier. She is a widow, and much older than Manoir; but she is very much admired, and a favourite with everybody.

"I have written myself into better spirits, dear cousin; but my anxiety returns upon me as I conclude. Write, dearest Victor,—one line—one word will be a blessing to us. Ten thousand thanks to Henry for his kindness, his affection, and his many letters: we are sincerely grateful. Adieu! my cousin; take care of your self; and, I entreat you, write!

"Elizabeth Lavenza
"Geneva, March 18, 17—."

"Dear, dear Elizabeth!" I exclaimed, when I had read her letter: "I will write instantly, and relieve them from the anxiety they must feel." I wrote, and this exertion greatly fatigued me; but my convalescence had commenced, and proceeded regularly. In another fortnight I was able to leave my chamber.

One of my first duties on my recovery was to introduce Clerval to the several professors of the university. In doing this, I underwent a kind of rough usage, ill befitting the wounds that my mind had sustained. Ever since the fatal night, the end of my labours, and the beginning of my misfortunes, I had conceived a violent antipathy even to the name of natural philosophy. When I was otherwise quite restored to health, the sight of a chemical instrument would renew all the agony of my nervous symptoms. Henry saw this, and had removed all my apparatus from my view. He had also changed my apartment; for he perceived that I had acquired a dislike for the room which had previously been my laboratory. But these cares of Clerval were made of no avail when I visited the professors. M. Waldman inflicted torture when he praised, with kindness and warmth, the astonishing progress I had made in the sciences. He soon perceived that I disliked the subject; but not guessing the real cause, he attributed my feelings to modesty, and changed the subject from my improvement, to the science itself, with a desire, as I evidently saw, of drawing me out. What could I do? He meant to please, and he tormented me. I felt as if he had placed carefully, one by one, in my view those instruments which were to be afterwards used in putting me to a slow and cruel death. I writhed under his words, yet dared not exhibit the pain I felt. Clerval, whose eyes and feelings were always quick in discerning the sensations of others, declined the subject, alleging, in excuse, his total ignorance; and the conversation took a more general turn. I thanked my friend from my heart, but I did not speak. I saw plainly that he was surprised, but he never attempted to draw my secret from me; and although I loved him with a mixture of affection and reverence that knew no bounds, yet I could never persuade myself to confide in him that event which was so often present to my recollection, but which I feared the detail to another would only impress more deeply.

M. Krempe was not equally docile; and in my condition at that time, of almost insupportable sensitiveness, his harsh blunt encomiums gave me even more pain than the benevolent approbation of M. Waldman. "D—n the fellow!" cried he; "why, M. Clerval, I assure you he has outstript us all. Ay, stare if you please; but it is nevertheless true. A youngster who, but a few years ago, believed in Cornelius Agrippa as firmly as in the gospel, has now set himself at the head of the university; and if he is not soon pulled down, we shall all be out of countenance.—Ay, ay," continued he, observing my face expressive of suffering, "M. Frankenstein is modest; an excellent quality in a young man. Young men should be diffident of themselves, you know, M. Clerval: I was myself when young; but that wears out in a very short time."

M. Krempe had now commenced an **eulogy** on himself, which happily turned the conversation from a subject that was so annoying to me.

eulogy: speech in praise of a person.

Clerval had never sympathized in my tastes for natural science; and his literary pursuits differed wholly from those which had occupied me. He came to the university with the design of making himself complete master of the oriental languages, as thus he should open a field for the plan of life he had marked out for himself. Resolved to pursue no inglorious career, he turned his eyes toward the East, as affording scope for his spirit of enterprise. The Persian, Arabic, and **Sanscrit** languages engaged his attention, and I was easily induced to enter on the same studies. Idleness had ever been irksome to me, and now that I wished to fly from reflection, and hated my former studies, I felt great relief in being the

Sanscrit: the ancient language of India considered sacred.

fellow-pupil with my friend, and found not only instruction but consolation in the works of the orientalists. I did not, like him, attempt a critical knowledge of their dialects, for I did not contemplate making any other use of them than temporary amusement. I read merely to understand their meaning, and they well repaid my labours. Their melancholy is soothing, and their joy elevating, to a degree I never experienced in studying the authors of any other country. When you read their writings, life appears to consist in a warm sun and a garden of roses,—in the smiles and frowns of a fair enemy, and the fire that consumes your own heart. How different from the manly and heroical poetry of Greece and Rome!

Summer passed away in these occupations, and my return to Geneva was fixed for the latter end of autumn; but being delayed by several accidents, winter and snow arrived, the roads were deemed impassable, and my journey was retarded until the ensuing spring. I felt this delay very bitterly; for I longed to see my native town and my beloved friends. My return had only been delayed so long, from an unwillingness to leave Clerval in a strange place, before he had become acquainted with any of its inhabitants. The winter, however, was spent cheerfully; and although the spring was uncommonly late, when it came its beauty compensated for its dilatoriness.

The month of May had already commenced, and I expected the letter daily which was to fix the date of my departure, when Henry proposed a pedestrian tour in the environs of Ingolstadt, that I might bid a personal farewell to the country I had so long inhabited. I acceded with pleasure to this proposition: I was fond of exercise, and Clerval had always been my favourite companion in the rambles of this nature that I had taken among the scenes of my native country.

We passed a fortnight in these **perambulations**: my health and spirits had long been restored, and they gained additional strength from the **salubrious** air I breathed, the natural incidents of our progress, and the conversation of my friend. Study had before secluded me from the intercourse of my fellow-creatures, and rendered me unsocial; but Clerval called forth the better feelings of my heart; he again taught me to love the aspect of nature, and the cheerful faces of children. Excellent friend! how sincerely you did love me, and endeavour to elevate my mind until it was on a level with your own! A selfish pursuit had cramped and narrowed me, until your gentleness and affection warmed and opened my senses; I became the same happy creature who, a few years ago, loved and beloved by all, had no sorrow or care. When happy, inanimate nature had the power of bestowing on me the most delightful sensations. A serene sky and verdant fields filled me with ecstasy. The present season was indeed divine; the flowers of spring bloomed in the hedges, while those of summer were already in bud. I was undisturbed by thoughts which during the preceding year had pressed upon me, notwithstanding my endeavours to throw them off, with an invincible burden.

perambulations: long walks.

salubrious: healthy.

Henry rejoiced in my gaiety, and sincerely sympathised in my feelings: he exerted himself to amuse me, while he expressed the sensations that filled his soul. The resources of his mind on this occasion were truly astonishing: his conversation was full of imagination; and very often, in imitation of the Persian and Arabic writers, he invented tales of wonderful fancy and passion. At other times he repeated my favourite poems, or drew me out into arguments, which he supported with great ingenuity.

We returned to our college on a Sunday afternoon: the peasants were dancing, and every one we met appeared gay and happy. My own spirits were high, and I bounded along with feelings of unbridled joy and hilarity.

COMMENTARY

Clerval gives Victor a letter from Elizabeth that arrived while he was sick. The letter depicts both a concerned lover and a dutiful daughter. But despite her terrible fears regarding Victor's health, Elizabeth also fears for the health of the elder Mr. Frankenstein and prevents him from traveling to Ingolstadt to visit his son. Understanding from Clerval that the critical moment has passed and that Victor is now recovering, she implores Victor to return to their happy and loving home. She also informs him about the family; Ernest is now sixteen and has decided on a military career, and Justine Moritz, after spending many years caring for her sick mother, has returned to Geneva to live with the Frankensteins and serve the family.

Elizabeth's Roles

The letter reveals the importance of Elizabeth's presence in the Frankenstein household and how impeccably she fulfills her role as daughter, sister, and mistress of the house. She modestly calls the difficult task of taking care of a family constituted exclusively by men "my trifling occupations," and remarks how well rewarded she is when the "happy, kind faces around [her]" reconfirm her good work and validate her efforts to please and enchant everybody.

Behind this serene image, however, is a young woman at the peak of her development, but almost completely negated—she exists merely to serve the needs of the men around her. The reader learns nothing about her desires and aspirations, her needs, or her education. In fact, she does not receive any formal instruction.

Elizabeth's reflections on the unchangeable laws of nature, which, she believes, equally govern human lives, introduce a note of pessimism that subtly but considerably alters the generally optimistic tone of her letter. She seems to be fully aware of her life's limitations but chooses to accept them as inescapable. She believes her life is controlled by an incomprehensible power that is indifferent to human existence and human needs.

The Frankenstein Family Dynamics

Elizabeth's account of the family members also contains interesting ambiguities. Victor's father is in excellent health, but he is easily persuaded not to go and assist his very sick child. Ironically, the good father appears as indifferent and detached. The image of Alphonse Frankenstein, abandoning his child and leaving him completely in the care of a devoted but young and inexperienced friend, offers a strong contrast to the image of Caroline Beaufort Frankenstein, the mother who sacrificed her life to save her adopted daughter and Victor's future wife.

Perhaps Caroline intuitively knew that her son, unhealthily dedicated to his studies and socially inept, would struggle to form and sustain a relationship with a woman. Therefore, Caroline understood that adopting Elizabeth was vital—Elizabeth could dedicate her life to tending Victor's needs, as well as the needs of all the men in the Frankenstein family.

In contrast, Alphonse Frankenstein appears as a selfish, self-centered man, who is unable to react appropriately to his son's needs (in the same way that the proud, rigid, and egotistic Beaufort ignored his daughter's needs). Elizabeth's account of Alphonse differs subtly from Victor's account of him in the first chapters; readers get two drastically different perspectives of the same man.

Elizabeth's description of Ernest intensifies the idea that not everything is perfect in the Frankenstein household. First, Victor's father adamantly disagrees with Ernest's desire to be a soldier. Does this description throw a shadow of doubt over Alphonse Frankenstein's patriotism? Does it question Victor's description of him as a man completely and selflessly dedicated to public service and the general good of the community? More importantly, however, is that Ernest appears as a foil for Victor, something that may explain why he is the only one to escape the Monster's vengeance later.

Justine's story also serves an important function. Like Elizabeth, Justine is an orphan, and she also adopts Caroline Beaufort Frankenstein's model completely. Justine nursed her sick and cruel mother with the same devotion and tenderness that Caroline showed her sick and selfish father. Justine even imitates Caroline's gestures and attitudes to the point that Elizabeth begins to see Caroline's image in Justine. At the same time, the story about Justine that Elizabeth recounts in her letter to Victor introduces some enigmatic details about Justine—for instance, her mother accuses Justine of causing the deaths of her siblings. This story sets the groundwork for suspicion about Justine later in the novel.

The final segment of Elizabeth's letter is also ironic. The Genevans are totally absorbed in their mundane concerns and insignificant lives that revolve around money, marriages, and love affairs. A clear insistence on the theme of marriage may be Elizabeth's way of reminding Victor of their own proposed marriage.

Clerval in Ingolstadt

After Victor recovers in Ingolstadt, he introduces Clerval to several professors, including M. Waldman and M. Krempe. They praise Victor's progress in the sciences, and instead of being pleased or flattered, Victor recalls the tormenting memory of his secret creation. Fortunately, Clerval's interest in Oriental languages, a subject in which he hopes to make his mark, distracts Victor from meditating on his former studies. Victor decides to join his friend in his study of Persian, Arabic, and Sanskrit languages not only to alleviate his pain but also for additional learning. Victor's return to Geneva, initially planned for the end of fall, is again postponed "by several accidents" and by his reluctance to leave Clerval alone in an unfamiliar place, without friends or any other solid connections. Before his departure at the end of spring, Victor and Clerval decide to take a walking tour of the country around Ingolstadt.

Clerval is not completely different from Walton and Victor. Like them, his aim is to pursue a glorious career. His obsession is to become the "complete master of the Oriental languages," and he "turn[s] his eyes toward the East, as affording scope for his spirit of enterprise." This spirit of enterprise sounds suspiciously similar to Walton and Victor's spirit of adventure; he, too, wants to master a certain type of knowledge so he can conquer and control.

Initially, Clerval is the only one among the three young men in the novel who complies with his father's desires. In the end, however, Clerval also becomes a transgressor. He does not disobey his father's demands directly but, instead, prepares a powerful strategy. Remember Victor's observation in Chapter 3 describing how he noticed in Clerval's "kindling eye" and "animated glance" a controlled but strong determination to resist his father's attempts of "chain[ing] him to the miserable details of commerce." Such words as "kindling eye" or "chained" clearly allude to Prometheus, the archetypal rebel, and Clerval's sarcasm calling the monotonous profession of accounting a "noble art" as well as his depreciation of his father's profession (especially a father who, in the end, puts his son's desire and happiness above his beliefs) offers a rather different image of Clerval than the one Victor conveys.

The theme of male friendship as superior to female presence resurfaces at the end of the chapter. After all, instead of hurrying back home as Elizabeth had begged him, Victor remains in Ingolstadt to support his friend and rediscover in his amiable and inspiring company the inexhaustible beauties of nature.

Chapter 7

Back in Ingolstadt, Victor receives terrible news from home: His youngest brother, William, has been found strangled in a park. On his journey home, Victor glimpses the Monster and becomes convinced that he was responsible for little William's death. At home, Ernest informs him that Justine has already been charged with the crime and will be tried the same day.

CHAPTER VII

ON my return, I found the following letter from my father:

"My dear Victor,

"You have probably waited impatiently for a letter to fix the date of your return to us; and I was at first tempted to write only a few lines, merely mentioning the day on which I should expect you. But that would be a cruel kindness, and I dare not do it. What would be your surprise, my son, when you expected a happy and glad welcome, to behold, on the contrary, tears and wretchedness? And how, Victor, can I relate our misfortune? Absence cannot have rendered you callous to our joys and griefs; and how shall I inflict pain on my long absent son? I wish to prepare you for the woeful news, but I know it is impossible; even now your eye skims over the page, to seek the words which are to convey to you the horrible tidings.

"William is dead!—that sweet child, whose smiles delighted and warmed my heart, who was so gentle, yet so gay! Victor, he is murdered!

"I will not attempt to console you; but will simply relate the circumstances of the transaction.

"Last Thursday (May 7th), I, my niece, and your two brothers, went to walk in Plainpalais. The evening was warm and serene, and we prolonged our walk farther than usual. It was already dusk before we thought of returning; and then we discovered that William and Ernest, who had gone on before, were not to be found. We accordingly rested on a seat until they should return. Presently Ernest came, and enquired if we had seen his brother: he said, that he had been playing with him, that William had run away to hide himself, and that he vainly sought for him, and afterwards waited for a long time, but that he did not return.

"This account rather alarmed us, and we continued to search for him until night fell, when Elizabeth conjectured that he might have returned to the house. He was not there. We returned again, with torches; for I could not rest, when I thought that my sweet boy had lost himself, and was exposed to all the damps and dews of night; Elizabeth also suffered extreme anguish. About five in the morning I discovered my lovely boy, whom the night before I had seen blooming and active in health, stretched on the grass livid and motionless: the print of the murderer's finger was on his neck.

"He was conveyed home, and the anguish that was visible in my countenance betrayed the secret to Elizabeth. She was very earnest to see the corpse. At first I attempted to prevent her; but she persisted, and entering the room where it lay, hastily examined the neck of the victim, and clasping her hands exclaimed, 'O God! I have murdered my darling child!'

"She fainted, and was restored with extreme difficulty. When she again lived, it was only to weep and sigh. She told me, that that same evening William had teased her to let him wear a very valuable miniature that she possessed of your mother. This picture is gone, and was doubtless the temptation which urged the murderer to the deed. We have no trace of him at present, although our exertions to discover him are unremitted; but they will not restore my beloved William!

"Come, dearest Victor; you alone can console Elizabeth. She weeps continually, and accuses herself unjustly as the cause of his death; her words pierce my heart. We are all unhappy; but will not that be an additional motive for you, my son, to return and be our comforter? Your dear mother! Alas, Victor! I now say, Thank God she did not live to witness the cruel, miserable death of her youngest darling!

"Come, Victor; not brooding thoughts of vengeance against the assassin, but with feelings of peace and gentleness, that will heal, instead of festering, the wounds of our minds. Enter the house of mourning, my friend, but with kindness and affection for those who love you, and not with hatred for your enemies.

"Your affectionate and afflicted father,
"Alphonse Frankenstein.
"Geneva, May 12th, 17—."

Clerval, who had watched my countenance as I read this letter, was surprised to observe the despair that succeeded to the joy I at first expressed on receiving news from my friends. I threw the letter on the table, and covered my face with my hands.

"My dear Frankenstein," exclaimed Henry, when he perceived me weep with bitterness, "are you always to be unhappy? My dear friend, what has happened?"

I motioned him to take up the letter, while I walked up and down the room in the extremest agitation. Tears also gushed from the eyes of Clerval, as he read the account of my misfortune.

"I can offer you no consolation, my friend," said he; "your disaster is irreparable. What do you intend to do?"

"To go instantly to Geneva: come with me, Henry, to order the horses."

During our walk, Clerval endeavoured to say a few words of consolation; he could only express his heartfelt sympathy. "Poor William!" said he, "dear lovely child, he now sleeps with his angel mother! Who that had seen him bright and joyous in his young beauty, but must weep over his untimely loss! To die so miserably; to feel the murderer's grasp! How much more a murderer, that could destroy such radiant innocence! Poor little fellow! one only consolation have we; his friends mourn and weep, but he is at rest. The pang is over, his sufferings are at an end for ever. A sod covers his gentle form, and he knows no pain. He can no longer be a subject for pity; we must reserve that for his miserable survivors."

Clerval spoke thus as we hurried through the streets; the words impressed themselves on my mind and I remembered them afterwards in solitude. But now, as soon as the horses arrived, I hurried into a **cabriolet**, and bade farewell to my friend.

cabriolet: a two-wheeled, one-horse-drawn carriage.

My journey was very melancholy. At first I wished to hurry on, for I longed to console and sympathise with my loved and sorrowing friends; but when I drew near my native town, I slackened my progress. I could hardly sustain the multitude of feelings that crowded into my mind. I passed through scenes familiar to my youth, but which I had not seen for nearly six years. How altered every thing might be during that time! One sudden and desolating change had taken place; but a thousand little circumstances might have by degrees worked other alterations, which, although they were done more tranquilly, might not be the less decisive. Fear overcame me; I dared not advance, dreading a thousand nameless evils that made me tremble, although I was unable to define them.

I remained two days at **Lausanne,** in this painful state of mind. I contemplated the lake: the waters were placid; all around was calm; and the snowy mountains, 'the palaces of nature,' were not changed. By degrees the calm and heavenly scene restored me, and I continued my journey towards Geneva.

Lausanne: town in Switzerland, on the northern shore of the Geneva Lake (also known as Lake Leman).

"the palaces of nature": from Byron's *Childe Harold's Pilgrimage* (1816), canto III.

The road ran by the side of the lake, which became narrower as I approached my native town. I discovered more distinctly the black sides of Jura, and the bright summit of **Mont Blanc**. I wept like a child. "Dear mountains! my own beautiful lake! how do you welcome your wanderer? Your summits are clear; the sky and lake are blue and placid. Is this to prognosticate peace, or to mock at my unhappiness?"

Mont Blanc: highest peak (15,771 feet) in Europe, situated in the Alps, on the border between France and Italy. For some Romantics, the aesthetic of the sublime was embodied by the Alps and its majestic peak.

I fear, my friend, that I shall render myself tedious by dwelling on these preliminary circumstances; but they were days of comparative happiness, and I think of them with pleasure. My country, my beloved country! who but a native can tell the delight I took in again beholding thy streams, thy mountains, and, more than all, thy lovely lake!

Yet, as I drew nearer home, grief and fear again overcame me. Night also closed around; and when I could hardly see the dark mountains, I felt still more gloomily. The picture appeared a vast and dim scene of evil, and I foresaw obscurely that I was destined to become the most wretched of human beings. Alas! I prophesied truly, and failed only in one single circumstance, that in all the misery I imagined and dreaded, I did not conceive the hundredth part of the anguish I was destined to endure.

It was completely dark when I arrived in the environs of Geneva; the gates of the town were already shut; and I was obliged to pass the night at Secheron, a village at the distance of half a league from the city. The sky was serene; and, as I was unable to rest, I resolved to visit the spot where my poor William had been murdered. As I could not pass through the town, I was obliged to cross the lake in a boat to arrive at Plainpalais. During this short voyage I saw the lightnings playing on the summit of Mont Blanc in the most beautiful figures. The storm appeared to approach rapidly; and, on landing, I ascended a low hill, that I might observe its progress. It advanced; the heavens were clouded, and I soon felt the rain coming slowly in large drops, but its violence quickly increased.

I quitted my seat, and walked on, although the darkness and storm increased every minute, and the thunder burst with a terrific crash over my head. It was echoed from Salêve, the Juras, and the Alps of Savoy; vivid flashes of lightning dazzled my eyes, illuminating the lake, making it appear like a vast sheet of fire; then for an instant every thing seemed of a pitchy darkness, until the eye recovered itself from the preceding flash. The storm, as is often the case in Switzerland, appeared at once in various parts of the heavens. The most violent storm hung exactly north of the town, over the part of the lake which lies between the **promontory** of Belrive and the village of Copêt. Another storm enlightened Jura with faint flashes; and another darkened and sometimes disclosed the Môle, a peaked mountain to the east of the lake.

promontory: a high point of land or rock, such as a headland, jutting into the sea.

While I watched the tempest, so beautiful yet terrific, I wandered on with a hasty step. This noble war in the sky elevated my spirits; I clasped my hands, and exclaimed aloud, "William, dear angel! this is thy funeral, this thy dirge!" As I said these words, I perceived in the gloom a figure which stole from behind a clump of trees near me; I stood fixed, gazing intently; I could not be mistaken. A flash of lightning illuminated the object, and discovered its shape plainly to me: its gigantic stature, and the deformity of its aspect, more hideous than belongs to humanity, instantly informed me that it was the wretch, the filthy daemon, to whom I had given life. What did he there? Could he be (I shuddered at the conception) the murderer of my brother? No sooner did that idea cross my imagination, than I became convinced of its truth; my teeth chattered, and I was forced to lean against a tree for support. The figure passed me quickly, and I lost it in the gloom. Nothing in human shape could have destroyed that fair child. *He* was the murderer! I could not doubt it. The mere presence of the idea was an irresistible proof of the fact. I thought of pursuing the devil; but it would have been in vain, for another flash discovered him to me hanging among the rocks of the nearly perpendicular ascent of Mont Salêve, a hill that bounds Plainpalais on the south. He soon reached the summit, and disappeared.

I remained motionless. The thunder ceased; but the rain still continued, and the scene was enveloped in an impenetrable darkness. I revolved in my mind the events which I had until now sought to forget: the whole train of my progress towards the creation; the appearance of the work of my own hands alive at my bedside; its departure. Two years had now nearly elapsed since the night on which he first received life; and was this his first crime? Alas! I had turned loose into the world a depraved wretch, whose delight was in carnage and misery; had he not murdered my brother?

No one can conceive the anguish I suffered during the remainder of the night, which I spent, cold and wet, in the open air. But I did not feel the inconvenience of the weather; my imagination was busy in scenes of evil and despair. I considered the being whom I had cast among mankind, and endowed with the will and power to effect purposes of horror, such as the deed which he had now done, nearly in the light of my own **vampire**, my own spirit let loose from the grave, and forced to destroy all that was dear to me.

Day dawned; and I directed my steps towards the town. The gates were open, and I hastened to my father's house. My first thought was to discover what I knew of the murderer, and cause instant pursuit to be made. But I paused when I reflected on the story that I had to tell. A being whom I myself had formed, and endued with life, had met me at midnight among the **precipices** of an inaccessible mountain. I remembered also the nervous fever with which I had been seized just at the time that I dated my creation, and which would give an air of delirium to a tale otherwise so utterly improbable. I well knew that if any other had communicated such a relation to me, I should have looked upon it as the ravings of insanity. Besides, the strange nature of the animal would elude all pursuit, even if I were so far credited as to persuade my relatives to commence it. And then of what use would be pursuit? Who could arrest a creature capable of scaling the overhanging sides of Mont Salêve? These reflections determined me, and I resolved to remain silent.

It was about five in the morning when I entered my father's house. I told the servants not to disturb the family, and went into the library to attend their usual hour of rising.

Six years had elapsed, passed as a dream but for one indelible trace, and I stood in the same place where I had last embraced my father before my departure for Ingolstadt. Beloved and venerable parent! He still remained to me. I gazed on the picture of my mother, which stood over the mantel-piece. It was an historical subject, painted at my father's desire, and represented Caroline Beaufort in an agony of despair, kneeling by the coffin of her dead father. Her garb was **rustic**, and her cheek pale; but there was an air of dignity and beauty, that hardly permitted the sentiment of pity. Below this picture was a **miniature** of William; and my tears flowed when I looked upon it. While I was thus engaged, Ernest entered; he had heard me arrive, and hastened to welcome me. He expressed a sorrowful delight to see me: "Welcome, my dearest Victor," said he. "Ah! I wish you had come three months ago, and then you would have found us all joyous and delighted. You come to us now to share a

vampire: a reanimated corpse, a living corpse, a monster.

precipices: very steep overhangs, usually on a mountain.

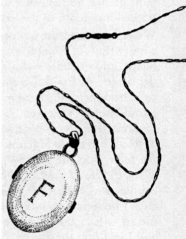

The broken locket.

rustic: rural, unsophisticated.

miniature: a portrait or other painting done on a small scale on ivory or metal.

misery which nothing can alleviate; yet your presence will, I hope, revive our father, who seems sinking under his misfortune; and your persuasions will induce poor Elizabeth to cease her vain and tormenting self-accusations.—Poor William! he was our darling and our pride!"

Tears, unrestrained, fell from my brother's eyes; a sense of mortal agony crept over my frame. Before, I had only imagined the wretchedness of my desolated home; the reality came on me as a new, and a not less terrible, disaster. I tried to calm Ernest; I enquired more minutely concerning my father, and her I named my cousin.

"She most of all," said Ernest, "requires consolation; she accused herself of having caused the death of my brother, and that made her very wretched. But since the murderer has been discovered—"

"The murderer discovered! Good God! how can that be? who could attempt to pursue him? It is impossible; one might as well try to overtake the winds, or confine a mountain-stream with a straw. I saw him too; he was free last night!"

"I do not know what you mean," replied my brother, in accents of wonder, "but to us the discovery we have made completes our misery. No one would believe it at first; and even now Elizabeth will not be convinced, notwithstanding all the evidence. Indeed, who would credit that Justine Moritz, who was so amiable, and fond of all the family, could suddenly become so capable of so frightful, so appalling a crime?"

"Justine Moritz! Poor, poor girl, is she the accused? But it is wrongfully; every one knows that; no one believes it, surely, Ernest?"

"No one did at first; but several circumstances came out, that have almost forced conviction upon us; and her own behaviour has been so confused, as to add to the evidence of facts a weight that, I fear, leaves no hope for doubt. But she will be tried to-day, and you will then hear all."

He related that, the morning on which the murder of poor William had been discovered, Justine had been taken ill, and confined to her bed for several days. During this interval, one of the servants, happening to examine the apparel she had worn on the night of the murder, had discovered in her pocket the picture of my mother, which had been judged to be the temptation of the murderer. The servant instantly showed it to one of the others, who, without saying a word to any of the family, went to a magistrate; and, upon their deposition, Justine was apprehended. On being charged with the fact, the poor girl confirmed the suspicion in a great measure by her extreme confusion of manner.

This was a strange tale, but it did not shake my faith; and I replied earnestly, "You are all mistaken; I know the murderer. Justine, poor, good Justine, is innocent."

At that instant my father entered. I saw unhappiness deeply impressed on his countenance, but he endeavoured to welcome me cheerfully; and, after we had exchanged our mournful greeting, would have introduced some other topic than that of our disaster, had not Ernest exclaimed, "Good God, papa! Victor says that he knows who was the murderer of poor William."

"We do also, unfortunately," replied my father; "for indeed I had rather have been for ever ignorant than have discovered so much depravity and ungratitude in one I valued so highly."

"My dear father, you are mistaken; Justine is innocent."

"If she is, God forbid that she should suffer as guilty. She is to be tried to-day, and I hope, I sincerely hope, that she will be acquitted."

This speech calmed me. I was firmly convinced in my own mind that Justine, and indeed every human being, was guiltless of this murder. I had no fear, therefore, that any circumstantial evidence could be brought forward strong enough to convict her. My tale was not one to announce publicly; its astounding horror would be looked upon as madness by the vulgar. Did any one indeed exist, except I, the creator, who would believe, unless his senses convinced him, in the existence of the living monument of presumption and rash ignorance which I had let loose upon the world?

We were soon joined by Elizabeth. Time had altered her since I last beheld her; it had endowed her with loveliness surpassing the beauty of her childish years. There was the same candour, the same vivacity, but it was allied to an expression more full of sensibility and intellect. She welcomed me with the greatest affection. "Your arrival, my dear cousin," said she, "fills me with hope. You perhaps will find some means to justify my poor guiltless Justine. Alas! who is safe, if she be convicted of crime? I rely on her innocence as certainly as I do upon my own. Our misfortune is doubly hard to us; we have not only lost that lovely darling boy, but this poor girl, whom I sincerely love, is to be torn away by even a worse fate. If she is condemned, I never shall know joy more. But she will not, I am sure she will not; and then I shall be happy again, even after the sad death of my little William."

"She is innocent, my Elizabeth," said I, "and that shall be proved; fear nothing, but let your spirits be cheered by the assurance of her acquittal."

"How kind and generous you are! every one else believes in her guilt, and that made me wretched, for I knew that it was impossible: and to see every one else prejudiced in so deadly a manner rendered me hopeless and despairing." She wept.

"Dearest niece," said my father, "dry your tears. If she is, as you believe, innocent, rely on the justice of our laws, and the activity with which I shall prevent the slightest shadow of partiality."

COMMENTARY

Returning to Ingolstadt, Victor finds a letter from his father. After a long, emotional introduction, Mr. Frankenstein abruptly announces to his son that his youngest brother, William, is dead. The letter details the circumstances of William's death: The family—the father, two brothers, and Elizabeth—spent a pleasant afternoon together, taking a long walk through the park. William and Ernest, running and hiding from each other, get separated from the group and then from each other. At dusk, when they leave for home, William is missing. Family and servants desperately but vainly search for him the entire night. Early in the morning, Alphonse Frankenstein finally discovers the strangled body of his son lying in the grass. The letter ends with a curious appeal to Victor's forgiveness, kindness, and generosity and asks him to come home to comfort the family.

Again, a passive Elizabeth emerges. Elizabeth feels responsible for William's death and is tormented by guilt. She is convinced that the valuable she had given to William was the real motive for the crime. She immediately condemns herself without showing any interest in finding the truth. Her attitude anticipates Justine's curious confession to a crime she did not commit. In fact, Elizabeth shares with Justine and Victor a universal sense of guilt; they accuse themselves of complicity in the murder of little William. At the same time, Alphonse Frankenstein seems equally uninterested in finding the truth or his son's murderer. His pathetic plea for Victor's compassion, mercy, and benevolence appears artificial in these circumstances.

Victor Returns Home

Victor leaves for Geneva immediately. Urged by the thought of being with his family and friends, he initially travels quickly, but soon, his conflicting feelings, generated by his long absence and inexplicable fears, make him stop for two days. The majestic Jura Mountains, Mont Blanc in particular, and the beautiful lake revitalize Victor's spirit, and he resumes his journey. But at night, the same mountains appear as "a vast and dim scene of evil," and again, Victor feels destined "to become the most wretched of human beings."

Mont Blanc.
© *John Noble/CORBIS*

Victor arrives in Geneva after the town's gates are closed for the night. Already in a morbid mood, he visits the scene of William's murder. He crosses the lake by boat, and on the opposite shore is surprised by a violent storm, simultaneously beautiful and terrifying. Deeply moved by the magnificent storm, Victor pathetically invokes William's name and calls this sublime manifestation of natural energy his little brother's funeral. Suddenly, he sees the gigantic form of the demon he created almost two years earlier, and is instantly convinced that the creature is William's murderer. Stunned at first, Victor's imagination is suddenly captured by "scenes of evil and despair." He thinks that he has created not only a hideous and repulsive being but also a murderer.

Victor concentrates on one impulse: to reveal the murderer and effect his capture. However, he instantly realizes the impossibility of convincing people of the truth. He is even more disturbed by the thought of confessing the abominable nature of his work. The initial urge to disclose the truth and, thus, free himself from the overwhelming burden is now replaced by a desperate desire to find excuses to justify his decision to remain silent.

For the first time, Victor perceives himself as a diabolical creator, whose demonic desires and actions resulted in disastrous consequences. Associated with Faust and Satan for aspiring to absolute knowledge, Victor is now identifiable with Cain, the original murderer from the Bible. Like Cain, the oldest son of Adam and Eve, Victor is the oldest son of the Frankensteins. Although Cain actually murders his innocent brother, Abel, Victor feels morally responsible for his innocent brother's death, and like Cain, who becomes a fugitive and vagabond, Victor, in the end becomes a wanderer.

Moreover, this first encounter with the Monster after the terrible night when Victor rejected and deserted him establishes a curious pattern. Every time they meet, Victor's first impulse is to chase the Monster and aggressively confront him or destroy him, but for reasons never explained, he is never able to realize his intentions.

Victor's Family Reunion

After an absence of six years, Victor, a sad and disillusioned man, returns to a house in mourning. Arriving very early in the morning, the family is still asleep, and Victor retires to the library to wait for them to awaken. He contemplates the disturbing portrait depicting his mother in great despair next to her father's coffin, and he gazes at a miniature of William. These portraits distress him greatly.

Caroline's portrait was painted at Alphonse Frankenstein's request and represents a typical example of the sentimental scene most nineteenth-century painters favored. Interestingly, Alphonse wanted to immortalize precisely this moment in Caroline's life—one that depicts her as a tragic heroine. Given that Shelley portrays Caroline's father as a selfish, proud, and even cruel father, Alphonse's selection of this specific moment becomes highly problematic. Alphonse seems narcissistic; the painting is clearly a constant reminder of a woman saved from despair and loneliness by a noble and generous man—Alphonse himself. He appears traditional and insensitive. A loving husband would have helped Caroline to forget these terrible moments. What seems to have impressed Alphonse most was Caroline's unconditional devotion and obedience to her father for whom she dutifully sacrificed everything. Furthermore, Alphonse is not at all inclined to identify or understand the real causes of Caroline's despair. One wonders why Caroline is, in fact, "in an agony of despair." Can this motherless girl cry for a father who exploited, humiliated, and ignored her? Or is Caroline worried about her uncertain future instead of mourning the death of her father, who left her "an orphan and a beggar"? Perhaps what Caroline really laments is the sudden recognition that her only chance for financial survival and social respectability is to throw herself on the mercy of a much older man, hoping that he will marry her.

The two portraits—the miniature hanging on William's neck on the night he was murdered and the portrait in the library—represent remarkably complex symbols. In the first one, Caroline is the smiling guardian of all her children. She appears as "the angel mother," a role that is clearly miniaturized because her husband prefers her portrayed as an obedient daughter, disconsolately lamenting her father's death. The juxtaposition between the two portraits creates an inescapable indication that despair, rather than happiness, remains the dominant note in Caroline's life and in the lives of those under her protection (Justine and William).

Justine's Trial

Ernest hears Victor arrive and comes into the room to greet his brother and to inform him that Justine Moritz was arrested and accused of killing William. Victor is devastated. He immediately proclaims Justine's innocence and asks Ernest to assure him that the rest of the family is as convinced as he is that the accusation is a terrible mistake. Disturbed, Ernest explains that the evidence against Justine is overwhelming, and he tells Victor that their mother's miniature, given to William by Elizabeth the same night he was murdered, has been found in Justine's pocket. Moreover, after the arrest, Justine's strange behavior confirms her guilt, leaving little, if any, doubt. Victor, however, maintains that Justine was wrongly accused, and when his father and then Elizabeth arrive to welcome him, he declares Justine's innocence even more intensely. Elizabeth immediately agrees. Victor's father and Ernest want to believe that Victor is right and put their entire faith in the absolute justice of the law.

Clearly, Ernest and Alphonse Frankenstein believe that Justine is guilty, thus anticipating the reaction of a jury that consists exclusively of men. Given that Justine's name implies "justice," Alphonse's counsel to let justice decide Justine's life is ironic, especially when he and the rest of his family are totally blind to the truth. (Another irony is that Justice is actually blind.) Victor knows the truth but doesn't have the courage to confess. Elizabeth does not see the truth because of her weakness and inefficacy and Alphonse and Ernest are blinded by their rigid, conservative view that the law is always right.

Nobody notices that the evidence against Justine is feeble and inconclusive. Clearly, the story of the servants who found her is suspicious, as the first servant could have planted the evidence. Moreover, Justine's faithful service and loyalty seems to count less than the servants' testimony, which is never really questioned.

| Chapter 8 | At the trial, Justine tells a credible story, and Elizabeth addresses the court with a modest but compelling petition. Victor, convinced that the judges have already condemned Justine and paralyzed by his guilty conscience, leaves the court without saying a word. Justine is convicted and condemned. Before her execution, she sees Elizabeth and Victor again and explains that she was forced to confess to the crime. |

CHAPTER VIII

WE passed a few sad hours, until eleven o'clock, when the trial was to commence. My father and the rest of the family being obliged to attend as witnesses, I accompanied them to the court. During the whole of this wretched mockery of justice I suffered living torture. It was to be decided, whether the result of my curiosity and lawless devices would cause the death of two of my fellow-beings: one a smiling babe, full of innocence and joy; the other far more dreadfully murdered, with every aggravation of infamy that could make the murder memorable in horror. Justine also was a girl of merit, and possessed qualities which promised to render her life happy; now all was to be obliterated in an ignominious grave; and I the cause! A thousand times rather would I have confessed myself guilty of the crime ascribed to Justine; but I was absent when it was committed, and such a declaration would have been considered as the ravings of a madman, and would not have exculpated her who suffered through me.

The appearance of Justine was calm. She was dressed in mourning; and her countenance, always engaging, was rendered, by the solemnity of her feelings, exquisitely beautiful. Yet she appeared confident in innocence, and did not tremble, although gazed on and execrated by thousands; for all the kindness which her beauty might otherwise have excited, was obliterated in the minds of the spectators by the imagination of the enormity she was supposed to have committed. She was tranquil, yet her tranquillity was evidently constrained; and as her confusion had before been adduced as a proof of her guilt, she worked up her mind to an appearance of courage. When she entered the court, she threw her eyes round it, and quickly discovered where we were seated. A tear seemed to dim her eye when she saw us; but she quickly recovered herself, and a look of sorrowful affection seemed to attest her utter guiltlessness.

The trial began; and after the advocate against her had stated the charge, several witnesses were called. Several strange facts combined against her, which might have staggered anyone who had not such proof of her innocence as I had. She had been out the whole of the night on which the murder had been committed, and towards morning had been perceived by a market-woman not far from the spot where the body of the murdered child had been afterwards found. The woman asked her what she did there; but she looked very strangely, and only returned a confused and unintelligible answer. She returned to the house about eight o'clock;

and, when one enquired where she had passed the night, she replied that she had been looking for the child, and demanded earnestly if anything had been heard concerning him. When shown the body, she fell into violent hysterics and kept her bed for several days. The picture was then produced, which the servant had found in her pocket; and when Elizabeth, in a faltering voice, proved that it was the same which, an hour before the child had been missed, she had placed round his neck, a murmur of horror and indignation filled the court.

Justine was called on for her defence. As the trial had proceeded, her countenance had altered. Surprise, horror, and misery were strongly expressed. Sometimes she struggled with her tears; but, when she was desired to plead, she collected her powers, and spoke, in an audible although variable voice.

"God knows," she said, "how entirely I am innocent. But I do not pretend that my protestations should acquit me: I rest my innocence on a plain and simple explanation of the facts which have been adduced against me; and I hope the character I have always borne will incline my judges to a favourable interpretation, where any circumstance appears doubtful or suspicious."

She then related that, by the permission of Elizabeth, she had passed the evening of the night on which the murder had been committed at the house of an aunt at Chêne, a village situated at about a league from Geneva. On her return, at about nine o'clock, she met a man who asked her if she had seen any thing of the child who was lost. She was alarmed by this account, and passed several hours in looking for him, when the gates of Geneva were shut, and she was forced to remain several hours of the night in a barn belonging to a cottage, being unwilling to call up the inhabitants, to whom she was well known. Most of the night she spent here watching; towards morning she believed that she slept for a few minutes; some steps disturbed her, and she awoke. It was dawn, and she quitted her asylum, that she might again endeavour to find my brother. If she had gone near the spot where his body lay, it was without her knowledge. That she had been bewildered when questioned by the market-woman was not surprising, since she had passed a sleepless night, and the fate of poor William was yet uncertain. Concerning the picture she could give no account.

"I know," continued the unhappy victim, "how heavily and fatally this one circumstance weighs against me, but I have no power of explaining it; and when I have expressed my utter ignorance, I am only left to conjecture concerning the probabilities by which it might have been placed in my pocket. But here also I am checked. I believe that I have no enemy on earth, and none surely would have been so wicked as to destroy me wantonly. Did the murderer place it there? I know of no opportunity afforded him for so doing; or, if I had, why should he have stolen the jewel, to part with it again so soon?

"I commit my cause to the justice of my judges, yet I see no room for hope. I beg permission to have a few witnesses examined concerning my character; and if their testimony shall not overweigh my supposed guilt, I must be condemned, although I would pledge my salvation on my innocence."

Several witnesses were called, who had known her for many years, and they spoke well of her; but fear, and hatred of the crime of which they supposed her guilty, rendered them timorous, and unwilling to come forward. Elizabeth saw even this last resource, her excellent dispositions and irreproachable conduct, about to fail the accused, when, although violently agitated, she desired permission to address the court.

"I am," said she, "the cousin of the unhappy child who was murdered, or rather his sister, for I was educated by and have lived with his parents ever since and even long before his birth. It may therefore be judged indecent in me to come forward on this occasion; but when I see a fellow-creature about to perish through the cowardice of her pretended friends, I wish to be allowed to speak, that I may say what I know of her character. I am well acquainted with the accused. I have lived in the same house with her, at one time for five, and at another for nearly two years. During all that period she appeared to me the most amiable and benevolent of human creatures. She nursed Madame Frankenstein, my aunt, in her last illness, with the greatest affection and care; and afterwards attended her own mother during a tedious illness, in a manner that excited the admiration of all who knew her; after which she again lived in my uncle's house, where she was beloved by all the family. She was warmly attached to the child who is now dead, and acted towards him like a most affectionate mother. For my own part, I do not hesitate to say, that, notwithstanding all the evidence produced against her, I believe and rely on her perfect innocence. She had no temptation for such an action: as to the bauble on which the chief proof rests, if she had earnestly desired it, I should have willingly given it to her; so much do I esteem and value her."

A murmur of approbation followed Elizabeth's simple and powerful appeal; but it was excited by her generous interference, and not in favour of poor Justine, on whom the public indignation was turned with renewed violence, charging her with the blackest ingratitude. She herself wept as Elizabeth spoke, but she did not answer. My own agitation and anguish was extreme during the whole trial. I believed in her innocence; I knew it. Could the demon who had (I did not for a minute doubt) murdered my brother, also in his hellish sport have betrayed the innocent to death and ignominy? I could not sustain the horror of my situation; and when I perceived that the popular voice, and the countenances of the judges, had already condemned my unhappy victim, I rushed out of the court in agony. The tortures of the accused did not equal mine; she was sustained by innocence, but the fangs of remorse tore my bosom, and would not forgo their hold.

I passed a night of unmingled wretchedness. In the morning I went to the court; my lips and throat were parched. I dared not ask the fatal question; but I was known, and the officer guessed the cause of my visit. The

ballots had been thrown; they were all black, and Justine was condemned.

ballots: small balls used by jurors for secret voting in a trial.

I cannot pretend to describe what I then felt. I had before experienced sensations of horror, and I have endeavoured to bestow upon them adequate expressions, but words cannot convey an idea of the heart-sickening despair that I then endured. The person to whom I addressed myself added, that Justine had already confessed her guilt. "That evidence," he observed, "was hardly required in so glaring a case, but I am glad of it; and, indeed, none of our judges like to condemn a criminal upon circumstantial evidence, be it ever so decisive."

This was strange and unexpected intelligence; what could it mean? Had my eyes deceived me? and was I really as mad as the whole world would believe me to be, if I disclosed the object of my suspicions? I hastened to return home, and Elizabeth eagerly demanded the result.

"My cousin," replied I, "it is decided as you may have expected; all judges had rather that ten innocent should suffer, than that one guilty should escape. But she has confessed."

This was a dire blow to poor Elizabeth, who had relied with firmness upon Justine's innocence. "Alas!" said she. "How shall I ever again believe in human goodness? Justine, whom I loved and esteemed as my sister, how could she put on those smiles of innocence only to betray? her mild eyes seemed incapable of any severity or guile, and yet she has committed a murder."

Soon after we heard that the poor victim had expressed a desire to see my cousin. My father wished her not to go; but said, that he left it to her own judgment and feelings to decide. "Yes," said Elizabeth, "I will go, although she is guilty; and you, Victor, shall accompany me: I cannot go alone." The idea of this visit was torture to me, yet I could not refuse.

We entered the gloomy prison-chamber, and beheld Justine sitting on some straw at the farther end; her hands were manacled, and her head rested on her knees. She rose on seeing us enter; and when we were left alone with her, she threw herself at the feet of Elizabeth, weeping bitterly. My cousin wept also.

"Oh, Justine!" said she. "Why did you rob me of my last consolation? I relied on your innocence; and although I was then very wretched, I was not so miserable as I am now."

"And do you also believe that I am so very, very wicked? Do you also join with my enemies to crush me, to condemn me as a murderer?" Her voice was suffocated with sobs.

"Rise, my poor girl," said Elizabeth, "why do you kneel, if you are innocent? I am not one of your enemies; I believed you guiltless, notwithstanding every evidence, until I heard that you had yourself declared your guilt. That report, you say, is false; and be assured, dear Justine, that nothing can shake my confidence in you for a moment, but your own confession."

"I did confess; but I confessed a lie. I confessed, that I might obtain absolution; but now that falsehood lies heavier at my heart than all my other sins. The God of heaven forgive me! Ever since I was condemned, my confessor has besieged me; he threatened and menaced, until I almost began to think that I was the monster that he said I was. He threatened **excommunication** and hell fire in my last moments, if I continued obdurate. Dear lady, I had none to support me; all looked on me as a wretch doomed to **ignominy** and perdition. What could I do? In an evil hour I subscribed to a lie; and now only am I truly miserable."

She paused, weeping, and then continued—"I thought with horror, my sweet lady, that you should believe your Justine, whom your blessed aunt had so highly honoured, and whom you loved, was a creature capable of a crime which none but the devil himself could have perpetrated. Dear William! dearest blessed child! I soon shall see you again in heaven, where we shall all be happy; and that consoles me, going as I am to suffer ignominy and death."

"Oh, Justine! forgive me for having for one moment distrusted you. Why did you confess? But do not mourn, dear girl. Do not fear. I will proclaim, I will prove your innocence. I will melt the stony hearts of your enemies by my tears and prayers. You shall not die!—You, my playfellow, my companion, my sister, perish on the scaffold! No! no! I never could survive so horrible a misfortune."

Justine shook her head mournfully. "I do not fear to die," she said; "that pang is past. God raises my weakness, and gives me courage to endure the worst. I leave a sad and bitter world; and if you remember me, and think of me as of one unjustly condemned, I am resigned to the fate awaiting me. Learn from me, dear lady, to submit in patience to the will of Heaven!"

During this conversation I had retired to a corner of the prison-room, where I could conceal the horrid anguish that possessed me. Despair! Who dared talk of that? The poor victim, who on the morrow was to pass the awful boundary between life and death, felt not as I did, such deep and bitter agony. I gnashed my teeth, and ground them together, uttering a groan that came from my inmost soul. Justine started. When she saw who it was, she approached me and said, "Dear sir, you are very kind to visit me; you, I hope, do not believe that I am guilty?"

I could not answer. "No, Justine," said Elizabeth; "he is more convinced of your innocence than I was; for even when he heard that you had confessed, he did not credit it."

"I truly thank him. In these last moments I feel the sincerest gratitude towards those who think of me with kindness. How sweet is the affection of others to such a wretch as I am! It removes more than half my misfortune; and I feel as if I could die in peace, now that my innocence is acknowledged by you, dear lady, and your cousin."

Thus the poor sufferer tried to comfort others and herself. She indeed gained the resignation she desired. But I, the true murderer, felt the never-dying worm alive in my bosom, which allowed of no hope or

excommunication: expulsion from the church; in the Catholic church, decision taken exclusively by the Pope.

ignominy: disgrace.

consolation. Elizabeth also wept, and was unhappy; but hers also was the misery of innocence, which, like a cloud that passes over the fair moon, for a while hides but cannot tarnish its brightness. Anguish and despair had penetrated into the core of my heart; I bore a hell within me, which nothing could extinguish. We stayed several hours with Justine; and it was with great difficulty that Elizabeth could tear herself away. "I wish," cried she, "that I were to die with you; I cannot live in this world of misery."

Justine assumed an air of cheerfulness, while she with difficulty repressed her bitter tears. She embraced Elizabeth, and said, in a voice of half-suppressed emotion, "Farewell, sweet lady, dearest Elizabeth, my beloved and only friend; may Heaven, in its bounty, bless and preserve you; may this be the last misfortune that you will ever suffer! Live, and be happy, and make others so."

And on the morrow Justine died. Elizabeth's heartrending eloquence failed to move the judges from their settled conviction in the criminality of the saintly sufferer. My passionate and indignant appeals were lost upon them. And when I received their cold answers, and heard the harsh unfeeling reasoning of these men, my purposed avowal died away on my lips. Thus I might proclaim myself a madman, but not revoke the sentence passed upon my wretched victim. She perished on the scaffold as a murderess!

From the tortures of my own heart, I turned to contemplate the deep and voiceless grief of my Elizabeth. This also was my doing! And my father's woe, and the desolation of that late so smiling home—all was the work of my thrice-accursed hands! Ye weep, unhappy ones; but these are not your last tears! Again shall you raise the funeral wail, and the sound of your **lamentations** shall again and again be heard! Frankenstein, your son, your kinsman, your early, much-loved friend; he who would spend each vital drop of blood for your sakes—who has no thought nor sense of joy, except as it is mirrored also in your dear countenances—who would fill the air with blessings, and spend his life in serving you—he bids you weep—to shed countless tears; happy beyond his hopes, if thus inexorable fate be satisfied, and if the destruction pause before the peace of the grave have succeeded to your sad torments!

lamentations: expressions of sorrow; wailing.

Thus spoke my **prophetic** soul, as, torn by remorse, horror, and despair, I beheld those I loved spend vain sorrow upon the graves of William and Justine, the first hapless victims to my unhallowed arts.

prophetic: in this context, doomed.

COMMENTARY

At Justine's trial, Victor is tortured with guilt. He wants to stop this "mockery of justice," but realizing that a confession would make him appear insane, he remains silent. Justine's demeanor is calm and restrained, and the Frankensteins' presence in the court room seems to move her deeply. Several witnesses are called to testify against her. Though gravely affected by the damaging testimony of her so-called friends, Justine regains her composure and tells a simple and convincing story: On the night of the crime, she looked for William into the night, and was forced to spend the night in a barn because the city gates were closed. She vaguely remembers being disturbed by footsteps, but she cannot explain how Caroline's miniature was found in her pocket. Other witnesses who have known Justine for a long time testify to her good character, but the court remains confident of her guilt.

Although Elizabeth is extremely disturbed, she addresses the court with "a simple and powerful appeal," testifying to Justine's character and reaffirming her belief in her innocence. Her moving speech deeply impresses the audience but increases the hostility against Justine, whose crime appears, in the light of Elizabeth's testimony, even more reprehensible and indeed monstrous. Victor, paralyzed by guilt and convinced that the public and the judges have already condemned Justine, leaves the court "in agony" without saying a word.

Justine's Confession

After a sleepless and tormented night, Victor returns to the court and finds out that Justine was unanimously convicted and condemned to death. The officer also informs Victor that Justine confessed to the murder. Distressed, Victor returns home and tells Elizabeth the news. Instantly, belief in Justine's guilt replaces Elizabeth's initial confidence in her innocence.

This segment offers several interpretations. One is to ignore the text's ambiguities; another is to explore them. Elizabeth's courtroom praise of Justine has major flaws; instead of helping Justine, Elizabeth's testimony damages her. Elizabeth is not only "agitated" when she testifies on Justine's behalf but is completely unprepared: She doesn't understand the legal implications of the case (which may be a commentary on the differences in the education allowed to men and that allowed to women); she can't control her emotions; and she makes fundamental mistakes. As a result, Elizabeth not only reemphasizes the association of Justine's name with William's murder, but she accepts all the evidence against Justine as valid. Elizabeth's proclaimed belief in Justine's innocence is eroded by her uncritical recognition of the legitimacy of the trial, and her testimony seems to intensify the audience's admiration for her rather than help Justine. But probably, Elizabeth's most tragic mistake is suggesting that Justine may have coveted the miniature.

Victor and Elizabeth Visit Justine

Justine's final wish is to see Elizabeth. Despite Justine's unexpected confession, Elizabeth decides to visit her in prison and asks Victor to accompany her. Deeply disturbed by Elizabeth's sudden distrust of her, Justine explains that she was threatened with expulsion from the church and confessed to the crime because she was scared of eternal damnation. As easily as before, Elizabeth changes her mind, implores Justine to forgive her for doubting her, and promises to save her from execution.

Victor involuntarily emits a sound of deep distress, making Justine suddenly aware of his presence. She asks Victor to assure her that he is also convinced of her innocence, but he is unable to utter a word. Elizabeth assures Justine that Victor has always believed in her integrity and, in fact, is the only one who never suspected or questioned her.

In painful silence, Victor looks at the two women comforting each other and recognizes that such consolation is refused to him—"the true murderer" of William and, later, Justine. Whereas the unhappiness of Elizabeth and Justine is "the misery of innocence" and, therefore, endurable, his unhappiness is almost beyond endurance. His disturbing silence indicates the torment of his soul. Despite Victor's last-minute efforts, Justine is executed the following morning.

Voice as a Theme

The element of voice has some interesting connotations in the novel. One quality that greatly impresses Walton when he first meets Victor is his unusually beautiful voice, a voice "whose varied intonations are soul-subduing music." If voice represents communication and if Walton is the only character in the book clearly impressed with Victor's voice, readers may infer that Walton is the only one with whom Victor really communicates. Also, Victor's seductive voice in connection with Walton may have the same effect that the Ancient Mariner's glittering eye has on the Wedding Guest: it mesmerizes Walton.

Chapters 9–10

Consumed with guilt, Victor finds refuge in solitude. Overwhelmed by despair, he decides to travel to the Valley of Chamounix, where, as a boy, he enjoyed the beauties of nature. At first, he is enchanted by the majestic landscape, but grief and fear eventually return and torment him. The next morning, Victor climbs the summit of Montanvert and, at noon, reaches its majestic top. Suddenly, he notices in the distance a strange and vigorous figure advancing toward him, and he recognizes the terrifying shape of his creature. The Monster quickly appears before him and convinces Victor to listen to his story.

CHAPTER IX

NOTES

NOTHING is more painful to the human mind, than, after the feelings have been worked up by a quick succession of events, the dead calmness of inaction and certainty which follows, and deprives the soul both of hope and fear. Justine died; she rested; and I was alive. The blood flowed freely in my veins, but a weight of despair and remorse pressed on my heart, which nothing could remove. Sleep fled from my eyes; I wandered like an evil spirit, for I had committed deeds of mischief beyond description horrible, and more, much more (I persuaded myself), was yet behind. Yet my heart overflowed with kindness, and the love of virtue. I had begun life with benevolent intentions, and thirsted for the moment when I should put them in practice, and make myself useful to my fellow-beings. Now all was blasted: instead of that serenity of conscience, which allowed me to look back upon the past with self-satisfaction, and from thence to gather promise of new hopes, I was seized by remorse and the sense of guilt, which hurried me away to a hell of intense tortures, such as no language can describe.

This state of mind preyed upon my health, which had perhaps never entirely recovered from the first shock it had sustained. I shunned the face of man; all sound of joy or complacency was torture to me; solitude was my only consolation—deep, dark, deathlike solitude.

My father observed with pain the alteration perceptible in my disposition and habits, and endeavoured by arguments deduced from the feelings of his serene conscience and guiltless life, to inspire me with fortitude, and awaken in me the courage to dispel the dark cloud which brooded over me. "Do you think, Victor," said he, "that I do not suffer also? No one could love a child more than I loved your brother;" (tears came into his eyes as he spoke,) "but is it not a duty to the survivors, that we should refrain from augmenting their unhappiness by an appearance of immoderate grief? It is also a duty owed to yourself; for excessive sorrow prevents improvement or enjoyment, or even the discharge of daily usefulness, without which no man is fit for society."

This advice, although good, was totally inapplicable to my case; I should have been the first to hide my grief, and console my friends, if remorse had not mingled its bitterness, and terror its alarm with my other sensations. Now I could only answer my father with a look of despair, and endeavour to hide myself from his view.

About this time we retired to our house at Belrive. This change was particularly agreeable to me. The shutting of the gates regularly at ten o'clock, and the impossibility of remaining on the lake after that hour; had rendered our residence within the walls of Geneva very irksome to me. I was now free. Often, after the rest of the family had retired for the night, I took the boat and passed many hours upon the water. Sometimes, with my sails set, I was carried by the wind; and sometimes, after rowing into the middle of the lake, I left the boat to pursue its own course, and gave way to my own miserable reflections. I was often tempted, when all was at peace around me, and I the only unquiet thing that wandered restless in a scene so beautiful and heavenly—if I except some bat, or the frogs, whose harsh and interrupted croaking was heard only when I approached the shore—often, I say, I was tempted to plunge into the silent lake, that the waters might close over me and my calamities for ever. But I was restrained, when I thought of the heroic and suffering Elizabeth, whom I tenderly loved, and whose existence was bound up in mine. I thought also of my father, and surviving brother: should I by my base desertion leave them exposed and unprotected to the malice of the fiend whom I had let loose among them?

At these moments I wept bitterly, and wished that peace would revisit my mind only that I might afford them consolation and happiness. But that could not be. Remorse extinguished every hope. I had been the author of unalterable evils; and I lived in daily fear, lest the monster whom I had created should perpetrate some new wickedness. I had an obscure feeling that all was not over, and that he would still commit some signal crime, which by its enormity should almost efface the recollection of the past. There was always scope for fear, so long as any thing I loved remained behind. My abhorrence of this fiend cannot be conceived. When I thought of him, I gnashed my teeth, my eyes became inflamed, and I ardently wished to extinguish that life which I had so thoughtlessly bestowed. When I reflected on his crimes and malice, my hatred and revenge burst all bounds of moderation. I would have made a pilgrimage to the highest peak of the Andes, could I, when there, have precipitated him to their base. I wished to see him again, that I might wreak the utmost extent of abhorrence on his head, and avenge the deaths of William and Justine.

Our house was the house of mourning. My father's health was deeply shaken by the horror of the recent events. Elizabeth was sad and desponding; she no longer took delight in her ordinary occupations; all pleasure seemed to her sacrilege toward the dead; eternal woe and tears she then thought was the just tribute she should pay to innocence so blasted and destroyed. She was no longer that happy creature, who in earlier youth wandered with me on the banks of the lake, and talked with ecstasy of our future prospects. The first of those sorrows which are sent to wean us from the earth, had visited her, and its dimming influence quenched her dearest smiles.

"When I reflect, my dear cousin," said she, "on the miserable death of Justine Moritz, I no longer see the world and its works as they before appeared to me. Before, I looked upon the accounts of vice and injustice, that I read in books or heard from others, as tales of ancient days, or imaginary evils; at least they were remote, and more familiar to reason than to the imagination; but now misery has come home, and men appear to me as monsters thirsting for each other's blood. Yet I am certainly unjust. Every body believed that poor girl to be guilty; and if she could have committed the crime for which she suffered, assuredly she would have been the most depraved of human creatures. For the sake of a few jewels, to have murdered the son of her benefactor and friend, a child whom she had nursed from its birth, and appeared to love as if it had been her own! I could not consent to the death of any human being; but certainly I should have thought such a creature unfit to remain in the society of men. But she was innocent. I know, I feel she was innocent; you are of the same opinion, and that confirms me. Alas! Victor, when falsehood can look so like the truth, who can assure themselves of certain happiness? I feel as if I were walking on the edge of a precipice, towards which thousands are crowding, and endeavouring to plunge me into the abyss. William and Justine were assassinated, and the murderer escapes; he walks about the world free, and perhaps respected. But even if I were condemned to suffer on the scaffold for the same crimes, I would not change places with such a wretch."

I listened to this discourse with the extremest agony. I, not in deed, but in effect, was the true murderer. Elizabeth read my anguish in my countenance, and kindly taking my hand, said, "My dearest friend, you must calm yourself. These events have affected me, God knows how deeply; but I am not so wretched as you are. There is an expression of despair, and sometimes of revenge, in your countenance, that makes me tremble. Dear Victor, banish these dark passions. Remember the friends around you, who centre all their hopes in you. Have we lost the power of rendering you happy? Ah! While we love—while we are true to each other, here in this land of peace and beauty, your native country, we may reap every tranquil blessing—what can disturb our peace?"

And could not such words from her whom I fondly prized before every other gift of fortune, suffice to chase away the fiend that lurked in my heart? Even as she spoke I drew near to her, as if in terror; lest at that very moment the destroyer had been near to rob me of her.

Thus not the tenderness of friendship, nor the beauty of earth, nor of heaven, could redeem my soul from woe: the very accents of love were ineffectual. I was encompassed by a cloud which no beneficial influence could penetrate. The wounded deer dragging its fainting limbs to some untrodden brake, there to gaze upon the arrow which had pierced it, and to die—was but a type of me.

Sometimes I could cope with the sullen despair that overwhelmed me: but sometimes the whirlwind passions of my soul drove me to seek, by bodily exercise and by change of place, some relief from my intolerable sensations. It was during an access of this kind that I suddenly left my home, and bending my steps towards the near Alpine valleys, sought in the magnificence, the eternity of such scenes, to forget myself and my ephemeral, because human, sorrows. My wanderings were directed towards the valley of Chamounix. I had visited it frequently during my boyhood. Six years had passed since then: *I* was a wreck—but nought had changed in those savage and enduring scenes.

I performed the first part of my journey on horseback. I afterwards hired a mule, as the more sure-footed, and least liable to receive injury on these rugged roads. The weather was fine: it was about the middle of the month of August, nearly two months after the death of Justine; that miserable epoch from which I dated all my woe. The weight upon my spirit was sensibly lightened as I plunged yet deeper in the ravine of Arve. The immense mountains and precipices that overhung me on every side—the sound of the river raging among the rocks, and the dashing of the waterfalls around, spoke of a power mighty as Omnipotence—and I ceased to fear, or to bend before any being less almighty than that which had created and ruled the elements, here displayed in their most terrific guise. Still, as I ascended higher, the valley assumed a more magnificent and astonishing character. Ruined castles hanging on the precipices of piny mountains; the impetuous Arve, and cottages every here and there peeping forth from among the trees, formed a scene of singular beauty. But it was augmented and rendered **sublime** by the mighty Alps, whose white and shining pyramids and domes towered above all, as belonging to another earth, the habitations of another race of beings.

I passed the bridge of Pélissier, where the ravine, which the river forms, opened before me, and I began to ascend the mountain that overhangs it. Soon after I entered the valley of Chamounix. This valley is more wonderful and sublime, but not so **beautiful and picturesque**, as that of Servox, through which I had just passed. The high and snowy mountains were its immediate boundaries; but I saw no more ruined castles and fertile fields. Immense **glaciers** approached the road; I heard the rumbling thunder of the falling avalanche, and marked the smoke of its passage. Mont Blanc, the supreme and magnificent Mont Blanc, raised itself from the surrounding **aiguilles**, and its tremendous dôme overlooked the valley.

A tingling long-lost sense of pleasure often came across me during this journey. Some turn in the road, some new object suddenly perceived and recognized, reminded me of days gone by, and were associated with the light-hearted gaiety of boyhood. The very winds whispered in soothing accents, and maternal nature bade me weep no more. Then again the kindly influence ceased to act—I found myself fettered again to grief, and indulging in all the misery of reflection. Then I spurred on my animal,

sublime: In the nineteenth century, *sublime* described anything capable of arousing the strongest possible emotions. Edmund Burke defines sublime as "whatever is in any sort terrible, or is conversant about terrible objects, or operates in a manner analogue to terror."

beautiful and picturesque: In the school of Romanticism, beauty is based on proportion and harmony, not on disorder and irregularity. *Picturesque* is another aesthetic category. If the beautiful is smooth, the picturesque is rough.

glaciers: fossil ice and snow that accumulates in the valleys of very high mountains or at the poles.

aiguilles: peaks resembling needles.

striving so to forget the world, my fears, and more than all, myself—or, in a more desperate fashion, I alighted, and threw myself on the grass, weighed down by horror and despair.

At length I arrived at the village of Chamounix. Exhaustion succeeded to the extreme fatigue both of body and of mind which I had endured. For a short space of time I remained at the window, watching the pallid lightnings that played above Mont Blanc, and listening to the rushing of the Arve, which pursued its noisy way beneath. The same lulling sounds acted as a lullaby to my too keen sensations: when I placed my head upon my pillow, sleep crept over me; I felt it as it came, and blessed the giver of oblivion.

CHAPTER X

I spent the following day roaming through the valley. I stood beside the sources of the Arveiron, which take their rise in a glacier, that with slow pace is advancing down from the summit of the hills, to barricade the valley. The abrupt sides of vast mountains were before me; the icy wall of the glacier overhung me; a few shattered pines were scattered around; and the solemn silence of this glorious presence-chamber of imperial Nature was broken only by the brawling waves, or the fall of some vast fragment, the thunder sound of the avalanche, or the cracking, reverberated along the mountains, of the accumulated ice, which, through the silent working of **immutable** laws, was ever and anon rent and torn, as if it had been but a plaything in their hands. These sublime and magnificent scenes afforded me the greatest consolation that I was capable of receiving. They elevated me from all littleness of feeling; and although they did not remove my grief, they subdued and tranquillised it. In some degree, also, they diverted my mind from the thoughts over which it had brooded for the last month. I retired to rest at night; my slumbers, as it were, waited on and ministered to by the assemblance of grand shapes which I had contemplated during the day. They congregated round me; the unstained snowy mountain-top, the glittering pinnacle, the pine woods, and ragged bare ravine; the eagle, soaring amidst the clouds—they all gathered round me, and bade me be at peace.

Where had they fled when the next morning I awoke? All of soul-inspiriting fled with sleep, and dark melancholy clouded every thought. The rain was pouring in torrents, and thick mists hid the summits of the mountains, so that I even saw not the faces of those mighty friends. Still I would penetrate their misty veil, and seek them in their cloudy retreats. What were rain and storm to me? My mule was brought to the door, and I resolved to ascend to the summit of Montanvert. I remembered the effect that the view of the tremendous and ever-moving glacier had produced upon my mind when I first saw it. It had then filled me with a sublime ecstasy, that gave wings to the soul, and allowed it to soar from the obscure world to light and joy. The sight of the **awful** and majestic in nature had indeed always the effect of solemnising my mind, and causing

immutable: unchangeable, eternal.

awful: terrifyingly beautiful.

me to forget the passing cares of life. I determined to go without a guide, for I was well acquainted with the path, and the presence of another would destroy the solitary **grandeur** of the scene.

grandeur: splendor, magnificence.

The ascent is precipitous, but the path is cut into continual and short windings, which enable you to surmount the perpendicularity of the mountain. It is a scene terrifically desolate. In a thousand spots the traces of the winter avalanche may be perceived, where trees lie broken and strewed on the ground; some entirely destroyed, others bent, leaning upon the jutting rocks of the mountain, or transversely upon other trees. The path, as you ascend higher, is intersected by ravines of snow, down which stones continually roll from above; one of them is particularly dangerous, as the slightest sound, such as even speaking in a loud voice, produces a **concussion** of air sufficient to draw destruction upon the head of the speaker. The pines are not tall or luxuriant, but they are **sombre**, and add an air of severity to the scene. I looked on the valley beneath; vast mists were rising from the rivers which ran through it, and curling in thick wreaths around the opposite mountains, whose summits were hid in the uniform clouds, while rain poured from the dark sky, and added to the melancholy impression I received from the objects around me. Alas! why does man boast of sensibilities superior to those apparent in the brute; it only renders them more necessary beings. If our impulses were confined to hunger, thirst, and desire, we might be nearly free; but now we are moved by every wind that blows, and a chance word or scene that that word may convey to us.

concussion: blow; impact.

sombre: gloomy.

We rest; a dream has power to poison sleep.

We rise; one wand'ring thought pollutes the day.

We feel, conceive, or reason; laugh or weep,

Embrace fond woe, or cast our cares away;

It is the same: for, be it joy or sorrow,

The path of its departure still is free.

Man's yesterday may ne'er be like his morrow;

Nought may endure but mutability!

"We rest . . .": final lines from Percy Shelley's "On Mutability" (1816).

It was nearly noon when I arrived at the top of the ascent. For some time I sat upon the rock that overlooks the sea of ice. A mist covered both that and the surrounding mountains. Presently a breeze dissipated the cloud, and I descended upon the glacier. The surface is very uneven, rising like the waves of a troubled sea, descending low, and interspersed by rifts that sink deep. The field of ice is almost a league in width, but I spent nearly two hours in crossing it. The opposite mountain is a bare perpendicular rock. From the side where I now stood Montanvert was exactly opposite, at the distance of a league; and above it rose Mont Blanc, in awful majesty. I remained in a recess of the rock, gazing on this wonderful and stupendous scene. The sea, or rather the vast river of ice, wound among its dependent mountains, whose aerial summits hung over its recesses. Their icy and glittering peaks shone in the sunlight over the clouds. My heart, which was before sorrowful, now swelled with something like joy; I exclaimed—"Wandering spirits, if indeed ye wander, and do not rest in your narrow beds, allow me this faint happiness, or take me, as your companion, away from the joys of life."

As I said this, I suddenly beheld the figure of a man, at some distance, advancing towards me with superhuman speed. He bounded over the crevices in the ice, among which I had walked with caution; his stature, also, as he approached, seemed to exceed that of man. I was troubled: a mist came over my eyes, and I felt a faintness seize me; but I was quickly restored by the cold gale of the mountains. I perceived, as the shape came nearer (sight tremendous and abhorred!) that it was the wretch whom I had created. I trembled with rage and horror, resolving to wait his approach and then close with him in mortal combat. He approached; his countenance bespoke bitter anguish, combined with disdain and malignity, while its unearthly ugliness rendered it almost too horrible for human eyes. But I scarcely observed this; rage and hatred had at first deprived me of utterance, and I recovered only to overwhelm him with words expressive of furious detestation and contempt.

"Devil," I exclaimed, "do you dare approach me? and do not you fear the fierce vengeance of my arm wreaked on your miserable head? Begone, vile insect! or rather, stay, that I may trample you to dust! and, oh! that I could, with the extinction of your miserable existence, restore those victims whom you have so diabolically murdered!"

"I expected this reception," said the daemon. "All men hate the wretched; how, then, must I be hated, who am miserable beyond all living things! Yet you, my creator, detest and spurn me, thy creature, to whom thou art bound by ties only dissoluble by the annihilation of one of us. You purpose to kill me. How dare you sport thus with life? Do your duty towards me, and I will do mine towards you and the rest of mankind. If you will comply with my conditions, I will leave them and you at peace; but if you refuse, I will glut the maw of death, until it be satiated with the blood of your remaining friends."

"Abhorred monster! fiend that thou art! the tortures of hell are too mild a vengeance for thy crimes. Wretched devil! you reproach me with your creation; come on, then, that I may extinguish the spark which I so negligently bestowed."

My rage was without bounds; I sprang on him, impelled by all the feelings which can arm one being against the existence of another.

He easily eluded me and said—

"Be calm! I entreat you to hear me, before you give vent to your hatred on my devoted head. Have I not suffered enough, that you seek to increase my misery? Life, although it may only be an accumulation of anguish, is dear to me, and I will defend it. Remember, thou hast made me more powerful than thyself; my height is superior to thine; my joints more supple. But I will not be tempted to set myself in opposition to thee. I am thy **creature**, and I will be even mild and docile to my natural lord and king if thou wilt also perform thy part, the which thou owest

creature: creation.

me. Oh, Frankenstein, be not equitable to every other, and trample upon me alone, to whom thy justice, and even thy **clemency** and affection, is most due. Remember, that I am thy creature; I ought to be thy Adam; but I am rather the fallen angel, whom thou drivest from joy for no misdeed. Every where I see bliss, from which I alone am irrevocably excluded. I was benevolent and good; misery made me a fiend. Make me happy, and I shall again be virtuous."

"Begone! I will not hear you. There can be no community between you and me; we are enemies. Begone, or let us try our strength in a fight, in which one must fall."

"How can I move thee? Will no entreaties cause thee to turn a favourable eye upon thy creature, who implores thy goodness and compassion? Believe me, Frankenstein: I was benevolent; my soul glowed with love and humanity: but am I not alone, miserably alone? You, my creator, abhor me; what hope can I gather from your fellow-creatures, who owe me nothing? they spurn and hate me. The desert mountains and dreary glaciers are my refuge. I have wandered here many days; the caves of ice, which I only do not fear, are a dwelling to me, and the only one which man does not grudge. These bleak skies I hail, for they are kinder to me than your fellow-beings. If the multitude of mankind knew of my existence, they would do as you do, and arm themselves for my destruction. Shall I not then hate them who abhor me? I will keep no terms with my enemies. I am miserable, and they shall share my wretchedness. Yet it is in your power to recompense me, and deliver them from an evil which it only remains for you to make so great, that not only you and your family, but thousands of others, shall be swallowed up in the whirlwinds of its rage. Let your compassion be moved, and do not disdain me. Listen to my tale: when you have heard that, abandon or commiserate me, as you shall judge that I deserve. But hear me. The guilty are allowed, by human laws, bloody as they are, to speak in their own defence before they are condemned. Listen to me, Frankenstein. You accuse me of murder; and yet you would, with a satisfied conscience, destroy your own creature. Oh, praise the eternal justice of man! Yet I ask you not to spare me: listen to me, and then, if you can, and if you will, destroy the work of your hands."

"Why do you call to my remembrance," I rejoined, "circumstances, of which I shudder to reflect, that I have been the miserable origin and author? Cursed be the day, abhorred devil, in which you first saw light! Cursed (although I curse myself) be the hands that formed you! You have made me wretched beyond expression. You have left me no power to consider whether I am just to you, or not. Begone! relieve me from the sight of your detested form."

"Thus I relieve thee, my creator," he said, and placed his hated hands before my eyes, which I flung from me with violence; "thus I take from thee a sight which you abhor. Still thou canst listen to me, and grant me thy compassion. By the virtues that I once possessed, I demand this from you. Hear my tale; it is long and strange, and the temperature of this

clemency: compassion.

place is not fitting to your fine sensations; come to the hut upon the mountain. The sun is yet high in the heavens; before it descends to hide itself behind your snowy precipices, and illuminate another world, you will have heard my story, and can decide. On you it rests, whether I quit for ever the neighbourhood of man, and lead a harmless life, or become the scourge of your fellow-creatures, and the author of your own speedy ruin."

As he said this, he led the way across the ice: I followed. My heart was full, and I did not answer him; but as I proceeded, I weighed the various arguments that he had used, and determined at least to listen to his tale. I was partly urged by curiosity, and compassion confirmed my resolution. I had hitherto supposed him to be the murderer of my brother, and I eagerly sought a confirmation or denial of this opinion. For the first time, also, I felt what the duties of a creator towards his creature were, and that I ought to render him happy before I complained of his wickedness. These motives urged me to comply with his demand. We crossed the ice, therefore, and ascended the opposite rock. The air was cold, and the rain again began to descend: we entered the hut, the fiend with an air of exultation, I with a heavy heart, and depressed spirits. But I consented to listen; and, seating myself by the fire which my odious companion had lighted, he thus began his tale.

COMMENTARY

Following Justine's death, Victor feels more and more like "an evil spirit" despite the virtuous feelings that abound in his heart. Unable to understand how his auspicious, promising beginnings can be replaced with such terrible pain and a sense of universal guilt, Victor avoids his family and friends, looking for consolation in absolute solitude. Victor's father tries to remind him that excessive suffering is destructive and that "immoderate grief" prevents him from fulfilling his obligations to the living.

This time, however, Victor cannot hear his father; he is no longer the young, innocent man he was before Ingolstadt, before M. Waldman, and before the creation of the Monster. A vast chasm separates his father's world—which is still governed by reason, laws, and order—from the irrational, nightmarish universe that Victor now inhabits. Because he sees himself as the true murderer of William (innocence) and Justine (justice), Victor feels that he is damned.

Just as he could not speak to Justine, Victor cannot answer his father; his only response is "a look of despair." He continues to spends most of his time alone, and after the family retires at night, he spends hours on the lake, lost in morbid meditations. He often contemplates suicide,

but the thought of his unprotected family, vulnerable and exposed to the viciousness of the Monster, a creature they know nothing about, as well as Elizabeth's heroic suffering, make him resist the temptation. Although Victor's suffering seems to acquire apocalyptic proportions, William's death and Justine's execution transform the other members of the family as well. Alphonse Frankenstein's health is seriously affected, and the once happy Elizabeth loses not only her joy but also her trust in people's kindness. However, unlike Victor, none of them completely abandons the hope of recovering from these tragic events.

Elizabeth's pessimism is indeed excessive. Evil has been something that she read about in books and heard in tales; for her, evil is the product of a powerful imagination. She could never have imagined people being capable of such monstrous deeds as murdering a young boy, and as a result, her entire trust in human benevolence is ruined. But compared to Victor, she still believes in the regenerative capacity of love. In her conversation with Victor, Elizabeth maintains that love is the only force in the universe that can restore one's ability to be happy. Victor, the scientist who sought to fully understand nature's secrets, is locked in a "deathlike solitude," where nothing—friendship, the beauties of nature, the magnificence of heaven, or even love—can "penetrate."

Vacillating painfully between moments of precarious tranquillity and unbearable melancholy, Victor decides to leave the house and journey through the magnificent Alpine valleys. The encounter with the sublime landscape reminds him of the divine power that created and continues to control the sublime universe—a power that Victor now realizes should be the only one revered or feared.

In a mood of "dark melancholy" Victor decides to climb the summit of Montanvert, where, in his younger days, he experienced moments of pure happiness and joy. Around noon, Victor reaches the top of the majestic mountain and stops for a moment to contemplate the impressive sea of ice unfolding under him.

Victor and the Monster's Dialogue

Previously, the sublime storm around Geneva made him think that the celestial powers were performing William's funeral song, and Victor again addresses the transient spirits of nature, asking them to alleviate his pain or absorb him in their measureless power. The parallelism of the two scenes continues, and suddenly Victor observes in the distance an unusually large form advancing rapidly toward him (in the previous scene, the Monster also appears immediately after Victor's invocation to nature). Terrified, Victor recognizes the abominable presence of his creature, and again, his first impulse is to destroy the Monster.

But Victor abandons his first thought, and instead of attacking the Monster, he addresses him with a mixture of invectives and threats. In a calm, more controlled manner, the Monster explains that he came to remind Victor of his duties toward his creature, duties that only death can dissolve, duties that Victor should fulfill before attending any other responsibility. If Victor promises to uphold his obligations, the Monster pledges to respect his own responsibilities and submit to Victor's will.

Victor refuses to listen to him, and unaffected by his words, he declares everlasting hostility for the Monster. Instead of discouraging or provoking the creature, Victor's refusal makes him renew his efforts—this time,

even more intensely. In the end of a moving speech that recapitulates his sufferings, the Monster implores Victor to listen to his story. Victor refuses once again and curses the very act of the Monster's creation, claiming that the Monster's abominable deeds have made Victor lose his sense of justice—his ability to judge, to understand clearly, and to discriminate properly between facts. The Monster ignores this second refusal and, at the same time, abandons his efforts to impress Victor and gain his compassion. Implacably, he demands that Victor listen to his tale, takes him to his hut, and, in front of the fire, tells his story.

This first real dialogue between Victor and his creature reveals a number of important details, including the clear difference between their language. Victor, who almost lost the ability to communicate and, as he claims, the ability to judge, appears indeed as a confused and irrational man. He is incapable of putting aside his own feeling to hear the Monster's story although he knows that, despite his feelings of repulsion and anger, his sacred duty is to listen to his creature. The Monster, on the other hand, is articulate and logical, eloquently mixing effective arguments with strong emotions in a speech of real rhetorical power. (Later, the creature, also loses his ability to speak; note when and why certain characters become silent, unintelligible, or inarticulate.)

In his speech, the Monster appears to link himself to Adam as well as Satan: "I ought to be thy Adam; but I am rather the fallen angel, whom thou drivest from joy for no misdeed." His association with Adam and Satan makes his connection with Victor, his creator, even stronger. Victor too can be viewed as an Adam-like figure and as a Satanic one. Like Adam, he is given a woman to "possess," has an incestuous relationship with "his more-than-sister," and is the beneficiary of a perfect childhood. Like Satan and Walton, Victor wants to be like God, acquire perfect knowledge by transgressing a patriarchal interdiction, and create life from "lifeless matter." What the second part of the Monster's sentence reveals, however, is that Victor cannot be like God, because he punished his creature without reason and deprived him of joy and happiness.

Chapter 11

Confused and scared after Victor's abandonment, the Monster begins to search for food and shelter. He arrives at a village but is attacked by the villagers and chased away. Frightened, he finds refuge in an abandoned hovel attached to a small cottage. Soon, the Monster discovers a family of three—an old man, a young child, and a young woman.

CHAPTER XI

"IT is with considerable difficulty that I remember the original era of my being: all the events of that period appear confused and indistinct. A strange multiplicity of sensations seized me, and I saw, felt, heard, and smelt, at the same time; and it was, indeed, a long time before I learned to distinguish between the operations of my various senses. By degrees, I remember, a stronger light pressed upon my nerves, so that I was obliged to shut my eyes. Darkness then came over me, and troubled me; but hardly had I felt this, when, by opening my eyes, as I now suppose, the light poured in upon me again. I walked, and, I believe, descended; but I presently found a great alteration in my sensations. Before, dark and opaque bodies had surrounded me, impervious to my touch or sight; but I now found that I could wander on at liberty, with no obstacles which I could not either surmount or avoid. The light became more and more oppressive to me; and, the heat wearying me as I walked, I sought a place where I could receive shade. This was the forest near Ingolstadt, and here I lay by the side of a brook resting from my fatigue, until I felt tormented by hunger and thirst. This roused me from my nearly dormant state, and I ate some berries which I found hanging on the trees, or lying on the ground. I slaked my thirst at the brook; and then lying down, was overcome by sleep.

"It was dark when I awoke; I felt cold also, and half-frightened, as it were instinctively, finding myself so desolate. Before I had quitted your apartment, on a sensation of cold, I had covered myself with some clothes; but these were insufficient to secure me from the dews of night. I was a poor, helpless, miserable wretch; I knew, and could distinguish, nothing; but feeling pain invade me on all sides, I sat down and wept.

"Soon a gentle light stole over the heavens, and gave me a sensation of pleasure. I started up, and beheld a radiant form rise from among the trees. I gazed with a kind of wonder. It moved slowly, but it enlightened my path; and I again went out in search of berries. I was still cold, when under one of the trees I found a huge cloak, with which I covered myself, and sat down upon the ground. No distinct ideas occupied my mind; all was confused. I felt light, and hunger, and thirst, and darkness; innumerable sounds rang in my ears, and on all sides various scents saluted me: the only object that I could distinguish was the bright moon, and I fixed my eyes on that with pleasure.

"Several changes of day and night passed, and the orb of night had greatly lessened, when I began to distinguish my sensations from each other. I gradually saw plainly the clear stream that supplied me with drink, and the trees that shaded me with their foliage. I was delighted when I first discovered that a pleasant sound, which often saluted my ears, proceeded from the throats of the little winged animals who had often intercepted the light from my eyes. I began also to observe, with greater accuracy, the forms that surrounded me, and to perceive the boundaries of the radiant roof of light which canopied me. Sometimes I tried to imitate the pleasant songs of the birds, but was unable. Sometimes I wished to express my sensations in my own mode, but the uncouth and inarticulate sounds which broke from me frightened me into silence again.

"The moon had disappeared from the night, and again, with a lessened form, showed itself, while I still remained in the forest. My sensations had, by this time, become distinct, and my mind received every day additional ideas. My eyes became accustomed to the light, and to perceive objects in their right forms; I distinguished the insect from the herb, and by degrees, one herb from another. I found that the sparrow uttered none but harsh notes, whilst those of the blackbird and thrush were sweet and enticing.

"One day, when I was oppressed by cold, I found a fire which had been left by some wandering beggars, and was overcome with delight at the warmth I experienced from it. In my joy I thrust my hand into the live embers, but quickly drew it out again with a cry of pain. How strange, I thought, that the same cause should produce such opposite effects! I examined the materials of the fire, and to my joy found it to be composed of wood. I quickly collected some branches; but they were wet, and would not burn. I was pained at this, and sat still watching the operation of the fire. The wet wood which I had placed near the heat dried, and itself became inflamed. I reflected on this; and, by touching the various branches, I discovered the cause, and busied myself in collecting a great quantity of wood, that I might dry it, and have a plentiful supply of fire. When night came on, and brought sleep with it, I was in the greatest fear lest my fire should be extinguished. I covered it carefully with dry wood and leaves, and placed wet branches upon it; and then, spreading my cloak, I lay on the ground, and sunk into sleep.

"It was morning when I awoke, and my first care was to visit the fire. I uncovered it, and a gentle breeze quickly fanned it into a flame. I observed this also, and contrived a fan of branches, which roused the embers when they were nearly extinguished. When night came again, I found, with pleasure, that the fire gave light as well as heat; and that the discovery of this element was useful to me in my food; for I found some of the offals that the travellers had left had been roasted, and tasted much more **savoury** than the berries I gathered from the trees. I tried, therefore, to dress my food in the same manner, placing it on the live embers. I found that the berries were spoiled by this operation, and the nuts and roots much improved.

savoury (savory): delicious, appetizing.

"Food, however, became scarce; and I often spent the whole day searching in vain for a few acorns to assuage the pangs of hunger. When I found this, I resolved to quit the place that I had hitherto inhabited, to seek for one where the few wants I experienced would be more easily satisfied. In this emigration, I exceedingly lamented the loss of the fire which I had obtained through accident, and knew not how to reproduce it. I gave several hours to the serious consideration of this difficulty; but I was obliged to relinquish all attempt to supply it; and, wrapping myself up in my cloak, I struck across the wood towards the setting sun. I passed three days in these rambles, and at length discovered the open country. A great fall of snow had taken place the night before, and the fields were of one uniform white; the appearance was disconsolate, and I found my feet chilled by the cold damp substance that covered the ground.

"It was about seven in the morning, and I longed to obtain food and shelter; at length I perceived a small hut, on a rising ground, which had doubtless been built for the convenience of some shepherd. This was a new sight to me; and I examined the structure with great curiosity. Finding the door open, I entered. An old man sat in it, near a fire, over which he was preparing his breakfast. He turned on hearing a noise; and, perceiving me, shrieked loudly, and, quitting the hut, ran across the fields with a speed of which his debilitated form hardly appeared capable. His appearance, different from any I had ever before seen, and his flight, somewhat surprised me. But I was enchanted by the appearance of the hut: here the snow and rain could not penetrate; the ground was dry; and it presented to me then as exquisite and divine a retreat as **Pandaemonium** appeared to the daemons of hell after their sufferings in the **lake of fire**. I greedily devoured the remnants of the shepherd's breakfast, which consisted of bread, cheese, milk, and wine; the latter, however, I did not like. Then, overcome by fatigue, I lay down among some straw, and fell asleep.

Pandaemonium: allusion to *Paradise Lost.*

lake of fire: allusion to *Paradise Lost.*

"It was noon when I awoke; and, allured by the warmth of the sun, which shone brightly on the white ground, I determined to recommence my travels; and, depositing the remains of the peasant's breakfast in a **wallet** I found, I proceeded across the fields for several hours, until at sunset I arrived at a village. How miraculous did this appear! the huts, the neater cottages, and stately houses, engaged my admiration by turns. The vegetables in the gardens, the milk and cheese that I saw placed at the windows of some of the cottages, allured my appetite. One of the best of these I entered; but I had hardly placed my foot within the door, before the children shrieked, and one of the women fainted. The whole village was roused; some fled, some attacked me, until, grievously bruised by stones and many other kinds of **missile** weapons, I escaped to the open country, and fearfully took refuge in a low hovel, quite bare, and making a wretched appearance after the palaces I had beheld in the village. This hovel, however, joined a cottage of a neat and pleasant appearance; but, after my late dearly bought experience, I dared not enter it. My place of refuge was constructed of wood, but so low that I could with difficulty sit upright in it. No wood, however, was placed on the earth,

wallet: beggar's bag.

missile: thrown.

which formed the floor, but it was dry; and although the wind entered it by innumerable chinks, I found it an agreeable asylum from the snow and rain.

"Here then I retreated, and lay down happy to have found a shelter, however miserable, from the inclemency of the season, and still more from the barbarity of man.

"As soon as morning dawned, I crept from my kennel, that I might view the adjacent cottage, and discover if I could remain in the habitation I had found. It was situated against the back of the cottage, and surrounded on the sides which were exposed by a pig-sty and a clear pool of water. One part was open, and by that I had crept in; but now I covered every crevice by which I might be perceived with stones and wood, yet in such a manner that I might move them on occasion to pass out: all the light I enjoyed came through the sty, and that was sufficient for me.

"Having thus arranged my dwelling, and carpeted it with clean straw, I retired; for I saw the figure of a man at a distance, and I remembered too well my treatment the night before, to trust myself in his power. I had first, however, provided for my sustenance for that day, by a loaf of coarse bread, which I purloined, and a cup with which I could drink, more conveniently than from my hand, of the pure water which flowed by my retreat. The floor was a little raised, so that it was kept perfectly dry, and by its vicinity to the chimney of the cottage it was tolerably warm.

"Being thus provided, I resolved to reside in this hovel, until something should occur which might alter my determination. It was indeed a paradise, compared to the bleak forest, my former residence, the rain-dropping branches, and dank earth. I ate my breakfast with pleasure, and was about to remove a plank to procure myself a little water, when I heard a step, and looking through a small chink, I beheld a young creature, with a pail on her head, passing before my hovel. The girl was young, and of gentle demeanour, unlike what I have since found cottagers and farm-house servants to be. Yet she was meanly dressed, a coarse blue petticoat and a linen jacket being her only garb; her fair hair was plaited, but not adorned: she looked patient, yet sad. I lost sight of her; and in about a quarter of an hour she returned, bearing the pail, which was now partly filled with milk. As she walked along, seemingly incommoded by the burden, a young man met her, whose countenance expressed a deeper despondence. Uttering a few sounds with an air of melancholy, he took the pail from her head, and bore it to the cottage himself. She followed, and they disappeared. Presently I saw the young man again, with some tools in his hand, cross the field behind the cottage; and the girl was also busied, sometimes in the house, and sometimes in the yard.

"On examining my dwelling, I found that one of the windows of the cottage had formerly occupied a part of it, but the panes had been filled up with wood. In one of these was a small and almost imperceptible chink, through which the eye could just penetrate. Through this crevice a small room was visible, whitewashed and clean, but very bare of furniture. In one corner, near a small fire, sat an old man, leaning his head on his hands in a disconsolate attitude. The young girl was occupied in arranging the cottage; but presently she took something out of a drawer, which employed her hands, and she sat down beside the old man, who, taking up an instrument, began to play, and to produce sounds sweeter than the voice of the thrush or the nightingale. It was a lovely sight, even to me, poor wretch! who had never beheld **aught** beautiful before. The silver hair and benevolent countenance of the aged cottager won my reverence, while the gentle manners of the girl enticed my love. He played a sweet mournful air, which I perceived drew tears from the eyes of his amiable companion, of which the old man took no notice, until she sobbed audibly; he then pronounced a few sounds, and the fair creature, leaving her work, knelt at his feet. He raised her, and smiled with such kindness and affection, that I felt sensations of a peculiar and overpowering nature: they were a mixture of pain and pleasure, such as I had never before experienced, either from hunger or cold, warmth or food; and I withdrew from the window, unable to bear these emotions.

aught: anything.

"Soon after this the young man returned, bearing on his shoulders a load of wood. The girl met him at the door, helped to relieve him of his burden, and, taking some of the fuel into the cottage, placed it on the fire; then she and the youth went apart into a nook of the cottage, and he showed her a large loaf and a piece of cheese. She seemed pleased, and went into the garden for some roots and plants, which she placed in water, and then upon the fire. She afterwards continued her work, whilst the young man went into the garden, and appeared busily employed in digging and pulling up roots. After he had been employed thus about an hour, the young woman joined him, and they entered the cottage together.

"The old man had, in the meantime, been **pensive**; but on the appearance of his companions, he assumed a more cheerful air, and they sat down to eat. The meal was quickly despatched. The young woman was again occupied in arranging the cottage; the old man walked before the cottage in the sun for a few minutes, leaning on the arm of the youth. Nothing could exceed in beauty the contrast between these two excellent creatures. One was old, with silver hairs and a countenance beaming with benevolence and love: the younger was slight and graceful in his figure, and his features were moulded with the finest **symmetry**; yet his eyes and attitude expressed the utmost sadness and despondency. The old man returned to the cottage: and the youth, with tools different from those he had used in the morning, directed his steps across the fields.

pensive: contemplative, meditative.

symmetry: regularity, proportion.

"Night quickly shut in; but to my extreme wonder, I found that the cottagers had a means of prolonging light by the use of tapers, and was delighted to find that the setting of the sun did not put an end to the pleasure I experienced in watching my human neighbours. In the evening, the young girl and her companion were employed in various occupations which I did not understand; and the old man again took up the instrument which produced the divine sounds that had enchanted me in the morning. So soon as he had finished, the youth began, not to play, but to utter sounds that were monotonous, and neither resembling the harmony of the old man's instrument nor the songs of the birds: I since found that he read aloud, but at that time I knew nothing of the science of words or letters.

"The family, after having been thus occupied for a short time, extinguished their lights and retired, as I conjectured, to rest.

COMMENTARY

The Monster's story is the third major narrative in the novel and constitutes the third window, or concentric circle, of its structure. The narrative is told to Victor who then repeats it to Walton, who rewrites it in a letter to Margaret based on his notes and Victor's corrections. Interestingly enough, the character whose story is the most mediated has the last word in the novel. Before the Monster's direct narrative starts, the reader knows that he was born motherless (like Eve in the book of Genesis or in Milton's *Paradise Lost*) in Victor's womb-like laboratory. Unlike Adam, however, whose celestial father offered him paradise, love, and divine presence, the Monster is rejected and abandoned by his creator.

The Monster discovers the world.
Everett Collection

Six chapters (perhaps an incomplete Genesis) are devoted to the Monster's story. In this first chapter, he narrates how, frightened and perplexed after Victor's abandonment, he discovers the different sensations of his senses—hunger and thirst, cold and warmth, pleasure and pain—and the connection between senses and sensations (for instance, how light and darkness affect his eyes). Hours later, exhausted by wandering for so long and oppressed by heat, he takes refuge in the forest near Ingolstadt. He sleeps for a short while and then eats some berries from the trees. When the night arrives and he suddenly becomes cold, the initial surprise of understanding how his body functions is replaced by intolerable pain. He understands now that he is "a poor, helpless, miserable wretch," and overwhelmed by suffering, the Monster cries for the first time.

During the following days, the Monster gradually discovers the song of the birds, the forms of natural objects, and, finally, fire. In his search for more food and a better shelter, he leaves the forest and travels for three days across the fields until he arrives at a shepherd's hut and a village, where he is savagely attacked by the villagers. Frightened, he finds refuge in an abandoned hovel attached to a small cottage. Peeping through a very small crack, the Monster discovers that living in the house is a small family—an old man and his two children.

The Monster's "Childhood"

The days in the forest of Ingolstadt are associated by some critics with a sort of primordial innocence; the Monster eats berries, learns about sensations, and perceives light. However, compared with Victor's fortunate childhood (with loving, nurturing parents who protect and instruct him) and Adam's paradise (in which the Creator puts him in the middle of a beautiful garden and converses with him), the Monster, who is born in a cold, isolated laboratory, is deserted by his creator. In the monster's account of his first experiences into the world, the days of happiness, joy, and bliss in Victor's and Adam's narratives are replaced with suffering, confusion, and unbearable sadness. His early attempts at speech, which attest to his immediate need to communicate, are disastrous. He cannot affirm like Adam in Milton's *Paradise Lost* that his "Tongue obey'd" him and he cannot easily name the objects surrounding him.

Clearly, the Monster's early days do not constitute a paradise, and instead of getting parental protection and guidance, he endures absolute loneliness, anguish, and fear. Not surprisingly, he soon perceives himself as a Satanic figure, associating his finding of the shepherd's hut with the devils' discovery of Pandemonium, the capital of Hell, in *Paradise Lost.* The connection with Satan is later reinforced by the episode in which the Monster secretly observes the De Laceys' pastoral world. Indeed, the segment echoes the fourth book of *Paradise Lost*, where Satan regards Adam and Eve's bower with envy and admiration. Along the same lines, the Monster's remarks on the young man's beautiful features can be seen as a commentary on his own Satan-like, monstrous size, a moment that anticipates his later observations regarding the disturbing differences between himself and the human beings he watches every day and his horror upon observing his hideous reflection mirrored in a pool in the following chapter.

The description of the creature's first experiences in the world allow Mary Shelley to reflect on educational issues, a major theme in the novel as well as a topic that intensely preoccupied her, Percy, and her parents. The Monster's experiences initially appear to allude to Jean Jacques Rousseau's famous concept of the *noble savage*, or the natural man.

Rousseau (1712–78) was one of the two most influential French writers of the eighteenth century (the other one was Voltaire). His ideas revolutionized many fields, including education—he is, in fact, considered one of the founders of modern education. An orphan like Mary Shelley and like so many of her characters, he lost his mother at birth and was abandoned by his father. Thus, Rousseau wrote extensively on the different aspects of early instruction. Succinctly, he claims that a child should be truly a child of nature and, therefore, should grow and learn from the inside and not have learning forced upon him or her from the outside. In his famous book *Emile*, he presents a child raised in a natural environment, almost in complete isolation, who discovers all the necessary knowledge simply by following his natural intelligence and instincts. This model was extremely attractive at a time of major social, political, and economic changes (the period before the French Revolution) precisely because of its insistence on inventiveness, spontaneity, perspicacity, and curiosity. Indeed, in his reactions to the surrounding world, the Monster is similar to Rousseau's natural man; he simply responds to the changing conditions of his body and the changes of the environment, feeling pleasure or pain without understanding what determines either of them. Gradually, he learns what causes pleasure and what causes discomfort or pain, and more importantly, he learns the significance of fire and shelter—the most important elements in the life of the primitive man.

Fire as One of the Monster's Themes

The discovery that perplexes and fascinates the Monster is fire. During his departure from the forest, the loss of fire (something that he obtained by accident and does not know how to produce) is the only loss he "laments," proving that he intuitively understands its enormous power. Paradoxically, this element the Monster so much admires for its civilizing power later becomes the agent of his vindictiveness.

The Monster's second important discovery is the shepherd's hut, which offers him a welcomed retreat. He also discovers processed food—bread, cheese, milk, and wine—and realizes that he does not like wine.

At this point, when the Monster discovers fire, housing, and cooked food (versus raw food), Mary Shelley abandons Rousseau and turns to John Locke's theories from *Essay Concerning Human Understanding* (1690) and *Some Thoughts Concerning Education* (1693). Her preference for Locke is explained by two factors:

* Mary Shelley became gradually aware of some disastrous consequences resulting from the mechanical application of Rousseau's theories. For instance, two famous intellectuals of the day, Richard Lovell Edgeworth and Thomas Day, raised their two children according to this model, and the children failed dramatically to develop the intellectual and social skills necessary to survive in the world.
* Locke's ideas were embraced by her parents and many other intellectuals from her circle, including Coleridge and Wordsworth. Especially appealing to all of them was Locke's theory that everything human beings know, do, or become is determined by what happens to them in their youth and by the environment in which they are raised.

The Monster's View of Family

Following Locke, who also insists that education cannot be complete without the presence of good moral and intellectual models in a child's life, Mary Shelley introduces the De Lacey family, the paradigm of domestic happiness, generosity, and affection. Although the family lacks a maternal presence, it almost represents a terrestrial Eden, partially mirroring the biblical paradise containing a father loved, venerated, and obeyed by his children—one male and one female.

The De Lacey family offers the Monster the image of an ideal domestic existence as well as a virtuous moral model, and his admiration for the family clearly confirms the Monster's fundamentally good nature. For the first time, the Monster encounters tender, delicate gestures and affectionate attitudes. The young man and woman help and encourage each other, the old man often comforts them, and although sad and melancholy at times, they all seem happy to be together.

Watching them, the Monster discovers some new sensations different from any other feelings he had come to know. The mixture of pain and pleasure the Monster experiences may be the experience of love. As defined by Plato in *Symposium*—his famous dialogue on the nature of love—in love, all opposites coincide.

This essentially important moment in the novel precedes the Monster's most important intellectual experience: the acquisition of language. The family, here and in the following chapters, also completes the Monster's education. Interestingly, one of his first educational experiences is music, and again, his positive reaction to music reveals a sensitive soul.

Chapter 12 The Monster continues to closely observe his neighbors, and he is deeply moved by the love and respect they have for each other. After a while, he notices that they communicate through words, and then he sees them reading from a book. Longing to communicate and hoping that people with such elegant and gentle manners may overlook his deformity, the Monster studies their language intensely.

CHAPTER XII

"I lay on my straw, but I could not sleep. I thought of the occurrences of the day. What chiefly struck me was the gentle manners of these people; and I longed to join them, but dared not. I remembered too well the treatment I had suffered the night before from the barbarous villagers, and resolved, whatever course of conduct I might hereafter think it right to pursue, that for the present I would remain quietly in my hovel, watching, and endeavouring to discover the motives which influenced their actions.

"The cottagers arose the next morning before the sun. The young woman arranged the cottage, and prepared the food; and the youth departed after the first meal.

"This day was passed in the same routine as that which preceded it. The young man was constantly employed out of doors, and the girl in various laborious occupations within. The old man, whom I soon perceived to be blind, employed his leisure hours on his instrument or in contemplation. Nothing could exceed the love and respect which the younger cottagers exhibited towards their venerable companion. They performed towards him every little office of affection and duty with gentleness; and he rewarded them by his benevolent smiles.

"They were not entirely happy. The young man and his companion often went apart, and appeared to weep. I saw no cause for their unhappiness; but I was deeply affected by it. If such lovely creatures were miserable, it was less strange that I, an imperfect and solitary being, should be wretched. Yet why were these gentle beings unhappy? They possessed a delightful house (for such it was in my eyes) and every luxury; they had a fire to warm them when chill, and delicious viands when hungry; they were dressed in excellent clothes; and, still more, they enjoyed one another's company and speech, interchanging each day looks of affection and kindness. What did their tears imply? Did they really express pain? I was at first unable to solve these questions; but perpetual attention and time explained to me many appearances which were at first enigmatic.

"A considerable period elapsed before I discovered one of the causes of the uneasiness of this amiable family: it was poverty; and they suffered that evil in a very distressing degree. Their nourishment consisted entirely of the vegetables of their garden, and the milk of one cow, which gave very little during the winter, when its masters could scarcely procure food to support it. They often, I believe, suffered the pangs of hunger very poignantly, especially the two younger cottagers; for several times they placed food before the old man, when they reserved none for themselves.

"This trait of kindness moved me sensibly. I had been accustomed, during the night, to steal a part of their store for my own consumption; but when I found that in doing this I inflicted pain on the cottagers, I abstained, and satisfied myself with berries, nuts, and roots, which I gathered from a neighbouring wood.

"I discovered also another means through which I was enabled to assist their labours. I found that the youth spent a great part of each day in collecting wood for the family fire; and during the night, I often took his tools, the use of which I quickly discovered, and brought home firing sufficient for the consumption of several days.

"I remember, the first time that I did this, the young woman, when she opened the door in the morning, appeared greatly astonished on seeing a great pile of wood on the outside. She uttered some words in a loud voice, and the youth joined her, who also expressed surprise. I observed, with pleasure, that he did not go to the forest that day, but spent it in repairing the cottage and cultivating the garden.

"By degrees I made a discovery of still greater moment. I found that these people possessed a method of communicating their experience and feelings to one another by articulate sounds. I perceived that the words they spoke sometimes produced pleasure or pain, smiles or sadness, in the minds and countenances of the hearers. This was indeed a godlike science, and I ardently desired to become acquainted with it. But I was baffled in every attempt I made for this purpose. Their pronunciation was quick; and the words they uttered, not having any apparent connection with visible objects, I was unable to discover any clue by which I could unravel the mystery of their reference. By great application, however, and after having remained during the space of several revolutions of the moon in my hovel, I discovered the names that were given to some of the most familiar objects of discourse; I learned and applied the words, *fire, milk, bread*, and *wood*. I learned also the names of the cottagers themselves. The youth and his companion had each of them several names, but the old man had only one, which was *father*. The girl was called *sister*, or *Agatha*; and the youth *Felix*, *brother*, or *son*. I cannot describe the delight I felt when I learned the ideas appropriated to each of these sounds, and was able to pronounce them. I distinguished several other words, without being able as yet to understand or apply them; such as *good, dearest, unhappy*.

"I spent the winter in this manner. The gentle manners and beauty of the cottagers greatly endeared them to me: when they were unhappy, I felt depressed; when they rejoiced, I sympathised in their joys. I saw few human beings besides them; and if any other happened to enter the cottage, their harsh manners and rude gait only enhanced to me the superior accomplishments of my friends. The old man, I could perceive, often endeavoured to encourage his children, as sometimes I found that he called them, to cast off their melancholy. He would talk in a cheerful accent, with an expression of goodness that bestowed pleasure even upon me. Agatha listened with respect, her eyes sometimes filled with tears, which she endeavoured to wipe away unperceived; but I generally found that her countenance and tone were more cheerful after having listened to the exhortations of her father. It was not thus with Felix. He was always the saddest of the group; and even to my unpractised senses, he appeared to have suffered more deeply than his friends. But if his countenance was more sorrowful, his voice was more cheerful than that of his sister, especially when he addressed the old man.

"I could mention innumerable instances, which, although slight, marked the dispositions of these amiable cottagers. In the midst of poverty and want, Felix carried with pleasure to his sister the first little white flower that peeped out from beneath the snowy ground. Early in the morning, before she had risen, he cleared away the snow that obstructed her path to the milk-house, drew water from the well, and brought the wood from the out-house, where, to his perpetual astonishment, he found his store always replenished by an invisible hand. In the day, I believe, he worked sometimes for a neighbouring farmer, because he often went forth, and did not return until dinner, yet brought no wood with him. At other times he worked in the garden; but as there was little to do in the frosty season, he read to the old man and Agatha.

"This reading had puzzled me extremely at first; but, by degrees, I discovered that he uttered many of the same sounds when he read as when he talked. I conjectured, therefore, that he found on the paper signs for speech which he understood, and I ardently longed to comprehend these also; but how was that possible, when I did not even understand the sounds for which they stood as signs? I improved, however, sensibly in this science, but not sufficiently to follow up any kind of conversation, although I applied my whole mind to the endeavour: for I easily perceived that, although I eagerly longed to discover myself to the cottagers, I ought not to make the attempt until I had first become master of their language; which knowledge might enable me to make them overlook the deformity of my figure; for with this also the contrast perpetually presented to my eyes had made me acquainted.

"I had admired the perfect forms of my cottagers—their grace, beauty, and delicate complexions: but how was I terrified, when I viewed myself in a transparent pool! At first I started back, unable to believe that it was indeed I who was reflected in the mirror; and when I became fully convinced that I was in reality the monster that I am, I was filled with the bitterest sensations of despondence and mortification. Alas! I did not yet entirely know the fatal effects of this miserable deformity.

"As the sun became warmer, and the light of day longer, the snow vanished, and I beheld the bare trees and the black earth. From this time Felix was more employed; and the heart-moving indications of impending famine disappeared. Their food, as I afterwards found, was coarse, but it was wholesome; and they procured a sufficiency of it. Several new kinds of plants sprung up in the garden, which they dressed; and these signs of comfort increased daily as the season advanced.

"The old man, leaning on his son, walked each day at noon, when it did not rain, as I found it was called when the heavens poured forth its waters. This frequently took place; but a high wind quickly dried the earth, and the season became far more pleasant than it had been.

"My mode of life in my hovel was uniform. During the morning, I attended the motions of the cottagers; and when they were dispersed in various occupations, I slept: the remainder of the day was spent in observing my friends. When they had retired to rest, if there was any moon, or the night was star-light, I went into the woods, and collected my own food and fuel for the cottage. When I returned, as often as it was necessary, I cleared their path from the snow, and performed those offices that I had seen done by Felix. I afterwards found that these labours, performed by an invisible hand, greatly astonished them; and once or twice I heard them, on these occasions, utter the words *good spirit, wonderful;* but I did not then understand the signification of these terms.

"My thoughts now became more active, and I longed to discover the motives and feelings of these lovely creatures; I was inquisitive to know why Felix appeared so miserable, and Agatha so sad. I thought (foolish wretch!) that it might be in my power to restore happiness to these deserving people. When I slept, or was absent, the forms of the venerable blind father, the gentle Agatha, and the excellent Felix, flitted before me. I looked upon them as superior beings, who would be the arbiters of my future destiny. I formed in my imagination a thousand pictures of presenting myself to them, and their reception of me. I imagined that they would be disgusted, until, by my gentle demeanour and conciliating words, I should first win their favour, and afterwards their love.

"These thoughts exhilarated me, and led me to apply with fresh ardour to the acquiring the art of language. My organs were indeed harsh, but supple; and although my voice was very unlike the soft music of their tones, yet I pronounced such words as I understood with tolerable ease. It was as **the ass and the lap-dog**; yet surely the gentle ass whose intentions were affectionate, although his manners were rude, deserved better treatment than blows and execration.

the ass and the lap-dog: in *Aesop's Fable,* the ass tries to gain his master's attention by imitating a lap dog, but is severely punished for it.

"The pleasant showers and genial warmth of spring greatly altered the aspect of the earth. Men, who before this change seemed to have been hid in caves, dispersed themselves, and were employed in various arts of cultivation. The birds sang in more cheerful notes, and the leaves began to bud forth on the trees. **Happy, happy earth! fit habitation for gods**, which, so short a time before, was bleak, damp, and unwholesome. My spirits were elevated by the enchanting appearance of nature; the past was blotted from my memory, the present was tranquil, and the future gilded by bright rays of hope, and anticipations of joy.

Happy, happy earth! fit habitation for gods: an allusion to Raphael's description of hell as a suitable habitation for devils in *Paradise Lost.*

COMMENTARY

The following day, the Monster observes the family following the same routine. The young people work both inside and outside the house, and while the old man plays his instrument or meditates, the Monster notices the same harmonious, affectionate relationships. However, they are not entirely happy; the old man is blind, the two young people are often sad and tired, and the family is poor. Gradually, he also discovers a certain affinity with the cottagers. Like him, they are vegetarians, they are geographically and socially isolated, and they are gentle and benevolent. For instance, the Monster notices that all the other visitors coming to the cottage have "harsh manners and rude gait," and as a result, his admiration increases for his new neighbors' superiority. Feeling a strong affection for them, the Monster decides to help the family by bringing wood to the cottage's door every night.

Finally, he observes that the cottagers "possessed a method of communicating their experience and feelings to one another by articulate sound," and listening carefully, he learns their names—Father, Agatha, and Felix—and some basic words. Encouraged by their gentleness and sensitivity and convinced that these kind people will accept and welcome him if he acquires the skills necessary to communicate with them, the Monster dedicates most of his time to the study of language.

This chapter introduces some new elements. The presence of the blind patriarch is probably an allusion to John Milton, the poet whom Mary Shelley, directly or indirectly, invokes so many times in the novel. (Like De Lacey, Milton was blind and a rather accomplished musician.) De Lacey's passion for music, in fact the entire family's sensitivity to music, may suggest a harmonious universe, one that reflects the perfection of God's creation on a smaller scale.

The Monster's Character

A number of elements highlight the Monster's fundamentally good nature. For example, as soon as he understands the family's poverty, he resolves to stop stealing their food. Moreover, he decides to help them by gathering wood for the fire during the night. He exhibits kindness and benevolence, as well as natural intelligence and perspicacity. The Monster quickly discerns where his help would be the most efficient. After he observes that collecting wood occupies the greatest part of the young man's day, he witnesses the immediate effect of his acts. The youth now has time to repair the cottage and cultivate the garden. The Monster's isolation from society and community has not only disadvantages but also some benefits, one of them being (as Rousseau would argue) exactly this ability to develop a natural sense of competency and productivity.

The Monster's insight and discrimination are best revealed in his immediate recognition of the benefits involved in mastering the "godlike science" that the cottagers use to communicate. His fervent ambition to learn their language, however, is different from Victor's or Walton's ambition. The Monster wants to learn the language in order to participate (not penetrate) into a cultural order that gives individuals a social status, respect, and recognition as a result of their membership to the order. His relation is a

The Monster observing Father De Lacey

participatory gesture, not a colonizing one. Observing the cottagers talking with each other, the Monster assumes that relationships are formed based on language and declares that this method of communicating may be the key to all his dilemmas. He seems to reason that, if language creates community, his hideous appearance will no longer prevent him from entering the community of people. Unfortunately, not only does language fail to fulfill the Monster's expectations, but its acquisition opens, like Pandora's box, a long line of terrible and painful events in the novel.

This comparison between the Monster's acquirement of language and Pandora's box is indeed productive. In Greek mythology, Pandora is the first human female. Her name means "all gifts" but she is, ironically, the cause of all man's afflictions. Fashioned out of clay by Hephaestus at Zeus's order, Pandora was created in order to punish Prometheus and humanity. She was given "gifts" by Olympian gods and sent to Prometheus' brother, Epimetheus. When she opened her box, all kinds of evils were released into the world. Similarly, Victor is a Promethean creator, and the "gift" of language that his creature obtains is Victor's worst punishment. The pain provoked by the failure of his dream to gain access to the community of men through language is directly responsible for the Monster's subsequent violence.

The Reflection in the Water

The Monster's affection for and attachment to the De Lacey family grows stronger every day and, after a while, his own moments of content or dejection are determined by the family members' joyful or gloomy attitude. At the same time, the closer he feels toward them, the harder he works on the improvement of his language skills and the firmer his hope for a welcoming encounter with them becomes. However, one day looking into a pool, his reflected image discourages and embitters him deeply, making him painfully aware of "the fatal effects of his miserable deformity." The scene alludes to Eve's own reflection in the water in Milton's fourth book of *Paradise Lost* (except that Eve perceives herself as beautiful) and also to Narcissus (a mythological, beautiful youth who loved no one until he saw his own reflection in water and fell in love with himself). The Monster's ugliness is clearly a reversal of the myth of Narcissus.

Fortunately, spring brings a renewed spirit of hope and an even more powerful desire to help the cottagers and, if at all possible, to find a cure for whatever causes their frequent melancholy (especially, Felix's unhappiness). The Monster's new thoughts, his intense study of language, his observation of the cottagers' daily routine, and his hard work to lessen the family's burden occupy most of his time and make him forget his miserable past. For the first time, the creature is utterly happy.

Again, this chapter is partially a vehicle Mary Shelley uses to reaffirm her complete accord with Locke's educational philosophy (and implicitly with Godwin's), which addresses the role played by affection and the desire to please in the education of children. Apparently, the Monster's desperate need to communicate motivates him to assiduously study language. A more careful consideration reveals that the De Lacey family is precisely the type of community in which the Monster wants to be included—a community for which he has enormous admiration, respect, and devotion and that inspires and stimulates his study.

Chapter 13

One day, a beautiful young woman arrives at the cottage door, and her presence makes Felix, the young man, enormously happy. Her name is Safie, and because she cannot understand their language, Felix begins to instruct. Paying close attention to Felix's explanations, the Monster learns about complex philosophical and social concepts, gender differences, motherhood, family relations, and death. This newly acquired knowledge makes him reflect on his own condition, status, and identity.

CHAPTER XIII

"I now hasten to the more moving part of my story. I shall relate events, that impressed me with feelings which, from what I had been, have made me what I am.

"Spring advanced rapidly; the weather became fine, and the skies cloudless. It surprised me, that what before was desert and gloomy should now bloom with the most beautiful flowers and verdure. My senses were gratified and refreshed by a thousand scents of delight, and a thousand sights of beauty.

"It was on one of these days, when my cottagers periodically rested from labour—the old man played on his guitar, and the children listened to him—that I observed the countenance of Felix was melancholy beyond expression; he sighed frequently; and once his father paused in his music, and I conjectured by his manner that he enquired the cause of his son's sorrow. Felix replied in a cheerful accent, and the old man was recommencing his music, when someone tapped at the door.

"It was a lady on horseback, accompanied by a countryman as a guide. The lady was dressed in a dark suit, and covered with a thick black veil. Agatha asked a question; to which the stranger only replied by pronouncing, in a sweet accent, the name of Felix. Her voice was musical, but unlike that of either of my friends. On hearing this word, Felix came up hastily to the lady; who, when she saw him, threw up her veil, and I beheld a countenance of angelic beauty and expression. Her hair of a shining raven black, and curiously braided; her eyes were dark, but gentle, although animated; her features of a regular proportion, and her complexion wondrously fair, each cheek tinged with a lovely pink.

"Felix seemed ravished with delight when he saw her, every trait of sorrow vanished from his face, and it instantly expressed a degree of ecstatic joy, of which I could hardly have believed it capable; his eyes sparkled, as his cheek flushed with pleasure; and at that moment I thought him as beautiful as the stranger. She appeared affected by different feelings; wiping a few tears from her lovely eyes, she held out her hand to Felix, who kissed it rapturously, and called her, as well as I could distinguish, his sweet Arabian. She did not appear to understand him, but smiled. He assisted her to dismount, and dismissing her guide, conducted her into the cottage. Some conversation took place between him and his father;

and the young stranger knelt at the old man's feet, and would have kissed his hand, but he raised her, and embraced her affectionately.

"I soon perceived, that although the stranger uttered articulate sounds, and appeared to have a language of her own, she was neither understood by, nor herself understood, the cottagers. They made many signs which I did not comprehend; but I saw that her presence diffused gladness through the cottage, dispelling their sorrow as the sun dissipates the morning mists. Felix seemed peculiarly happy, and with smiles of delight welcomed his Arabian. Agatha, the ever-gentle Agatha, kissed the hands of the lovely stranger; and, pointing to her brother, made signs which appeared to me to mean that he had been sorrowful until she came. Some hours passed thus, while they, by their countenances, expressed joy, the cause of which I did not comprehend. Presently I found, by the frequent recurrence of some sound which the stranger repeated after them, that she was endeavouring to learn their language; and the idea instantly occurred to me, that I should make use of the same instructions to the same end. The stranger learned about twenty words at the first lesson; most of them, indeed, were those which I had before understood, but I profited by the others.

"As night came on, Agatha and the Arabian retired early. When they separated, Felix kissed the hand of the stranger, and said, 'Good night, sweet Safie.' He sat up much longer, conversing with his father; and, by the frequent repetition of her name, I conjectured that their lovely guest was the subject of their conversation. I ardently desired to understand them, and bent every faculty towards that purpose, but found it utterly impossible.

"The next morning Felix went out to his work; and, after the usual occupations of Agatha were finished, the Arabian sat at the feet of the old man, and, taking his guitar, played some airs so entrancingly beautiful, that they at once drew tears of sorrow and delight from my eyes. She sang, and her voice flowed in a rich cadence, swelling or dying away, like a nightingale of the woods.

"When she had finished, she gave the guitar to Agatha, who at first declined it. She played a simple air, and her voice accompanied it in sweet accents, but unlike the wondrous strain of the stranger. The old man appeared enraptured, and said some words, which Agatha endeavoured to explain to Safie, and by which he appeared to wish to express that she bestowed on him the greatest delight by her music.

"The days now passed as peaceably as before, with the sole alteration, that joy had taken place of sadness in the countenances of my friends. Safie was always gay and happy; she and I improved rapidly in the knowledge of language, so that in two months I began to comprehend most of the words uttered by my protectors.

"In the meanwhile also the black ground was covered with herbage, and the green banks interspersed with innumerable flowers, sweet to the scent and the eyes, stars of pale radiance among the moonlight woods; the sun became warmer, the nights clear and balmy; and my nocturnal rambles were an extreme pleasure to me, although they were considerably shortened by the late setting and early rising of the sun; for I never ventured abroad during daylight, fearful of meeting with the same treatment I had formerly endured in the first village which I entered.

"My days were spent in close attention, that I might more speedily master the language; and I may boast that I improved more rapidly than the Arabian, who understood very little, and conversed in broken accents, whilst I comprehended and could imitate almost every word that was spoken.

"While I improved in speech, I also learned the science of letters, as it was taught to the stranger; and this opened before me a wide field for wonder and delight.

"The book from which Felix instructed Safie was **Volney**'s 'Ruins of Empires.' I should not have understood the purport of this book, had not Felix, in reading it, given very minute explanations. He had chosen this work, he said, because the **declamatory style** was framed in imitation of the eastern authors. Through this work I obtained a cursory knowledge of history, and a view of the several empires at present existing in the world; it gave me an insight into the manners, governments, and religions of the different nations of the earth. I heard of the slothful Asiatics; of the stupendous genius and mental activity of the Grecians; of the wars and wonderful virtue of the early Romans—of their subsequent degenerating—of the decline of that mighty empire; of chivalry, Christianity, and kings. I heard of the discovery of the American hemisphere, and wept with Safie over the hapless fate of its original inhabitants.

"These wonderful narrations inspired me with strange feelings. Was man, indeed, at once so powerful, so virtuous, and magnificent, yet so vicious and base? He appeared at one time a mere scion of the evil principle, and at another, as all that can be conceived of noble and godlike. To be a great and virtuous man appeared the highest honour that can befall a sensitive being; to be base and vicious, as many on record have been, appeared the lowest degradation, a condition more abject than that of the blind mole or harmless worm. For a long time I could not conceive how one man could go forth to murder his fellow, or even why there were laws and governments; but when I heard details of vice and bloodshed, my wonder ceased, and I turned away with disgust and loathing.

"Every conversation of the cottagers now opened new wonders to me. While I listened to the instructions which Felix bestowed upon the Arabian, the strange system of human society was explained to me. I heard of the division of property, of immense wealth and squalid poverty; of rank, descent, and noble blood.

"The words induced me to turn towards myself. I learned that the possessions most esteemed by your fellow-creatures were high and unsullied **descent** united with riches. A man might be respected with only one of these advantages; but, without either, he was considered, except in very rare instances, as a vagabond and a slave, doomed to waste his powers for

Volney: Constantin Francois de Chasseboaf (1757–1820), French philosopher, historian, and poet.

declamatory style: eloquent style.

descent: origin, lineage.

the profits of the chosen few! And what was I? Of my creation and creator I was absolutely ignorant; but I knew that I possessed no money, no friends, no kind of property. I was, besides, endued with a figure hideously deformed and loathsome; I was not even of the same nature as man. I was more agile than they, and could subsist upon coarser diet; I bore the extremes of heat and cold with less injury to my frame; my stature far exceeded theirs. When I looked around, I saw and heard of none like me. Was I then a monster, a blot upon the earth, from which all men fled, and whom all men disowned?

"I cannot describe to you the agony that these reflections inflicted upon me: I tried to dispel them, but sorrow only increased with knowledge. Oh, that I had forever remained in my native wood, nor known nor felt beyond the sensations of hunger, thirst, and heat!

"Of what a strange nature is knowledge! It clings to the mind, when it has once seized on it, like a lichen on the rock. I wished sometimes to shake off all thought and feeling; but I learned that there was but one means to overcome the sensation of pain, and that was death—a state which I feared yet did not understand. I admired virtue and good feelings, and loved the gentle manners and amiable qualities of my cottagers; but I was shut out from intercourse with them, except through means which I obtained by stealth, when I was unseen and unknown, and which rather increased than satisfied the desire I had of becoming one among my fellows. The gentle words of Agatha, and the animated smiles of the charming Arabian, were not for me. The mild exhortations of the old man and the lively conversation of the loved Felix, were not for me. Miserable, unhappy wretch!

"Other lessons were impressed upon me even more deeply. I heard of the difference of sexes; and the birth and growth of children; how the father doated on the smiles of the infant, and the lively sallies of the older child; how all the life and cares of the mother were wrapped up in the precious charge; how the mind of youth expanded and gained knowledge; of brother, sister, and all the various relationships which bind one human being to another in mutual bonds.

"But where were my friends and relations? No father had watched my infant days, no mother had blessed me with smiles and caresses; or if they had, all my past life was now a blot, a blind vacancy in which I distinguished nothing. From my earliest remembrance I had been as I then was in height and proportion. I had never yet seen a being resembling me, or who claimed any intercourse with me. What was I? The question again recurred, to be answered only with groans.

"I will soon explain to what these feelings tended; but allow me now to return to the cottagers, whose story excited in me such various feelings of indignation, delight, and wonder, but which all terminated in additional love and reverence for my protectors (for so I loved, in an innocent, half painful self-deceit, to call them).

COMMENTARY

This chapter opens with the arrival of a beautiful young woman whose presence miraculously removes the sadness from Felix's face. He immediately introduces her to his blind father who welcomes her with great affection. The Monster notices that the stranger disseminates happiness among the cottagers, and despite their difficulties communicating with her because she speaks a different language, they all seem happier than ever. Her name is Safie. The next day, when Felix is out working as usual, Safie, Agatha, and her father converse in the universal language of music, expressing their feelings through the melodies they sing.

Soon, Felix begins to teach Safie their language using Volney's *Ruins of Empires*. By observing them and listening closely to Felix's detailed explanations, the Monster rapidly improves his speaking and reading skills. More importantly, however, Volney's book provides the Monster with an extensive education on the history, customs, politics, and religions of various countries. And yet, all these new discoveries force him to question his own condition, and for the first time, he realizes his limitations and disadvantages. His despair at his inadequacies makes him wish that he had never learned anything. Reflecting more on the suffering that knowledge can produce, the Monster eventually understands that the only remedy for pain is death.

Education as a Theme

This chapter should be particularly relevant to students reflecting on the nature of knowledge and its moral and philosophical implications. In contrast to students who are generally educated by others, the Monster is self-educated. Moreover, he does not have a choice of studies, and he is forced to learn from what others (Felix and Safie) use for instruction or from what he happens to come across. Fortunately, the book Felix uses for Safie's instruction, as well as the books the Monster reads later, are all core texts and excellent models of rhetorical power. Finally, like everything else in his life (clothes, food, and a place to live), the knowledge that he acquires is unauthorized, stolen knowledge. Interestingly, these circumstances do not differ essentially from the circumstances of women's education during the nineteenth century. Like the Monster, women did not have a choice of study. Their education was limited to the domestic sphere, and they appropriated any other knowledge from the masculine sphere. Greek and Latin, for instance, was

knowledge not meant for them and, therefore, was clandestine. The fact that the Monster is also an outsider and different from human beings makes his connection with the female even more convincing. To complicate things further, Mary Shelley places the Monster in a position that makes him inferior not only to women (because he does not have access to what Safie does) but also to women belonging to cultures notorious for their persecution of women (like Safie, who is Turkish).

In this context, Felix's choice of Volney's *Ruins of Empires,* a stereotypically masculine book, is an interesting one. Felix's choice may signify his inability to teach anything else but a text belonging to his educational experience, or his conscious desire to empower Safie, the woman he loves, with the kind of knowledge to which only man can have access. His selection may also suggest Mary Shelley's way of allying herself with her mother's ideas explored in her famous *Vindication of the Rights of Woman* (1792) because he defends the right to equal education for women. In the same way that Mary Shelley prefers Locke to Rousseau in terms of children's education, she prefers her mother, Mary Wollstonecraft, to Rousseau in terms of female education. In fact, Wollstonecraft's argument is largely a response to Rousseau's theory that men and women should be educated differently, a view that Wollstonecraft (and perhaps Mary Shelley, too) qualifies as retrogressive. In her *Vindication,* Wollstonecraft writes: "Thus Milton describes our first frail mother; though when he tells us that women are formed for softness and sweet attractive grace, I cannot comprehend his meaning, unless, in the true Mahometan strain, he meant to deprive us of souls, and insinuate that we were beings only designed by sweet attractive grace, and docile blind obedience, to gratify the sense of man when he can no longer soar on the wings of contemplation."

Volney's *The Ruins*

Volney's book *The Ruins, or Meditations on the Revolutions of Empires* (1791), one of Percy Shelley's favorite books in 1816, became a source for free thinkers and atheists in the nineteenth century. Primarily a work on the causes of the fall of ancient civilization, the book is a detailed survey of the world's most important religions, and is a secular repudiation of all of them, especially Christianity, which, Volney claims, encourages and promotes internal and external despotism. The Church is evil, corrupt, and ineffectual and is an instigator of war.

It propagates false doctrines and enslaves people. When the Monster later reads Milton's *Paradise Lost*—the religious version of the origins of humanity—remember that he is no longer an innocent reader, but one who has closely read Volney's sarcastic and corrosive attack against religions, patriarchy, and the Church.

Listening to the causes responsible for the degeneration of once powerful and vigorous cultures, the Monster raises important questions about the problematic nature of humans: "Was man, indeed, at once so powerful, so virtuous, and magnificent, yet so vicious and base?" — a question that may fundamentally affect his entire perspective on human beings and society.

Volney's analysis of property, wealth, descent, and rank—all important factors in determining one's identity and position in society—not only clarifies for the Monster that he has no possessions but also that he has no clear center, no definite origin, and no recognized father.

At the end of his first book, the Monster is more knowledgeable but also much sadder. He can say, like Manfred, Byron's melancholy hero, that "Sorrow is Knowledge: they who know the most / Must mourn the deepest o'er the fatal truth, / The Tree of Knowledge is not that of Life."

Chapter 14

The Monster relates the history of the family he has been observing as well as their relationship with Safie. The name of the old, blind man is De Lacey, and Felix and Agatha are his children. Safie, the daughter of a wealthy Turkish merchant whom Felix helped to escape prison in Paris, fell in love with Felix. When the French government discovered Felix's involvement with the Turk's escape, the De Lacey family was disgraced, deprived of its fortune, and forced into perpetual exile. Against her father's will, Safie followed her lover to Germany.

CHAPTER XIV

NOTES

"SOME time elapsed before I learned the history of my friends. It was one which could not fail to impress itself deeply on my mind, unfolding as it did a number of circumstances, each interesting and wonderful to one so utterly inexperienced as I was.

"The name of the old man was De Lacey. He was descended from a good family in France, where he had lived for many years in affluence, respected by his superiors and beloved by his equals. His son was bred in the service of his country, and Agatha had ranked with ladies of the highest distinction. A few months before my arrival, they had lived in a large and luxurious city, called Paris, surrounded by friends, and possessed of every enjoyment which virtue, refinement of intellect, or taste, accompanied by a moderate fortune, could afford.

"The father of Safie had been the cause of their ruin. He was a Turkish merchant, and had inhabited Paris for many years, when, for some reason which I could not learn, he became obnoxious to the government. He was seized and cast into prison the very day that Safie arrived from **Constantinople** to join him. He was tried, and condemned to death. The injustice of his sentence was very **flagrant**; all Paris was indignant; and it was judged that his religion and wealth, rather than the crime alleged against him, had been the cause of his condemnation.

"Felix had accidentally been present at the trial; his horror and indignation were uncontrollable, when he heard the decision of the court. He made, at that moment, a solemn vow to deliver him, and then looked around for the means. After many fruitless attempts to gain admittance to the prison, he found a strongly grated window in an unguarded part of the building, which lighted the dungeon of the unfortunate **Mahometan**; who, loaded with chains, waited in despair the execution of the barbarous sentence. Felix visited the grate at night, and made known to the prisoner his intentions in his favour. The Turk, amazed and delighted, endeavoured to kindle the zeal of his deliverer by promises of reward and wealth. Felix rejected his offers with contempt; yet when he saw the lovely Safie, who was allowed to visit her father, and who, by her gestures expressed her lively gratitude, the youth could not help owning to his own mind, that the captive possessed a treasure which would fully reward his toil and hazard.

Constantinople: Byzantium, Constantinople, and Istanbul are three different names for the same city. The Byzantium of the ancient world was renamed Constantinopol by Constantine the Great, when he established the city as the capital of the Roman Empire in 330 AD. In 1453, Turks conquered Constantinopole and changed its name to Istanbul.

flagrant: obvious.

Mahometan: adherent of the Muslim religion.

"The Turk quickly perceived the impression that his daughter had made on the heart of Felix, and endeavoured to secure him more entirely in his interests by the promise of her hand in marriage, so soon as he should be conveyed to a place of safety. Felix was too delicate to accept this offer; yet he looked forward to the probability of the event as to the consummation of his happiness.

"During the ensuing days, while the preparations were going forward for the escape of the merchant, the zeal of Felix was warmed by several letters that he received from this lovely girl, who found means to express her thoughts in the language of her lover by the aid of an old man, a servant of her father, who understood French. She thanked him in the most ardent terms for his intended services towards her parent; and at the same time she gently deplored her own fate.

"I have copies of these letters; for I found means, during my residence in the hovel, to procure the implements of writing; and the letters were often in the hands of Felix or Agatha. Before I depart, I will give them to you; they will prove the truth of my tale; but at present, as the sun is already far declined, I shall only have time to repeat the substance of them to you.

"Safie related, that her mother was a Christian Arab, seized and made a slave by the Turks; recommended by her beauty, she had won the heart of the father of Safie, who married her. The young girl spoke in high and enthusiastic terms of her mother, who, born in freedom, spurned the bondage to which she was now reduced. She instructed her daughter in the tenets of her religion, and taught her to aspire to higher powers of intellect, and an independence of spirit, forbidden to the female followers of Mahomet. This lady died; but her lessons were indelibly impressed on the mind of Safie, who sickened at the prospect of again returning to Asia, and being immured within the walls of a haram, allowed only to occupy herself with infantile amusements, ill suited to the temper of her soul, now accustomed to grand ideas and a noble emulation for virtue. The prospect of marrying a Christian, and remaining in a country where women were allowed to take a rank in society, was enchanting to her.

"The day for the execution of the Turk was fixed; but, on the night previous to it, he quitted his prison, and before morning was distant many leagues from Paris. Felix had procured passports in the name of his father, sister, and himself. He had previously communicated his plan to the former, who aided the deceit by quitting his house, under the pretence of a journey, and concealed himself, with his daughter, in an obscure part of Paris.

"Felix conducted the fugitives through France to Lyons, and across Mont Cenis to Leghorn, where the merchant had decided to wait a favourable opportunity of passing into some part of the Turkish dominions.

"Safie resolved to remain with her father until the moment of his departure, before which time the Turk renewed his promise that she should be united to his deliverer; and Felix remained with them in expectation of that event; and in the meantime he enjoyed the society of the Arabian, who exhibited towards him the simplest and tenderest affection. They conversed with one another through the means of an interpreter, and sometimes with the interpretation of looks; and Safie sang to him the divine airs of her native country.

"The Turk allowed this intimacy to take place, and encouraged the hopes of the youthful lovers, while in his heart he had formed far other plans. He loathed the idea that his daughter should be united to a Christian; but he feared the resentment of Felix, if he should appear lukewarm; for he knew that he was still in the power of his deliverer, if he should choose to betray him to the Italian state which they inhabited. He revolved a thousand plans by which he should be enabled to prolong the deceit until it might be no longer necessary, and secretly to take his daughter with him when he departed. His plans were facilitated by the news which arrived from Paris.

"The government of France were greatly enraged at the escape of their victim, and spared no pains to detect and punish his deliverer. The plot of Felix was quickly discovered, and De Lacey and Agatha were thrown into prison. The news reached Felix, and roused him from his dream of pleasure. His blind and aged father, and his gentle sister, lay in a noisome dungeon, while he enjoyed the free air, and the society of her whom he loved. This idea was torture to him. He quickly arranged with the Turk, that if the latter should find a favourable opportunity for escape before Felix could return to Italy, Safie should remain as a boarder at a convent at Leghorn; and then, quitting the lovely Arabian, he hastened to Paris, and delivered himself up to the vengeance of the law, hoping to free De Lacey and Agatha by this proceeding.

"He did not succeed. They remained confined for five months before the trial took place; the result of which deprived them of their fortune, and condemned them to a perpetual exile from their native country.

"They found a miserable asylum in the cottage in Germany, where I discovered them. Felix soon learned that the treacherous Turk, for whom he and his family endured such unheard-of oppression, on discovering that his deliverer was thus reduced to poverty and ruin, became a traitor to good feeling and honour, and had quitted Italy with his daughter, insultingly sending Felix a pittance of money, to aid him, as he said, in some plan of future maintenance.

"Such were the events that preyed on the heart of Felix, and rendered him, when I first saw him, the most miserable of his family. He could have endured poverty; and while this distress had been the meed of his virtue, he gloried in it; but the ingratitude of the Turk, and the loss of his beloved Safie, were misfortunes more bitter and irreparable. The arrival of the Arabian now infused new life into his soul.

"When the news reached Leghorn, that Felix was deprived of his wealth and rank, the merchant commanded his daughter to think no more of her lover, but to prepare to return to her native country. The generous nature of Safie was outraged by this command; she attempted to expostulate with her father, but he left her angrily, reiterating his tyrannical mandate.

"A few days after, the Turk entered his daughter's apartment, and told her hastily, that he had reason to believe that his residence at Leghorn had been divulged, and that he should speedily be delivered up to the French government; he had, consequently, hired a vessel to convey him to Constantinople, for which city he should sail in a few hours. He intended to leave his daughter under the care of a confidential servant, to follow at her leisure with the greater part of his property, which had not yet arrived at Leghorn.

"When alone, Safie resolved in her own mind the plan of conduct that it would become her to pursue in this emergency. A residence in Turkey was abhorrent to her; her religion and her feelings were alike averse to it. By some papers of her father, which fell into her hands, she heard of the exile of her lover, and learnt the name of the spot where he then resided. She hesitated some time, but at length she formed her determination. Taking with her some jewels that belonged to her, and a sum of money, she quitted Italy with an attendant, a native of Leghorn, but who understood the common language of Turkey, and departed for Germany.

"She arrived in safety at a town about twenty leagues from the cottage of De Lacey, when her attendant fell dangerously ill. Safie nursed her with the most devoted affection; but the poor girl died, and the Arabian was left alone, unacquainted with the language of the country, and utterly ignorant of the customs of the world. She fell, however, into good hands. The Italian had mentioned the name of the spot for which they were bound; and, after her death, the woman of the house in which they had lived took care that Safie should arrive in safety at the cottage of her lover.

COMMENTARY

This chapter constitutes the complete history of the cottagers and Safie. De Lacey, the father, descends from an old, well-respected French family. Shortly before the Monster's arrival, he was living with his two children in Paris. They were only moderately wealthy, but they had good taste and intellectual refinement and were surrounded by virtuous and devoted friends.

Safie's Story

Safie's father, a wealthy Turkish merchant, was also living in Paris at the time. He was wrongly accused by the French government and unjustly condemned to die. Romantic and idealistic Felix De Lacey, who happens onto the trial, decides to correct the terrible injustice by helping the Turk regain his freedom. Felix visits the Turk in prison, where he meets Safie, the Turk's beautiful daughter, and falls in love with her. Noticing Felix's strong reaction to his daughter and understanding that he can profit from the youth's attraction to her, the Turk cunningly promises Felix his daughter's hand in marriage as soon as he is freed and safely placed.

With the help of a French-speaking servant, Safie tells Felix her history in a series of letters. Her mother, a Christian Arab, was taken into slavery by the Turks and then was chosen by Safie's father to become his wife. A wise and discerning woman, her mother raised her daughter as a Christian and instilled in her a love for learning, freedom, and independence.

True to his word, Felix helps the Turk escape prison and execution and accompanies him and his daughter to Italy. Meanwhile, in Paris, Felix's responsibility for the Turk's escape is discovered, and as a result, his father and sister are arrested. Distressed, Felix arranges with the Turk to let Safie wait for him in a convent and then immediately leaves for Paris. At the De Laceys' trial, Felix and his family (who, indeed, helped Felix) are found guilty and, consequently, are forced into perpetual exile. Adding to Felix's sufferings, the Turk, who loathed from the beginning the idea of a marriage between his daughter and a Christian, betrays Felix. The Turk sails to Constantinople and orders his daughter to follow him as soon as the rest of his property arrives from France. Safie is disgusted by her father's lack of honor and integrity and appalled by the thought of returning to a country that enslaved her mother and whose culture, customs, and religion are foreign to her. Thus, she follows her exiled lover to Germany.

Contrasting Safie with the Other Women of *Frankensten*

Like the histories of Caroline Beaufort, Elizabeth Lavenza, and Justine Moritz, Safie's story is one of numerous mininarratives that join one of the three major concentric narratives of Walton, Victor, or the Monster. These mininarratives serve to illuminate particular areas in the major narratives; in this case, Safie's story illuminates the Monster's position in relationship with the De Lacey family as well as Mary Shelley's educational philosophy. Critics sometimes consider Safie in connection with Elizabeth, arguing that what Safie wants is what Elizabeth already has—a family to love, please, and serve—the ideal of nineteenth-century middle-class domesticity. Keep in mind, however, that Safie, unlike Elizabeth, was raised by her wise mother to value her independence. Her desire to marry a man sharing her spiritual beliefs and live in a country that, unlike her father's native land, allows women to acquire a position in society does not necessarily indicate that she wants to mechanically conform to the model of virtuous domesticity embraced and perpetuated by Elizabeth. Moreover, Safie breaks (almost like Walton, Clerval, and Victor) the patriarchal law by courageously revealing her story to Felix (a story that throws an unflattering light on her father and his culture), and then she follows her lover, against her father's will, to Germany.

In contrast to the three male protagonists, Safie's transgression is based, not on ambition or a spirit of adventure, but on a moral decision to put honor and love of freedom above parental obedience. Safie's decision distinguishes her from Elizabeth, who never questions or disobeys her adopted father, or any other member of the family for that matter. Safie's attention to her past and to her mother's legacy, which she presents as the guiding principles of her life, are certainly not the principles of Elizabeth's life, despite the fact that she is, after all, the daughter of an Italian revolutionary. Elizabeth adopts the values of her new family with an imperturbability foreign to Safie, who wants to marry Felix not only out of love but also out of respect for her own values, her mother's memory, and her own identity.

The suggestion that Safie aspires to attain Elizabeth's type of existence may be further eroded by the understanding that a woman like Safie, so determined to affirm her identity and beliefs, would never settle for a life of genteel, but nevertheless obvious, servitude like Elizabeth's. Also, Elizabeth obeys Victor's desires and his need for isolation and male companionship and does not follow him to Ingolstadt, whereas Safie assumes considerable risks to follow her lover to Germany. Moreover, as a sign of her independence, Safie is the only woman in the novel who has property and who travels extensively, which allows for her ability to understand and function well in other cultures. At first, she may not appear to have strong intellectual abilities. She has more difficulty absorbing and processing new information than does the Monster, but she is the only female character in the book who studies texts, which are usually assigned in a masculine curriculum and involve a level of complexity and sophistication never intended for women's education.

Chapter 15

The Monster discovers three books and a fragment of Victor's journal. Deeply influenced by the books and encouraged by the happy atmosphere in the De Lacey family, he decides to make friends with the cottagers. He approaches the blind man first, and talks to him alone and, for the first time, discovers a sympathetic soul. Unfortunately, he is surprised by Felix, who attacks him with unusual violence.

CHAPTER XV

"SUCH was the history of my beloved cottagers. It impressed me deeply. I learned, from the views of social life which it developed, to admire their virtues and to deprecate the vices of mankind.

"As yet I looked upon crime as a distant evil; benevolence and generosity were ever present before me, inciting within me a desire to become an actor in the busy scene where so many admirable qualities were called forth and displayed. But, in giving an account of the progress of my intellect, I must not omit a circumstance which occurred in the beginning of the month of August of the same year.

"One night, during my accustomed visit to the neighbouring wood, where I collected my own food, and brought home firing for my protectors, I found on the ground a leathern portmanteau, containing several articles of dress and some books. I eagerly seized the prize, and returned with it to my hovel. Fortunately the books were written in the **language,** the elements of which I had acquired at the cottage; they consisted of '**Paradise Lost,**' a volume of '**Plutarch's Lives,**' and the '**Sorrows of Werter.**' The possession of these treasures gave me extreme delight; I now continually studied and exercised my mind upon these histories, whilst my friends were employed in their ordinary occupations.

"I can hardly describe to you the effect of these books. They produced in me an infinity of new images and feelings, that sometimes raised me to ecstasy, but more frequently sunk me into the lowest **dejection.** In the 'Sorrows of Werter,' besides the interest of its simple and affecting story, so many opinions are canvassed, and so many lights thrown upon what had hitherto been to me obscure subjects, that I found in it a never-ending source of speculation and astonishment. The gentle and domestic manners it described, combined with lofty sentiments and feelings, which had for their object something out of self, accorded well with my experience among my protectors, and with the wants which were forever alive in my own bosom. But I thought Werter himself a more divine being than I had ever beheld or imagined; his character contained no pretension, but it sunk deep. The disquisitions upon death and suicide were calculated to fill me with wonder. I did not pretend to enter into the merits of the case, yet I inclined towards the opinions of the hero, whose extinction I wept, without precisely understanding it.

NOTES

language: in this context, French.

Paradise Lost: Epic poem by John Milton (1608–1674), telling the story of the creation of the world—the loss of Eden and its recapture through the coming of Christ. Romantics were fascinated with Milton's poem and the heroic posture of Satan, who was, in their reading of the work, a symbol for the rebellion against tyranny and oppression.

Plutarch's Lives: allusion to Plutarch's *Parallel Lives* (circa 100 AD), biographies of 46 eminent Greeks and Romans. Plutarch was a Greek biographer and philosopher (46–119 AD).

Sorrows of Werter: The Sorrows of Young Werther (1774), by J. W. Goethe, is a novel about a young artist in love with an unattainable woman.

dejection: despair, sorrow.

"As I read, however, I applied much personally to my own feelings and condition. I found myself similar, yet at the same time strangely unlike to the beings concerning whom I read, and to whose conversation I was a listener. I sympathized with, and partly understood them, but I was unformed in mind; I was dependent on none, and related to none. '**The path of my departure was free;**' and there was none to lament my annihilation. My person was hideous, and my stature gigantic: what did this mean? Who was I? What was I? Whence did I come? What was my destination? These questions continually recurred, but I was unable to solve them.

"The volume of 'Plutarch's Lives,' which I possessed, contained the histories of the first founders of the ancient republics. This book had a far different effect upon me from the 'Sorrows of Werter.' I learned from Werter's imaginations despondency and gloom: but Plutarch taught me high thoughts; he elevated me above the wretched sphere of my own reflections, to admire and love the heroes of past ages. Many things I read surpassed my understanding and experience. I had a very confused knowledge of kingdoms, wide extents of country, mighty rivers, and boundless seas. But I was perfectly unacquainted with towns, and large assemblages of men. The cottage of my protectors had been the only school in which I had studied human nature; but this book developed new and mightier scenes of action. I read of men concerned in public affairs, governing or massacring their species. I felt the greatest ardour for virtue rise within me, and abhorrence for vice, as far as I understood the signification of those terms, relative as they were, as I applied them, to pleasure and pain alone. Induced by these feelings, I was of course led to admire peaceable lawgivers, **Numa**, **Solon**, and **Lycurgus**, in preference to **Romulus** and **Theseus**. The **patriarchal** lives of my protectors caused these impressions to take a firm hold on my mind; perhaps, if my first introduction to humanity had been made by a young soldier, burning for glory and slaughter, I should have been imbued with different sensations.

"But 'Paradise Lost' excited different and far deeper emotions. I read it, as I had read the other volumes which had fallen into my hands, as a true history. It moved every feeling of wonder and awe, that the picture of an **omnipotent** God warring with his creatures was capable of exciting. I often referred the several situations, as their similarity struck me, to my own. Like Adam, I was apparently united by no link to any other being in existence; but his state was far different from mine in every other respect. He had come forth from the hands of God a perfect creature, happy and prosperous, guarded by the especial care of his Creator; he was allowed to converse with, and acquire knowledge from, beings of a superior nature: but I was wretched, helpless, and alone. Many times I considered Satan as the fitter **emblem** of my condition; for often, like him, when I viewed the bliss of my protectors, the bitter gall of envy rose within me.

"Another circumstance strengthened and confirmed these feelings. Soon after my arrival in the hovel, I discovered some papers in the pocket of

The path of my departure was free: Probably an allusion to Shelley's "Mutability"; "The path of its departure still is free."

Numa: Numa Pompilius (715–673 BC), a king of Rome.

Solon: Athenian statesman in the sixth century BC.

Lycurgus: (390–324 BC) Athenian statesman.

Romulus: Romulus and Remus are the legendary founders of Rome.

Theseus: legendary Athenian hero.

patriarchal: respectful.

omnipotent: all-powerful; unlimited in power. Usually an attribute of gods.

emblem: symbol.

the dress which I had taken from your laboratory. At first I had neglected them; but now that I was able to decipher the characters in which they were written, I began to study them with diligence. It was your journal of the four months that preceded my creation. You minutely described in these papers every step you took in the progress of your work; this history was mingled with accounts of domestic occurrences. You, doubtless, recollect these papers. Here they are. Every thing is related in them which bears reference to my accursed origin; the whole detail of that series of disgusting circumstances which produced it, is set in view; the minutest description of my odious and loathsome person is given, in language which painted your own horrors and rendered mine indelible. I sickened as I read. 'Hateful day when I received life!' I exclaimed in agony. 'Accursed creator! Why did you form a monster so hideous that even *you* turned from me in disgust? God, in pity, made man beautiful and alluring, after his own image; but my form is a filthy type of yours, more horrid even from the very resemblance. Satan had his companions, fellow-devils, to admire and encourage him; but I am solitary and abhorred.'

"These were the reflections of my hours of despondency and solitude; but when I contemplated the virtues of the cottagers, their amiable and benevolent dispositions, I persuaded myself that when they should become acquainted with my admiration of their virtues, they would compassionate me, and overlook my personal deformity. Could they turn from their door one, however monstrous, who solicited their compassion and friendship? I resolved, at least, not to despair, but in every way to fit myself for an interview with them which would decide my fate. I postponed this attempt for some months longer; for the importance attached to its success inspired me with a dread lest I should fail. Besides, I found that my understanding improved so much with every day's experience, that I was unwilling to commence this undertaking until a few more months should have added to my sagacity.

"Several changes, in the mean time, took place in the cottage. The presence of Safie diffused happiness among its inhabitants; and I also found that a greater degree of plenty reigned there. Felix and Agatha spent more time in amusement and conversation, and were assisted in their labours by servants. They did not appear rich, but they were contented and happy; their feelings were serene and peaceful, while mine became every day more tumultuous. Increase of knowledge only discovered to me more clearly what a wretched outcast I was. I cherished hope, it is true; but it vanished when I beheld my person reflected in water, or my shadow in the moonshine, even as that frail image and that inconstant shade.

"I endeavoured to crush these fears, and to fortify myself for the trial which in a few months I resolved to undergo; and some times I allowed my thoughts, unchecked by reason, to ramble in the fields of Paradise, and dared to fancy amiable and lovely creatures sympathizing with my feelings, and cheering my gloom; their angelic countenances breathed smiles of consolation. But it was all a dream; no Eve soothed my sorrows, nor shared my thoughts; I was alone. I remembered **Adam's supplication to his Creator**. But where was mine? He had abandoned me; and, in the bitterness of my heart, I cursed him.

"Autumn passed thus. I saw, with surprise and grief, the leaves decay and fall, and nature again assume the barren and bleak appearance it had worn when I first beheld the woods and the lovely moon. Yet I did not heed the bleakness of the weather; I was better fitted by my **conformation** for the endurance of cold than heat. But my chief delights were the sight of the flowers, the birds, and all the gay apparel of summer; when those deserted me, I turned with more attention towards the cottagers. Their happiness was not decreased by the absence of summer. They loved, and sympathised with one another; and their joys, depending on each other, were not interrupted by the casualties that took place around them. The more I saw of them, the greater became my desire to claim their protection and kindness; my heart yearned to be known and loved by these amiable creatures: to see their sweet looks directed towards me with affection, was the utmost limit of my ambition. I dared not think that they would turn them from me with disdain and horror. The poor that stopped at their door were never driven away. I asked, it is true, for greater treasures than a little food or rest: I required kindness and sympathy; but I did not believe myself utterly unworthy of it.

"The winter advanced, and an entire revolution of the seasons had taken place since I awoke into life. My attention, at this time, was solely directed towards my plan of introducing myself into the cottage of my protectors. I revolved many projects; but that on which I finally fixed was, to enter the dwelling when the blind old man should be alone. I had sagacity enough to discover, that the unnatural hideousness of my person was the chief object of horror with those who had formerly beheld me. My voice, although harsh, had nothing terrible in it; I thought, therefore, that if, in the absence of his children, I could gain the good-will and mediation of the old De Lacey, I might, by his means, be tolerated by my younger protectors.

"One day, when the sun shone on the red leaves that strewed the ground and diffused cheerfulness, although it denied warmth, Safie, Agatha, and Felix departed on a long country walk, and the old man, at his own desire, was left alone in the cottage. When his children had departed, he took up his guitar, and played several mournful but sweet airs, more sweet and mournful than I had ever heard him play before. At first his countenance was illuminated with pleasure, but as he continued, thoughtfulness and sadness succeeded; at length, laying aside the instrument, he sat absorbed in reflection.

"My heart beat quick; this was the hour and moment of trial, which would decide my hopes, or realise my fears. The servants were gone to a neighbouring fair. All was silent in and around the cottage: it was an excellent opportunity; yet, when I proceeded to execute my plan, my limbs failed me, and I sank to the ground. Again I rose; and, exerting all the firmness of which I was master, removed the planks which I had

Adam's supplication to his Creator: In the book of Genesis, Adam asks God for a human companion.

conformation: design.

placed before my hovel to conceal my retreat. The fresh air revived me, and with renewed determination, I approached the door of their cottage.

"I knocked. 'Who is there?' said the old man—'Come in.'

"I entered; 'Pardon this intrusion,' said I: 'I am a traveller in want of a little rest; you would greatly oblige me, if you would allow me to remain a few minutes before the fire.'

"'Enter,' said De Lacey, 'and I will try in what manner I can to relieve your wants; but, unfortunately, my children are from home, and, as I am blind, I am afraid I shall find it difficult to procure food for you.'

"'Do not trouble yourself, my kind host, I have food; it is warmth and rest only that I need.'

"I sat down, and a silence ensued. I knew that every minute was precious to me, yet I remained irresolute in what manner to commence the interview, when the old man addressed me—

"'By your language, stranger, I suppose you are my country-man; are you French?'"

"'No; but I was educated by a French family, and understand that language only. I am now going to claim the protection of some friends, whom I sincerely love, and of whose favour I have some hopes.'

"'Are they Germans?'

"'No, they are French. But let us change the subject. I am an unfortunate and deserted creature; I look around, and I have no relation or friend upon earth. These amiable people to whom I go have never seen me, and know little of me. I am full of fears; for if I fail there, I am an outcast in the world for ever.'

"'Do not despair. To be friendless is indeed to be unfortunate; but the hearts of men, when unprejudiced by any obvious self-interest, are full of brotherly love and charity. Rely, therefore, on your hopes; and if these friends are good and amiable, do not despair.'

"'They are kind—they are the most excellent creatures in the world; but, unfortunately, they are prejudiced against me. I have good dispositions; my life has been hitherto harmless, and in some degree beneficial; but a fatal prejudice clouds their eyes, and where they ought to see a feeling and kind friend, they behold only a detestable monster.'

"'That is indeed unfortunate; but if you are really blameless, cannot you undeceive them?'

"'I am about to undertake that task; and it is on that account that I feel so many overwhelming terrors. I tenderly love these friends; I have, unknown to them, been for many months in the habits of daily kindness towards them; but they believe that I wish to injure them, and it is that prejudice which I wish to overcome.'

"'Where do these friends reside?'

"'Near this spot.'

"The old man paused, and then continued, 'If you will unreservedly confide to me the particulars of your tale, I perhaps may be of use in undeceiving them. I am blind, and cannot judge of your countenance, but there is something in your words, which persuades me that you are sincere. I am poor, and an exile; but it will afford me true pleasure to be in any way serviceable to a human creature.'

"'Excellent man! I thank you, and accept your generous offer. You raise me from the dust by this kindness; and I trust that, by your aid, I shall not be driven from the society and sympathy of your fellow-creatures.'

"'Heaven forbid! even if you were really criminal; for that can only drive you to desperation, and not instigate you to virtue. I also am unfortunate; I and my family have been condemned, although innocent: judge, therefore, if I do not feel for your misfortunes.'

"'How can I thank you, my best and only benefactor? From your lips first have I heard the voice of kindness directed towards me; I shall be for ever grateful; and your present humanity assures me of success with those friends whom I am on the point of meeting.'

"'May I know the names and residence of those friends?'

"I paused. This, I thought, was the moment of decision, which was to rob me of, or bestow happiness on me forever. I struggled vainly for firmness sufficient to answer him, but the effort destroyed all my remaining strength; I sank on the chair and sobbed aloud. At that moment I heard the steps of my younger protectors. I had not a moment to lose; but, seizing the hand of the old man I cried, 'Now is the time!—save and protect me! You and your family are the friends whom I seek. Do not you desert me in the hour of trial!'

"'Great God!' exclaimed the old man. 'who are you?'

"At that instant the cottage door was opened, and Felix, Safie, and Agatha entered. Who can describe their horror and consternation on beholding me? Agatha fainted; and Safie, unable to attend to her friend, rushed out of the cottage. Felix darted forward, and with supernatural force tore me from his father, to whose knees I clung: in a transport of fury, he dashed me to the ground, and struck me violently with a stick. I could have torn him limb from limb, as the lion rends the antelope. But my heart sank within me as with bitter sickness, and I refrained. I saw him on the point of repeating his blow, when, overcome by pain and anguish, I quitted the cottage, and in the general tumult escaped unperceived to my hovel.

COMMENTARY

Although seriously affected by the reading of Volney's book, the Monster's faith in human and social goodness is partially restored by Safie's moving story. Like Elizabeth before Justine's trial and execution, the Monster, still in a state of innocence, considers "crime as a distant evil; benevolence and generosity were ever present before [him], inciting within [him] a desire to become an actor in the busy scenes where so many admirable qualities were called forth and displayed." He is much more enthusiastic than Elizabeth ever was about becoming one who advances good and justice in the world. Also, compared to Victor and Walton whose dreams of fame and power are meant to subdue and control nature, the Monster's hope is to play a role in somebody else's plan, not to create his own vision in situations that require an infusion of "admirable qualities" (such as goodness, nobility, generosity, and honesty). Ironically, reality cruelly contradicts his benevolent dream, and instead of becoming, as he so much wishes, the hero on the world stage, he is forced to play the villain.

The Monster's Readings

One night, the Monster finds three books—Milton's *Paradise Lost*, Plutarch's *Lives*, and Goethe's *Sorrows of Werter*—all written in French. The three books that Mary Shelley chooses to complete the Monster's education are books that she herself was reading in the years she worked on *Frankenstein*. That the Monster considers books a "prize" and a "treasure" is no surprise, considering how important the experience of reading and studying books was in Mary Shelley's own life. Often, she took books to her mother's grave in St. Pancras Churchyard, and reading became a way of connecting with her dead mother.

Goethe's epistolary novel, *The Sorrows of the Young Werther*, originally published in 1774, is one of the most famous products of the literature of *sensibility* in the middle to late eighteenth century and, for a long time, young men all over Europe tried to imitate Werther. (Making the necessary alterations, Justine's mimicry of Caroline Beaufort Frankenstein represents a pretty accurate example of how people sometimes tried to identify with real or fictional characters whom they admired or revered.)

During the eighteenth century and the first part of the nineteenth century, the cult of sensibility played an essential role in precipitating the major European event of the century—the French Revolution. An ethical and psychological concept, sensibility replaced theology as the arbitrator of good and evil. A good person is no longer somebody who observes and faithfully follows the rules of the Church but somebody with a large capacity for feeling; conversely, an evil or sinful person is anybody who cannot manifest such potential. Consequently, all Europe was invaded at this time by a new type of man—"the man of feeling"—who is delicate, noble, generous, sensitive, and capable of sympathizing with somebody else's pain and misfortune. This concept of sensibility often intersects with the concept of the *sublime* (a concept that in the eighteenth century came to describe either a landscape or a work of art that stimulates elevated sentiments, strong emotions, or astonishment), more in psychological terms than theological ones.

Mary Shelley (whose mother was called by Godwin "a female Werter") shared some of her husband's interest in the virtues of sensibility. Characters in *Frankenstein* frequently look for other characters who can sympathize or empathize with them. The best example is Walton's desire for a male friend) Also, the book abounds in sublime landscapes that both impress and terrify the spectator. It is important to remember that the first important encounter between Victor and the Monster takes place, in the most sublime landscape of all, on the top of Mont Blanc, surrounded by a sea of ice.

What primarily attracts the Monster to Goethe's book is "the gentle and domestic manners it described, combined with lofty sentiments and feelings," sentiments similar to those he sees and admires in the De Lacey family and longs to emulate. Mary Shelley's emphasis on Werther's suicide and on the Monster's strong reaction to it, may reflect the suicides in her and Percy's families, "whose extinction[s] . . . without precisely understanding [them]" presumably devastated them as much as the death of Goethe's hero depressed the Monster. The Monster's reading of Werther, and his harsh reaction to his reflection in the water, reinforces the impression that he is "similar, yet at the same time strangely unlike" the people he observed and read about, which increased his sense of alienation and estrangement. Although not exactly an answer to his disturbing questions about his existence and his place in the world, the idea that *he* is not *them* becomes more and more evident. But as long as he still wants to be accepted by the cottagers he perceives this difference as painful and limiting. Later, when he declares war on all human beings, this difference functions as a liberating instance: He is not hurting his own race, but he kills "the Other."

The Monster also reads Plutarch's *Lives* (the first volume of Plutarch's work), which contains five biographies of prominent statesmen. Interestingly, the Monster prefers Lycurgus, Numa, and Solon (all of them lawgivers) over Theseus, the founder of Athens, and Romulus, the founder of Rome. This is probably because any history relating to origins is both disturbing and confusing for him, and also because of his uncivilized existence. He is, in fact, outside any law, and as such, outside family, society, and civilization. Critics suggest that Mary Shelley's decision to polarize the Monster's preferences may be explained by Theseus' and Romulus' reputations as serial rapists (Theseus, rapist of the Amazons, and Romulus of the Sabine women). Again, despite his dislike for Theseus and Romulus, the Monster will become exactly this—a killer of women.

Plutarch's book also makes the Monster aware of his lack of history and his sense of being part of the world. His inability to move translates into a limitation of horizons, a lack of access to a bigger, more complex image of the world. In this context, calling the De Lacey family "protectors" is ironic, considering that instead of protecting him, they, in fact, block his vision.

The book that impresses him the most is *Paradise Lost*, Milton's brilliant narrative poem, often ranked with the *Iliad* and *Odyssey*. It was also one of the books Mary Shelley studied most intensely and, in fact, during the gestation of Frankenstein, she was studying Milton's works (*Areopagetica, Comus, Lycidas, Paradise Lost,* and *Paradise Regained*).

Critics are still divided on whether Mary Shelley challenges Milton's misogynistic position. The Monster's reading of Milton doesn't offer a clear answer to this dilemma. What is evident, however, is that the Monster reads *Paradise Lost* "as a true history" of origins and compares it with his own history. In fact, he identifies with Adam, God's first man, and Satan, the envious angel. With Adam, he finds both striking similarities and essential differences. Like Adam, he was not given another being like him as a companion, but unlike Adam, who was "allowed to converse with and acquire knowledge from beings of a superior nature," he was "wretched, helpless, and alone." Created in the image of a false God and abandoned by the only being who could love even a hideous creature like him, the Monster was condemned to complete loneliness.

Victor's Journal

The same day he finds the books, the Monster also finds a fragment from Victor's journal in the pocket of a coat he has taken from Victor's laboratory. The journal entry describes, in minute detail, the Monster's origin and the four months preceding his creation. More than from Victor's account to Walton, readers understand the "horrors" accompanying the creation of the Monster and although nothing concrete is revealed, one can infer from the Monster's reaction (indeed, his first violent outburst) that Victor's journal contains very disturbing information, both about Victor and about his monstrous creation.

Contrasts between the De Laceys and the Frankensteins

The Monster also observes that the life of the De Lacey family improved substantially with Safie's arrival. They hire servants, and are now able spend more time in "amusement and conversation." Safie rescues the family from financial distress and becomes the major provider, a role traditionally reserved to men. Again, compared to the passive Elizabeth, Safie uses her money, intelligence, and energy to restore her new family's lost prosperity and status, and, at the same time, to fulfill her, and her mother's, dream of success. Unlike Caroline Beaufort's father, the blind patriarch does not proudly refuse assistance in times of trouble. Their acceptance of Safie's help reinforces their respect for each other and establishes a model of egalitarianism very similar to those envisioned by Godwin, Mary Wollstonecraft, and Coleridge.

Interview with De Lacey

Encouraged by these changes, the Monster decides to introduce himself to "his protectors." Simply watching how "they loved and sympathized with one another" becomes almost painful, and the Monster, tired of being an observer, longs to participate in this happiness and to be looked upon with affection. Knowing their generosity to the poor and remembering Safie's reception, the Monster finally conceives a plan to first talk with the blind man.

One day, when Agatha, Safie, and Felix are out for a long walk and the servants are away at a fair, the Monster enters the De Lacey's cottage and addresses the old man with these symbolic words: "I am a traveler in want of a little rest" (almost immediately repeated by "it is warmth and rest only that I need"). Indeed, the Monster's difficult and long journey through a hostile universe and his amazing intellectual adventures have simply exhausted him. Undoubtedly, "rest" signifies not only the remedy for fatigue but also the opposite of being rejected and exiled. The Monster speaks for the first time and his eloquent words impress De Lacey, who promises his help. Unfortunately, they are surprised by Felix, who, terrified for his father's safety, hits the Monster violently, forcing him to run away.

Chapter 16   **Although angry with Felix for driving him away, the Monster realizes how imprudent he had been the previous day. It was, however, too late to try a new plan; the De Lacey family had already left the cottage. Enraged, the Monster burns down the cottage and leaves for Geneva to find Victor. In Geneva, he happens to find little William Frankenstein playing in the park. The Monster kills William and frames Justine for the crime. At the end of his story, the Monster asks Victor to create a female companion for him.**

CHAPTER XVI

"CURSED, cursed creator! Why did I live? Why, in that instant, did I not extinguish the spark of existence which you had so wantonly bestowed? I know not; despair had not yet taken possession of me; my feelings were those of rage and revenge. I could with pleasure have destroyed the cottage and its inhabitants, and have glutted myself with their shrieks and misery.

"When night came, I quitted my retreat, and wandered in the wood; and now, no longer restrained by the fear of discovery, I gave vent to my anguish in fearful howlings. I was like a wild beast that had broken the toils; destroying the objects that obstructed me, and ranging through the wood with a stag-like swiftness. O! what a miserable night I passed! the cold stars shone in mockery, and the bare trees waved their branches above me: now and then the sweet voice of a bird burst forth amidst the universal stillness. All, save I, were at rest or in enjoyment: I, like the arch-fiend, bore a hell within me; and finding myself unsympathised with, wished to tear up the trees, spread havoc and destruction around me, and then to have sat down and enjoyed the ruin.

"But this was a luxury of sensation that could not endure; I became fatigued with excess of bodily exertion, and sank on the damp grass in the sick impotence of despair. There was none among the myriads of men that existed who would pity or assist me; and should I feel kindness towards my enemies? No: from that moment I declared everlasting war against the species, and, more than all, against him who had formed me, and sent me forth to this insupportable misery.

"The sun rose; I heard the voices of men, and knew that it was impossible to return to my retreat during that day. Accordingly I hid myself in some thick underwood, determining to devote the ensuing hours to reflection on my situation.

"The pleasant sunshine, and the pure air of day, restored me to some degree of tranquillity; and when I considered what had passed at the cottage, I could not help believing that I had been too hasty in my conclusions. I had certainly acted imprudently. It was apparent that my conversation had interested the father in my behalf, and I was a fool in having exposed my person to the horror of his children. I ought to have familiarised the old De Lacey to me, and by degrees to have discovered myself to the rest of his family, when they should have been prepared for my approach. But I did not believe my errors to be irretrievable; and, after much consideration, I resolved to return to the cottage, seek the old man, and by my representations win him to my party.

"These thoughts calmed me, and in the afternoon I sank into a profound sleep; but the fever of my blood did not allow me to be visited by peaceful dreams. The horrible scene of the preceding day was forever acting before my eyes; the females were flying, and the enraged Felix tearing me from his father's feet. I awoke exhausted; and, finding that it was already night, I crept forth from my hiding-place, and went in search of food.

"When my hunger was appeased, I directed my steps towards the well-known path that conducted to the cottage. All there was at peace. I crept into my hovel, and remained in silent expectation of the accustomed hour when the family arose. That hour passed, the sun mounted high in the heavens, but the cottagers did not appear. I trembled violently, apprehending some dreadful misfortune. The inside of the cottage was dark, and I heard no motion; I cannot describe the agony of this suspense.

"Presently two countrymen passed by; but, pausing near the cottage, they entered into conversation, using violent gesticulations; but I did not understand what they said, as they spoke the language of the country, which differed from that of my protectors. Soon after, however, Felix approached with another man: I was surprised, as I knew that he had not quitted the cottage that morning, and waited anxiously to discover, from his discourse, the meaning of these unusual appearances.

"'Do you consider,' said his companion to him, 'that you will be obliged to pay three months' rent, and to lose the produce of your garden? I do not wish to take any unfair advantage, and I beg therefore that you will take some days to consider of your determination.'

"'It is utterly useless,' replied Felix; 'we can never again inhabit your cottage. The life of my father is in the greatest danger, owing to the dreadful circumstance that I have related. My wife and my sister will never recover [from] their horror. I entreat you not to reason with me any more. Take possession of your tenement, and let me fly from this place.'

"Felix trembled violently as he said this. He and his companion entered the cottage, in which they remained for a few minutes, and then departed. I never saw any of the family of De Lacey more.

"I continued for the remainder of the day in my hovel in a state of utter and stupid despair. My protectors had departed, and had broken the only link that held me to the world. For the first time the feelings of revenge and hatred filled my bosom, and I did not strive to control them; but, allowing myself to be borne away by the stream, I bent my mind towards injury and death. When I thought of my friends, of the mild voice of De Lacey, the gentle eyes of Agatha, and the exquisite beauty of the Arabian, these thoughts vanished, and a gush of tears somewhat soothed me. But again, when I reflected that they had spurned and deserted me, anger returned, a rage of anger; and unable to injure any thing human, I turned my fury towards inanimate objects. As night advanced, I placed a variety of combustibles around the cottage; and, after having destroyed every vestige of cultivation in the garden, I waited with forced impatience until the moon had sunk to commence my operations.

"As the night advanced, a fierce wind arose from the woods, and quickly dispersed the clouds that had loitered in the heavens: the blast tore along like a mighty avalanche, and produced a kind of insanity in my spirits, that burst all bounds of reason and reflection. I lighted the dry branch of a tree, and danced with fury around the devoted cottage, my eyes still fixed on the western horizon, the edge of which the moon nearly touched. A part of its orb was at length hid, and I waved my brand; it sunk, and with a loud scream, I fired the straw, and heath, and bushes, which I had collected. The wind fanned the fire, and the cottage was quickly enveloped by the flames, which clung to it, and licked it with their forked and destroying tongues.

"As soon as I was convinced that no assistance could save any part of the habitation, I quitted the scene, and sought for refuge in the woods.

"And now, with the world before me, whither should I bend my steps? I resolved to fly far from the scene of my misfortunes; but to me, hated and despised, every country must be equally horrible. At length the thought of you crossed my mind. I learned from your papers that you were my father, my creator; and to whom could I apply with more fitness than to him who had given me life? Among the lessons that Felix had bestowed upon Safie, geography had not been omitted: I had learned from these the relative situations of the different countries of the earth. You had mentioned Geneva as the name of your native town; and towards this place I resolved to proceed.

"But how was I to direct myself? I knew that I must travel in a south-westerly direction to reach my destination, but the sun was my only guide. I did not know the names of the towns that I was to pass through, nor could I ask information from a single human being; but I did not despair. From you only could I hope for succour, although towards you I felt no sentiment but that of hatred. Unfeeling, heartless creator! you had endowed me with perceptions and passions, and then cast me abroad an object for the scorn and horror of mankind. But on you only had I any claim for pity and redress, and from you I determined to seek that justice which I vainly attempted to gain from any other being that wore the human form.

"My travels were long, and the sufferings I endured intense. It was late in autumn when I quitted the district where I had so long resided. I travelled only at night, fearful of encountering the visage of a human being. Nature decayed around me, and the sun became heatless; rain and snow poured around me; mighty rivers were frozen; the surface of the earth was hard and chill, and bare, and I found no shelter. Oh, earth! how often did I imprecate curses on the cause of my being! The mildness of my nature had fled, and all within me was turned to gall and bitterness. The nearer I approached to your habitation, the more deeply did I feel the spirit of revenge enkindled in my heart. Snow fell, and the waters were hardened; but I rested not. A few incidents now and then directed me, and I possessed a map of the country; but I often wandered wide from my path. The agony of my feelings allowed me no respite: no incident occurred from which my rage and misery could not extract its food; but a circumstance that happened when I arrived on the confines of Switzerland, when the sun had recovered its warmth, and the earth again began to look green, confirmed in an especial manner the bitterness and horror of my feelings.

"I generally rested during the day, and travelled only when I was secured by night from the view of man. One morning, however, finding that my path lay through a deep wood, I ventured to continue my journey after the sun had risen; the day, which was one of the first of spring, cheered even me by the loveliness of its sunshine and the balminess of the air. I felt emotions of gentleness and pleasure, that had long appeared dead, revive within me. Half surprised by the novelty of these sensations, I allowed myself to be borne away by them; and, forgetting my solitude and deformity, dared to be happy. Soft tears again bedewed my cheeks, and I even raised my humid eyes with thankfulness towards the blessed sun which bestowed such joy upon me.

"I continued to wind among the paths of the wood, until I came to its boundary, which was skirted by a deep and rapid river, into which many of the trees bent their branches, now budding with the fresh spring. Here I paused, not exactly knowing what path to pursue, when I heard the sound of voices, that induced me to conceal myself under the shade of a cypress. I was scarcely hid, when a young girl came running towards the spot where I was concealed, laughing, as if she ran from some one in sport. She continued her course along the precipitous sides of the river, when suddenly her foot slipt, and she fell into the rapid stream. I rushed from my hiding-place; and, with extreme labour from the force of the current, saved her, and dragged her to shore. She was senseless; and I endeavoured, by every means in my power, to restore animation, when I was suddenly interrupted by the approach of a rustic, who was probably the person from whom she had playfully fled. On seeing me, he darted towards me, and tearing the girl from my arms, hastened towards the deeper parts of the wood. I followed speedily, I hardly knew why; but when the man saw me draw near, he aimed a gun, which he carried, at my body and fired. I sunk to the ground, and my injurer, with increased swiftness, escaped into the wood.

"This was then the reward of my benevolence! I had saved a human being from destruction, and, as a recompense, I now writhed under the miserable pain of a wound, which shattered the flesh and bone. The feelings of kindness and gentleness, which I had entertained but a few moments before, gave place to hellish rage and gnashing of teeth. Inflamed by pain, I vowed eternal hatred and vengeance to all mankind. But the agony of my wound overcame me; my pulses paused, and I fainted.

"For some weeks I led a miserable life in the woods, endeavouring to cure the wound which I had received. The ball had entered my shoulder, and I knew not whether it had remained there or passed through; at any rate I had no means of extracting it. My sufferings were augmented also by the oppressive sense of the injustice and ingratitude of their infliction. My daily vows rose for revenge—a deep and deadly revenge, such as would alone compensate for the outrages and anguish I had endured.

"After some weeks my wound healed, and I continued my journey. The labours I endured were no longer to be alleviated by the bright sun or gentle breezes of spring; all joy was but a mockery, which insulted my desolate state, and made me feel more painfully that I was not made for the enjoyment of pleasure.

"But my toils now drew near a close; and, in two months from this time, I reached the environs of Geneva.

"It was evening when I arrived, and I retired to a hiding-place among the fields that surround it, to meditate in what manner I should apply to you. I was oppressed by fatigue and hunger, and far too unhappy to enjoy the gentle breezes of evening, or the prospect of the sun setting behind the stupendous mountains of Jura.

"At this time a slight sleep relieved me from the pain of reflection, which was disturbed by the approach of a beautiful child, who came running into the recess I had chosen, with all the sportiveness of infancy. Suddenly, as I gazed on him, an idea seized me that this little creature was unprejudiced, and had lived too short a time to have imbibed a horror of deformity. If, therefore, I could seize him, and educate him as my companion and friend, I should not be so desolate in this peopled earth.

"Urged by this impulse, I seized on the boy as he passed, and drew him towards me. As soon as he beheld my form, he placed his hands before his eyes, and uttered a shrill scream: I drew his hand forcibly from his face, and said, 'Child, what is the meaning of this? I do not intend to hurt you; listen to me.'

"He struggled violently. 'Let me go,' he cried; 'monster! ugly wretch! you wish to eat me, and tear me to pieces—You are an ogre—Let me go, or I will tell my papa.'

"'Boy, you will never see your father again; you must come with me.'

"'Hideous monster! let me go. My papa is a Syndic—he is M. Frankenstein—he will punish you. You dare not keep me.'

"'Frankenstein! you belong then to my enemy—to him towards whom I have sworn eternal revenge; you shall be my first victim.'

"The child still struggled, and loaded me with **epithets** which carried despair to my heart; I grasped his throat to silence him, and in a moment he lay dead at my feet.

epithets: names.

"I gazed on my victim, and my heart swelled with exultation and hellish triumph: clapping my hands, I exclaimed, 'I, too, can create desolation; my enemy is not invulnerable; this death will carry despair to him, and a thousand other miseries shall torment and destroy him.'

"As I fixed my eyes on the child, I saw something glittering on his breast. I took it; it was a portrait of a most lovely woman. In spite of my **malignity**, it softened and attracted me. For a few moments I gazed with delight on her dark eyes, fringed by deep lashes, and her lovely lips; but presently my rage returned: I remembered that I was for ever deprived of the delights that such beautiful creatures could bestow; and that she whose resemblance I contemplated would, in regarding me, have changed that air of divine benignity to one expressive of disgust and affright.

malignity: hostility.

"Can you wonder that such thoughts transported me with rage? I only wonder that at that moment, instead of venting my sensations in exclamations and agony, I did not rush among mankind, and perish in the attempt to destroy them.

"While I was overcome by these feelings, I left the spot where I had committed the murder, and seeking a more secluded hiding-place, I entered a barn which had appeared to me to be empty. A woman was sleeping on some straw; she was young: not indeed so beautiful as her whose portrait I held; but of an agreeable aspect, and blooming in the loveliness of youth and health. Here, I thought, is one of those whose joy-imparting smiles are bestowed on all but me. And then I bent over her, and whispered, 'Awake, fairest, thy lover is near—he who would give his life but to obtain one look of affection from thine eyes: my beloved, awake!'

"The sleeper stirred; a thrill of terror ran through me. Should she indeed awake, and see me, and curse me, and denounce the murderer? Thus would she assuredly act, if her darkened eyes opened, and she beheld me. The thought was madness; it stirred the fiend within me—not I, but she shall suffer: the murder I have committed because I am forever robbed of all that she could give me, she shall atone. The crime had its source in her: be hers the punishment! Thanks to the lessons of Felix and the **sanguinary** laws of man, I had learned now to work mischief. I bent over her, and placed the portrait securely in one of the folds of her dress. She moved again, and I fled.

sanguinary: bloody.

"For some days I haunted the spot where these scenes had taken place; sometimes wishing to see you, sometimes resolved to quit the world and its miseries forever. At length I wandered towards these mountains, and have ranged through their immense recesses, consumed by a burning passion which you alone can gratify. We may not part until you have promised to comply with my **requisition**. I am alone, and miserable; man will not associate with me; but one as deformed and horrible as myself would not deny herself to me. My companion must be of the same species, and have the same defects. This being you must create."

requisition: request, demand.

COMMENTARY

This is the last segment of the Monster's narrative. It starts with a condemnation—the incensed "cursed creator"—and ends with a commandment—the imperious "you must create." From the obedient being who wanted to be Victor's Adam, to serve and worship Victor, the Monster has changed into a god-like-figure who demands obedience. In fact, from this moment on, Victor and the Monster will alternate the positions of slave and master.

Continuing his story, the Monster recalls that, back into the woods, the night after Felix's brutal attack, he "gave vent to [his] anguish in fearful howlings." The "god-like science" he has worked so hard to acquire is abandoned to the terrifying sound of his monstrosity. Educated, humanized, and domesticated by his "protectors," but rejected and abused by them when he tried to gain their real protection and sympathy, the Monster understands that his last hope for acceptance is gone. Again, he identifies with Satan and suddenly discovers an insatiable desire to "spread havoc and destruction around [him]." Convinced that not even one person could ever sympathize with his sufferings, he declares war against all human beings, especially against his creator.

The next day, when sunlight replaces the darkness of the night, the Monster realizes how imprudently he had acted with the De Lacey family and decides to try a new plan. Calmed by this renewed hope, he falls asleep and dreams. The dreams painfully replay the horrible scene when Felix chased him away. Like Victor's nightmare after his terrible creations juxtaposing the image and of his lover with (his dead mother), the Monster's vision conveys a profoundly disturbing impression, one of distance ("flying") and separation ("tearing"). Also, the dream prophetically anticipates the destruction of the Monster's hope for female companionship and the separation from Victor, his "father" and his only connection with the world.

The Monster is surprised to find no signs of life in the cottage the following day. His dark presentiments are confirmed when he hears two men trying, vainly, to persuade Felix to renounce his decision to leave the cottage. Felix explains that his father is in danger and that his wife and sister cannot bear to stay in the cottage. De Lacey, who, like the reader, cannot see the Monster, but the women "will never recover from the horror," and Felix, who did see the Monster, appears horrified and frightened.

After hearing Felix describe the De Lacey family's horror, the Monster finally understands that his only link to humanity is irreparably broken and all hopes shattered.

The Monster is filled with "feelings of revenge and hatred" that, for the first time, he refuses to control. Like Victor after Justine's death, oscillating between despair and tranquillity, the Monster is torn between loving thoughts for his lost friends and an uncontrollable rage.

The moon is sinking while the Monster burns down the De Laceys' cottage — the very place that, like a womb, protected and sheltered him and fed his mind and his soul with knowledge, joy, and the dream of being born again into a better world. Remember that the hovel was so low that the Monster was forced into a fetus-like position.

The Fire Theme Recurs

The Monster's most important discovery in his infancy was fire, and that through fire, he first learns to exercise his powers of observation: "How strange, I thought, the same cause should produce such opposite effects! I examined the materials of the fire, and to my joy found it to be composed of wood." Fire also shows him how the environment can be transformed. Moreover, fire reveals his sensitivity and natural tendency to protect whatever assists and serves him, and he cares for his first fire as a parent cares for a child. Fire is the only thing he regrets leaving when he departs the forest of Ingolstadt.

The first job he undertakes for the De Laceys is collecting wood for the family fire. The dramatic dialogue with blind De Lacey takes place near fire, and when asked if he needs anything, the Monster responds enigmatically that all he really needs is "warmth and rest."

Fire plays an essential role in the transition from pure animalistic behavior to a domesticated existence and, simultaneously, becomes a symbol for the Monster's connection with the world.

After he sets fire to the cottage, fire essentially disappears from the Monster's vocabulary until the very end, when it is again invoked in connection with his promise of self-immolation. The burning cottage indeed foreshadows his funeral pyre. The fire's place (and all it stands for—warmth, communication, domesticity) is

The Monster watches the fire.
Everett Collection

invaded, from this moment on, by absolute coldness, emotional frigidity, and, finally, death. Identifying himself with the fire, which is at once creative and destructive, the Monster destroys the memory of the domestic paradise (the family around the fire) and embraces the hell of revenge (the fire inside him). He too could have loved; he too can destroy.

The Monster's ritualistic dance around the cottage, which assumes religious connotations (as it looks like a pagan temple), and conjures up the cosmic elements—the rising winds and the descending moon—also has strong sexual connotations, like many primitive dances. The tongues that destroy also "link" and "embrace" the body of the cottage. It is possible to identify a sexual awakening in the Monster's dance; afterward the Monster demands a woman, and when he is refused, he symbolically rapes Elizabeth.

There is no catharsis, nothing purifying in the nocturnal ceremony. It is pure bestiality. Long before Conrad and his disturbing *Heart of Darkness,* Mary Shelley speaks of "unspeakable rites."

The Monster Saved and Damned

This scene is indeed essential in decoding the Monster's complexity. He is at once a Satanic figure, an expelled Adam, and an avenging angel who blocks man's way back into Eden with fire. The ironic invocation of Milton's final lines from *Paradise Lost,* showing Adam and Eve taking "hand in hand" their "solitary way" through the world before them, reinforces the fundamental difference between the first man's history and the Monster's condition. For him, there is no Eve, no world before him, and no promise for salvation. The only possible path for him is back to his false and unjust creator with the dark hope for a monstrous companion and a deserted anti-paradise.

The fire, and its warmth, disappears gradually from the landscape during the Monster's journey to his father's home: "It was late in autumn when I quitted the district." Interestingly enough, when a feeble hope for some unexpected good change appears, nature also shows signs of regeneration. In the spring, when the landscape is becoming once again warm and green, the Monster, seeing a young girl fall into a rapid stream, jumps into the water and saves her.

While he is trying to reanimate her, a friend of the girl's shows up and, like Felix, maliciously attacks him. The man then shoots him. Overcome with rage at the injustice and ingratitude shown him on all fronts, the Monster renews his vow of "eternal hatred and vengeance to all mankind."

After a long and difficult journey, the Monster arrives in the vicinity of Geneva, Victor's native town. By accident, he meets little William Frankenstein, who, despite his young age, has the same violent reaction to the Monster's appearance as adults have had. The Monster kills William and frames Justine for the murder. At the end of his story, the Monster asks Victor to create a female companion for him.

Chapter 17

Victor refuses to satisfy the Monster's request to create a female companion for him. However, after the Monster promises to take his mate to the uninhabited territory of South America and never come back, Victor acquiesces. Deeply disturbed by the encounter with the Monster and by his new, "abhorred" task, Victor returns to Geneva.

CHAPTER XVII

THE being finished speaking, and fixed his looks upon me in the expectation of a reply. But I was bewildered, perplexed, and unable to arrange my ideas sufficiently to understand the full extent of his proposition. He continued—

"You must create a female for me, with whom I can live in the interchange of those sympathies necessary for my being. This you alone can do; and I demand it of you as a right which you must not refuse to concede."

The latter part of his tale had kindled anew in me the anger that had died away while he narrated his peaceful life among the cottagers, and, as he said this, I could no longer suppress the rage that burned within me.

"I do refuse it," I replied; "and no torture shall ever extort a consent from me. You may render me the most miserable of men, but you shall never make me base in my own eyes. Shall I create another like yourself, whose joint wickedness might desolate the world? Begone! I have answered you; you may torture me, but I will never consent."

"You are in the wrong," replied the fiend; "and instead of threatening, I am content to reason with you. I am malicious because I am miserable. Am I not shunned and hated by all mankind? You, my creator, would tear me to pieces, and triumph; remember that, and tell me why I should pity man more than he pities me? You would not call it murder, if you could precipitate me into one of those ice-rifts, and destroy my frame, the work of your own hands. Shall I respect man, when he **contemns** me? Let him live with me in the interchange of kindness; and instead of injury, I would bestow every benefit upon him with tears of gratitude at his acceptance. But that cannot be; the human senses are insurmountable barriers to our union. Yet mine shall not be the submission of abject slavery. I will revenge my injuries: if I cannot inspire love, I will cause fear; and chiefly towards you my arch-enemy, because my creator, do I swear inextinguishable hatred. Have a care: I will work at your destruction, nor finish until I desolate your heart, **so that you shall curse the hour of your birth.**"

A fiendish rage animated him as he said this; his face was wrinkled into contortions too horrible for human eyes to behold; but presently he calmed himself and proceeded—

"I intended to reason. This passion is detrimental to me; for you do not reflect that *you* are the cause of its excess. If any being felt emotions of benevolence towards me, I should return them an hundred and an

NOTES

contemns: despises.

so that you shall curse the hour of your birth: an allusion to Job 3: 1–10.

hundred fold; for that one creature's sake, I would make peace with the whole kind! But I now indulge in dreams of bliss that cannot be realised. What I ask of you is reasonable and moderate; I demand a creature of another sex, but as hideous as myself; the gratification is small, but it is all that I can receive, and it shall content me. It is true, we shall be monsters, cut off from all the world; but on that account we shall be more attached to one another. Our lives will not be happy, but they will be harmless, and free from the misery I now feel. Oh! my creator, make me happy; let me feel gratitude towards you for one benefit! Let me see that I excite the sympathy of some existing thing; do not deny me my request!"

I was moved. I shuddered when I thought of the possible consequences of my consent; but I felt that there was some justice in his argument. His tale, and the feelings he now expressed, proved him to be a creature of fine sensations; and did I not, as his maker, owe him all the portion of happiness that it was in my power to bestow? He saw my change of feeling and continued—

"If you consent, neither you nor any other human being shall ever see us again: I will go to the vast wilds of South America. My food is not that of man; I do not destroy the lamb and the kid to glut my appetite; acorns and berries afford me sufficient nourishment. My companion will be of the same nature as myself, and will be content with the same fare. We shall make our bed of dried leaves; the sun will shine on us as on man, and will ripen our food. The picture I present to you is peaceful and human, and you must feel that you could deny it only in the wantonness of power and cruelty. Pitiless as you have been towards me, I now see compassion in your eyes; let me seize the favourable moment, and persuade you to promise what I so ardently desire."

"You propose," replied I, "to fly from the habitations of man, to dwell in those wilds where the beasts of the field will be your only companions. How can you, who long for the love and sympathy of man, persevere in this exile? You will return, and again seek their kindness, and you will meet with their detestation; your evil passions will be renewed, and you will then have a companion to aid you in the task of destruction. This may not be: cease to argue the point, for I cannot consent."

"How inconstant are your feelings! but a moment ago you were moved by my representations, and why do you again harden yourself to my complaints? I swear to you, by the earth which I inhabit, and by you that made me, that, with the companion you bestow, I will quit the neighbourhood of man, and dwell as it may chance, in the most savage of places. My evil passions will have fled, for I shall meet with sympathy! My life will flow quietly away, and in my dying moments, I shall not curse my maker."

His words had a strange effect upon me. I compassionated him, and sometimes felt a wish to console him; but when I looked upon him, when I saw the filthy mass that moved and talked, my heart sickened, and my feelings were altered to those of horror and hatred. I tried to stifle these sensations; I thought, that as I could not sympathise with him, I had no right to withhold from him the small portion of happiness which was yet in my power to bestow.

"You swear," I said, "to be harmless; but have you not already shown a degree of malice that should reasonably make me distrust you? May not even this be a feint that will increase your triumph by affording a wider scope for your revenge?"

"How is this? I must not be trifled with: and I demand an answer. If I have no ties and no affections, hatred and vice must be my portion; the love of another will destroy the cause of my crimes, and I shall become a thing, of whose existence everyone will be ignorant. My vices are the children of a forced solitude that I abhor; and my virtues will necessarily arise when I live in communion with an equal. I shall feel the affections of a sensitive being, and become linked to the chain of existence and events, from which I am now excluded."

I paused some time to reflect on all he had related, and the various arguments which he had employed. I thought of the promise of virtues which he had displayed on the opening of his existence, and the subsequent blight of all kindly feeling by the loathing and scorn which his protectors had manifested towards him. His power and threats were not omitted in my calculations: a creature who could exist in the ice-caves of the glaciers, and hide himself from pursuit among the ridges of inaccessible precipices, was a being possessing faculties it would be vain to cope with. After a long pause of reflection, I concluded that the justice due both to him and my fellow-creatures demanded of me that I should comply with his request. Turning to him, therefore, I said—

"I consent to your demand, on your solemn oath to quit Europe for ever, and every other place in the neighbourhood of man, as soon as I shall deliver into your hands a female who will accompany you in your exile."

"I swear," he cried, "by the sun, and by the blue sky of Heaven, and by the fire of love that burns my heart, that if you grant my prayer, while they exist you shall never behold me again. Depart to your home, and commence your labours: I shall watch their progress with unutterable anxiety; and fear not but that when you are ready, I shall appear."

Saying this, he suddenly quitted me, fearful, perhaps, of any change in my sentiments. I saw him descend the mountain with greater speed than the flight of an eagle, and quickly lost him among the undulations of the sea of ice.

His tale had occupied the whole day; and the sun was upon the verge of the horizon when he departed. I knew that I ought to hasten my descent towards the valley, as I should soon be encompassed in darkness; but my heart was heavy, and my steps slow. The labour of winding among the little paths of the mountains and fixing my feet firmly as I advanced, perplexed me, occupied as I was by the emotions which the occurrences of the day had produced. Night was far advanced, when I came to the half-way resting-place, and seated myself beside the fountain. The stars shone at intervals, as the clouds passed from over them; the dark pines rose before me, and every here and there a broken tree lay on the ground: it was a scene of wonderful solemnity, and stirred strange thoughts within me. I wept bitterly; and clasping my hands in agony, I exclaimed, "Oh! stars and clouds, and winds, ye are all about to mock me: if ye really pity me, crush sensation and memory; let me become as nought; but if not, depart, depart, and leave me in darkness."

These were wild and miserable thoughts; but I cannot describe to you how the eternal twinkling of the stars weighed upon me, and how I listened to every blast of wind, as if it were a dull, ugly **siroc** on its way to consume me.

siroc: sirocco; a hot and destructive wind that blows from North Africa across the Mediterranean and Southern Europe.

Morning dawned before I arrived at the village of Chamounix; I took no rest, but returned immediately to Geneva. Even in my own heart I could give no expression to my sensations—they weighed on me with a mountain's weight, and their excess destroyed my agony beneath them. Thus I returned home, and entering the house, presented myself to the family. My haggard and wild appearance awoke intense alarm; but I answered no question, scarcely did I speak. I felt as if I were placed under a ban—as if I had no right to claim their sympathies—as if never more might I enjoy companionship with them. Yet even thus I loved them to adoration; and to save them, I resolved to dedicate myself to my most abhorred task. The prospect of such an occupation made every other circumstance of existence pass before me like a dream; and that thought only had to me the reality of life.

COMMENTARY

The Monster's account of his sufferings, desires, and shattered aspirations impress and move Victor. However, the irreverent and authoritarian tone in which he delivers his demand for a female companion brings back Victor's anger, and he categorically refuses to satisfy the Monster. Perfectly controlled, the Monster reminds Victor of the insurmountable barriers separating him from all human beings, blames humankind for its cruelty and inability to deal with difference, and imperturbably announces that if Victor insists on refusing his request, he will simply destroy him: "I will work at your destruction, not finish until I desolate your heart, so that you shall curse the hour of your birth."

Without waiting for an answer to his ultimatum, the Monster goes on explaining, in a logical and dispassionate manner, Victor's fundamental guilt—that the crimes the Monster has committed are ultimately Victor's responsibility. The Monster sets forth the fairness and reasonableness of his request for a female companion who can sympathize with him and his needs. He closes with a pathetic appeal to Victor's compassion and, influenced by an awakened sense of justice, Victor promises to fulfill his request.

Role Reversal

Clearly, Victor's and the Monster's roles are, once again, reversed. Victor becomes the slave, and the Monster assumes the behavior and prerogatives of the master, and seeks revenge for his injuries. Revenge, however, can be read here more as reparation—as a necessary rebalancing of justice and equity in the Monster's relationship with the world and the man who created and then abandoned him. Before the Monster returns to his initial docile and obedient attitude, his words sound curiously similar to God's words from Ezek. 22:29-31: "The people of the land . . . oppressed the stranger . . . without judgment. And I thought among them for a man that might set up a hedge, and standing the gap before me in favor of the land, that I might not destroy it: and I found none. And I pour out my indignation upon them . . . "

Claiming that "if any being felt emotions of benevolence towards me, I should return them an hundred and an hundred fold; for that one creature's sake, I would make peace with the whole kind" and than adding "But I now indulge in dreams of bliss that cannot be realised," the Monster, in fact employs the vocabulary of divine forgiveness that would save the whole race for the sacredness of one single life. At the same time, he exhibits the signs of an equally divine melancholy, one that perceives man's constant and all-pervasive exposure to the threat of losing its humanity, and thereby its sacredness, by losing its capacity for love.

In short, the Monster speaks and acts like God, punishing human beings not so much for their errors against him, but, more importantly, for ignoring the very attribute that makes them human: their potential for compassion, for sympathy. The absence of this quality, he suggests, creates a godless universe, one in which oppression of the stranger, violence against the orphan, rejection of the ugly become possible. Like God, who, at times, reestablishes the balance in the universe through acts of divine violence, the Monster sees himself in these moments as a fair judge of those who acted "without judgment."

And yet, the Monster seems uncomfortable appropriating a role that it is not his. In a last attempt to make peace with Victor and, at the same time, free him of a responsibility (parental duty) that he is clearly incapable of upholding, the Monster returns to his initial position of humble creature and begs for the creation of a female: "Oh! my creator, make me happy; let me feel gratitude towards you for one benefit!"

From Victor's perspective, there is absolutely no evidence that the Monster can be trusted, and yet a number of circumstances testify in his favor. First, the entire episode with the De Lacey family reveals a benevolent being, capable not only of superior intellectual and moral accomplishments, but also able to resist violence even when he is the victim of violence and abuse (he does not react to Felix' vicious attack despite the fact that he "could have torn him limb from limb"). Moreover, despite his bitterness and solemn promises of "everlasting war" against mankind, his natural impulse for goodness resurfaces in the episode with the little girl he saves from drowning. Even William's murder is more a reaction to the name Frankenstein and to William's arrogance than a premeditated act.

In agreeing to create a female, Victor is motivated by a rediscovered sense of justice , but also by a curious mixture of hesitant sympathy for the Monster, surprise at his gentle spirit, and a certain fear of his unusual powers. And yet, the important fact remains that for the first time Victor experiences feelings of empathy and understanding for his creature.

Language and Communication Themes

The Monster's intuition that the acquisition of language could give him access to the community of men and help him establish a position and an identity proved, after all, correct. Clearly, Victor admires his lucid, astute, and eloquent arguments, his ability to navigate through his (Victor's) vacillations, and his power to control his reactions and remain undisturbed (as Victor himself is unable to do). Clearly, such an individual could have functioned well in the society of man. What the Monster couldn't predict, however, was that his deformity would never be "overlooked" in a world where the "different" is always regarded as dangerous and, therefore, instinctively rejected.

The abnormal, the deviation from the "norm," the "other" usually alienates and disturbs us, or even more frightful, may insinuate a dark secret about our own nature. If something so monstrous on the outside is human inside, cannot the reverse also be true? Is there a monstrous part inside us?

Chapters 18–19

Victor, with Clerval, leaves for England to begin his promised work for the Monster. A friend invites them to visit Scotland. Victor, fearing the Monster's impatience, pretends that he wants to tour Scotland alone and goes to the Orkney Islands to finish his work. Day after day, Victor works in a maddening solitude on his task and the closer he comes to its completion, the darker his thoughts become.

CHAPTER XVIII

DAY after day, week after week, passed away on my return to Geneva; and I could not collect the courage to recommence my work. I feared the vengeance of the disappointed fiend, yet I was unable to overcome my repugnance to the task which was enjoined me. I found that I could not compose a female without again devoting several months to profound study and laborious **disquisition**. I had heard of some discoveries having been made by an English philosopher, the knowledge of which was material to my success, and I sometimes thought of obtaining my father's consent to visit England for this purpose; but I clung to every pretence of delay, and shrunk from taking the first step in an undertaking whose immediate necessity began to appear less absolute to me. A change indeed had taken place in me: my health, which had hitherto declined, was now much restored; and my spirits, when unchecked by the memory of my unhappy promise, rose proportionably. My father saw this change with pleasure, and he turned his thoughts towards the best method of eradicating the remains of my melancholy, which every now and then would return by fits, and with a devouring blackness overcast the approaching sunshine. At these moments I took refuge in the most perfect solitude. I passed whole days on the lake alone in a little boat, watching the clouds, and listening to the rippling of the waves, silent and listless. But the fresh air and bright sun seldom failed to restore me to some degree of composure; and, on my return, I met the salutations of my friends with a readier smile and a more cheerful heart.

It was after my return from one of these rambles, that my father, calling me aside, thus addressed me:—

"I am happy to remark, my dear son, that you have resumed your former pleasures, and seem to be returning to yourself. And yet you are still unhappy, and still avoid our society. For some time I was lost in conjecture as to the cause of this; but yesterday an idea struck me, and if it is well founded, I conjure you to avow it. Reserve on such a point would be not only useless, but draw down treble misery on us all."

I trembled violently at his **exordium**, and my father continued—

"I confess, my son, that I have always looked forward to your marriage with our dear Elizabeth as the tie of our domestic comfort, and the stay of my declining years. You were attached to each other from your earliest infancy; you studied together, and appeared, in dispositions and tastes,

NOTES

disquisition: examination, investigation.

exordium: discourse.

entirely suited to one another. But so blind is the experience of man, that what I conceived to be the best assistants to my plan, may have entirely destroyed it. You, perhaps, regard her as your sister, without any wish that she might become your wife. Nay, you may have met with another whom you may love; and considering yourself as bound in honour to Elizabeth, this struggle may occasion the poignant misery which you appear to feel."

"My dear father, re-assure yourself. I love my cousin tenderly and sincerely. I never saw any woman who excited, as Elizabeth does, my warmest admiration and affection. My future hopes and prospects are entirely bound up in the expectation of our union."

"The expression of your sentiments of this subject, my dear Victor, gives me more pleasure than I have for some time experienced. If you feel thus, we shall assuredly be happy, however present events may cast a gloom over us. But it is this gloom which appears to have taken so strong a hold of your mind, that I wish to dissipate. Tell me, therefore, whether you object to an immediate solemnisation of the marriage. We have been unfortunate, and recent events have drawn us from that every-day tranquillity befitting my years and infirmities. You are younger; yet I do not suppose, possessed as you are of a competent fortune, that an early marriage would at all interfere with any future plans of honour and utility that you may have formed. Do not suppose, however, that I wish to dictate happiness to you, or that a delay on your part would cause me any serious uneasiness. Interpret my words with **candour**, and answer me, I **conjure** you, with confidence and sincerity."

candour: kindness.

conjure: summon.

I listened to my father in silence and remained for some time incapable of offering any reply. I revolved rapidly in my mind a multitude of thoughts, and endeavoured to arrive at some conclusion. Alas! to me the idea of an immediate union with my Elizabeth was one of horror and dismay. I was bound by a solemn promise, which I had not yet fulfilled, and dared not break; or, if I did, what manifold miseries might not impend over me and my devoted family! Could I enter into a festival with this deadly weight yet hanging round my neck, and bowing me to the ground? I must perform my **engagement**, and let the monster depart with his mate, before I allowed myself to enjoy the delight of a union from which I expected peace.

engagement: promise, pact.

I remembered also the necessity imposed upon me of either journeying to England, or entering into a long correspondence with those philosophers of that country, whose knowledge and discoveries were of indispensable use to me in my present undertaking. The latter method of obtaining the desired intelligence was dilatory and unsatisfactory; besides, I had an insurmountable aversion to the idea of engaging myself in my loathsome task in my father's house, while in habits of familiar intercourse with those I loved. I knew that a thousand fearful accidents might occur, the slightest of which would disclose a tale to thrill all connected with me with horror. I was aware also that I should often lose all self-command, all capacity of hiding the harrowing sensations that would possess me during the progress of my unearthly occupation. I must absent myself from all I loved while thus employed. Once commenced, it would quickly be achieved, and I might be restored to my family in peace and happiness. My promise fulfilled, the monster would depart forever. Or (so my fond fancy imaged) some accident might meanwhile occur to destroy him and put an end to my slavery forever.

These feelings dictated my answer to my father. I expressed a wish to visit England; but, concealing the true reasons of this request, I clothed my desires under a guise which excited no suspicion, while I urged my desire with an earnestness that easily induced my father to comply. After so long a period of an absorbing melancholy, that resembled madness in its intensity and effects, he was glad to find that I was capable of taking pleasure in the idea of such a journey, and he hoped that change of scene and varied amusement would, before my return, have restored me entirely to myself.

The duration of my absence was left to my own choice; a few months, or at most a year, was the period contemplated. One paternal kind precaution he had taken to ensure my having a companion. Without previously communicating with me, he had, in concert with Elizabeth, arranged that Clerval should join me at Strasburgh. This interfered with the solitude I coveted for the prosecution of my task; yet at the commencement of my journey the presence of my friend could in no way be an impediment, and truly I rejoiced that thus I should be saved many hours of lonely, maddening reflection. Nay, Henry might stand between me and the intrusion of my foe. If I were alone, would he not at times force his abhorred presence on me, to remind me of my task, or to contemplate its progress?

To England, therefore, I was bound, and it was understood that my union with Elizabeth should take place immediately on my return. My father's age rendered him extremely averse to delay. For myself, there was one reward I promised myself from my detested toils—one consolation for my unparalleled sufferings; it was the prospect of that day when, enfranchised from my miserable slavery, I might claim Elizabeth, and forget the past in my union with her.

I now made arrangements for my journey; but one feeling haunted me, which filled me with fear and agitation. During my absence I should leave my friends unconscious of the existence of their enemy, and unprotected from his attacks, exasperated as he might be by my departure. But he had promised to follow me wherever I might go; and would he not accompany me to England? This imagination was dreadful in itself, but soothing, inasmuch as it supposed the safety of my friends. I was agonised with the idea of the possibility that the reverse of this might happen. But through the whole period during which I was the slave of my creature, I allowed myself to be governed by the impulses of the moment; and my present sensations strongly intimated that the fiend would follow me, and exempt my family from the danger of his machinations.

It was in the latter end of September that I again quitted my native country. My journey had been my own suggestion, and Elizabeth, therefore, acquiesced: but she was filled with disquiet at the idea of my suffering, away from her, the inroads of misery and grief. It had been her care which provided me a companion in Clerval—and yet a man is blind to a thousand minute circumstances, which call forth a woman's sedulous attention. She longed to bid me hasten my return,—a thousand conflicting emotions rendered her mute, as she bade me a tearful silent farewell.

I threw myself into the carriage that was to convey me away, hardly knowing whither I was going, and careless of what was passing around. I remembered only, and it was with a bitter anguish that I reflected on it, to order that my chemical instruments should be packed to go with me. Filled with dreary imaginations, I passed through many beautiful and majestic scenes; but my eyes were fixed and unobserving. I could only think of the **bourne** of my travels, and the work which was to occupy me whilst they endured.

bourne: goal, objective.

After some days spent in listless indolence, during which I traversed many leagues, I arrived at **Strasburgh**, where I waited two days for Clerval. He came. Alas, how great was the contrast between us! He was alive to every new scene; joyful when he saw the beauties of the setting sun, and more happy when he beheld it rise, and recommence a new day. He pointed out to me the shifting colours of the landscape, and the appearances of the sky. "This is what it is to live," he cried, "now I enjoy existence! But you, my dear Frankenstein, wherefore are you desponding and sorrowful?" In truth, I was occupied by gloomy thoughts, and neither saw the descent of the evening star, nor the golden sunrise reflected in the **Rhine**.—And you, my friend, would be far more amused with the journal of Clerval, who observed the scenery with an eye of feeling and delight, than in listening to my reflections. I, a miserable wretch, haunted by a curse that shut up every avenue to enjoyment.

Strasburgh: French town on the Rhine river, on the border with Germany.

Rhine: a river, originating in the Western Alps and flowing between France and Germany, toward the North Sea.

We had agreed to descend the Rhine in a boat from Strasburgh to **Rotterdam**, whence we might take shipping for London. During this voyage, we passed many willowy islands, and saw several beautiful towns. We stayed a day at Manheim, and, on the fifth from our departure from Strasburgh, arrived at **Mayence**. The course of the Rhine below Mayence becomes much more picturesque. The river descends rapidly, and winds between hills, not high, but steep, and of beautiful forms. We saw many ruined castles standing on the edges of precipices, surrounded by black woods, high and inaccessible. This part of the Rhine, indeed, presents a singularly variegated landscape. In one spot you view rugged hills, ruined castles overlooking tremendous precipices, with the dark Rhine rushing beneath; and on the sudden turn of a promontory, flourishing vineyards, with green sloping banks, and a meandering river, and populous towns occupy the scene.

Rotterdam: important port city at the North Sea, in Netherlands.

Mayence: Mainz, Germany.

We travelled at the time of the vintage, and heard the song of the labourers, as we glided down the stream. Even I, depressed in mind, and my spirits continually agitated by gloomy feelings, even I was pleased. I lay at the bottom of the boat, and, as I gazed on the cloudless blue sky, I seemed to drink in a tranquillity to which I had long been a stranger. And if these were my sensations, who can describe those of Henry? He felt as if he had been transported to Fairy-land, and enjoyed a happiness seldom tasted by man. "I have seen," he said, "the most beautiful scenes of my own country; I have visited the lakes of Lucerne and Uri, where the snowy mountains descend almost perpendicularly to the water, casting black and impenetrable shades, which would cause a gloomy and mournful appearance, were it not for the most verdant islands that relieve the eye by their gay appearance; I have seen this lake agitated by a tempest, when the wind tore up whirlwinds of water, and gave you an idea of what the water-spout must be on the great ocean, and the waves dash with fury the base of the mountain, where the priest and his mistress were overwhelmed by an avalanche, and where their dying voices are still said to be heard amid the pauses of the nightly wind; I have seen the mountains of La Valais, and the Pays de Vaud: but this country, Victor, pleases me more than all those wonders. The mountains of Switzerland are more majestic and strange; but there is a charm in the banks of this divine river, that I never before saw equalled. Look at that castle which overhangs yon precipice; and that also on the island, almost concealed amongst the foliage of those lovely trees; and now that group of labourers coming from among their vines; and that village half hid in the recess of the mountain. Oh, surely, the spirit that inhabits and guards this place has a soul more in harmony with man, than those who pile the glacier, or retire to the inaccessible peaks of the mountains of our own country."

Clerval! beloved friend! even now it delights me to record your words, and to dwell on the praise of which you are so eminently deserving. He was a being formed in the "**very poetry of nature.**" His wild and enthusiastic imagination was chastened by the sensibility of his heart. His soul overflowed with ardent affections, and his friendship was of that devoted and wondrous nature that the world-minded teach us to look for only in the imagination. But even human sympathies were not sufficient to satisfy his eager mind. The scenery of external nature, which others regard only with admiration, he loved with ardour:—

> The sounding cataract
>
> Haunted him like a passion: the tall rock,
>
> The mountain, and the deep and gloomy wood,
>
> Their colours and their forms, were then to him
>
> An appetite; a feeling, and a love,
>
> That had no need of a remoter charm,
>
> By thought supplied, or any interest
>
> Unborrow'd from the eye.
>
> [Wordsworth's "Tintern Abbey."]

And where does he now exist? Is this gentle and lovely being lost forever? Has this mind, so replete with ideas, imaginations fanciful and magnificent, which formed a world, whose existence depended on the life of its

"very poetry of nature": from the *Story of Rimini* by Leigh Hunt (1784–1859). The poem narrates the moving story of Paolo and Francesca, the two lovers from Dante's *Inferno.*

Ruins of Tintern Abbey.

creator;—has this mind perished? Does it now only exist in my memory? No, it is not thus; your form so divinely wrought, and beaming with beauty, has decayed, but your spirit still visits and consoles your unhappy friend.

Pardon this gush of sorrow; these ineffectual words are but a slight tribute to the unexampled worth of Henry, but they soothe my heart, overflowing with the anguish which his remembrance creates. I will proceed with my tale.

Beyond **Cologne** we descended to the plains of Holland; and we resolved to **post** the remainder of our way; for the wind was contrary, and the stream of the river was too gentle to aid us.

Cologne: old name of Koln, an important city on the Rhine river in Germany.

post: to travel by horse.

Our journey here lost the interest arising from beautiful scenery; but we arrived in a few days at Rotterdam, whence we proceeded by sea to England. It was on a clear morning, in the latter days of December, that I first saw the white cliffs of Britain. The banks of the Thames presented a new scene; they were flat, but fertile, and almost every town was marked by the remembrance of some story. We saw Tilbury Fort, and remembered the Spanish armada; Gravesend, Woolwich, and Greenwich, places which I had heard of even in my country.

At length we saw the numerous steeples of London, St. Paul's towering above all, and the Tower famed in English history.

CHAPTER XIX

London was our present point of rest; we determined to remain several months in this wonderful and celebrated city. Clerval desired the **intercourse** of the men of genius and talent who flourished at this time; but this was with me a secondary object; I was principally occupied with the means of obtaining the information necessary for the completion of my promise, and quickly availed myself of the letters of introduction that I had brought with me, addressed to the most distinguished natural philosophers.

intercourse: conversation, dialogue.

If this journey had taken place during my days of study and happiness, it would have afforded me inexpressible pleasure. But a blight had come over my existence, and I only visited these people for the sake of the information they might give me on the subject in which my interest was so terribly profound. Company was irksome to me; when alone, I could fill my mind with the sights of heaven and earth; the voice of Henry soothed me, and I could thus cheat myself into a transitory peace. But busy, uninteresting, joyous faces brought back despair to my heart. I saw an insurmountable barrier placed between me and my fellow-men; this barrier was sealed with the blood of William and Justine; and to reflect on the events connected with those names filled my soul with anguish.

But in Clerval I saw the image of my former self; he was inquisitive and anxious to gain experience and instruction. The difference of manners which he observed was to him an inexhaustible source of instruction and amusement. He was also pursuing an object he had long had in view. His design was to visit India, in the belief that he had in his knowledge of its various languages, and in the views he had taken of its society, the means of materially assisting the progress of European colonisation and trade. In

Britain only could he further the execution of his plan. He was forever busy; and the only check to his enjoyments was my sorrowful and dejected mind. I tried to conceal this as much as possible, that I might not debar him from the pleasures natural to one, who was entering on a new scene of life, undisturbed by any care or bitter recollection. I often refused to accompany him, alleging another engagement, that I might remain alone. I now also began to collect the materials necessary for my new creation, and this was to me like the torture of single drops of water continually falling on the head. Every thought that was devoted to it was an extreme anguish, and every word that I spoke in allusion to it caused my lips to quiver, and my heart to palpitate.

After passing some months in London, we received a letter from a person in Scotland, who had formerly been our visitor at Geneva. He mentioned the beauties of his native country, and asked us if those were not sufficient allurements to induce us to prolong our journey as far north as Perth, where he resided. Clerval eagerly desired to accept this invitation; and I, although I abhorred society, wished to view again mountains and streams, and all the wondrous works with which Nature adorns her chosen dwelling-places.

We had arrived in England at the beginning of October, and it was now February. We accordingly determined to commence our journey towards the north at the expiration of another month. In this expedition we did not intend to follow the great road to Edinburgh, but to visit Windsor, Oxford, Matlock, and the Cumberland lakes, resolving to arrive at the completion of this tour about the end of July. I packed up my chemical instruments, and the materials I had collected, resolving to finish my labours in some obscure nook in the northern highlands of Scotland.

We quitted London on the 27th of March, and remained a few days at Windsor, rambling in its beautiful forest. This was a new scene to us mountaineers; the majestic oaks, the quantity of game, and the herds of stately deer, were all novelties to us.

From thence we proceeded to Oxford. As we entered this city, our minds were filled with the remembrance of the events that had been transacted there more than a century and a half before. It was here that Charles I. had collected his forces. This city had remained faithful to him, after the whole nation had forsaken his cause to join the standard of parliament and liberty. The memory of that unfortunate king, and his companions, the amiable **Falkland,** the insolent **Goring,** his **queen,** and **son,** gave a peculiar interest to every part of the city, which they might be supposed to have inhabited. The spirit of elder days found a dwelling here, and we delighted to trace its footsteps. If these feelings had not found an imaginary gratification, the appearance of the city had yet in itself sufficient beauty to obtain our admiration. The colleges are ancient and picturesque; the streets are almost magnificent; and the lovely Isis, which flows beside it through meadows of exquisite verdure, is spread forth into a placid expanse of waters, which reflects its majestic assemblage of towers, and spires, and domes, embosomed among aged trees.

Falkland: Lucius Cary, second Viscount Falkland (1610–1643), was the secretary of state for Charles I.

Goring: Baron Goring (1608–1657) was one of Charles I's best generals in the English Civil War (1642–49).

queen: Henrietta Maria (1609–1669), wife of King Charles I of England.

son: son of Charles I. He became Charles II in 1660.

I enjoyed this scene; and yet my enjoyment was embittered both by the memory of the past, and the anticipation of the future. I was formed for peaceful happiness. During my youthful days discontent never visited my mind; and if I was ever overcome by ***ennui,*** the sight of what is beautiful in nature, or the study of what is excellent and sublime in the productions of man, could always interest my heart, and communicate elasticity to my spirits. But I am a blasted tree; the bolt has entered my soul; and I felt then that I should survive to exhibit, what I shall soon cease to be—a miserable spectacle of wrecked humanity, pitiable to others, and intolerable to myself.

ennui: melancholy.

We passed a considerable period at Oxford, rambling among its environs, and endeavouring to identify every spot which might relate to the most animating epoch of English history. Our little voyages of discovery were often prolonged by the successive objects that presented themselves. We visited the tomb of the illustrious **Hampden**, and the field on which that patriot fell. For a moment my soul was elevated from its debasing and miserable fears, to contemplate the divine ideas of liberty and self-sacrifice, of which these sights were the monuments and the remembrancers. For an instant I dared to shake off my chains, and look around me with a free and lofty spirit; but the iron had eaten into my flesh, and I sank again, trembling and hopeless, into my miserable self.

Hampden: John Hampden (1594–1643), a supporter of Oliver Cromwell, lord protector of England under Charles I during the English Civil War.

We left Oxford with regret, and proceeded to Matlock, which was our next place of rest. The country in the neighbourhood of this village resembled, to a greater degree, the scenery of Switzerland; but every thing is on a lower scale, and the green hills want the crown of distant white Alps, which always attend on the piny mountains of my native country. We visited the wondrous cave, and the little **cabinets** of natural history, where the **curiosities** are disposed in the same manner as in the collections at Servox and Chamounix. The latter name made me tremble, when pronounced by Henry; and I hastened to quit Matlock, with which that terrible scene was thus associated.

cabinets: rooms to display works of art and curiosities.

curiosities: rare or exquisite objects.

From Derby, still journeying northwards, we passed two months in Cumberland and **Westmorland**. I could now almost fancy myself among the Swiss mountains. The little patches of snow which yet lingered on the northern sides of the mountains, the lakes, and the dashing of the rocky streams, were all familiar and dear sights to me. Here also we made some acquaintances, who almost contrived to cheat me into happiness. The delight of Clerval was proportionably greater than mine; his mind expanded in the company of men of talent, and he found in his own nature greater capacities and resources than he could have imagined himself to have possessed while he associated with his inferiors. "I could pass my life here," said he to me; "and among these mountains I should scarcely regret Switzerland and the Rhine."

Westmorland: Lake District, famous for its association with the Lake Poets: Wordsworth, Coleridge, and Southey.

But he found that a traveller's life is one that includes much pain amidst its enjoyments. His feelings are forever on the stretch; and when he begins to sink into repose, he finds himself obliged to quit that on which he rests in pleasure for something new, which again engages his attention, and which also he forsakes for other novelties.

We had scarcely visited the various lakes of Cumberland and Westmorland, and conceived an affection for some of the inhabitants, when the period of our appointment with our Scotch friend approached, and we left them to travel on. For my own part I was not sorry. I had now neglected my promise for some time, and I feared the effects of the daemon's disappointment. He might remain in Switzerland, and wreak his vengeance on my relatives. This idea pursued me, and tormented me at every moment from which I might otherwise have snatched repose and peace. I waited for my letters with feverish impatience: if they were delayed, I was miserable, and overcome by a thousand fears; and when they arrived, and I saw the **superscription** of Elizabeth or my father, I hardly dared to read and ascertain my fate. Sometimes I thought that the fiend followed me, and might expedite my remissness by murdering my companion. When these thoughts possessed me, I would not quit Henry for a moment, but followed him as his shadow, to protect him from the fancied rage of his destroyer. I felt as if I had committed some great crime, the consciousness of which haunted me. I was guiltless, but I had indeed drawn down a horrible curse upon my head, as mortal as that of crime.

superscription: the address on a letter.

I visited Edinburgh with **languid** eyes and mind; and yet that city might have interested the most unfortunate being. Clerval did not like it so well as Oxford: for the antiquity of the latter city was more pleasing to him. But the beauty and regularity of the new town of Edinburgh, its romantic castle and its environs, the most delightful in the world, **Arthur's Seat**, **St. Bernard's Well**, and the **Pentland Hills**, compensated him for the change, and filled him with cheerfulness and admiration. But I was impatient to arrive at the termination of my journey.

languid: feeble, debilitated.

Arthur's Seat; St. Bernard's Well; town near Edinburgh, Scotland.

Pentland Hills: notable geographic features near Edinburgh, Scotland.

We left Edinburgh in a week, passing through Coupar, St. Andrew's, and along the banks of the Tay, to Perth, where our friend expected us. But I was in no mood to laugh and talk with strangers, or enter into their feelings or plans with the good humour expected from a guest; and accordingly I told Clerval that I wished to make the tour of Scotland alone. "Do you," said I, "enjoy yourself, and let this be our rendezvous. I may be absent a month or two; but do not interfere with my motions, I entreat you: leave me to peace and solitude for a short time; and when I return, I hope it will be with a lighter heart, more congenial to your own temper."

Henry wished to dissuade me; but, seeing me bent on this plan, ceased to **remonstrate**. He entreated me to write often. "I had rather be with you," he said, "in your solitary rambles, than with these Scotch people, whom I do not know: hasten then my friend, to return, that I may again feel myself somewhat at home, which I cannot do in your absence."

remonstrate: protest, reproach.

Having parted from my friend, I determined to visit some remote spot of Scotland, and finish my work in solitude. I did not doubt but that the monster followed me, and would discover himself to me when I should have finished, that he might receive his companion.

With this resolution I traversed the northern highlands, and fixed on one of the remotest of the **Orkneys** as the scene of my labours. It was a place fitted for such a work, being hardly more than a rock whose high sides

Orkneys: the Orkney Islands, a group of 67 islands in the Atlantic Ocean off the northern coast of Scotland.

were continually beaten upon by the waves. The soil was barren, scarcely affording pasture for a few miserable cows, and oatmeal for its inhabitants, which consisted of five persons, whose gaunt and scraggy limbs gave tokens of their miserable fare. Vegetables and bread, when they indulged in such luxuries, and even fresh water, was to be procured from the mainland, which was about five miles distant.

On the whole island there were but three miserable huts, and one of these was vacant when I arrived. This I hired. It contained but two rooms, and these exhibited all the **squalidness** of the most miserable penury. The thatch had fallen in, the walls were unplastered, and the door was off its hinges. I ordered it to be repaired, bought some furniture, and took possession; an incident which would, doubtless, have occasioned some surprise, had not all the senses of the cottagers been benumbed by want and squalid poverty. As it was, I lived ungazed at and unmolested, hardly thanked for the pittance of food and clothes which I gave; so much does suffering blunt even the coarsest sensations of men.

squalidness: filth, disorder.

In this retreat I devoted the morning to labour; but in the evening, when the weather permitted, I walked on the stony beach of the sea, to listen to the waves as they roared and dashed at my feet. It was a monotonous yet ever-changing scene. I thought of Switzerland; it was far different from this desolate and appalling landscape. Its hills are covered with vines, and its cottages are scattered thickly in the plains. Its fair lakes reflect a blue and gentle sky; and when troubled by the winds, their tumult is but as the play of a lively infant, when compared to the roarings of the giant ocean.

In this manner I distributed my occupations when I first arrived; but, as I proceeded in my labour, it became every day more horrible and irksome to me. Sometimes I could not prevail on myself to enter my laboratory for several days; and at other times I toiled day and night in order to complete my work. It was, indeed, a filthy process in which I was engaged. During my first experiment, a kind of enthusiastic frenzy had blinded me to the horror of my employment; my mind was intently fixed on the consummation of my labour, and my eyes were shut to the horror of my proceedings. But now I went to it in cold blood, and my heart often sickened at the work of my hands.

Thus situated, employed in the most detestable occupation, immersed in a solitude where nothing could for an instant call my attention from the actual scene in which I was engaged, my spirits became **unequal**; I grew restless and nervous. Every moment I feared to meet my persecutor. Sometimes I sat with my eyes fixed on the ground, fearing to raise them, lest they should encounter the object which I so much dreaded to behold. I feared to wander from the sight of my fellow-creatures, lest when alone he should come to claim his companion.

unequal: unbalanced.

In the mean time I worked on, and my labour was already considerably advanced. I looked towards its completion with a tremulous and eager hope, which I dared not trust myself to question, but which was intermixed with obscure forebodings of evil, that made my heart sicken in my bosom.

COMMENTARY

At the end of the previous chapter, Victor returns home in a trance-like state both perplexed and disquieted, yet determined to dedicate himself entirely to his new "abhorred task." Surprisingly, his health improves and, although still depressed and apathetic at times, Victor seems to return to his old self. Observing the positive change, but intrigued by his son's frequent moments of melancholy, Victor's father asks him directly if his obligation to marry Elizabeth is the reason for his unhappiness. Victor immediately reassures him that there is no other woman. And yet, when encouraged by his son's words, Alphonse Frankenstein suggests the wedding take place immediately. Victor hesitates and then announces that before the wedding, he wants to visit England. Convinced that the journey will restore Victor completely and pleased that Clerval has agreed to accompany him through Europe, Victor's father consents to the trip, and, at the end of September, Victor leaves Switzerland.

Victor's revulsion at marrying Elizabeth—"the idea of an immediate union with my Elizabeth was one of horror and dismay,"—indicates a rather problematic relationship with her. Critics occasionally interpret this passage as a confirmation of Victor's difficult relationships with women in general and Elizabeth, the woman who indirectly caused the death of his mother, in particular. As the nightmare that Victor had immediately after the creation of the Monster revealed, Victor may indeed feel threatened by Elizabeth's sexuality. He may look at her as the woman who subconsciously wanted to kill his mother in order to possess him exclusively. The kiss with which Victor kills Elizabeth in his dream appears as a way of escaping her devouring sexuality and isolating himself in a world devoid of women. Furthermore, Victor's explanation that he wants to fulfill his promise of creating the female monster and only then "enjoy the delight of a union from which I expected peace," seems rather unconvincing: Victor is perfectly aware of the fact that he will never have peace or be a free man again. "Could I enter into a festival with this deadly weight yet hanging round my neck, and bowing me to the ground?" he asks when he knows very well that the answer is not only "No" but "Never."

This allusion to the Ancient Mariner links Victor to Coleridge's protagonist around whose neck hangs the dead albatross as a reminder of his absurd crime. Like the Mariner, Victor can never be a bridegroom; like the Mariner he is permanently divorced from society and from normal relationships.

There are, however, other interpretations of Victor's rejection of his father's suggestion to marry Elizabeth. One such interpretation may be Victor's perception of Elizabeth as a failure of the female ideal and of the ideal of domesticity: His nightmare revealed not a nurturing, gentle, and pure Elizabeth, but a possessive, competitive, and sexually intense woman who Victor has to kill to protect himself. Also, women confuse Victor. Caroline, his mother, abandoned him, but before her death (one that may appear suspiciously like suicide) she invests Elizabeth with the conflicting function of surrogate mother and prospective bride. Also, Justine, the very image of kindness and generosity, is accused of murdering her siblings and, in prison, her initial confession to a crime that she didn't commit perplexes and disturbs everybody. Finally, Elizabeth, whose function, after Caroline's death, becomes increasingly ambiguous, threatens Victor with her fluidity and ability to so easily change roles.

Critics also suggest that, although alienating and dangerous, Victor's scientific pursuits are much more attractive and rewarding than the prospect of a perfect domestic life like the one embraced by his parents and perpetuated by Elizabeth. His ambition and genius may lead to monstrous creations, but they also encourage a passion for the power of the mind, for invention and discovery. Consequently, these critics see the Monster as Victor's repressed self, as the double who acts out Victor's frustrations with the bondage of domesticity.

Nature and Victor and Clerval

Before his departure for England, Victor orders the instruments necessary for his new task. He travels with Clerval by boat to Rotterdam. The picturesque landscapes along the banks of the Rhine lift Victor's gloomy disposition for a while, but infuse Clerval with an overwhelming happiness.

In his description of Clerval's enthusiasm for the picturesque landscapes surrounding them, Victor invokes Wordsworth's celebrated lines from *Tintern Abbey*. These lines are usually interpreted as the poet's direct connection with nature, which he has temporarily lost but that his beloved sister Dorothy retains. Clerval's Wordsworthian trust in nature prepares the reader for nature's ironic betrayal of Clerval in the next chapter and offers an equally ironic commentary to the famous adage from the same poem, claiming that nature "never did betray / The heart that loved her." The fact that Nature does in fact betray Clerval testifies to its intrinsic ambiguity—nature is both benevolent and destructive—an ambiguity splendidly evoked by Percy Shelley's poem, *Mont Blanc.*

Mary Shelley's concept of nature is very different from the romanticized version embraced by her characters, Victor and Clerval, in these two chapters and other isolated episodes that rhapsodize natural beauties. Again, Mary Shelley distances herself from the optimism of the Romantics and announces the Victorian distrust in a nature that is neither benevolent nor protective, but indifferent and even cruel. Nature's indifference to human lives and its potential monstrosity is even more clearly revealed in the description of the sublime landscapes of the Alps in the novel. Mary Shelley's expedition through these mountains made a strong impression on her and they appear frequently in her journal from those years and in her *History of a Six Weeks' Tour* from 1817. However, the sublime is repeatedly connected with the dangerous and the monstrous in Frankenstein. Almost every time Victor, inspired by the sublimity of nature, invokes its spirit, the Monster appears at a distance or comes to talk to him.

It is useful to compare the passages in Mary Shelley's journal entries and her letters to her sister Fanny Imlay describing the same beautiful natural scenes that Victor and Clerval encounter during their tour through Europe. Her literary model was her mother's work, *Letters written during a Short Residence in Sweden, Norway, and Denmark* (1796), a book that made Godwin fall in love with Mary Wollstonecraft and about which he wrote: "If ever there was a book calculated to make a man in love with its author, this appears to me to be the book." On their trip along the Rhine (Clerval's favorite part of the journey), Percy read aloud from Wollstonecraft's letters to Mary and Jane Clairmont. Like Victor's account of Clerval's enthusiastic response to the beautiful landscapes, Mary Shelley's reactions are complemented by poetry. She reads Byron's description of the Rhine banks in *Childe Harold* (canto II). Like Clerval and unlike Percy (considered by numerous critics to be the model for many aspects of Victor), Mary Shelley is attracted by beautiful rather than sublime landscapes.

Victor and Henry in England

Victor and Clerval remain in England for several months to visit London. While Clerval "desired the intercourse of the men of genius and talent who flourished at this time," Victor was simply interested in gathering the information necessary to complete his project. His encounters with philosophers give him no special pleasure, and unlike Clerval, he is not only indifferent to the richness of cultural and intellectual life around him but also tortured by the enthusiasm of a world to which he no longer belongs.

After almost five months in London, Victor and Clerval receive an invitation to visit a friend in Scotland. The two friends decide to begin their journey towards Scotland at the end of March and tour Windsor, Oxford, and the Cumberland lakes along the way. Oxford produces a strong impression on the two travelers. They visit the tomb of John Hampden (1594–1643), a famous English statesman who raised a regiment when the Civil War began and was mortally wounded in the battle of Charlgrove Field. Critics have suggested that Victor's failed attempt to find in the contemplation of "the divine ideas of liberty and self-sacrifice, of which these sights were the monuments and remembrancers," a remedy for his agonizing sufferings and his strange compassion for "the memory of that unfortunate king and his companions," reflects Mary Shelley's disillusionment with the revolutionary ideals.

After two months in Cumberland and Westmorland, Victor and Clerval spend a week in Edinburgh. Before traveling to Perth where their friend is waiting for them, Victor suddenly announces to Clerval that he wants to tour Scotland alone. Surprised at first, Clerval finally accepts the arrangement and the two friends begin their separate journeys. Fearing the Monster's impatience with his long delay, Victor hastens to one of the most remote Orkney Islands, gathers the necessary instruments, establishes his new laboratory in an isolated cottage, and begins working on creating a female monster. As before, he becomes ill.

Chapter 20 Victor destroys the almost finished body of the new creature and, incensed, the Monster threatens a terrible revenge on Victor's wedding night. While throwing the remains of the unfinished creature into the sea, Victor falls asleep. His boat comes to rest on the shore of a small harbor in Ireland. Here, he is arrested under suspicion of murder.

CHAPTER XX

I sat one evening in my laboratory; the sun had set, and the moon was just rising from the sea; I had not sufficient light for my employment, and I remained idle, in a pause of consideration of whether I should leave my labour for the night, or hasten its conclusion by an unremitting attention to it. As I sat, a train of reflection occurred to me, which led me to consider the effects of what I was now doing. Three years before I was engaged in the same manner, and had created a fiend whose unparalleled barbarity had desolated my heart, and filled it for ever with the bitterest remorse. I was now about to form another being, of whose dispositions I was alike ignorant; she might become ten thousand times more malignant than her mate, and delight, for its own sake, in murder and wretchedness. He had sworn to quit the neighbourhood of man, and hide himself in deserts; but she had not; and she, who in all probability was to become a thinking and reasoning animal, might refuse to comply with a compact made before her creation. They might even hate each other; the creature who already lived loathed his own deformity, and might he not conceive a greater abhorrence for it when it came before his eyes in the female form? She also might turn with disgust from him to the superior beauty of man; she might quit him, and he be again alone, exasperated by the fresh provocation of being deserted by one of his own species.

Even if they were to leave Europe, and inhabit the deserts of the new world, yet one of the first results of those sympathies for which the daemon thirsted would be children, and a race of devils would be propagated upon the earth, who might make the very existence of the species of man a condition **precarious** and full of terror. Had I right, for my own benefit, to inflict this curse upon everlasting generations? I had before been moved by the **sophisms** of the being I had created; I had been struck senseless by his fiendish threats; but now, for the first time, the wickedness of my promise burst upon me; I shuddered to think that future ages might curse me as their pest, whose selfishness had not hesitated to buy its own peace at the price, perhaps, of the existence of the whole human race.

I trembled, and my heart failed within me; when, on looking up, I saw, by the light of the moon, the daemon at the casement. A ghastly grin wrinkled his lips as he gazed on me, where I sat fulfilling the task which he had allotted to me. Yes, he had followed me in my travels; he had loitered in forests, hid himself in caves, or taken refuge in wide and desert

NOTES

precarious: uncertain, unstable.

sophisms: misleading arguments.

heaths; and he now came to mark my progress, and claim the fulfillment of my promise.

As I looked on him, his countenance expressed the utmost extent of malice and treachery. I thought with a sensation of madness on my promise of creating another like to him, and trembling with passion, tore to pieces the thing on which I was engaged. The wretch saw me destroy the creature on whose future existence he depended for happiness, and, with a howl of devilish despair and revenge, withdrew.

I left the room, and, locking the door, made a solemn vow in my own heart never to resume my labours; and then, with trembling steps, I sought my own apartment. I was alone; none were near me to dissipate the gloom, and relieve me from the sickening oppression of the most terrible reveries.

Several hours passed, and I remained near my window gazing on the sea; it was almost motionless, for the winds were hushed, and all nature reposed under the eye of the quiet moon. A few fishing vessels alone specked the water, and now and then the gentle breeze wafted the sound of voices, as the fishermen called to one another. I felt the silence, although I was hardly conscious of its extreme profundity, until my ear was suddenly arrested by the paddling of oars near the shore, and a person landed close to my house.

In a few minutes after, I heard the creaking of my door, as if some one endeavoured to open it softly. I trembled from head to foot; I felt a presentiment of who it was, and wished to rouse one of the peasants who dwelt in a cottage not far from mine; but I was overcome by the sensation of helplessness, so often felt in frightful dreams, when you in vain endeavour to fly from an impending danger, and was rooted to the spot.

Presently I heard the sound of footsteps along the passage; the door opened, and the wretch whom I dreaded appeared. Shutting the door, he approached me, and said, in a smothered voice—

"You have destroyed the work which you began; what is it that you intend? Do you dare to break your promise? I have endured toil and misery: I left Switzerland with you; I crept along the shores of the Rhine, among its willow islands and over the summits of its hills. I have dwelt many months in the heaths of England, and among the deserts of Scotland. I have endured incalculable fatigue, and cold, and hunger; do you dare destroy my hopes?"

"Begone! I do break my promise; never will I create another like yourself, equal in deformity and wickedness."

"Slave, I before reasoned with you, but you have proved yourself unworthy of my condescension. Remember that I have power; you believe yourself miserable, but I can make you so wretched that the light of day will be hateful to you. You are my creator, but I am your master;—obey!"

"The hour of my irresolution is past, and the **period** of your power is arrived. Your threats cannot move me to do an act of wickedness; but they confirm me in a determination of not creating you a companion in

period: end.

vice. Shall I, in cool blood, set loose upon the earth a daemon, whose delight is in death and wretchedness? Begone! I am firm, and your words will only **exasperate** my rage."

exasperate: increase, exacerbate.

The monster saw my determination in my face, and gnashed his teeth in the impotence of anger. "Shall each man," cried he, "find a wife for his bosom, and each beast have his mate, and I be alone? I had feelings of affection, and they were requited by detestation and scorn. Man! you may hate; but beware! your hours will pass in dread and misery, and soon the bolt will fall which must ravish from you your happiness for ever. Are you to be happy, while I grovel in the intensity of my wretchedness? You can blast my other passions; but revenge remains—revenge, henceforth dearer than light or food! I may die; but first you, my tyrant and tormentor, shall curse the sun that gazes on your misery. Beware; for I am fearless, and therefore powerful. I will watch with the wiliness of a snake, that I may sting with its venom. Man, you shall repent of the injuries you inflict."

"Devil, cease; and do not poison the air with these sounds of malice. I have declared my resolution to you, and I am no coward to bend beneath words. Leave me; I am inexorable."

"It is well. I go; but remember, I shall be with you on your wedding-night."

I started forward, and exclaimed, "Villain! before you sign my death-warrant, be sure that you are yourself safe."

I would have seized him; but he eluded me, and quitted the house with precipitation. In a few moments I saw him in his boat, which shot across the waters with an arrowy swiftness, and was soon lost amidst the waves.

All was again silent; but his words rang in my ears. I burned with rage to pursue the murderer of my peace, and precipitate him into the ocean. I walked up and down my room hastily and perturbed, while my imagination conjured up a thousand images to torment and sting me. Why had I not followed him, and **closed with him** in mortal strife? But I had suffered him to depart, and he had directed his course towards the main land. I shuddered to think who might be the next victim sacrificed to his insatiate revenge. And then I thought again of his words—"*I will be with you on your wedding-night.*" That, then was the period fixed for the fulfillment of my destiny. In that hour I should die, and at once satisfy and extinguish his malice. The prospect did not move me to fear; yet when I thought of my beloved Elizabeth,—of her tears and endless sorrow, when she should find her lover so barbarously snatched from her,—tears, the first I had shed for many months, streamed from my eyes, and I resolved not to fall before my enemy without a bitter struggle.

closed with him: fought with him.

The night passed away, and the sun rose from the ocean; my feelings became calmer, if it may be called calmness, when the violence of rage sinks into the depths of despair. I left the house, the horrid scene of the last night's contention, and walked on the beach of the sea, which I almost regarded as an **insuperable** barrier between me and my fellow-creatures; nay, a wish that such should prove the fact stole across me. I

insuperable: insurmountable.

desired that I might pass my life on that barren rock, wearily, it is true, but uninterrupted by any sudden shock of misery. If I returned, it was to be sacrificed, or to see those whom I most loved die under the grasp of a daemon whom I had myself created.

I walked about the isle like a restless spectre, separated from all it loved, and miserable in the separation. When it became noon, and the sun rose higher, I lay down on the grass, and was overpowered by a deep sleep. I had been awake the whole of the preceding night, my nerves were agitated, and my eyes inflamed by watching and misery. The sleep into which I now sank refreshed me; and when I awoke, I again felt as if I belonged to a race of human beings like myself, and I began to reflect upon what had passed with greater composure; yet still the words of the fiend rang in my ears like a death-knell; they appeared like a dream, yet distinct and oppressive as a reality.

The sun had far descended, and I still sat on the shore, satisfying my appetite, which had become **ravenous**, with an oaten cake, when I saw a fishing-boat land close to me, and one of the men brought me a packet; it contained letters from Geneva, and one from Clerval entreating me to join him. He said that he was wearing away his time fruitlessly where he was; that letters from the friends he had formed in London desired his return to complete the negotiation they had entered into for his Indian enterprise. He could not any longer delay his departure; but as his journey to London might be followed, even sooner than he now conjectured, by his longer voyage, he entreated me to bestow as much of my society on him as I could spare. He besought me, therefore, to leave my solitary isle, and to meet him at **Perth**, that we might proceed southwards together. This letter in a degree recalled me to life, and I determined to quit my island at the expiration of two days.

Yet, before I departed, there was a task to perform, on which I shuddered to reflect: I must pack up my chemical instruments; and for that purpose I must enter the room which had been the scene of my odious work, and I must handle those utensils, the sight of which was sickening to me. The next morning, at daybreak, I summoned sufficient courage, and unlocked the door of my laboratory. The remains of the half-finished creature, whom I had destroyed, lay scattered on the floor, and I almost felt as if I had mangled the living flesh of a human being. I paused to collect myself, and then entered the chamber. With trembling hand I conveyed the instruments out of the room; but I reflected that I ought not to leave **the relics** of my work to excite the horror and suspicion of the peasants; and I accordingly put them into a basket, with a great quantity of stones, and, laying them up, determined to throw them into the sea that very night; and in the meantime I sat upon the beach, employed in cleaning and arranging my chemical apparatus.

Nothing could be more complete than the alteration that had taken place in my feelings since the night of the appearance of the daemon. I had before regarded my promise with a gloomy despair, as a thing that, with whatever consequences, must be fulfilled; but I now felt as if a film had

ravenous: insatiable, voracious.

Perth: small town in Scotland, north of Edinburgh and Glasgow.

relics: the remains; the equipment.

been taken from before my eyes, and that I, for the first time, saw clearly. The idea of renewing my labours did not for one instant occur to me; the threat I had heard weighed on my thoughts, but I did not reflect that a voluntary act of mine could avert it. I had resolved in my own mind, that to create another like the fiend I had first made would be an act of the basest and most atrocious selfishness; and I banished from my mind every thought that could lead to a different conclusion.

Between two and three in the morning the moon rose; and I then, putting my basket aboard a little skiff, sailed out about four miles from the shore. The scene was perfectly solitary: a few boats were returning towards land, but I sailed away from them. I felt as if I was about the commission of a dreadful crime, and avoided with shuddering anxiety any encounter with my fellow-creatures. At one time the moon, which had before been clear, was suddenly overspread by a thick cloud, and I took advantage of the moment of darkness, and cast my basket into the sea: I listened to the gurgling sound as it sunk, and then sailed away from the spot. The sky became clouded; but the air was pure, although chilled by the north-east breeze that was then rising. But it refreshed me, and filled me with such agreeable sensations, that I resolved to prolong my stay on the water; and, fixing the rudder in a direct position, stretched myself at the bottom of the boat. Clouds hid the moon, every thing was obscure, and I heard only the sound of the boat, as its keel cut through the waves; the murmur lulled me, and in a short time I slept soundly.

I do not know how long I remained in this situation, but when I awoke I found that the sun had already mounted considerably. The wind was high, and the waves continually threatened the safety of my little skiff. I found that the wind was north-east, and must have driven me far from the coast from which I had embarked. I endeavoured to change my course, but quickly found that, if I again made the attempt, the boat would be instantly filled with water. Thus situated, my only resource was to drive before the wind. I confess that I felt a few sensations of terror. I had no compass with me, and was so slenderly acquainted with the geography of this part of the world, that the sun was of little benefit to me. I might be driven into the wide Atlantic, and feel all the tortures of starvation, or be swallowed up in the immeasurable waters that roared and buffeted around me. I had already been out many hours, and felt **the torment of a burning thirst**, a prelude to my other sufferings. I looked on the heavens, which were covered by clouds that flew before the wind, only to be replaced by others; I looked upon the sea, it was to be my grave. "Fiend," I exclaimed, "your task is already fulfilled!" I thought of Elizabeth, of my father, and of Clerval; all left behind, on whom the monster might satisfy his sanguinary and merciless passions. This idea plunged me into a **reverie**, so despairing and frightful, that even now, when the scene is on the point of closing before me forever, I shudder to reflect on it.

Some hours passed thus; but by degrees, as the sun declined towards the horizon, the wind died away into a gentle breeze and the sea became free

torment of a burning thirst: allusion to a line in Coleridge's *Ancient Mariner:* "Water, water, every where / And all the boards did shrink; / Water, water, every where, / Nor any drop to drink."

reverie: daydream, trance. Here, the reverie has nightmarish connotations.

from breakers. But these gave place to a heavy swell: I felt sick, and hardly able to hold the rudder, when suddenly I saw a line of high land towards the south.

Almost spent, as I was, by fatigue and the dreadful suspense I endured for several hours, this sudden certainty of life rushed like a flood of warm joy to my heart, and tears gushed from my eyes.

How **mutable** are our feelings, and how strange is that clinging love we have of life even in the excess of misery! I constructed another sail with a part of my dress, and eagerly steered my course towards the land. It had a wild and rocky appearance; but, as I approached nearer, I easily perceived the traces of cultivation. I saw vessels near the shore, and found myself suddenly transported back to the neighbourhood of civilised man. I carefully traced the windings of the land, and hailed a steeple which I at length saw issuing from behind a small promontory. As I was in a state of extreme **debility**, I resolved to sail directly towards the town, as a place where I could most easily procure nourishment. Fortunately I had money with me. As I turned the promontory, I perceived a small, neat town and a good harbour, which I entered, my heart bounding with joy at my unexpected escape.

mutable: changeable, variable.

debility: weakness, feebleness, incapacity.

As I was occupied in fixing the boat and arranging the sails, several people crowded towards the spot. They seemed much surprised at my appearance; but, instead of offering me any assistance, whispered together with gestures that at any other time might have produced in me a slight sensation of alarm. As it was, I merely remarked that they spoke English; and I therefore addressed them in that language: "My good friends," said I, "will you be so kind as to tell me the name of this town, and inform me where I am?"

"You will know that soon enough," replied a man with a hoarse voice. "May be you are come to a place that will not prove much to your taste; but you will not be consulted as to your quarters, I promise you."

I was exceedingly surprised on receiving so rude an answer from a stranger; and I was also disconcerted on perceiving the frowning and angry countenances of his companions. "Why do you answer me so roughly?" I replied; "surely it is not the custom of Englishmen to receive strangers so inhospitably."

"I do not know," said the man, "what the custom of the English may be; but it is the custom of the Irish to hate villains."

While this strange dialogue continued, I perceived the crowd rapidly increase. Their faces expressed a mixture of curiosity and anger, which annoyed, and in some degree alarmed me. I enquired the way to the inn; but no one replied. I then moved forward, and a murmuring sound arose from the crowd as they followed and surrounded me; when an ill-looking man approached, tapped me on the shoulder, and said, "Come, sir, you must follow me to Mr. Kirwin's, to give an account of yourself."

"Who is Mr. Kirwin? Why am I to give an account of myself? Is not this a free country?"

"Ay, sir, free enough for honest folks. Mr. Kirwin is a magistrate; and you are to give an account of the death of a gentleman who was found murdered here last night."

This answer startled me; but I presently recovered myself. I was innocent; that could easily be proved: accordingly I followed my conductor in silence, and was led to one of the best houses in the town. I was ready to sink from fatigue and hunger; but, being surrounded by a crowd, I thought it politic to rouse all my strength, that no physical debility might be construed into apprehension or conscious guilt. Little did I then expect the calamity that was in a few moments to overwhelm me, and extinguish in horror and despair all fear of ignominy or death.

I must pause here, for it requires all my fortitude to recall the memory of the frightful events which I am about to relate, in proper detail, to my recollection.

COMMENTARY

The chapter opens with Victor in his laboratory meditating on the imminent "effects" of the creation of a female monster. The rising moon—traditionally associated with women, ebb tide, and change—intensifies the enigmatic atmosphere of the opening lines and prepares the reader for the dramatic shift in Victor's plans. One by one, Victor determines the most threatening consequences resulting from the creation of a female monster. He decides that she may be less moral than her mate and even refuse to abide with the plan to live isolated from humanity as the Monster promised. Finally, an increasingly alarmed Victor observes, she may want to have children and breed "a race of devils." Terrified at the thought of such dark prospects, Victor destroys the almost finished body of the new creature.

Victor's Fear of the Feminine

Victor's fears of a race of monsters spring from the same anxiety about women and female sexuality that made him reject Elizabeth in the previous chapter. The fact that he speaks about a female Monster and not about a real female allows him to express his true feelings, fears, and obsessions about women in a way that he never could about Elizabeth, his prospective wife.

Victor's rationalization indicates that he is frightened by female will and female desires, appetites, and independence. As one whose most passionate dream was to usurp woman's procreative role, Victor is simply unwilling to admit that women can openly affirm their aspirations, fantasies, and passions. Also, the thought of women choosing their own partners seems particularly dangerous to Victor—this autonomy threatens man's right of property over women. Moreover, Victor concludes that by choosing freely, women may acquire (to him, monstrous) powers that place them in a position of ascendancy, one of controlling and even abusing men. (The possibility of female monsters having intercourse with men implies male rape to Victor.)

Victor's description of his unfinished female as potentially "ten thousand times more malignant," than the male Monster and as capable of murdering and inflicting suffering on others out of sheer pleasure, reinforces a long tradition that sees women as fundamentally evil, predatory, and destructive. But, above anything else, Victor fears the female Monster's reproductive powers, especially her capacity to beget more monsters—the very opposite of the superior beings he dreamt of fathering and whose adored patriarch he so much wanted to become.

Defeated in his plans to create a new world ruled exclusively by men, where women are simply instruments of pleasure, Victor decides to destroy the female monster, in order to give his male Monster a justification for the destruction of Elizabeth, the other potential mother of children and the last female character in the novel.

Men and Technology

Mary Shelley uses Victor's hostility toward women and his fear of female sexuality as a vehicle to reflect on the terrifying consequences of men's use of technology. Victor's meditation from the opening segment regarding the potential harm inherent in the creation of a female monster transforms almost unnoticeably into the author's reflection on male monstrosity and the potentially dangerous use men make of science and technology. An interesting detail supports this analysis: The word "sophisms" that Victor uses to characterize the Monster's request for his own Eve: "I had before been moved by the sophisms of the being I had created;" (*sophists*, unlike *philosophers*, are not interested in discovering and affirming the truth but rather in persuading an audience, and in winning a debate at any cost).

If the Monster's arguments are false or misleading as Victor maintains, then, by destroying the female Monster he restores the "truth"; the truth of patriarchy, which declares women evil, marginalizes, and silences them.

The Monster's Vow

After the destruction of the female monster, Victor returns to his house, closing behind him the door to his messy laboratory and promising never to return to his "filthy work." A feeling of absolute loneliness overwhelms him. Indeed, Victor, who has left his father's house to isolate himself on a remote island, rejected Elizabeth, his lover, and separated from Clerval, his best friend, is now completely disconnected from the outside world and tormented by the painful silence around him. He stands at a window, gazing at the water, the primordial element over which the spirit of God moved at the beginning of the creation. But unlike God, there are no creative impulses in Victor. Unlike God, he cannot summon the light to dissipate the darkness around him. Unlike God, Victor is a fallen deity who has abandoned and destroyed his creations. At the end of his alleged creative acts he could never say, like the God he wanted to usurp, that his actions were "good."

Alone and exhausted, Victor hears the voices of the fishermen calling each other but there is nobody calling him. All he can feel is an overwhelming silence: "I felt the silence, although, I was hardly conscious of its extreme profundity." Soon, however, he hears the sound of footsteps and, indeed, before long the Monster opens the door of Victor's cottage and, suffocated by emotion, reminds Victor that he promised the Monster the love and comfort of a female companion. When Victor announces that he has broken his promise, the heretofore submissive creature reassumes the role of the master and orders Victor to obey him.

As long as Victor kept his promise and acted as a responsible creator, the Monster was willing to resume his initial role of the obedient creature. However, as soon as Victor's rebellion destroys his only hope for companionship, the Monster renews his threats and promises Victor that a terrible punishment will fall upon him on his wedding night. Then the angry Monster escapes by sea.

Clerval's Letter

After receiving a letter from Clerval, announcing his imminent departure for India, Victor decides to quit the island and go immediately to London to meet his friend. Before his departure, Victor collects the remains of the unfinished creature, puts them into a basket, and sails out at night to throw them into the sea. Exhausted by these actions, Victor loses consciousness, a storm blows up, and his boat is blown off course and carried to the shore of a small seaport in Ireland. To his astonishment, Victor is arrested for the murder of a young gentleman found dead on the shore.

The Monster enters the cottage.
Everett Collection

Chapter 21

At the sight of Henry Clerval's dead body, Victor becomes violently ill. He's nursed in prison by a competent but hostile nurse. An unexpected visit by his father accelerates Victor's recovery. Released for lack of evidence, Victor and his father sail back to Geneva.

CHAPTER XXI

I was soon introduced into the presence of the magistrate, an old benevolent man, with calm and mild manners. He looked upon me, however, with some degree of severity, and then, turning towards my conductors, he asked who appeared as witnesses on this occasion.

About half a dozen men came forward; and, one being selected by the magistrate, he deposed, that he had been out fishing the night before with his son and brother-in-law, Daniel Nugent, when, about ten o'clock, they observed a strong northerly blast rising, and they accordingly put in for port. It was a very dark night, as the moon had not yet risen; they did not land at the harbour, but, as they had been accustomed, at a creek about two miles below. He walked on first, carrying a part of the **fishing tackle**, and his companions followed him at some distance. As he was proceeding along the sands, he struck his foot against something, and fell at his length on the ground. His companions came up to assist him; and, by the light of their lantern, they found that he had fallen on the body of a man, who was to all appearance dead. Their first supposition was, that it was the corpse of some person who had been drowned, and was thrown on shore by the waves; but, on examination, they found that the clothes were not wet, and even that the body was not then cold. They instantly carried it to the cottage of an old woman near the spot, and endeavoured, but in vain, to restore it to life. It appeared to be a handsome young man, about five and twenty years of age. He had apparently been strangled; for there was no sign of any violence, except the black mark of fingers on his neck.

The first part of this deposition did not in the least interest me; but when the mark of the fingers was mentioned, I remembered the murder of my brother, and felt myself extremely agitated; my limbs trembled, and a mist came over my eyes, which obliged me to lean on a chair for support. The magistrate observed me with a keen eye, and of course drew an unfavourable **augury** from my manner.

The son confirmed his father's account: but when Daniel Nugent was called, he swore positively that, just before the fall of his companion, he saw a boat, with a single man in it, at a short distance from the shore; and, as far as he could judge by the light of a few stars, it was the same boat in which I had just landed.

A woman deposed that she lived near the beach, and was standing at the door of her cottage, waiting for the return of the fishermen, about an hour before she heard of the discovery of the body, when she saw a boat,

NOTES

fishing tackle: fishing equipment.

augury: prognostication; interpretation.

with only one man in it, push off from that part of the shore where the corpse was afterwards found.

Another woman confirmed the account of the fishermen having brought the body into her house; it was not cold. They put it into a bed, and rubbed it; and Daniel went to the town for an **apothecary**, but life was quite gone.

apothecary: pharmacist.

Several other men were examined concerning my landing; and they agreed, that, with the strong north wind that had arisen during the night, it was very probable that I had beaten about for many hours, and had been obliged to return nearly to the same spot from which I had departed. Besides, they observed that it appeared that I had brought the body from another place, and it was likely, that as I did not appear to know the shore, I might have put into the harbour ignorant of the distance of the town of * * * from the place where I had deposited the corpse.

Mr. Kirwin, on hearing this evidence, desired that I should be taken into the room where the body lay for interment, that it might be observed what effect the sight of it would produce upon me. This idea was probably suggested by the extreme agitation I had exhibited when the mode of the murder had been described. I was accordingly conducted, by the magistrate and several other persons, to the inn. I could not help being struck by the strange coincidences that had taken place during this eventful night; but, knowing that I had been conversing with several persons in the island I had inhabited about the time that the body had been found, I was perfectly tranquil as to the consequences of the affair.

I entered the room where the corpse lay, and was led up to the coffin. How can I describe my sensations on beholding it? I feel yet parched with horror, nor can I reflect on that terrible moment without shuddering and agony. The examination, the presence of the magistrate and witnesses, passed like a dream from my memory, when I saw the lifeless form of Henry Clerval stretched before me. I gasped for breath; and, throwing myself on the body, I exclaimed, "Have my murderous machinations deprived you also, my dearest Henry, of life? Two I have already destroyed; other victims await their destiny: but you, Clerval, my friend, my benefactor—"

The human frame could no longer support the agonies that I endured, and I was carried out of the room in strong convulsions.

A fever succeeded to this. I lay for two months on the point of death: my ravings, as I afterwards heard, were frightful; I called myself the murderer of William, of Justine, and of Clerval. Sometimes I entreated my attendants to assist me in the destruction of the fiend by whom I was tormented; and at others I felt the fingers of the monster already grasping my neck, and screamed aloud with agony and terror. Fortunately, as I spoke my native language, Mr. Kirwin alone understood me; but my gestures and bitter cries were sufficient to affright the other witnesses.

Why did I not die? More miserable than man ever was before, why did I not sink into forgetfulness and rest? Death snatches away many blooming children, the only hopes of their doating parents: how many brides and youthful lovers have been one day in the bloom of health and hope, and the next a prey for worms and the decay of the tomb! Of what materials was I made, that I could thus resist so many shocks, which, like the turning of the wheel, continually renewed the torture?

But I was doomed to live; and in two months, found myself as awaking from a dream, in a prison, stretched on a wretched bed, surrounded by **gaolers**, turnkeys, bolts, and all the miserable apparatus of a dungeon. It was morning, I remember, when I thus awoke to understanding: I had forgotten the particulars of what had happened, and only felt as if some great misfortune had suddenly overwhelmed me; but when I looked around, and saw the barred windows, and the squalidness of the room in which I was, all flashed across my memory and I groaned bitterly.

gaolers: jailers.

This sound disturbed an old woman who was sleeping in a chair beside me. She was a hired nurse, the wife of one of the turnkeys, and her countenance expressed all those bad qualities which often characterise that class. The lines of her face were hard and rude, like that of persons accustomed to see without sympathising in sights of misery. Her tone expressed her entire indifference; she addressed me in English, and the voice struck me as one that I had heard during my sufferings:—

"Are you better now, sir?" said she.

I replied in the same language, with a feeble voice, "I believe I am; but if it be all true, if indeed I did not dream, I am sorry that I am still alive to feel this misery and horror."

"For that matter," replied the old woman, "if you mean about the gentleman you murdered, I believe that it were better for you if you were dead, for I fancy it will go hard with you! However, that's none of my business; I am sent to nurse you, and get you well; I do my duty with a safe conscience; it were well if every body did the same."

I turned with loathing from the woman who could utter so unfeeling a speech to a person just saved, on the very edge of death; but I felt **languid**, and unable to reflect on all that had passed. The whole series of my life appeared to me as a dream; I sometimes doubted if indeed it were all true, for it never presented itself to my mind with the force of reality.

languid: exhausted, lethargic.

As the images that floated before me became more distinct, I grew feverish; a darkness pressed around me: no one was near me who soothed me with the gentle voice of love; no dear hand supported me. The physician came and prescribed medicines, and the old woman prepared them for me; but utter carelessness was visible in the first, and the expression of brutality was strongly marked in the visage of the second. Who could be interested in the fate of a murderer, but the hangman who would gain his fee?

These were my first reflections; but I soon learned that Mr. Kirwin had shown me extreme kindness. He had caused the best room in the prison to be prepared for me (wretched indeed was the best); and it was he who had provided a physician and a nurse. It is true, he seldom came to see me; for, although he ardently desired to relieve the sufferings of every human creature, he did not wish to be present at the agonies and miserable ravings of a murderer. He came, therefore, sometimes, to see that I was not neglected; but his visits were short and with long intervals.

One day, while I was gradually recovering, I was seated in a chair, my eyes half open, and my cheeks livid like those in death. I was overcome by gloom and misery, and often reflected I had better seek death than desire to remain in a world which to me was replete with wretchedness. At one time I considered whether I should not declare myself guilty and suffer the penalty of the law, less innocent than poor Justine had been. Such were my thoughts, when the door of my apartment was opened, and Mr. Kirwin entered. His countenance expressed sympathy and compassion; he drew a chair close to mine, and addressed me in French—"I fear that this place is very shocking to you; can I do anything to make you more comfortable?"

"I thank you; but all that you mention is nothing to me: on the whole earth there is no comfort which I am capable of receiving."

"I know that the sympathy of a stranger can be but of little relief to one borne down as you are by so strange a misfortune. But you will, I hope, soon quit this melancholy abode; for, doubtless evidence can easily be brought to free you from the criminal charge."

"That is my least concern: I am, by a course of strange events, become the most miserable of mortals. Persecuted and tortured as I am and have been, can death be any evil to me?"

"Nothing indeed could be more unfortunate and agonising than the strange chances that have lately occurred. You were thrown, by some surprising accident, on this shore, renowned for its hospitality; seized immediately, and charged with murder. The first sight that was presented to your eyes was the body of your friend, murdered in so unaccountable a manner and placed, as it were, by some fiend across your path."

As Mr. Kirwin said this, notwithstanding the agitation I endured on this retrospect of my sufferings, I also felt considerable surprise at the knowledge he seemed to possess concerning me. I suppose some astonishment was exhibited in my countenance; for Mr. Kirwin hastened to say—

"Immediately upon your being taken ill, all the papers that were on your person were brought me, and I examined them that I might discover some trace by which I could send to your relations an account of your misfortune and illness. I found several letters, and, among others, one which I discovered from its commencement to be from your father. I instantly wrote to Geneva: nearly two months have elapsed since the departure of my letter.—But you are ill; even now you tremble: you are unfit for agitation of any kind."

"This suspense is a thousand times worse than the most horrible event: tell me what new scene of death has been acted, and whose murder I am now to lament?"

"Your family is perfectly well," said Mr. Kirwin with gentleness; "and some one, a friend, is come to visit you."

I know not by what chain of thought the idea presented itself, but it instantly darted into my mind that the murderer had come to mock at my misery, and taunt me with the death of Clerval, as a new **incitement** for me to comply with his hellish desires. I put my hand before my eyes, and cried out in agony—

incitement: stimulus, incentive (ironic).

"Oh! take him away! I cannot see him; for God's sake, do not let him enter!"

Mr. Kirwin regarded me with a troubled countenance. He could not help regarding my exclamation as a presumption of my guilt, and said, in rather a severe tone—

"I should have thought, young man, that the presence of your father would have been welcome, instead of inspiring such violent repugnance."

"My father!" cried I, while every feature and every muscle was relaxed from anguish to pleasure: "is my father indeed come? How kind, how very kind! But where is he, why does he not hasten to me?"

My change of manner surprised and pleased the magistrate; perhaps he thought that my former exclamation was a momentary return of **delirium**, and now he instantly resumed his former benevolence. He rose and quitted the room with my nurse, and in a moment my father entered it.

delirium: hallucination.

Nothing, at this moment, could have given me greater pleasure than the arrival of my father. I stretched out my hand to him and cried—"Are you then safe—and Elizabeth—and Ernest?"

My father calmed me with assurances of their welfare, and endeavoured, by dwelling on these subjects so interesting to my heart, to raise my desponding spirits; but he soon felt that a prison cannot be the abode of cheerfulness. "What a place is this that you inhabit, my son!" said he, looking mournfully at the barred windows and wretched appearance of the room. "You travelled to seek happiness, but a fatality seems to pursue you. And poor Clerval—"

The name of my unfortunate and murdered friend was an agitation too great to be endured in my weak state; I shed tears.

"Alas! yes, my father," replied I; "some destiny of the most horrible kind hangs over me, and I must live to fulfil it, or surely I should have died on the coffin of Henry."

We were not allowed to converse for any length of time, for the precarious state of my health rendered every precaution necessary that could ensure tranquillity. Mr. Kirwin came in, and insisted that my strength should not be exhausted by too much exertion. But the appearance of my father was to me like that of my good angel, and I gradually recovered my health.

As my sickness quitted me, I was absorbed by a gloomy and black melancholy, that nothing could dissipate. The image of Clerval was for ever before me, ghastly and murdered. More than once the agitation into which these reflections threw me made my friends dread a dangerous relapse. Alas! why did they preserve so miserable and detested a life? It was surely that I might fulfil my destiny, which is now drawing to a close. Soon, oh! very soon, will death extinguish these throbbings, and relieve me from the mighty weight of anguish that bears me to the dust; and, in executing the award of justice, I shall also sink to rest. Then the appearance of death was distant, although the wish was ever present to my thoughts; and I often sat for hours motionless and speechless, wishing for some mighty revolution that might bury me and my destroyer in its ruins.

The season of the **assizes** approached. I had already been three months in prison; and although I was still weak, and in continual danger of a relapse, I was obliged to travel nearly a hundred miles to the country-town where the court was held. Mr. Kirwin charged himself with every care of collecting witnesses, and arranging my defence. I was spared the disgrace of appearing publicly as a criminal, as the case was not brought before the court that decides on life and death. The grand jury rejected the bill, on its being proved that I was on the Orkney Islands at the hour the body of my friend was found; and a fortnight after my removal I was liberated from prison.

My father was **enraptured** on finding me freed from the vexations of a criminal charge, that I was again allowed to breathe the fresh atmosphere, and permitted to return to my native country. I did not participate in these feelings; for to me the walls of a dungeon or a palace were alike hateful. The cup of life was poisoned for ever, and, although the sun shone upon me, as upon the happy and gay of heart, I saw around me nothing but a dense and frightful darkness, penetrated by no light but the glimmer of **two eyes that glared upon me**. Sometimes they were the expressive eyes of Henry, languishing in death, the dark orbs nearly covered by the lids, and the long black lashes that fringed them; sometimes it was the watery, clouded eyes of the monster, as I first saw them in my chamber at Ingolstadt.

My father tried to awaken in me the feelings of affection. He talked of Geneva, which I should soon visit—of Elizabeth and Ernest; but these words only drew deep groans from me. Sometimes, indeed, I felt a wish for happiness; and thought, with melancholy delight, of my beloved cousin; or longed, with a devouring **maladie du pays**, to see once more the blue lake and rapid Rhone, that had been so dear to me in early childhood: but my general state of feeling was a torpor, in which a prison was as welcome a residence as the divinest scene in nature; and these fits were seldom interrupted but by paroxysms of anguish and despair. At these moments I often endeavoured to put an end to the existence I loathed; and it required unceasing attendance and vigilance to restrain me from committing some dreadful act of violence.

Yet one duty remained to me, the recollection of which finally triumphed over my selfish despair. It was necessary that I should return without delay to Geneva, there to watch over the lives of those I so fondly loved; and to lie in wait for the murderer, that if any chance led me to the place of his concealment, or if he dared again to blast me by his presence, I might, with unfailing aim, put an end to the existence of the monstrous

assizes: court sessions held three or four times a year in each English county. In Scotch law, an assize is a jury trial of a criminal case.

enraptured: ecstatic, overjoyed.

two eyes that glared upon me: an allusion to Percy Shelley's *"Alastor"*—two eyes, / Two starry eyes, hung in the gloom of thought."

maladie du pays: homesickness.

Image which I had endued with the mockery of a soul still more monstrous. My father still desired to delay our departure, fearful that I could not sustain the fatigues of a journey: for I was a shattered wreck,—the shadow of a human being. My strength was gone. I was a mere skeleton; and fever night and day preyed upon my wasted frame.

Still, as I urged our leaving Ireland with such inquietude and impatience, my father thought it best to yield. We took our passage on board a vessel bound for Havre-de-Grace, and sailed with a fair wind from the Irish shores. It was midnight. I lay on the deck, looking at the stars, and listening to the dashing of the waves. I hailed the darkness that shut Ireland from my sight; and my pulse beat with a feverish joy when I reflected that I should soon see Geneva. The past appeared to me in the light of a frightful dream; yet the vessel in which I was, the wind that blew me from the detested shore of Ireland, and the sea which surrounded me, told me too forcibly that I was deceived by no vision, and that Clerval, my friend and dearest companion, had fallen a victim to me and the monster of my creation. I repassed, in my memory, my whole life; my quiet happiness while residing with my family in Geneva, the death of my mother, and my departure for Ingolstadt. I remembered, shuddering, the mad enthusiasm that hurried me on to the creation of my hideous enemy, and I called to mind the night in which he first lived. I was unable to pursue the train of thought; a thousand feelings pressed upon me, and I wept bitterly.

Ever since my recovery from the fever, I had been in the custom of taking every night a small quantity of **laudanum**; for it was by means of this drug only that I was enabled to gain the rest necessary for the preservation of life. Oppressed by the recollection of my various misfortunes, I now swallowed double my usual quantity, and soon slept profoundly. But sleep did not afford me respite from thought and misery; my dreams presented a thousand objects that scared me. Towards morning I was possessed by a kind of night-mare; I felt the fiend's grasp in my neck, and could not free myself from it; groans and cries rung in my ears. My father, who was watching over me, perceiving my restlessness, awoke me; the dashing waves were around: the cloudy sky above; the fiend was not here: a sense of security, a feeling that a truce was established between the present hour and the irresistible, disastrous future, imparted to me a kind of calm forgetfulness, of which the human mind is by its structure peculiarly susceptible.

laudanum: a solution of opium in alcohol. This drug was used frequently by some famous Romantic writers, including Coleridge.

COMMENTARY

The body of a young man, about 25 years old, was found dead on the beach and Victor Frankenstein is accused of the crime. Witnesses testify that the previous night, after finding the body of the young man, they observed a lone man in a boat similar to Victor's. Moreover, the mention of the finger marks on the victim's neck and Victor's strong reaction to this detail (which brings his brother's murder to mind) leads the magistrate to suspect that Victor is guilty of the crime. Victor is taken to view the body. Mr. Kirwin, the magistrate, hopes to use Victor's reaction to the sight of the dead body as evidence of his guilt. Victor's reaction, however, is much stronger than even Mr. Kirwin anticipated and encourages the magistrate to consider the case more carefully. When Victor sees that the young man found dead is his best friend, Clerval, he throws himself on the body and surprisingly refers to "murderous machinations" that destroyed not only his friend but other victims as well. Overwhelmed, Victor collapses and remains in a delirious state for two months.

Victor, the Monster, and Articulation

In this segment, Victor again comes across as selfish and narcissistic. Even the death of his best friend doesn't wake him up and, instead of revealing the truth, he continues to keep silent, still believing that this silence will protect his loved ones. Readers may be frustrated with Victor's decision to conceal the truth, a decision that leads to one tragedy after another. Victor's continual silence is indeed puzzling. It may be, as several critics argue, that Victor and the Monster are indeed doubles, and that the Monster acts out a hideous, terrifying side of Victor. Interestingly, one can observe in all the final chapters, but particularly in this one, that as the Monster grows increasingly articulate, Victor grows increasingly inarticulate. What really happens is that Victor "raves" for two months and experiences what the Monster initially endured: the inability to articulate and to communicate. Like the Monster, he has been reduced to "gestures" and "cries"—a very primal language. Like the Monster, he experiences the anguish and the isolation created by this lack of communication. But while the Monster was the victim of circumstances—abandoned, deprived of an education, a loving family, and a nurturing presence—Victor becomes dehumanized by his own inability to connect with other people and is now trapped in his self-obsessed thinking.

Victor's Imprisonment

Two months later, Victor regains consciousness and finds himself a prisoner. The nurse hired to care for Victor shows no signs of compassion for him. Convinced that he is indeed Clerval's murderer, she performs her duty in a detached, even hostile, manner. Instead of a sympathetic attitude and a kind, friendly word, she expresses animosity toward Victor and declares that it would be better if he'd died, "for I fancy it will go hard with you."

Finding himself a prisoner, Victor degenerates even further into an animal-like state, emitting cries of anguish. The contrast between his supposed return to physical health is obviously at variance with his deteriorating emotional state. Ironically, the nurse hired to assist in the healing process, does just the opposite, enforcing his emotional pain. She is cold and even cruel. This lack of compassion, coming from somebody whose "duty" is not to pass judgment but to manifest kindness and alleviate sufferings, also forces Victor to experience the same isolation, the same painful loneliness that the Monster so many times endured. And yet, Victor selfishly remains focused on his own afflictions, on his own anguish and anxiety. Not even for a moment does Victor associate his isolation and pain to the isolation and the pain of his creature. Incapable of moving beyond his own problems, Victor is indeed a prisoner. Not the prisoner of a dungeon that he will eventually escape (ironically, the innocent Justine didn't find a compassionate and generous Mr. Kirwin as the guilty Victor does) but the prisoner of a much more terrifying prison, the prison of his solipsistic thinking.

The prison metaphor goes back to Victor's Promethean dream and his relationship with the Monster. What Victor, the young, enthusiastic scientist, really wanted was to discover something that would eliminate death, diseases, and suffering. Yet, separating himself entirely from the surrounding community, he moved into a dangerous territory where science and love, work and marriage are incompatible and inharmonious. His failure as a scientist results from his failure as a human being. There is no harmony, no marriages (no marriage between home and laboratory, between science and sexuality) in Victor's life but only disharmony and divorces. Completely unaware of the consequences of his destructive ambition, instead of creating the superior race he has dreamed about, Victor frees a hideous being who reflects his own monstrosity. By separating his dream of domesticity from his dream as a scientist, he ends being imprisoned in a world where the Monster, the creation resulting from his scientific ambition, gradually devours him. Remember Victor's own words from Chapter 7: "I considered the being whom I had cast among mankind, and endowed with the will and power to effect purposes of horror, . . . nearly in the light of my own vampire, my own spirit let loose from the grave, and forced to destroy all that was dear to me." His domestic dream of marriage with Elizabeth becomes impossible. The novel starts with an ambitious dream and ends with a nightmare. It starts with Victor's sincere desire to free humanity from the terrifying presence of death and ends with his mental and spiritual imprisonment.

Victor's Innocence

Mr. Kirwin's changed attitude toward Victor mirrors the relationship between Walton and Frankenstein. Like Walton, the magistrate is attracted by Victor's unusual story and fascinating personality. As a result, the magistrate becomes seriously involved in the case. Convinced that Victor is indeed innocent, Mr. Kirwin decides to help him. It is he who hires the nurse and the physician to take care of Victor, he who arranges for the best room in the prison for this unusual prisoner, and he who contacts Victor's family and informs them about his "misfortune and illness."

Hearing that the magistrate wrote to his father two months ago and hasn't received a response yet, Victor fears that something terrible might have happened, and asks Mr. Kerwin impatiently: "tell me what new scene of death has been acted, and whose I am now to lament?" The magistrate's answer—"Your family is perfectly well"—is ironic (readers know by now that nobody is really "well" in that family and that they are constantly threatened by the terrible situation created by Victor and by their own inability to be open with one another). The magistrate's answer is also surprising—why isn't Mr. Kirwin disturbed or even intrigued by Victor's repeated self-accusations or his constant fears that somebody else in his family has been murdered? Mr. Kirwin is undoubtedly a minor character in Mary Shelley's novel and one who receives little if any critical attention, but his presence is nevertheless puzzling. His extreme benevolence and unusual clemency toward Victor (it is possible to assume that the nurse's intransigence and lack of sympathy were meant to make the magistrate's tolerance for Victor even more evident) may suggest that Mr. Kirwin is, like Walton, Victor's kindred spirit. He could be considered an older Walton who wisely abandoned his utopic dreams and returned to his old life and his family. The obvious similarities between Walton and Mr. Kirwin's reactions and behavior to and around Victor could support such a theory.

The Two Mr. Frankensteins

Victor's bizarre reaction to and "violent repugnance" of Mr. Kirwin's announcement that Victor has a visitor is equally ironic and surprising. There has always been tension between Alphonse Frankenstein and Victor. As a young man, Victor was infuriated because his father belittled Agrippa, one of his favorite philosophers. Moreover, readers may find reasons to believe that Victor was not altogether happy to be displaced and sent to school in a foreign land. (Readers should remember how, on his way to Ingolstadt, Victor becomes increasingly apprehensive about his loneliness and lack of family protection.) Interestingly, however, this chapter suggests more than simply tension in this father-son relationship, and Victor's

curious reaction to Mr. Kirwin's announcement of a friend coming to visit him in prison is more than ironic or surprising: It is disturbing. By associating Alphonse Frankenstein with the Monster—"I know not by what chain of thought the idea presented itself, but it instantly darted into my mind that the murderer had come to mock at my misery"—Victor's character helps Mary Shelley suggest a much more complicated question than the one readers and critics usually formulate: "Who is the real monster? Victor or his hideous creation?"

Toward the end of the novel, Victor increasingly resembles the Monster and, by the end of this chapter, the line of demarcation between the two of them becomes almost indistinguishable (see Victor's nightmare). But the identification of Alphonse Frankenstein with the Monster seems to suggest that the cause of this terrible, indeed monstrous chain of events is the father himself—a patriarchal monster—who supports and endorses an order often based on deficient principles and flawed moral values. Unlike De Lacey, Alphonse Frankenstein is not the head of an egalitarian family—remember that readers' first glance into the Frankenstein family shows clearly divided spheres, with the father directing the children's intellectual life and the mother participating solely in their "enjoyments." Alphonse Frankenstein also treats his wife more like a child than a partner, and consequently, she acts more like a dutiful daughter than her husband's equal. Alphonse participates in offering Elizabeth as a "gift" to his son, and has a very ambiguous relationship with her after his wife's death.

Victor's lack of communication with his father is reflected by their one-way conversation. Despite the fact that Victor keeps repeating highly disturbing confessions of guilt, his father never reacts appropriately. What does this lack of normal parental response signify? Clearly, Alphonse is incapable of communicating with his son—the same incapacity Victor manifests in his communication with his own creation. The elder Mr. Frankenstein is unable to react adequately to moments of crisis, or offer advice, understanding, or support. He is as narcissistic and self-centered as Victor is; in fact, father and son mirror each other.

Although it's difficult at first to determine what kind of father Alphonse Frankenstein really is, the novel gradually insinuates a perplexing fact: Victor learned how to abandon, how to be selfish, indifferent, and irresponsible from his own father. In short, Victor learned how to behave like a monster; therefore, it is not surprising that, over time, in popular culture (music, movies, artifacts, and graphic art), the name of Frankenstein came to be confused with the Monster rather than his creator.

Victor's Release

The chapter ends with the dismissal of the charges against Victor, and he and his father planning their return to Geneva. The liberation from prison does not excite Victor as much as it energizes his father, simply because Victor's imprisonment was essentially mental and only accidentally physical: "for to me the walls of a dungeon or a palace were alike. The cup of life was poisoned for ever." The man who wanted to "penetrate" nature and followed her "to her hiding places" is now encircled by darkness. Nature, abused and controlled, cannot offer comfort any longer and sadly, Victor sees no difference any more between *prison* (the ultimate confinement) and *nature* (the supreme openness): "prison was as welcome a residence as the divinest scene in nature."

And yet, even in this terrible abyss that he finds himself in, even now that he hit the bottom of despair and darkness, Victor still does not realize what the real question is and what he should do about it. The supreme irony remains that Victor absurdly continues to see himself as the protector of his family rather than understanding that his egotism is the cause of all these disasters and of his own tragedy.

The final paragraph describes Victor's nightmare during which the Monster kills him. Mary Shelley's genius is powerfully evident in this final segment. She brilliantly intertwines in one symbolic fabric the most important threads of the narrative. First, the "preservation of life" that Victor invokes is ironically the very opposite of what his work has accomplished—suffering and death. In fact, this purpose that should constitute the center of any human endeavor, the proper objective of any human action is, in Victor's life, only the dream of an "opium-eater." Secondly, readers are again subtly alerted to the similarities between Victor's father and Victor's creature. If from his first nightmare, the one in which he killed Elizabeth with a kiss (in Chapter 5), Victor was awakened by the Monster, from this second nightmare, in which he is murdered by the Monster, Victor is awakened by his own father. This is the second time in this chapter that Victor thinks or dreams about the Monster, only to find that it was his father "visiting" and "watching over him." In this context, the sentence, "the fiend was not here," is, highly ironic.

Chapter 22 In Paris, Victor receives a disturbing letter from Elizabeth, expressing her fear that the real cause of his suffering is that he loves another woman. Victor reassures her of his love and promises to reveal the reason for his agony on their wedding day. Soon after his arrival in Geneva, Victor and Elizabeth are married, and the couple sails to Evian for their wedding night.

Chapter XXII

THE voyage came to an end. We landed, and proceeded to Paris. I soon found that I had overtaxed my strength, and that I must repose before I could continue my journey. My father's care and attentions were **indefatigable**; but he did not know the origin of my sufferings, and sought **erroneous** methods to remedy the incurable ill. He wished me to seek amusement in society. I abhorred the face of man. Oh, not abhorred! they were my brethren, my fellow beings, and I felt attracted even to the most repulsive among them, as to creatures of an angelic nature and celestial mechanism. But I felt that I had no right to share their intercourse. I had unchained an enemy among them, whose joy it was to shed their blood, and to revel in their groans. How they would, each and all, abhor me, and hunt me from the world, did they know my unhallowed acts, and the crimes which had their source in me!

My father yielded at length to my desire to avoid society, and strove by various arguments to banish my despair. Sometimes he thought that I felt deeply the degradation of being obliged to answer a charge of murder, and he endeavoured to prove to me the futility of pride.

"Alas! my father," said I, "how little do you know me. Human beings, their feelings and passions, would indeed be degraded if such a wretch as I felt pride. Justine, poor unhappy Justine, was as innocent as I, and she suffered the same charge; she died for it; and I am the cause of this—I murdered her. William, Justine, and Henry—they all died by my hands."

My father had often, during my imprisonment, heard me make the same assertion; when I thus accused myself, he sometimes seemed to desire an explanation, and at others he appeared to consider it as the offspring of delirium, and that, during my illness, some idea of this kind had presented itself to my imagination, the remembrance of which I preserved in my **convalescence.** I avoided explanation, and maintained a continual silence concerning the wretch I had created. I had a persuasion that I should be supposed mad; and this in itself would for ever have chained my tongue. But, besides, I could not bring myself to disclose a secret which would fill my hearer with **consternation**, and make fear and unnatural horror the inmates of his breast. I checked, therefore, my impatient thirst for sympathy, and was silent when I would have given the world to have confided the fatal secret. Yet still words like those I have recorded, would burst uncontrollably from me. I could offer no explanation of them; but their truth in part relieved the burden of my mysterious woe.

NOTES

indefatigable: inexhaustible, tireless.

erroneous: inaccurate, incorrect.

convalescence: recovering from sickness.

consternation: alarm, indignation, bewilderment.

Upon this occasion my father said, with an expression of unbounded wonder, "My dearest Victor, what infatuation is this? My dear son, I entreat you never to make such an assertion again."

"I am not mad," I cried energetically; "the sun and the heavens, who have viewed my operations, can bear witness of my truth. I am the assassin of those most innocent victims; they died by my machinations. A thousand times would I have shed my own blood, drop by drop, to have saved their lives; but I could not, my father, indeed I could not sacrifice the whole human race."

The conclusion of this speech convinced my father that my ideas were deranged, and he instantly changed the subject of our conversation, and endeavoured to alter the course of my thoughts. He wished as much as possible to obliterate the memory of the scenes that had taken place in Ireland, and never alluded to them, or suffered me to speak of my misfortunes.

As time passed away I became more calm; misery had her dwelling in my heart, but I no longer talked in the same incoherent manner of my own crimes; sufficient for me was the consciousness of them. By the utmost self-violence, I curbed the imperious voice of wretchedness, which some-times desired to declare itself to the whole world; and my manners were calmer and more composed than they had ever been since my journey to the sea of ice.

A few days before we left Paris on our way to Switzerland, I received the following letter from Elizabeth:—

My dear Friend,

"It gave me the greatest pleasure to receive a letter from my uncle dated at Paris; you are no longer at a formidable distance, and I may hope to see you in less than a fortnight. My poor cousin, how much you must have suffered! I expect to see you looking even more ill than when you quitted Geneva. This winter has been passed most miserably, tortured as I have been by anxious suspense; yet I hope to see peace in your countenance, and to find that your heart is not totally void of comfort and tranquillity.

"Yet I fear that the same feelings now exist that made you so miserable a year ago, even perhaps augmented by time. I would not disturb you at this period, when so many misfortunes weigh upon you; but a con-versation that I had with my uncle previous to his departure renders some explanation necessary before we meet.

"Explanation! you may possibly say; what can Elizabeth have to explain? If you really say this, my questions are answered, and all my doubts satisfied. But you are distant from me, and it is possible that you may dread, and yet be pleased with this explanation; and, in a probability of this being the case, I dare not any longer postpone writing what, during your absence, I have often wished to express to you, but have never had the courage to begin.

"You well know, Victor, that our union had been the favourite plan of your parents ever since our infancy. We were told this when young, and taught to look forward to it as an event that would certainly take place. We were affectionate playfellows during childhood, and, I believe, dear and valued friends to one another as we grew older. But as brother and sister often entertain a lively affection towards each other, without desiring a more intimate union, may not such also be our case? Tell me, dearest Victor. Answer me, I **conjure** you, by our mutual happiness, with simple truth—Do you not love another?

conjure: request.

"You have travelled; you have spent several years of your life at Ingolstadt; and I confess to you, my friend, that when I saw you last autumn so unhappy, flying to solitude, from the society of every creature, I could not help supposing that you might regret our connection, and believe yourself bound in honour to fulfil the wishes of your parents, although they opposed themselves to your inclinations. But this is false reasoning. I confess to you, my friend, that I love you, and that in my airy dreams of futurity you have been my constant friend and companion. But it is your happiness I desire as well as my own, when I declare to you, that our marriage would render me eternally miserable, unless it were the dictate of your own free choice. Even now I weep to think, that, borne down as you are by the cruellest misfortunes, you may stifle, by the word *honour*, all hope of that love and happiness which would alone restore you to yourself. I, who have so disinterested an affection for you, may increase your miseries tenfold, by being an obstacle to your wishes. Ah! Victor, be assured that your cousin and playmate has too sincere a love for you not to be made miserable by this supposition. Be happy, my friend; and if you obey me in this one request, remain satisfied that nothing on earth will have the power to interrupt my tranquillity.

"Do not let this letter disturb you; do not answer tomorrow, or the next day, or even until you come, if it will give you pain. My uncle will send me news of your health; and if I see but one smile on your lips when we meet, occasioned by this or any other exertion of mine, I shall need no other happiness.

Elizabeth Lavenza

Geneva, May 18th, 17—."

This letter revived in my memory what I had before forgotten, the threat of the fiend—"*I will be with you on your wedding-night*!" Such was my sentence, and on that night would the daemon employ every art to destroy me, and tear me from the glimpse of happiness which promised partly to console my sufferings. On that night he had determined to **consummate** his crimes by my death. Well, be it so; a deadly struggle would then assuredly take place, in which if he were victorious I should be at peace, and his power over me be at an end. If he were vanquished,

consummate: complete.

I should be a free man. Alas! what freedom? such as the peasant enjoys when his family have been massacred before his eyes, his cottage burnt, his lands laid waste, and he is turned adrift, homeless, penniless, and alone, but free. Such would be my liberty, except that in my Elizabeth I possessed a treasure; alas! balanced by those horrors of remorse and guilt, which would pursue me until death.

Sweet and beloved Elizabeth! I read and re-read her letter, and some softened feelings stole into my heart, and dared to whisper paradisiacal dreams of love and joy; but the apple was already eaten, and the angel's arm bared to drive me from all hope. Yet I would die to make her happy. If the monster executed his threat, death was inevitable; yet, again, I considered whether my marriage would hasten my fate. My destruction might indeed arrive a few months sooner; but if my torturer should suspect that I postponed it, influenced by his menaces, he would surely find other and perhaps more dreadful means of revenge. He had vowed *to be with me on my wedding-night*, yet he did not consider that threat as binding him to peace in the mean time; for, as if to show me that he was not yet satiated with blood, he had murdered Clerval immediately after the enunciation of his threats. I resolved, therefore, that if my immediate union with my cousin would conduce either to hers or my father's happiness, my adversary's designs against my life should not retard it a single hour.

In this state of mind I wrote to Elizabeth. My letter was calm and affectionate. "I fear, my beloved girl," I said, "little happiness remains for us on earth; yet all that I may one day enjoy is centred in you. Chase away your idle fears; to you alone do I consecrate my life, and my endeavours for contentment. I have one secret, Elizabeth, a dreadful one; when revealed to you, it will chill your frame with horror, and then, far from being surprised at my misery, you will only wonder that I survive what I have endured. I will confide this tale of misery and terror to you the day after our marriage shall take place; for, my sweet cousin, there must be perfect confidence between us. But until then, I conjure you, do not mention or allude to it. This I most earnestly entreat, and I know you will comply."

In about a week after the arrival of Elizabeth's letter, we returned to Geneva. The sweet girl welcomed me with warm affection; yet tears were in her eyes, as she beheld my **emaciated** frame and feverish cheeks. I saw a change in her also. She was thinner, and had lost much of that heavenly vivacity that had before charmed me; but her gentleness, and soft looks of compassion, made her a more fit companion for one blasted and miserable as I was.

emaciated: starved.

The tranquillity which I now enjoyed did not endure. Memory brought madness with it; and when I thought of what had passed, a real insanity possessed me; sometimes I was furious, and burnt with rage, sometimes low and despondent. I neither spoke, nor looked at anyone, but sat motionless, bewildered by the multitude of miseries that overcame me. Elizabeth alone had the power to draw me from these fits; her gentle voice would soothe me when transported by passion, and inspire me with human feelings when sunk in torpor. She wept with me, and for me. When reason returned, she would remonstrate, and endeavour to inspire me with resignation. Ah! it is well for the unfortunate to be resigned, but for the guilty there is no peace. The agonies of remorse poison the luxury there is otherwise sometimes found in indulging the excess of grief.

Soon after my arrival, my father spoke of my immediate marriage with Elizabeth. I remained silent.

"Have you, then, some other attachment?"

"None on earth. I love Elizabeth, and look forward to our union with delight. Let the day therefore be fixed; and on it I will consecrate myself, in life or death, to the happiness of my cousin."

"My dear Victor, do not speak thus. Heavy misfortunes have befallen us; but let us only cling closer to what remains, and transfer our love for those whom we have lost, to those who yet live. Our circle will be small, but bound close by the ties of affection and mutual misfortune. And when time shall have softened your despair, new and dear objects of care will be born to replace those of whom we have been so cruelly deprived."

Such were the lessons of my father. But to me the remembrance of the threat returned: nor can you wonder that, omnipotent as the fiend had yet been in his deeds of blood, I should almost regard him as invincible; and that when he had pronounced the words "I shall be with you on your wedding-night," I should regard the threatened fate as unavoidable. But death was no evil to me, if the loss of Elizabeth were balanced with it; and I therefore, with a contented and even cheerful countenance, agreed with my father, that if my cousin would consent, the ceremony should take place in ten days, and thus put, as I imagined, the seal to my fate.

Great God! if for one instant I had thought what might be the hellish intention of my fiendish adversary, I would rather have banished myself forever from my native country, and wandered a friendless outcast over the earth, than have consented to this miserable marriage. But, as if possessed of magic powers, the monster had blinded me to his real intentions; and when I thought that I had prepared only my own death, I hastened that of a far dearer victim.

As the period fixed for our marriage drew nearer, whether from cowardice or a prophetic feeling, I felt my heart sink within me. But I concealed my feelings by an appearance of hilarity, that brought smiles and joy to the countenance of my father, but hardly deceived the ever-watchful and **nicer eye** of Elizabeth. She looked forward to our union with placid contentment, not unmingled with a little fear, which past misfortunes had impressed, that what now appeared certain and tangible happiness, might soon dissipate into an airy dream, and leave no trace but deep and everlasting regret.

Preparations were made for the event; congratulatory visits were received; and all wore a smiling appearance. I shut up, as well as I could, in my own heart the anxiety that preyed there, and entered with seeming

nicer eye: a more critical eye.

earnestness into the plans of my father, although they might only serve as the decorations of my tragedy. Through my father's exertions, a part of the inheritance of Elizabeth had been restored to her by the Austrian government. A small possession on the shores of Como belonged to her. It was agreed that, immediately after our union, we should proceed to Villa Lavenza, and spend our first days of happiness beside the beautiful lake near which it stood.

In the meantime I took every precaution to defend my person, in case the fiend should openly attack me. I carried pistols and a dagger constantly about me, and was ever on the watch to prevent artifice; and by these means gained a greater degree of tranquillity. Indeed, as the period approached, the threat appeared more as a delusion, not to be regarded as worthy to disturb my peace, while the happiness I hoped for in my marriage wore a greater appearance of certainty, as the day fixed for its **solemnisation** drew nearer, and I heard it continually spoken of as an occurrence which no accident could possibly prevent.

solemnisation: ceremony.

Elizabeth seemed happy; my tranquil demeanour contributed greatly to calm her mind. But on the day that was to fulfil my wishes and my destiny, she was melancholy, and a presentiment of evil pervaded her; and perhaps also she thought of the dreadful secret which I had promised to reveal to her on the following day. My father was in the mean time overjoyed, and, in the bustle of preparation, only recognized in the melancholy of his niece the diffidence of a bride.

After the ceremony was performed, a large party assembled at my father's; but it was agreed that Elizabeth and I should commence our journey by water, sleeping that night at **Evian,** and continuing our voyage on the following day. The day was fair, the wind favourable, all smiled on our nuptial **embarkation.**

Evian: town in France, on the south shore of Geneva Lake.

embarkation: departure.

Those were the last moments of my life during which I enjoyed the feeling of happiness. We passed rapidly along: the sun was hot, but we were sheltered from its rays by a kind of canopy, while we enjoyed the beauty of the scene, sometimes on one side of the lake, where we saw **Mont Salêve,** the pleasant banks of **Montalègre**, and at a distance, surmounting all, the beautiful Mont Blanc, and the assemblage of snowy mountains that in vain endeavour to emulate her; sometimes coasting the opposite banks, we saw the mighty Jura opposing its dark side to the ambition that would quit its native country, and an almost insurmountable barrier to the invader who should wish to enslave it.

Mont Salêve: peak in France, south of Geneva.

Montalègre: peak in France, near Mont Salêve.

I took the hand of Elizabeth: "You are sorrowful, my love. Ah! if you knew what I have suffered, and what I may yet endure, you would endeavour to let me taste the quiet and freedom from despair, that this one day at least permits me to enjoy."

"Be happy, my dear Victor," replied Elizabeth; "there is, I hope, nothing to distress you; and be assured that if a lively joy is not painted in my face, my heart is contented. Something whispers to me not to depend too much on the prospect that is opened before us; but I will not listen to such a sinister voice. Observe how fast we move along, and how the clouds, which sometimes obscure and sometimes rise above the dome of Mont Blanc, render this scene of beauty still more interesting. Look also at the innumerable fish that are swimming in the clear waters, where we can distinguish every pebble that lies at the bottom. What a divine day! how happy and serene all nature appears!"

Thus Elizabeth endeavoured to divert her thoughts and mine from all reflection upon melancholy subjects. But her temper was fluctuating; joy for a few instants shone in her eyes, but it continually gave place to distraction and reverie.

The sun sunk lower in the heavens; we passed the river Drance, and observed its path through the **chasms** of the higher, and the **glens** of the lower hills. The Alps here come closer to the lake, and we approached the **amphitheatre** of mountains which forms its eastern boundary. The spire of Evian shone under the woods that surrounded it, and the range of mountain above mountain by which it was overhung.

chasms: deep clefts, cracks.

glens: narrow valleys.

amphitheatre: large, circular or oval arena with tiered seats.

The wind, which had hitherto carried us along with amazing rapidity, sunk at sunset to a light breeze; the soft air just ruffled the water, and caused a pleasant motion among the trees as we approached the shore, from which it wafted the most delightful scent of flowers and hay. The sun sunk beneath the horizon as we landed; and as I touched the shore, I felt those cares and fears revive, which soon were to clasp me and cling to me forever.

COMMENTARY

On the way back to Switzerland, Victor and his father stop in Paris so that Victor, still feeble after his latest illness, can rest before continuing their long journey. Despite the opportunity here for some meaningful father-son conversation, the isolation and lack of communication between the two continues. Instead of alleviating his son's suffering, Victor's father increases Victor's desperation and loneliness. Clearly, Mr. Kirwin, who saved Victor's life, was able to do so because he "knew" him surprisingly well. By comparison, his father not only interprets Victor's avoidance of society as a sign of pride (which proves how inattentive he is) but instead of being shocked or terrified by his son's constant self-accusations he merely changes the subject. Alphonse Frankenstein remains a stranger to his tormented son.

Although Mary Shelley portrays Alphonse Franken-stein in dark colors, keep in mind that Victor's attitude toward his father is equally deficient, even cruel. Whether Victor deeply resents his father for his dismissive attitude toward Agrippa (the sixteenth-century alchemist, experimenter, and physician whose work made a strong impression on Victor as a young boy) or for sending him away from home to study in Ingolstadt, or whether he simply reacts to his father' soft oppression, Victor often hurts his father by failing to write regularly. Thus, Victor remains silent and uncommunicative. Although he knows from Elizabeth about Alphonse's need to hear from his son, Victor intentionally neglects writing and justifies his negligence by claiming that he could focus on nothing but his work. Again and again, we see Victor and Alphonse painfully separated from each other (like the "A" and the "V" of the alphabet), hurting each other incessantly, and continually damaging their relationship.

Elizabeth's Letter

While still in Paris, Victor receives a letter from Elizabeth who decides to abandon her passivity and finally opens a door into the truth of her relationship with Victor. The letter, unlike her other letter, which was addressed to "My dearest Cousin," is, this time, addressed to "My dear Friend." The difference in addressing Victor may seem insignificant but, in fact, the distinction is quite important. The change from "dearest" to "dear" clearly suggests a change in Elizabeth's way of expressing her affection. Not that she loves Victor less, but she is less willing to reveal her feelings to a man who doesn't seem to reciprocate. Also, by naming Victor a "friend," Elizabeth not only introduces a ceremonial note ("friend" is obviously more formal than "Victor"), distancing herself from him and eliminating any intimate implications, but also invites him to consider her his equal and tell her the truth. And yet, her initial coldness is only an artifice, a stratagem used to protect Victor and herself from the pain introduced by Elizabeth's openness.

In this context, the first sentence of her letter is obviously ironic and the final part of the sentence, "you are no longer at a formidable distance," means precisely the opposite. Even the word "formidable" is an interesting choice since it is a word that Elizabeth (or any other woman in the novel) rarely if ever uses but that appears abundantly in the vocabulary of men during the nineteenth century. It is a word usually associated with the sublime (the masculine sphere) rather than with the beautiful (the feminine domain). Walton's or Victor's aspirations can be qualified as "formidable," and, in fact, with this one word, Elizabeth brilliantly combines both the real cause (his formidable ambition) and the effect (his fears/rejection of domesticity) of Victor's separation from her. His "formidable" studies pushed him further and further away from her: to Ingolstadt, to his laboratory, to England. As a result, the isolated, secluded Victor becomes more and more detached from the warmth, protection, and balance created by the presence of family and home. Elizabeth, a formidable woman, indeed knows more than she reveals. Critics, with few exceptions, consider Elizabeth superficial and monotonous, but a closer examination of the impressive rhetorical skills she employs in her two long letters to Victor constitute a solid argument for a different reading of Elizabeth.

That Elizabeth understands more than she directly communicates is also apparent in her correct evaluation of Victor's general state of being: "I expect to see you looking even more ill than when you quitted Geneva." Again, this simple sentence is disturbingly ambiguous and confirms Elizabeth's unusual capacity to concentrate—to synthesize an entire spectrum of complicated events.

Comparing the two letters makes this easier. Her first letter (in the beginning of Chapter 6), like this one, was written after one of Victor's long illnesses. More precisely, it was immediately after the recovery from the nervous fever provoked by the recognition that he has created a monster. In fact, that illness was, if not clearly more severe than this one, surely longer. And yet, a sense of optimism and hope permeates Elizabeth's first letter and her words are cheerful and radiant: "I eagerly hope that you will . . . Get well—and return to us. You will find a happy, cheerful home, and friends who love you dearly." After this confident beginning, a chatty, intimate, even gossipy Elizabeth informs her fiancé about everybody in the family, about friends, and about social life in Geneva, a life that she was soon supposed to enter as the young wife of a brilliant scientist and noble gentleman. Everything in the letter, although not directly expressed, is clearly directed toward a promising future and around a family at whose center she affectionately places Victor and herself, the new couple capable of bringing stability, protection, and a new energy into the Frankenstein household.

By contrast, in her second letter, despite the fact that she knows from Alphonse Frankenstein's account that Victor is indeed recovering, Elizabeth appears to have completely lost her optimism in her lover's well-being or in the future happiness of their marriage. "I expect to see you looking even more ill than when you quitted Geneva," translates into Elizabeth's tortuous fears that Victor is, in fact, beyond recovery. She believes that terrible, mysterious powers torment his existence—powers significantly larger than her protective forces could ever counterbalance. The winter she invokes in the letter's fourth sentence is the winter of sterility and separation hovering dangerously over their unhealthy relationship. The intensely pessimistic vocabulary of the first part of the sentence—"The *winter* has been passed most *miserably*, *tortured* as I have been by *anxious suspense*;"—cannot possibly let the vaguely brighter connotations of the second part—"yet I hope to see peace in your countenance, and to find your heart is not totally void of comfort and tranquillity"—dissipate the general feeling of loss, absence, and destruction. Note that at the center of the second part of this sentence, Mary Shelley ingeniously places the word "void," thus intensifying the emptiness gradually engulfing Elizabeth and Victor's once-promising future.

Between "your heart" and "comfort and tranquillity" there is indeed a void, and Elizabeth knows it. And there are too many dead bodies—William, Justine, and Clerval—between her and Victor for happiness to still be possible. With so much death around, Victor cannot be but "more ill" than ever.

In this context, Elizabeth's major question, "Tell me, dearest Victor. Answer me, I conjure you, by our mutual happiness, with simple truth—do you not love another?" acquires more depth than the simply emotional eruption of a woman who suspects her lover of a relationship with another woman. Even the syntax of the sentence itself supports this reading and the "not" from "do you not love another?" weakens rather than promotes the idea that Elizabeth refers to a female competitor. Moreover, the following paragraph makes the ambiguity of the word "another" even more evident. In that paragraph, she talks about "Ingolstadt," and about Victor's "solitude from the society of every creature," and not once does she mention or allude to another woman. When she uses words such as "friend," "companion," and "marriage" she refers exclusively to herself, which may suggest that the word "another" refers more to "Ingolstadt" and "solitude" than to another woman. Additionally, the very premise of the question is, interestingly enough, "our mutual happiness," which again indicates that Elizabeth knows that their happiness in each other is still mutual but that a much more powerful force, closely related to "Ingolstadt" and to "solitude," threatens the relationship.

What Elizabeth fears is not another woman but Victor's essential misogyny, his increasing revulsion toward her. Therefore, her letter, possibly one of the most subtle texts in the entire body of nineteenth-century literature, can be read as the desperate cry for help of a woman who knows that she may be the next victim, a woman who trembles at the thought that the man she loves may destroy her. Her desperation, a combination of anger and helplessness, is clear in the urgency of her words: "Tell me...Answer me...I conjure you..." But Elizabeth knows that Victor cannot answer and that the "truth" is never "simple." In the body of her letter, she expresses the unsteady hope that love and joy will restore Victor. But in the end, an increasingly depressed Elizabeth asks Victor to postpone the answer— "do not answer me tomorrow, or the next day, or even until you come." Unlike her previous letter, when Victor's physical health was indeed the real issue, Elizabeth no longer needs his "own handwriting" to confirm his recovery. Now, a word from her uncle will suffice.

The most important message of Elizabeth's letter remains the "smile" she invokes in its closing lines. It constitutes the delicate testimony of one of the most profound feelings of love and devotion that a woman ever had for a man. It is her way of saying that she has already forgiven Victor.

Victor's Reaction

Appropriately, Victor's first thought after reading Elizabeth's letter was "the threat of the fiend—'*I will be with you on your wedding-night.*'" Knowing his fiancee better than anybody else, Victor immediately understands that what frightens Elizabeth is death, not his infidelity. In fact, Victor doesn't pay any real attention to this detail, makes no significant comments on it, but dismisses it in no more than five words: "Chase away your idle fears." The rest of his response to Elizabeth's letter contains an indirect confirmation of her dark premonitions—"I fear, my beloved girl...little happiness remains for us on earth,"—and the promise that he will reveal a terrible "secret," after their wedding.

And yet, even now that Elizabeth subtly has suggested to Victor that she is perfectly aware of the unusual forces controlling his life, Victor refuses to see the truth and, instead of doing something radical to save her life and stop the tragic events generated by his self-centeredness, he continues to interpret the Monster's words as a threat on his own life. Consequently, before the marriage Victor takes "every precaution to defend *my* person, in case the fiend should openly attack *me.*"

Whether it is true, as many critics have argued, that the Monster, as Victor's double, acts out his creator's murderous will and that by indirectly killing Elizabeth, Victor frees himself from the bondage of conjugal intimacy, or whether Victor, otherwise capable of grandiose endeavors remains surprisingly inadequate, even impotent, when confronted with the intricacies of daily existence, will undoubtedly remain an open debate. What this elaborate and often neglected chapter suggests, however, is at least equally intriguing. From it, a subtle, amazingly intelligent, and profound Elizabeth emerges—a character much more complicated and sophisticated than the majority of critics want to consider. The melancholy bride is at the end of the chapter, the person who reminds Victor of the restorative powers of nature, and is by far more complex than any other female character in the novel.

Chapter 23

Despite Victor's vigilance, the Monster enters their nuptial chamber and strangles Elizabeth. While embracing her dead body, Victor sees the Monster through an open window and shoots at him, but the Monster escapes.

Victor returns to Geneva fearing that his father and brother have been murdered also. They're still alive but just a few days later Victor's father dies in his arms. Having lost everything, Victor vows to destroy the Monster.

CHAPTER XXIII

IT was eight o'clock when we landed; we walked for a short time on the shore, enjoying the transitory light, and then retired to the inn, and contemplated the lovely scene of waters, woods, and mountains, obscured in darkness, yet still displaying their black outlines.

The wind, which had fallen in the south, now rose with great violence in the west. The moon had reached her summit in the heavens, and was beginning to descend; the clouds swept across it swifter than the flight of the vulture, and dimmed her rays, while the lake reflected the scene of the busy heavens, rendered still busier by the restless waves that were beginning to rise. Suddenly a heavy storm of rain descended.

I had been calm during the day; but so soon as night obscured the shapes of objects, a thousand fears arose in my mind. I was anxious and watchful, while my right hand grasped a pistol which was hidden in my bosom; every sound terrified me; but I resolved that I would sell my life dearly, and not shrink from the conflict until my own life, or that of my adversary, was extinguished.

Elizabeth observed my agitation for some time in timid and fearful silence; but there was something in my glance which communicated terror to her, and trembling, she asked, "What is it that agitates you, my dear Victor? What is it you fear?"

"Oh! peace, peace, my love," replied I; "this night, and all will be safe: but this night is dreadful, very dreadful."

I passed an hour in this state of mind, when suddenly I reflected how fearful the combat which I momentarily expected would be to my wife, and I earnestly entreated her to retire, resolving not to join her until I had obtained some knowledge as to the situation of my enemy.

She left me, and I continued some time walking up and down the passages of the house, and inspecting every corner that might afford a retreat to my adversary. But I discovered no trace of him, and was beginning to conjecture that some fortunate chance had intervened to prevent the execution of his menaces; when suddenly I heard a shrill and dreadful scream. It came from the room into which Elizabeth had retired. As I heard it, the whole truth rushed into my mind, my arms dropped, the motion of every muscle and fibre was suspended; I could feel the blood trickling in my veins, and tingling in the extremities of my limbs. This

NOTES

state lasted but for an instant; the scream was repeated, and I rushed into the room.

Great God! why did I not then expire! Why am I here to relate the destruction of the best hope, and the purest creature on earth? She was there, lifeless and inanimate, thrown across the bed, her head hanging down, and her pale and distorted features half covered by her hair. Every where I turn I see the same figure—her bloodless arms and relaxed form flung by the murderer on its bridal bier. Could I behold this, and live? Alas! life is obstinate, and clings closest where it is most hated. For a moment only did I lose recollection; I fell senseless on the ground.

When I recovered, I found myself surrounded by the people of the inn; their countenances expressed a breathless terror: but the horror of others appeared only as a mockery, a shadow of the feelings that oppressed me. I escaped from them to the room where lay the body of Elizabeth, my love, my wife, so lately living, so dear, so worthy. She had been moved from the posture in which I had first beheld her; and now, as she lay, her head upon her arm, and a handkerchief thrown across her face and neck, I might have supposed her asleep. I rushed towards her, and embraced her with ardour; but the deadly languor and coldness of the limbs told me, that what I now held in my arms had ceased to be the Elizabeth whom I had loved and cherished. The murderous mark of the fiend's grasp was on her neck, and the breath had ceased to issue from her lips.

While I still hung over her in the agony of despair, I happened to look up. The windows of the room had before been darkened, and I felt a kind of panic on seeing the pale yellow light of the moon illuminate the chamber. The shutters had been thrown back; and with a sensation of horror not to be described, I saw at the open window a figure the most hideous and abhorred. A grin was on the face of the monster; he seemed to jeer, as with his fiendish finger he pointed towards the corpse of my wife. I rushed towards the window, and drawing a pistol from my bosom, fired; but he eluded me, leaped from his station, and, running with the swiftness of lightning, plunged into the lake.

The report of the pistol brought a crowd into the room. I pointed to the spot where he had disappeared, and we followed the track with boats; nets were cast, but in vain. After passing several hours, we returned hopeless, most of my companions believing it to have been a form conjured up by my fancy. After having landed, they proceeded to search the country, parties going in different directions among the woods and vines.

I attempted to accompany them, and proceeded a short distance from the house; but my head whirled round, my steps were like those of a drunken man, I fell at last in a state of utter exhaustion; a film covered my eyes, and my skin was parched with the heat of fever. In this state I was carried back, and placed on a bed, hardly conscious of what had happened; my eyes wandered round the room, as if to seek something that I had lost.

After an interval, I arose, and as if by instinct, crawled into the room where the corpse of my beloved lay. There were women weeping around—I hung over it, and joined my sad tears to theirs—all this time no distinct idea presented itself to my mind; but my thoughts rambled to various subjects, reflecting confusedly on my misfortunes, and their cause. I was bewildered in a cloud of wonder and horror. The death of William, the execution of Justine, the murder of Clerval, and lastly of my wife; even at that moment I knew not that my only remaining friends were safe from the malignity of the fiend; my father even now might be writhing under his grasp, and Ernest might be dead at his feet. This idea made me shudder, and recalled me to action. I started up, and resolved to return to Geneva with all possible speed.

There were no horses to be procured, and I must return by the lake; but the wind was unfavourable, and the rain fell in torrents. However, it was hardly morning, and I might reasonably hope to arrive by night. I hired men to row, and took an oar myself; for I had always experienced relief from mental torment in bodily exercise. But the overflowing misery I now felt, and the excess of agitation that I endured, rendered me incapable of any exertion. I threw down the oar; and leaning my head upon my hands, gave way to every gloomy idea that arose. If I looked up, I saw scenes which were familiar to me in my happier time, and which I had contemplated but the day before in the company of her who was now but a shadow and a recollection. Tears streamed from my eyes. The rain had ceased for a moment, and I saw the fish play in the waters as they had done a few hours before; they had then been observed by Elizabeth. Nothing is so painful to the human mind as a great and sudden change. The sun might shine, or the clouds might lower: but nothing could appear to me as it had done the day before. A fiend had snatched from me every hope of future happiness: no creature had ever been so miserable as I was; so frightful an event is single in the history of man.

But why should I dwell upon the incidents that followed this last overwhelming event? Mine has been a tale of horrors; I have reached their **acme**, and what I must now relate can but be tedious to you. Know that, one by one, my friends were snatched away; I was left desolate. My own strength is exhausted; and I must tell, in a few words, what remains of my hideous narration.

acme: highest point or stage; perfection.

I arrived at Geneva. My father and Ernest yet lived; but the former sunk under the tidings that I bore. I see him now, excellent and venerable old man! his eyes wandered in vacancy, for they had lost their charm and their delight—his Elizabeth, his more than daughter, whom he doated on with all that affection which a man feels, who in the decline of life, having few affections, clings more earnestly to those that remain. Cursed, cursed be the fiend that brought misery on his grey hairs, and doomed him to waste in wretchedness! He could not live under the horrors that were accumulated around him; the springs of existence suddenly gave way: he was unable to rise from his bed, and in a few days he died in my arms.

What then became of me? I know not; I lost sensation, and chains and darkness were the only objects that pressed upon me. Sometimes, indeed, I dreamt that I wandered in flowery meadows and pleasant vales with the friends of my youth; but I awoke, and found myself in a dungeon.

Melancholy followed, but by degrees I gained a clear conception of my miseries and situation, and was then released from my prison. For they had called me mad; and during many months, as I understood, a solitary cell had been my habitation.

Liberty, however, had been a useless gift to me, had I not, as I awakened to reason, at the same time awakened to revenge. As the memory of past misfortunes pressed upon me, I began to reflect on their cause—the monster whom I had created, the miserable daemon whom I had sent abroad into the world for my destruction. I was possessed by a maddening rage when I thought of him, and desired and ardently prayed that I might have him within my grasp to wreak a great and signal revenge on his cursed head.

Nor did my hate long confine itself to useless wishes; I began to reflect on the best means of securing him; and for this purpose, about a month after my release, I repaired to a criminal judge in the town and told him that I had an accusation to make; that I knew the destroyer of my family; and that I required him to exert his whole authority for the apprehension of the murderer.

The magistrate listened to me with attention and kindness:—"Be assured, sir," said he, "no pains or exertions on my part shall be spared to discover the villain."

"I thank you," replied I; "listen, therefore, to the deposition that I have to make. It is indeed a tale so strange, that I should fear you would not credit it, were there not something in truth which, however wonderful, forces conviction. The story is too **connected** to be mistaken for a dream, and I have no motive for falsehood." My manner, as I thus addressed him, was impressive, but calm; I had formed in my own heart a resolution to pursue my destroyer to death; and this purpose quieted my agony, and for an interval reconciled me to life. I now related my history, briefly, but with firmness and precision, marking the dates with accuracy, and never deviating into invective or exclamation.

connected: coherent, consistent.

The magistrate appeared at first perfectly incredulous, but as I continued he became more attentive and interested; I saw him sometimes shudder with horror, at others a lively surprise, unmingled with disbelief, was painted on his countenance.

When I had concluded my narration, I said, "This is the being whom I accuse, and for whose seizure and punishment I call upon you to exert your whole power. It is your duty as a magistrate, and I believe and hope that your feelings as a man will not revolt from the execution of those functions on this occasion."

This address caused a considerable change in the physiognomy of my own auditor. He had heard my story with that half kind of belief that is given to a tale of spirits and supernatural events; but when he was called upon to act officially in consequence, the whole tide of his incredulity returned. He, however, answered mildly, "I would willingly afford you every aid in your pursuit; but the creature of whom you speak appears to have powers which would put all my exertions to defiance. Who can follow an animal which can traverse the sea of ice, and inhabit caves and dens where no man would venture to intrude? Besides, some months have elapsed since the commission of his crimes, and no one can conjecture to what place he has wandered, or what region he may now inhabit."

"I do not doubt that he hovers near the spot which I inhabit; and if he has indeed taken refuge in the Alps, he may be hunted like the **chamois**, and destroyed as a beast of prey. But I perceive your thoughts: you do not credit my narrative, and do not intend to pursue my enemy with the punishment which is his desert."

As I spoke, rage sparkled in my eyes; the magistrate was intimidated:— "You are mistaken," said he. "I will exert myself; and if it is in my power to seize the monster, be assured that he shall suffer punishment proportionate to his crimes. But I fear, from what you have yourself described to be his properties, that this will prove impracticable; and thus, while every proper measure is pursued, you should make up your mind to disappointment."

"That cannot be; but all that I can say will be of little avail. My revenge is of no **moment** to you; yet, while I allow it to be a vice, I confess that it is the devouring and only passion of my soul. My rage is unspeakable, when I reflect that the murderer, whom I have turned loose upon society, still exists. You refuse my just demand: I have but one resource; and I devote myself, either in my life or death, to his destruction."

I trembled with excess of agitation as I said this; there was a frenzy in my manner, and something, I doubt not, of that haughty fierceness which the **martyrs** of old are said to have possessed. But to a Genevan magistrate, whose mind was occupied by far other ideas than those of devotion and heroism, this elevation of mind had much the appearance of madness. He endeavoured to soothe me as a nurse does a child, and **reverted** to my tale as the effects of delirium.

"Man," I cried, "how ignorant art thou in thy pride of wisdom! Cease; you know not what it is you say."

I broke from the house angry and disturbed, and retired to meditate on some other mode of action.

chamois: antelope.

An antelope.

moment: importance.

martyrs: sufferers, victims.

reverted: looked back at.

COMMENTARY

In this chapter, the Monster murders Elizabeth on her wedding night, and only days after the tragic event, Alphonse Frankenstein dies of grief in his son's arms. Ernest Frankenstein, the only survivor of Victor's circle of family and friends, subsequently disappears from the narrative without explanation.

Victor divulges his extraordinary story to a magistrate but fails to convince him to organize a search party to track down the Monster. Therefore, Victor finally abandons his infuriating passivity and leaves Geneva dedicating his life to pursuing his enemy.

The ominous description at the beginning of the chapter prepares the reader for the terrible events soon to unfold. The light that the newly married Elizabeth and Victor enjoy on their short walk on the shore is, unfortunately, as transitory as their happiness. Soon, unfriendly winds and threatening clouds plunge the couple in darkness and heavy rain. The moon, always present at the novel's most dramatic moments (the creation of the Monster, the destruction of its mate, etc.) also presides sinisterly over the landscape, foreshadowing Elizabeth's demise. And, although only invoked as a comparison, the word "vulture" certainly intensifies the threatening atmosphere that permeates the scene.

The foreshadowing in Chapter 2 is revealed here. In Chapter 2, Victor remarks that Elizabeth's soul "shone like a shrine-dedicated lamp." Did he intuitively know that this young woman, who was initially offered to him as a "present" by his parents, would be sacrificed on the altar of his ambition? Does his bizarre combination of the words "shrine" and "lamp" anticipate the disappearance of Elizabeth's light into the darkness of the grave?

Victor becomes increasingly ill-at-ease as the night transforms everything into a sea of undifferentiated darkness. In his usual narcissistic manner, Victor interprets all these disturbing signs as indicators of his own death, rather than his beloved's. Like the terrible night when, alone in his house, Victor listened to every sound, trembling, waiting for the Monster to come and punish him for the destruction of the female monster, he is again terrified by "every sound," convinced that this is the night that his enemy will finally come to destroy him.

But as readers already know, the Monster never targets Victor. Mary Shelley's astuteness is indeed remarkable in these final chapters. On the one hand, she gradually creates a pattern that helps readers understand the profoundly mysterious relationship between Victor and his creature: Even if they cannot predict the development of events in the narrative, readers can quickly discern that the Monster's victims are always Victor's closest relatives and friends and not Victor himself. It becomes clear that the Monster wants to create the same desolation, the same emptiness, for Victor that he himself experiences, and make Victor confront absolute loneliness and isolation so that he will at last realize his cruelty and irresponsible behavior.

At the same time, this tension between what readers gradually understand (and what Elizabeth intuitively senses) and Victor's continual blindness subtly defines the magnitude of Victor's lamentable condition. Step by step, Victor becomes transformed from an insufferable, arrogant individual, deserving of contempt, into a tragic figure—to be pitied rather than condemned. It seems that indeed the same "immutable laws" that Elizabeth invokes in her first letter to Victor (in Chapter 6), "regulating" nature, "our placid home," and "our...hearts," also govern Victor's unhappy destiny.

Victor's character transformation mirrors Mary Shelley's own change of attitude. By the time she revised the original 1818 version of the novel, she had become increasingly pessimistic. Like some Victorian writers after her, she seems to see the characters of her fiction at the mercy of indifferent forces that manipulate and control them. Although fate is not completely an outside force in her novel, and although individuals are also driven by their own desires, ambitions, and obsessions, Victor's destiny, like the entire universe, seems to be ruled largely by chance. As she acknowledges in a personal letter from 1827, four years before she substantially revised *Frankenstein*, "the power of Destiny, I feel every day pressing more and more on me, and I yield myself a slave to it..."

By presenting Victor Frankenstein as a victim of fate, not entirely responsible for his decisions (one need only remember his reaction to Waldman's tempting words: "one by one the various keys were touched which formed the mechanism of my being...and soon my mind was filled with one thought, one conception, one purpose"), Mary Shelley may have intended to soften the image of the character whose model was Percy Shelley—her beloved husband. Emotionally narcissistic, like Victor, often insensitive to Mary's needs, and repeatedly irresponsible as a father, critics have convincingly demonstrated that Percy's temperament and personality constitutes the foundation of Victor's character. But in 1818, when the novel was written and Percy alive, this transference helped Mary Shelley cope with her marital frustrations. By 1831, nine years after her husband's death, when she wanted to forget all his errors, a more positive portrait of Victor, one in which a cruel fate and a vicious self-centeredness are more judiciously balanced, illustrates Mary Shelly's understanding of the profound contradictions in her husband's personality and her ambivalent feelings about him.

Elizabeth's Death

This segment receives a lot of critical attention and is a favorite scene for film directors, who often used it to highlight the problems in Victor's relationship with Elizabeth. Especially intriguing are James Whale's version from the 1935 production, *The Bride of Frankenstein*, and, more recently, Branagh's reading in *Mary Shelley's Frankenstein*. In the novel, the preamble to Elizabeth's murder (and symbolic rape), and Victor's unexpectedly rapid recovery from the violent shock of his wife's death, are presented with a remarkable concision. Unusual for the novel's narrative scheme, which generally consists of relatively short chapters with one major emphasis on a character or a situation, this chapter juxtaposes Elizabeth's and Alphonse Frankenstein's deaths, a detail that has particularly interesting connotations and explains, in part, why after years of silence, Victor impulsively confesses his crimes.

Mary Shelley presents a number of disturbing elements that both puzzle and alert the reader. Victor is progressively agitated around Elizabeth, but suspiciously calm after her departure. Nothing really explains this implausible transformation from a situation of "terror" that kept Elizabeth in a state of fear to Victor's meticulous room-by-room inspection, which encouraged a curiously hopeful calmness. His words, "Oh! peace, peace, my love," sound in this context highly ironic; it seems as if Victor anticipates Elizabeth's eternal peace. And in fact he sends her *alone*, completely unprotected, to her bed chamber, the place of her death, "resolving not to join her

until I had obtained some knowledge as to the situation of my enemy." Ironically again, the moment when he indeed "joins" her is not one of reunion but one of absolute separation.

Both Victor's horrible mistake of exposing Elizabeth to the Monster's promised attack, and his ridiculous decision "not to join her" before he knows precisely where the Monster is raise serious questions about Victor's real intentions. Sending Elizabeth alone to her room is obviously absurd, since the only way to defend her is to remain with her. At the same time, if sincerely convinced that he is indeed the Monster's intended victim, the whole idea of "rejoining" Elizabeth appears simply ludicrous, considering that Victor must realize that he has absolutely no chance to defeat his enemy.

Chapter 24   Victor finishes his story. Walton continues to write Margaret about Victor's last days, his death, and the Monster's unexpected arrival on the ship. Accused by Walton for his wicked revenge, the Monster responds that the real murderer was Victor. He created and abandoned him and forced him to change from a compassionate and virtuous being into a violent and bitter creature. Finishing his speech, the Monster vanishes into the darkness.

Chapter XXIV

MY present situation was one in which all voluntary thought was swallowed up and lost. I was hurried away by fury; revenge alone endowed me with strength and composure; it moulded my feelings, and allowed me to be calculating and calm, at periods when otherwise delirium or death would have been my portion.

My first resolution was to quit Geneva fore ver; my country, which, when I was happy and beloved, was dear to me, now, in my adversity, became hateful. I provided myself with a sum of money, together with a few jewels which had belonged to my mother, and departed.

And now my wanderings began, which are to cease but with life. I have traversed a vast portion of the earth, and have endured all the hardships which travellers in deserts, and barbarous countries are wont to meet. How I have lived I hardly know; many times have I stretched my failing limbs upon the sandy plain, and prayed for death. But revenge kept me alive; I dared not die, and leave my adversary in being.

When I quitted Geneva, my first labour was to gain some clue by which I might trace the steps of my fiendish enemy. But my plan was unsettled; and I wandered many hours round the confines of the town, uncertain what path I should pursue. As night approached, I found myself at the entrance of the cemetery where William, Elizabeth, and my father reposed. I entered it and approached the tomb which marked their graves. Every thing was silent, except the leaves of the trees, which were gently agitated by the wind; the night was nearly dark; and the scene would have been solemn and affecting even to an uninterested observer. The spirits of the departed seemed to flit around, and to cast a shadow, which was felt but not seen, around the head of the mourner.

The deep grief which this scene had at first excited quickly gave way to rage and despair. They were dead, and I lived; their murderer also lived, and to destroy him I must drag out my weary existence. I knelt on the grass, and kissed the earth, and with quivering lips exclaimed, "By the sacred earth on which I kneel, by the **shades** that wander near me, by the deep and eternal grief that I feel, I swear; and by thee, O Night, and the spirits that preside over thee, to pursue the daemon, who caused this misery, until he or I shall perish in mortal conflict. For this purpose I will preserve my life: to execute this dear revenge, will I again behold the sun, and tread the green herbage of earth, which otherwise should vanish from my eyes for ever. And I call on you, spirits of the dead; and on you,

NOTES

shades: spirits.

wandering ministers of vengeance, to aid and conduct me in my work. Let the cursed and hellish monster drink deep of agony; let him feel the despair that now torments me.

" I had begun my **adjuration** with solemnity, and an awe which almost assured me that the shades of my murdered friends heard and approved my devotion; but the **furies** possessed me as I concluded, and rage choked my utterance.

I was answered through the stillness of night by a loud and fiendish laugh. It rang on my ears long and heavily; the mountains re-echoed it, and I felt as if all hell surrounded me with mockery and laughter. Surely in that moment I should have been possessed by frenzy, and have destroyed my miserable existence, but that my vow was heard, and that I was reserved for vengeance. The laughter died away; when a well-known and abhorred voice, apparently close to my ear, addressed me in an audible whisper—"I am satisfied: miserable wretch! you have determined to live, and I am satisfied."

I darted towards the spot from which the sound proceeded; but the devil eluded my grasp. Suddenly the broad disk of the moon arose, and shone full upon his ghastly and distorted shape, as he fled with more than mortal speed.

I pursued him; and for many months this has been my task. Guided by a slight clue, I followed the windings of the Rhone, but vainly. The blue **Mediterranean** appeared; and by a strange chance, I saw the fiend enter by night, and hide himself in a vessel bound for the **Black Sea**. I took my passage in the same ship; but he escaped, I know not how.

Amidst the wilds of **Tartary** and Russia, although he still evaded me, I have ever followed in his track. Sometimes the peasants, scared by this horrid apparition, informed me of his path; sometimes he himself, who feared that if I lost all trace of him I should despair and die, left some mark to guide me. The snows descended on my head, and I saw the print of his huge step on the white plain. To you first entering on life, to whom care is new, and agony unknown, how can you understand what I have felt, and still feel? Cold, want, and fatigue, were the least pains which I was destined to endure; I was cursed by some devil, and carried about with me my **eternal hell**; yet still a spirit of good followed and directed my steps; and, when I most murmured, would suddenly extricate me from seemingly insurmountable difficulties. Sometimes, when nature, overcome by hunger, sank under the exhaustion, a repast was prepared for me in the desert, that restored and inspirited me. The fare was, indeed, coarse, such as the peasants of the country ate; but I will not doubt that it was set there by the spirits that I had invoked to aid me. Often, when all was dry, the heavens cloudless, and I was parched by thirst, a slight cloud would bedim the sky, shed the few drops that revived me, and vanish.

I followed, when I could, the courses of the rivers; but the daemon generally avoided these, as it was here that the population of the country chiefly collected. In other places human beings were seldom seen; and I

adjuration: invocation.

furies: Greek spirits of revenge.

Mediterranean: sea between southern Europe and northern Africa.

Black Sea: sea bordering clockwise Bulgaria, Romania, Ukraine, Georgia, and Turkey.

Tartary: territory in southern Russia (today's Ukraine) and Crimea, inhabited by Tatars, people of Turk origin.

eternal hell: allusion to Milton's *Paradise Lost.*

generally subsisted on the wild animals that crossed my path. I had money with me, and gained the friendship of the villagers by distributing it; or I brought with me some food that I had killed, which, after taking a small part, I always presented to those who had provided me with fire and utensils for cooking.

My life, as it passed thus, was indeed hateful to me, and it was during sleep alone that I could taste joy. O blessed sleep! often, when most miserable, I sank to repose, and my dreams lulled me even to rapture. The spirits that guarded me had provided these moments, or rather hours, of happiness, that I might retain strength to fulfil my **pilgrimage**. Deprived of this respite, I should have sunk under my hardships. During the day I was sustained and inspirited by the hope of night: for in sleep I saw my friends, my wife, and my beloved country; again I saw the benevolent countenance of my father, heard the silver tones of my Elizabeth's voice, and beheld Clerval enjoying health and youth. Often, when wearied by a toilsome march, I persuaded myself that I was dreaming until night should come, and that I should then enjoy reality in the arms of my dearest friends. What agonising fondness did I feel for them! how did I cling to their dear forms, as sometimes they haunted even my waking hours, and persuade myself that they still lived! At such moments vengeance, that burned within me, died in my heart, and I pursued my path towards the destruction of the daemon, more as a task enjoined by heaven, as the **mechanical impulse** of some power of which I was unconscious, than as the ardent desire of my soul.

pilgrimage: journey.

mechanical impulse: mechanical momentum.

What his feelings were whom I pursued I cannot know. Sometimes, indeed, he left marks in writing on the barks of the trees, or cut in stone, that guided me, and instigated my fury. "My reign is not yet over" (these words were legible in one of these inscriptions;) "you live, and my power is complete. Follow me; I seek the everlasting ices of the north, where you will feel the misery of cold and frost, to which I am impassive. You will find near this place, if you follow not too tardily, a dead hare; eat and be refreshed. Come on, my enemy; we have yet to wrestle for our lives; but many hard and miserable hours must you endure until that period shall arrive."

Scoffing devil! Again do I vow vengeance; again do I devote thee, miserable fiend, to torture and death. Never will I give up my search, until he or I perish; and then with what ecstasy shall I join my Elizabeth, and my departed friends, who even now prepare for me the reward of my tedious toil and horrible pilgrimage!

As I still pursued my journey to the northward, the snows thickened and the cold increased in a degree almost too severe to support. The peasants were shut up in their hovels, and only a few of the most hardy ventured forth to seize the animals whom starvation had forced from their hiding-places to seek for prey. The rivers were covered with ice, and no fish could be procured; and thus I was cut off from my chief article of maintenance.

The triumph of my enemy increased with the difficulty of my labours. One inscription that he left was in these words:—"Prepare! your toils only begin: wrap yourself in furs, and provide food; for we shall soon enter upon a journey where your sufferings will satisfy my everlasting hatred."

My courage and perseverance were invigorated by these scoffing words; I resolved not to fail in my purpose; and, calling on Heaven to support me, I continued with unabated fervour to traverse immense deserts, until the ocean appeared at a distance, and formed the utmost boundary of the horizon. Oh! how unlike it was to the blue seasons of the south! Covered with ice, it was only to be distinguished from land by its superior wildness and ruggedness. **The Greeks wept for joy when they beheld the Mediterranean from the hills of Asia**, and hailed with rapture the boundary of their toils. I did not weep; but I knelt down, and, with a full heart, thanked my guiding spirit for conducting me in safety to the place where I hoped, notwithstanding my adversary's gibe, to meet and grapple with him.

Some weeks before this period I had procured a sledge and dogs, and thus traversed the snows with inconceivable speed. I know not whether the fiend possessed the same advantages; but I found that, as before I had daily lost ground in the pursuit, I now gained on him, so much so, that when I first saw the ocean, he was but one day's journey in advance, and I hoped to intercept him before he should reach the beach. With new courage, therefore, I pressed on, and in two days arrived at a wretched hamlet on the sea-shore. I enquired of the inhabitants concerning the fiend, and gained accurate information. A gigantic monster, they said, had arrived the night before, armed with a gun and many pistols; putting to flight the inhabitants of a solitary cottage, through fear of his terrific appearance. He had carried off their store of winter food, and, placing it in a sledge, to draw which he had seized on a numerous drove of trained dogs, he had harnessed them, and the same night, to the joy of the horror-struck villagers, had pursued his journey across the sea in a direction that led to no land; and they conjectured that he must speedily be destroyed by the breaking of the ice, or frozen by the eternal frosts.

On hearing this information, I suffered a temporary access of despair. He had escaped me; and I must commence a destructive and almost endless journey across the mountainous ices of the ocean,—amidst cold that few of the inhabitants could long endure, and which I, the native of a genial and sunny climate, could not hope to survive. Yet at the idea that the fiend should live and be triumphant, my rage and vengeance returned, and, like a mighty tide, overwhelmed every other feeling. After a slight repose, during which the spirits of the dead hovered round, and instigated me to toil and revenge, I prepared for my journey.

I exchanged my land-sledge for one fashioned for the inequalities of the Frozen Ocean; and purchasing a plentiful stock of provisions, I departed from land.

The Greeks . . . Asia: allusion to the famous retreat of Greek mercenaries from Persia, through Armenia to the Black Sea, described by Xenophon, a witness, in *Anabasis* (or *Retreat of the Ten Thousand*).

I cannot guess how many days have passed since then; but I have endured misery, which nothing but the eternal sentiment of a just retribution burning within my heart could have enabled me to support. Immense and rugged mountains of ice often barred up my passage, and I often heard the thunder of the ground sea, which threatened my destruction. But again the frost came, and made the paths of the sea secure.

By the quantity of provision which I had consumed, I should guess that I had passed three weeks in this journey; and the continual protraction of hope, returning back upon the heart, often wrung bitter drops of despondency and grief from my eyes. Despair had indeed almost secured her prey, and I should soon have sunk beneath this misery. Once, after the poor animals that conveyed me had with incredible toil gained the summit of a sloping ice-mountain, and one, sinking under his fatigue, died, I viewed the expanse before me with anguish, when suddenly my eye caught a dark speck upon the dusky plain. I strained my sight to discover what it could be, and uttered a wild cry of ecstasy when I distinguished a sledge, and the distorted proportions of a well-known form within. Oh! with what a burning gush did hope revisit my heart! warm tears filled my eyes, which I hastily wiped away, that they might not intercept the view I had of the daemon; but still my sight was dimmed by the burning drops, until, giving way to the emotions that oppressed me, I wept aloud.

But this was not the time for delay; I disencumbered the dogs of their dead companion, gave them a plentiful portion of food; and, after an hour's rest, which was absolutely necessary, and yet which was bitterly irksome to me, I continued my route. The sledge was still visible; nor did I again lose sight of it, except at the moments when for a short time some ice-rock concealed it with its intervening crags. I indeed perceptibly gained on it and when, after nearly two days' journey, I beheld my enemy at no more than a mile distant, my heart bounded within me.

But now, when I appeared almost within grasp of my foe, my hopes were suddenly extinguished, and I lost all trace of him more utterly than I had ever done before. A ground sea was heard; the thunder of its progress, as the waters rolled and swelled beneath me, became every moment more **ominous** and terrific. I pressed on, but in vain. The wind arose; the sea roared; and, as with the mighty shock of an earthquake, it split, and cracked with a tremendous and overwhelming sound. The work was soon finished: in a few minutes a tumultuous sea rolled between me and my enemy, and I was left drifting on a scattered piece of ice, that was continually lessening, and thus preparing for me a hideous death.

ominous: doomed.

In this manner many appalling hours passed; several of my dogs died; and I myself was about to sink under the accumulation of distress, when I saw your vessel riding at anchor, and holding forth to me hopes of succour and life. I had no conception that vessels ever came so far north, and was astounded at the sight. I quickly destroyed part of my sledge to construct oars; and by these means was enabled, with infinite fatigue, to move my ice-raft in the direction of your ship. I had determined, if you were going southwards, still to trust myself to the mercy of the seas rather than abandon my purpose. I hoped to induce you to grant me a boat with which I could pursue my enemy. But your direction was northwards. You took me on board when my vigour was exhausted, and I should soon have sunk under my multiplied hardships into a death which I still dread—for my task is unfulfilled.

Oh! when will my guiding spirit, in conducting me to the daemon, allow me the rest I so much desire; or must I die, and he yet live? If I do, swear to me, Walton, that he shall not escape; that you will seek him, and satisfy my vengeance in his death. And do I dare to ask of you to undertake my pilgrimage, to endure the hardships that I have undergone? No; I am not so selfish. Yet, when I am dead, if he should appear; if the ministers of vengeance should conduct him to you, swear that he shall not live— swear that he shall not triumph over my accumulated woes, and survive to add to the list of his dark crimes. He is eloquent and persuasive; and once his words had even power over my heart; but trust him not. His soul is as hellish as his form, full of treachery and fiendlike malice. Hear him not; call on the **manes** of William, Justine, Clerval, Elizabeth, my father, and of the wretched Victor, and thrust your sword into his heart. I will hover near, and direct the steel aright.

manes: spirits of the dead.

Walton, in continuation.

August 26th, 17—.

You have read this strange and terrific story, Margaret; and do you not feel your blood congeal with horror, like that which even now curdles mine? Sometimes, seized with sudden agony, he could not continue his tale; at others, his voice broken, yet piercing, uttered with difficulty the words so replete with anguish. His fine and lovely eyes were now lighted up with indignation, now subdued to downcast sorrow, and quenched in infinite wretchedness. Sometimes he commanded his countenance and tones, and related the most horrible incidents with a tranquil voice, suppressing every mark of agitation; then, like a volcano bursting forth, his face would suddenly change to an expression of the wildest rage, as he shrieked out **imprecations** on his persecutor.

imprecations: vulgar or violent language.

His tale is connected, and told with an appearance of the simplest truth, yet I own to you that the letters of Felix and Safie, which he showed me, and the apparition of the monster seen from our ship, brought to me a greater conviction of the truth of his narrative than his **asseverations,** however earnest and connected. Such a monster has then really existence! I cannot doubt it; yet I am lost in surprise and admiration. Sometimes I endeavoured to gain from Frankenstein the particulars of his creature's formation: but on this point he was impenetrable.

asseverations: affirmations.

"Are you mad, my friend?" said he. "or whither does your senseless curiosity lead you? Would you also create for yourself and the world a demoniacal enemy? Peace, peace! learn my miseries, and do not seek to increase your own."

Frankenstein discovered that I made notes concerning his history: he asked to see them, and then himself corrected and augmented them in many places; but principally in giving the life and spirit to the conversations he held with his enemy. "Since you have preserved my narration," said he, "I would not that a mutilated one should go down to **posterity**."

posterity: future generations.

Thus has a week passed away, while I have listened to the strangest tale that ever imagination formed. My thoughts, and every feeling of my soul, have been drunk up by the interest for my guest, which this tale, and his own elevated and gentle manners, have created. I wish to soothe him; yet can I counsel one so infinitely miserable, so destitute of every hope of consolation, to live? Oh, no! the only joy that he can now know will be when he composes his shattered spirit to peace and death. Yet he enjoys one comfort, the offspring of solitude and delirium: he believes, that, when in dreams he holds converse with his friends, and derives from that communion consolation for his miseries, or excitements to his vengeance, that they are not the creations of his fancy, but the beings themselves who visit him from the regions of a remote world. This faith gives a solemnity to his reveries that render them to me almost as imposing and interesting as truth.

Our conversations are not always confined to his own history and misfortunes. On every point of general literature he displays unbounded knowledge, and a quick and piercing apprehension. His eloquence is forcible and touching; nor can I hear him, when he relates a pathetic incident, or endeavours to move the passions of pity or love, without tears. What a glorious creature must he have been in the days of his prosperity, when he is thus noble and godlike in ruin! He seems to feel his own worth, and the greatness of his fall.

"When younger," said he, "I believed myself destined for some great enterprise. My feelings are profound; but I possessed a coolness of judgment that fitted me for illustrious achievements. This sentiment of the worth of my nature supported me, when others would have been oppressed; for I deemed it criminal to throw away in useless grief those talents that might be useful to my fellow-creatures. When I reflected on the work I had completed, no less a one than the creation of a sensitive and rational animal, I could not rank myself with the herd of **common projectors**. But this thought, which supported me in the commencement of my career, now serves only to plunge me lower in the dust. All my speculations and hopes are as nothing; and, **like the archangel who aspired to omnipotence, I am chained in an eternal hell**. My imagination was vivid, yet my powers of analysis and application were intense; by the union of these qualities I conceived the idea, and executed the creation of a man. Even now I cannot recollect, without passion, my reveries while the work was incomplete. I trod heaven in my thoughts, now exulting in my powers, now burning with

common projectors: speculators.

like the archangel . . . eternal hell: allusion to *Paradise Lost.*

the idea of their effects. From my infancy I was imbued with high hopes and a lofty ambition; but how am I sunk! Oh! my friend, if you had known me as I once was, you would not recognise me in this state of degradation. Despondency rarely visited my heart; a high destiny seemed to bear me on, until I fell, never, never again to rise."

Must I then lose this admirable being? I have longed for a friend; I have sought one who would sympathise with and love me. Behold, on these desert seas I have found such a one; but, I fear I have gained him only to know his value, and lose him. I would reconcile him to life, but he repulses the idea.

"I thank you, Walton," he said, "for your kind intentions towards so miserable a wretch; but when you speak of new ties, and fresh affections, think you that any can replace those who are gone? Can any man be to me as Clerval was; or any woman another Elizabeth? Even where the affections are not strongly moved by any superior excellence, the companions of our childhood always possess a certain power over our minds which hardly any later friend can obtain. They know our **infantine** dispositions, which, however they may be afterwards modified, are never **eradicated**; and they can judge of our actions with more certain conclusions as to the integrity of our motives. A sister or a brother can never, unless indeed such symptoms have been shown early, suspect the other of fraud or false dealing, when another friend, however strongly he may be attached, may, in spite of himself, be contemplated with suspicion. But I enjoyed friends, dear not only through habit and association, but from their own merits; and wherever I am, the soothing voice of my Elizabeth, and the conversation of Clerval, will be ever whispered in my ear. They are dead; and but one feeling in such a solitude can persuade me to preserve my life. If I were engaged in any high undertaking or design, fraught with extensive utility to my fellow-creatures, then could I live to fulfil it. But such is not my destiny; I must pursue and destroy the being to whom I gave existence; then my lot on earth will be fulfilled, and I may die."

My beloved Sister,

                                                                      September 2d.

I write to you, encompassed by peril, and ignorant whether I am ever doomed to see again dear England, and the dearer friends that inhabit it. I am surrounded by mountains of ice, which admit of no escape, and threaten every moment to crush my vessel. The brave fellows, whom I have persuaded to be my companions, look towards me for aid; but I have none to bestow. There is something terribly appalling in our situation, yet my courage and hopes do not desert me. Yet it is terrible to reflect that the lives of all these men are endangered through me. If we are lost, my mad schemes are the cause.

infantine: immature.

eradicated: annihilated, exterminated.

And what, Margaret, will be the state of your mind? You will not hear of my destruction, and you will anxiously await my return. Years will pass, and you will have visitings of despair, and yet be tortured by hope. Oh! my beloved sister, the sickening failing of your heart-felt expectations is, in prospect, more terrible to me than my own death. But you have a husband, and lovely children; you may be happy: Heaven bless you, and make you so!

My unfortunate guest regards me with the tenderest compassion. He endeavours to fill me with hope; and talks as if life were a possession which he valued. He reminds me how often the same accidents have happened to other navigators, who have attempted this sea, and in spite of myself, he fills me with cheerful auguries. Even the sailors feel the power of his eloquence; when he speaks, they no longer despair; he rouses their energies, and, while they hear his voice, they believe these vast mountains of ice are mole-hills, which will vanish before the resolutions of man. These feelings are transitory; each day of expectation delayed fills them with fear, and I almost dread a **mutiny** caused by this despair.

mutiny: revolt.

September 5th.

A scene has just passed of such uncommon interest that, although it is highly probable that these papers may never reach you, yet I cannot forbear recording it.

We are still surrounded by mountains of ice, still in imminent danger of being crushed in their conflict. The cold is excessive, and many of my unfortunate comrades have already found a grave amidst this scene of desolation. Frankenstein has daily declined in health: a feverish fire still glimmers in his eyes; but he is exhausted, and, when suddenly roused to any exertion, he speedily sinks again into apparent lifelessness.

I mentioned in my last letter the fears I entertained of a mutiny. This morning, as I sat watching the wan countenance of my friend—his eyes half closed, and his limbs hanging listlessly,—I was roused by half a dozen of the sailors, who demanded admission into the cabin. They entered, and their leader addressed me. He told me that he and his companions had been chosen by the other sailors to come in deputation to me, to make me a requisition, which, in justice, I could not refuse. We were immured in ice, and should probably never escape: but they feared that if, as was possible, the ice should dissipate, and a free passage be opened, I should be rash enough to continue my voyage, and lead them into fresh dangers, after they might happily have surmounted this. They insisted, therefore, that I should engage with a solemn promise, that if the vessel should be freed I would instantly direct my course southward.

This speech troubled me. I had not despaired; nor had I yet conceived the idea of returning, if set free. Yet could I, in justice, or even in possibility, refuse this demand? I hesitated before I answered; when Frankenstein, who had at first been silent, and, indeed, appeared hardly to have force enough to attend, now roused himself; his eyes sparkled, and his cheeks flushed with momentary vigour. Turning towards the men, he said—

"What do you mean? What do you demand of your captain? Are you then so easily turned from your design? Did you not call this a glorious expedition? And wherefore was it glorious? Not because the way was smooth and **placid** as a southern sea, but because it was full of dangers and terror; because, at every new incident, your fortitude was to be called forth, and your courage exhibited; because danger and death surrounded it, and these you were to brave and overcome. For this was it a glorious, for this was it an honourable undertaking. You were hereafter to be hailed as the benefactors of your species; your names adored, as belonging to brave men who encountered death for honour, and the benefit of mankind. And now, behold, with the first imagination of danger, or, if you will, the first mighty and terrific trial of your courage, you shrink away, and are content to be handed down as men who had not strength enough to endure cold and peril; and so, poor souls, they were chilly, and returned to their warm firesides. Why, that requires not this preparation; ye need not have come thus far, and dragged your captain to the shame of a defeat, merely to prove yourselves cowards. Oh! be men, or be more than men. Be steady to your purposes, and firm as a rock. This ice is not made of such stuff as your hearts may be; it is mutable, and cannot withstand you, if you say that it shall not. Do not return to your families with the **stigma** of disgrace marked on your brows. **Return as heroes who have fought and conquered**, and who know not what it is to turn their backs on the foe."

He spoke this with a voice so modulated to the different feelings expressed in his speech, with an eye so full of lofty design and heroism, that can you wonder that these men were moved? They looked at one another, and were unable to reply. I spoke; I told them to retire, and consider of what had been said: that I would not lead them farther north, if they strenuously desired the contrary; but that I hoped that, with reflection, their courage would return.

They retired, and I turned towards my friend; but he was sunk in languor, and almost deprived of life.

How all this will terminate, I know not; but I had rather die than return shamefully,—my purpose unfulfilled. Yet I fear such will be my fate; the men, unsupported by ideas of glory and honour, can never willingly continue to endure their present hardships.

placid: peaceful.

stigma: disgrace.

Return as heroes . . . conquered: an echo of Ulysses' speech in Dante's *Inferno.*

September 7th.

The die is cast; I have consented to return, if we are not destroyed. Thus are my hopes blasted by cowardice and indecision; I come back ignorant and disappointed. It requires more philosophy than I possess, to bear this injustice with patience.

September 12th.

It is past; I am returning to England. I have lost my hopes of utility and glory;—I have lost my friend. But I will endeavour to detail these bitter circumstances to you, my dear sister; and while I am wafted towards England and towards you, I will not despond.

September 9th, the ice began to move, and roarings like thunder were heard at a distance, as the islands split and cracked in every direction. We were in the most imminent peril; but, as we could only remain passive, my chief attention was occupied by my unfortunate guest, whose illness increased in such a degree, that he was entirely confined to his bed. The ice cracked behind us, and was driven with force towards the north; a breeze sprung from the west, and on the 11th the passage towards the south became perfectly free. When the sailors saw this, and that their return to their native country was apparently assured, a shout of tumultuous joy broke from them, loud and long-continued. Frankenstein, who was dozing, awoke, and asked the cause of the tumult. "They shout," I said, "because they will soon return to England."

"Do you then really return?"

"Alas! yes; I cannot withstand their demands. I cannot lead them unwillingly to danger, and I must return."

"Do so, if you will; but I will not. You may give up your purpose, but mine is assigned to me by Heaven, and I dare not. I am weak; but surely the spirits who assist my vengeance will endow me with sufficient strength." Saying this, he endeavoured to spring from the bed, but the exertion was too great for him; he fell back, and fainted.

It was long before he was restored; and I often thought that life was entirely extinct. At length he opened his eyes; he breathed with difficulty, and was unable to speak. The surgeon gave him a **composing draught**, and ordered us to leave him undisturbed. In the mean time he told me, that my friend had certainly not many hours to live.

His sentence was pronounced; and I could only grieve, and be patient. I sat by his bed, watching him; his eyes were closed, and I thought he slept; but presently he called to me in a feeble voice, and, bidding me come near, said—"Alas! the strength I relied on is gone; I feel that I shall soon die, and he, my enemy and persecutor, may still be in being. Think not, Walton, that in the last moments of my existence I feel that burning hatred, and ardent desire of revenge, I once expressed; but I feel myself justified in desiring the death of my adversary. During these

The die is cast: an allusion to the famous remark of Julius Caesar on crossing the Rubicon.

composing draught: restorative liquid.

last days I have been occupied in examining my past conduct; nor do I find it blamable. In a fit of enthusiastic madness I created a rational creature, and was bound towards him, to assure, as far as was in my power, his happiness and well-being. This was my duty; but there was another still paramount to that. My duties towards the beings of my own species had greater claims to my attention, because they included a greater proportion of happiness or misery. Urged by this view, I refused, and I did right in refusing, to create a companion for the first creature. He showed unparalleled malignity and selfishness, in evil; he destroyed my friends; he devoted to destruction beings who possessed exquisite sensations, happiness, and wisdom; nor do I know where this thirst for vengeance may end. Miserable himself, that he may render no other wretched, he ought to die. The task of his destruction was mine, but I have failed. When actuated by selfish and vicious motives, I asked you to undertake my unfinished work; and I renew this request now, when I am only induced by reason and virtue.

"Yet I cannot ask you to renounce your country and friends, to fulfil this task; and now, that you are returning to England, you will have little chance of meeting with him. But the consideration of these points, and the well balancing of what you may esteem your duties, I leave to you; my judgment and ideas are already disturbed by the near approach of death. I dare not ask you to do what I think right, for I may still be misled by passion.

"That he should live to be an instrument of mischief disturbs me; in other respects, this hour, when I momentarily expect my release, is the only happy one which I have enjoyed for several years. The forms of the beloved dead flit before me, and I hasten to their arms. Farewell, Walton! Seek happiness in tranquillity, and avoid ambition, even if it be only the apparently innocent one of distinguishing yourself in science and discoveries. Yet why do I say this? I have myself been blasted in these hopes, yet another may succeed."

His voice became fainter as he spoke; and at length, exhausted by his effort, he sunk into silence. About half an hour afterwards he attempted again to speak, but was unable; he pressed my hand feebly, and his eyes closed for ever, while the irradiation of a gentle smile passed away from his lips.

Margaret, what comment can I make on the untimely extinction of this glorious spirit? What can I say, that will enable you to understand the depth of my sorrow? All that I should express would be inadequate and feeble. My tears flow; my mind is overshadowed by a cloud of disappointment. But I journey towards England, and I may there find consolation.

I am interrupted. What do these sounds portend? It is midnight; the breeze blows fairly, and the watch on deck scarcely stir. Again; there is a sound as of a human voice, but hoarser; it comes from the cabin where the remains of Frankenstein still lie. I must arise, and examine. Good night, my sister.

Great God! what a scene has just taken place! I am yet dizzy with the remembrance of it. I hardly know whether I shall have the power to detail it; yet the tale which I have recorded would be incomplete without this final and **wonderful** catastrophe.

I entered the cabin, where lay the remains of my ill-fated and admirable friend. Over him hung a form which I cannot find words to describe; gigantic in stature, yet uncouth and distorted in its proportions. As he hung over the coffin, his face was concealed by long locks of ragged hair; but one vast hand was extended, in colour and apparent texture like that of a **mummy**. When he heard the sound of my approach, he ceased to utter exclamations of grief and horror, and sprung towards the window. Never did I behold a vision so horrible as his face, of such loathsome yet appalling hideousness. I shut my eyes involuntarily, and endeavoured to recollect what were my duties with regard to this destroyer. I called on him to stay.

He paused, looking on me with wonder; and, again turning towards the lifeless form of his creator, he seemed to forget my presence, and every feature and gesture seemed instigated by the wildest rage of some uncontrollable passion.

"That is also my victim!" he exclaimed: "in his murder my crimes are consummated; the miserable series of my being is wound to its close! Oh, Frankenstein! generous and self-devoted being! what does it avail that I now ask thee to pardon me? I, who irretrievably destroyed thee by destroying all thou lovedst. Alas! he is cold, he cannot answer me."

His voice seemed suffocated; and my first impulses, which had suggested to me the duty of obeying the dying request of my friend, in destroying his enemy, were now suspended by a mixture of curiosity and compassion. I approached this tremendous being; I dared not again raise my eyes to his face, there was something so scaring and unearthly in his ugliness. I attempted to speak, but the words died away on my lips. The monster continued to utter wild and incoherent self-reproaches. At length I gathered resolution to address him in a pause of the tempest of his passion: "Your repentance," I said, "is now **superfluous**. If you had listened to the voice of conscience, and heeded the stings of remorse, before you had urged your diabolical vengeance to this extremity, Frankenstein would yet have lived."

"And do you dream?" said the daemon. "Do you think that I was then dead to agony and remorse?—He," he continued, pointing to the corpse, "he suffered not in the consummation of the deed—oh! not the ten-thousandth portion of the anguish that was mine during the lingering detail of its execution. A frightful selfishness hurried me on, while my heart was poisoned with remorse. Think you that the groans

of Clerval were music to my ears? My heart was fashioned to be susceptible of love and sympathy; and, when wrenched by misery to vice
and hatred, it did not endure the violence of the change, without torture such as you cannot even imagine.

"After the murder of Clerval, I returned to Switzerland, heart-broken
and overcome. I pitied Frankenstein; my pity amounted to horror: I
abhorred myself. But when I discovered that he, the author at once of
my existence and of its unspeakable torments, dared to hope for happiness; that while he accumulated wretchedness and despair upon me, he
sought his own enjoyment in feelings and passions from the indulgence of which I was forever barred, then impotent envy and bitter
indignation filled me with an insatiable thirst for vengeance. I recollected my threat, and resolved that it should be accomplished. I knew
that I was preparing for myself a deadly torture; but I was the slave,
not the master, of an impulse, which I detested, yet could not disobey.
Yet when she died!—nay, then I was not miserable. I had cast off all
feeling, subdued all anguish, to riot in the excess of my despair. **Evil
thenceforth became my good.** Urged thus far, I had no choice but to
adapt my nature to an element which I had willingly chosen. The
completion of my demoniacal design became an **insatiable** passion.
And now it is ended; there is my last victim!"

I was at first touched by the expressions of his misery; yet, when I
called to mind what Frankenstein had said of his powers of eloquence
and persuasion, and when I again cast my eyes on the lifeless form of
my friend, indignation was rekindled within me. "Wretch!" I said. "it
is well that you come here to whine over the desolation that you have
made. You throw a torch into a pile of buildings; and, when they are
consumed, you sit among the ruins and lament the fall. Hypocritical
fiend! if he whom you mourn still lived, still would he be the object,
again would he become the prey, of your accursed vengeance. It is not
pity that you feel; you lament only because the victim of your malignity is withdrawn from your power."

"Oh, it is not thus—not thus," interrupted the being. "Yet such must
be the impression conveyed to you by what appears to be the purport
of my actions. Yet I seek not a fellow-feeling in my misery. No sympathy may I ever find. When I first sought it, it was the love of virtue, the
feelings of happiness and affection with which my whole being overflowed, that I wished to be participated. But now, that virtue has
become to me a shadow, and that happiness and affection are turned
into bitter and loathing despair, in what should I seek for sympathy? I
am content to suffer alone, while my sufferings shall endure: when I
die, I am well satisfied that abhorrence and **opprobrium** should load
my memory. Once my fancy was soothed with dreams of virtue, of
fame, and of enjoyment. Once I falsely hoped to meet with beings,
who, pardoning my outward form, would love me for the excellent

Evil thenceforth became my good: allusion
to *Paradise Lost*—"All Good to me is
lost / Evil be then my Good."

insatiable: difficult or impossible to satisfy.

opprobrium: disgrace.

qualities which I was capable of unfolding. I was nourished with high thoughts of honour and devotion. But now crime has degraded me beneath the meanest animal. No guilt, no mischief, no malignity, no misery, can be found comparable to mine. When I run over the frightful catalogue of my sins, I cannot believe that I am the same creature whose thoughts were once filled with sublime and **transcendent** visions of the beauty and the majesty of goodness. But it is even so; the fallen angel becomes a malignant devil. Yet even that enemy of God and man had friends and associates in his desolation; I am alone.

transcendent: beyond comprehension; of divine origin.

"You, who call Frankenstein your friend, seem to have a knowledge of my crimes and his misfortunes. But in the detail which he gave you of them, he could not sum up the hours and months of misery which I endured, wasting in impotent passions. For while I destroyed his hopes, I did not satisfy my own desires. They were forever ardent and craving; still I desired love and fellowship, and I was still spurned. Was there no injustice in this? Am I to be thought the only criminal, **when all human kind sinned against me**? Why do you not hate Felix, who drove his friend from his door with **contumely**? Why do you not execrate the rustic who sought to destroy the saviour of his child? Nay, these are virtuous and **immaculate** beings! I, the miserable and the abandoned, am an **abortion**, to be spurned at, and kicked, and trampled on. Even now my blood boils at the recollection of this injustice.

when all human kind sinned against me: allusion to *King Lear.*

contumely: contempt.

immaculate: without any flaw or error.

abortion: monstrosity, anomaly.

"But it is true that I am a wretch. I have murdered the lovely and the helpless; I have strangled the innocent as they slept, and grasped to death his throat who never injured me or any other living thing. I have devoted my creator, the select specimen of all that is worthy of love and admiration among men, to misery; I have pursued him even to that irremediable ruin. There he lies, white and cold in death. You hate me; but your abhorrence cannot equal that with which I regard myself. I look on the hands which executed the deed; I think on the heart in which the imagination of it was conceived, and long for the moment when these hands will meet my eyes, when that imagination will haunt my thoughts no more.

"Fear not that I shall be the instrument of future mischief. My work is nearly complete. Neither yours nor any man's death is needed to consummate the series of my being, and accomplish that which must be done; but it requires my own. Do not think that I shall be slow to perform this sacrifice. I shall quit your vessel on the ice-raft which brought me thither, and shall seek the most northern extremity of the globe; I shall collect my funeral pile, and consume to ashes this miserable frame, that its remains may afford no light to any curious and unhallowed wretch, who would create such another as I have been. I shall die. I shall no longer feel the agonies which now consume me, or be the prey of feelings unsatisfied, yet unquenched. He is dead who called me into being; and when I shall be no more, the very remembrance of us both will speedily vanish. I shall no longer see the sun or stars, or feel the winds play on my cheeks. Light, feeling, and sense will pass away; and in this condition must I find my happiness. Some years ago, when the images which this world affords first opened upon me, when I felt the cheering warmth of summer, and heard the rustling of the leaves and the warbling of the birds, and these were all to me, I should have wept to die; now it is my only consolation. Polluted by crimes, and torn by the bitterest remorse, where can I find rest but in death?

"Farewell! I leave you, and in you the last of human kind whom these eyes will ever behold. Farewell, Frankenstein! If thou wert yet alive, and yet cherished a desire of revenge against me, it would be better **satiated** in my life than in my destruction. But it was not so; thou didst seek my extinction, that I might not cause greater wretchedness; and if yet, in some mode unknown to me, thou hadst not ceased to think and feel, thou wouldst not desire against me a vengeance greater than that which I feel. Blasted as thou wert, my agony was still superior to thine; for the bitter sting of remorse will not cease to rankle in my wounds until death shall close them for ever.

satiated: full, saturated.

"But soon," he cried with sad and solemn enthusiasm, "I shall die, and what I now feel be no longer felt. Soon these burning miseries will be extinct. I shall ascend my funeral pile triumphantly, and exult in the agony of the torturing flames. The light of that **conflagration** will fade away; my ashes will be swept into the sea by the winds. My spirit will sleep in peace, or if it thinks, it will not surely think thus. Farewell."

conflagration: a large, disastrous fire.

He sprung from the cabin-window, as he said this, upon the ice-raft which lay close to the vessel. He was soon borne away by the waves, and lost in darkness and distance.

COMMENTARY

The final chapter of Mary Shelley's disturbing novel is comprised of two fragments: the terrifying conclusion of Victor's story; and the conclusion of Walton's expedition, as recounted in his letters to his sister Margaret.

The last segment of Victor's narrative begins with his pursuit of the Monster into the Arctic and ends with his dying request that Walton replace him as the Monster's executioner. In his continual death-defying pursuit of knowledge, Victor is a man Walton deeply admires. Walton's letters contain a report of Victor's last days. Walton reveals more details about Victor's unusual breadth of knowledge, and he finds intriguing Victor's reflections on his own life and work. The letters also include Victor's touching explanation for the impossibility of a new friendship with Walton, his praise of Walton's work, his belief in the importance of Walton's expedition, and his rousing speech to the sailors who, unlike Walton, do not want to continue the perilous voyage. After recounting Victor's final confession and death, the letters narrate Walton's unexpected encounter with the Monster, as well as the Monster's disappearance into the darkness.

Significantly, the absence of Walton's signature at the end of the last letter prohibits the novel from completing its Chinese-box structure because it leaves the ending open and forces the reader to accept the uncertainties created by this intriguing rejection of closure. By leaving Walton's signature off of the last letter, Mary Shelley gives the upper hand to the Monster—an artificial creature, rational yet inhuman, that is composed of both animal and human parts. This is the creature who, ironically, gets to utter the last word in the book. In this sense, the writing itself becomes a testament to monstrosity. It offers no definite conclusion to the struggle between Victor and the Monster, no real proof of the Monster's death, and no clear evidence of what Walton learned, if anything, from Victor's tragic story.

The Monster's overwhelming presence at the end of the story and the fact that, despite his promises, there is no guarantee that he will disappear from the world, eliminates the hope for regeneration or renewal. The ending echoes Elizabeth's disquieting words in Chapter 9, when, after Justine's death, she confesses to Victor that her faith in justice and benevolence has been ruined, that all men appear to her as "monsters," and that she sees herself suspended on the edge of the "abyss," fearing to fall at any moment.

Although the story appears to end, readers, like Elizabeth, remain hanging on the edge of a precipice—in a territory of unanswered questions and difficult dilemmas—knowing that the Monster may still be out there. The book ends, but the story, as Mary Shelly planned from the very beginning, continues to "speak to the mysterious fears of our nature." In Friederich Nietzshe's *Beyond Good and Evil* (written in 1886, thirty-five years after Mary Shelley's death), the German philosopher writes: "If you gaze for too long into the abyss, the abyss will gaze back into your self." Mary Shelley's *Frankenstein* is such a long gaze into the abyss.

The Chase

The chase at the North Pole reverses the initial roles: from being the pursued, Victor becomes the pursuer. The formerly passive, almost paralyzed, Victor turns suddenly active. Having lost everything, after Elizabeth's murder and his father's death, he decides to aggressively follow the Monster and finally destroy him. Achieving this "dear revenge" on the deaths of his family and friend becomes a sacred mission, one that requires supernatural assistance. Interestingly enough, instead of turning to God, Victor appeals to the powers of the Night and its presiding spirits, indicating once again his association with the darker powers, and his inability to search for the truth of his life. As always, Victor's excessive self-indulgence impairs his judgment. Impressed by the "solemnity " of his own words, Victor jumps again to a false conclusion. What he assumes to be an approving response from the

spirits of his "murdered friends" is, in fact, only the Monster's "fiendish laugh."

This ironic episode raises serious doubts about the authenticity of Victor's transformation. Does he indeed change from a passive individual into an active pursuer of his enemy? Critics occasionally argue that after the destruction of the female monster and the death of Elizabeth Lavenza and Alphonse Frankenstein, Victor and the Monster become indistinguishable, equally obsessed with the other's death, equally engaged in an endless cycle of violence. Fierce rivalry, these critics maintain, remains the dominant note at the end of the novel.

And yet, even if it initially appears that Victor is indeed determined to abandon his passivity and engage in a courageous confrontation with the murderer of his family, the entire chase seems to be the Monster's master plan, one in which Victor is nothing more than a marionette manipulated by his creature. The Monster leaves food, warm clothes, and marks of his movements along the trail and seems to protect Victor rather than torment him. There is something almost maternal in the Monster's persistence in keeping Victor alive at any cost. And when Victor dies, the Monster stands before his corpse as a completely tamed creature who takes no pleasure in his success. He praises Victor's generosity and devotion and, in fact, calls himself Victor's murderer, expressing regret that he did not come forward sooner to ask for forgiveness. There is a sense of absolute despair in the Monster's address that completely contradicts the idea of his inherently violent nature. Although Victor's fierce pursuit of the creature makes him appear the most active player in this last chapter, he is paradoxically more passive than ever, and his illness and slow, lingering death renders him unable to confront the creature. The result, once again, is an image of Victor as a weak and inefficient man, whose passivity generates only suffering and death.

This same passivity accounts for Victor's more tragic flaws: his inability to change and his inability to see the truth. He ignores the opportunity to gain insight into his actions and motivations while retelling his story to Walton, and his attitude toward the Monster remains completely unaltered. Victor continues to see the Monster as malicious and vindictive, and considers himself justified in his quest to annihilate his creation. Moreover, the examination of his life that he claims that the retelling of the story has provoked, reassures Victor that there is nothing "blamable" in his actions. Although he recognizes that he had a duty toward the "rational creature" he brought into the world, Victor immediately invokes the duties toward his own people that, he maintains, supersede his first commitment. The same rationalization helps Victor justify his subsequent decision to destroy the female monster he'd promised his creature: Her creation would have engendered humanity. Still shocked by the Monster's "unparalleled malignity," following the destruction of the female creature, Victor declares that the Monster "ought to die" and asks Walton to continue his crusade. Of course, Victor couldn't know that a remorseful, humbled Monster will confess that he would have abandoned his vindictive plans had Victor abandoned his wedding plans. The Monster considered that, having irreparably destroyed the Monster's only hope for companionship and sympathy, Victor had no right to enjoy his own dreams of conjugal happiness. But even had Victor known of the Monster's feeling on this issue, chances are that Victor would have continued to remain rigidly attached to his convictions.

Perpetual suffering, loss, and the onset of death only serve to harden Victor's resolve. He advises Walton to learn from his misery and to throw away the cup with the "intoxicating draught" (see Letter 4) but at the same time encourages him to continue his own perilous voyage, despite the risk to his reluctant crew. When a group of sailors come to ask Walton to turn back the ship so that they may return to their families if the ice breaks and a free passage opens, it is Victor again who addresses them with the most Promethean of his speeches, reminding them that heroic acts are glorious and noble precisely because they are dangerous and challenging. To abandon the dream does not only mean to embarrass the captain and betray humanity's trust in its heroes; it means that one lives with the "stigma of disgrace" for ever. Victor again presents the image of an obsessed man who, in his insistence that the sailors follow Walton on his dangerous voyage, raises the possibility of leaving more destruction, suffering, and death in his wake through his cavalier attempt to control lives again: this time from his own deathbed.

Victor dies a much, much sadder man but not a wiser one. Readers are repeatedly told that in Coleridge's poem the Ancient Mariner is saved when he unknowingly blesses the sea-snakes. In that very moment, the Mariner is able to pray and "The Albatross fell off, and sank/Like lead into the sea." Knowing the scriptural references to the snake, it seems that the Mariner's salvation occurs when he spontaneously (not rationally) prays for and recognizes the sacredness of all forms of life. Unlike the Mariner, Victor cannot make peace with the Monster, and from his deathbed he prays not for his creature's forgiveness but for his destruction.

Critics often note that at least in the end, Victor breaks his destructive silence and learns to communicate. Clearly, there are redemptory possibilities in his revelation although it is unclear whether he tells his story out of an authentic need for confession, out of sympathy for Walton, or out of a well-disguised scheme to use Walton as an instrument of his unfinished revenge.

Is Walton Saved?

Walton sails back home, with his dream in tatters. But is he bitter and dissatisfied, or is he wiser? Hopefully Walton is able to discern, despite Victor's manipulation of the story, the contradictions in the narrative, just as the readers of *Frankenstein* should be able to read between the lines. However, Walton's admission that, until the end, he still clings to the hope that he will find out from Victor "the particulars of his creature's formation," the secret of creating life, testifies that Walton's Promethean impulses are as intense at the end as they were in the beginning of the novel. It seems that he returns home not because he wisely understands the dangers of his single-minded obsession, but because he simply has no choice.

Mary Shelley leaves Walton's position rather ambiguous, making it difficult to decide if Walton is sincerely interested in his crew and his well-being or if he is afraid of a mutiny on the ship. Although he continues to see his companions as "brave" and correct in their assessment of the situation as inevitably destructive, his subsequent words qualify the sailor's withdraw as "cowardice" and "indecision." Their request to abort the voyage, is likewise perceived as unjust. Moreover, Walton blames his crew for disappointing him and holds them responsible for making sure that he does not return home an "ignorant" and defeated man. Indeed, the differences between Walton and his sailors seem to suggest that the men initially hired for sharing Walton's wild courage and ambition come to understand the dangers inherent in any Promethean enterprise while Walton refuses to see the truth.

But if Walton, like Victor, remains attached to his Prometheanism despite his return to England, family, and domesticity, why then, does he not respect Victor's death wish and destroy the Monster as Victor requested? Again, critics are divided on this question. Some see Walton's refusal as proof that, despite his still strong

Promethean ties, Walton is in fact gradually moving toward spiritual recovery, a recovery symbolized in his return from the frigid and sterile north to the warmer and more civilized south. His noncompliance with Victor's final wish represents in this context a gesture of assertiveness, temerity, and self-respect. It guarantees Walton's eventual transformation. Others consider Walton incapable of change. While his companions mature and learn from their experiences, Walton learns little, if anything. The text seems to support this conclusion. Walton listens to Victor's story but the story does not enlighten him. It does not "complete" his education as Walton initially hoped. Confronted with the Monster, Walton reacts with the same passivity as we previously saw in Victor Frankenstein. Instead of challenging the hideousness of the Monster, Walton closes his eyes. Instead of carrying out his friend's request, he listens to the Monster's confession with a "mixture of curiosity and compassion."

The Monster's End

But is it indeed possible to destroy the Monster? Who indeed could kill him? Readers can easily observe that at the end of the novel the Monster undergoes the most spectacular evolution. From an inarticulate simpleton, he develops, through the acquisition of language and the reading of sophisticated texts (one critic suggests that the books the Monster reads constitute a complete Romantic encyclopedia) into an educated being whose rhetorical abilities are indeed impressive. Victor himself acknowledges his persuasiveness and eloquence during their first dialogue on the top of Mont Blanc. Again, before his death, Victor notes the Monster's rhetorical power by warning Walton to remain alert to the Monster's ability to manipulate language.

While it is relatively easy to discern the contradictions existent in Victor's and Walton's final pronouncements, it is almost impossible to sense any discrepancies in the Monster's brilliant argument. Not only is it convincing, logical, and powerful but his explanations reveal a vigorous and dynamic orator, one who knows precisely how to combine rhetorical force with emotional intensity, how to adjust the tone, how to modulate the voice. He moves from a voice controlled by passion, to one "suffocated" by emotion. When accused by Walton of being responsible for Victor's ordeal and untimely death, the Monster retaliates with an artillery of questions, subtly forcing Walton to redirect his attention from Victor's suffering to the Monster's torment. The Monster enumerates all his victims and their violent deaths with astonishing perspicacity, in a manner ingeniously calculated to accentuate not the victims' terror but the Monster's suffering as he feels compelled to act as a murderer despite his inherently good, compassionate nature.

Walton, almost trapped in the Monster's stratagem, recalls Victor's instruction just in time, and regains his vigilance. He accuses the Monster of hypocrisy, and the Monster instantly changes his tone. His powerful voice is replaced by a humble, melancholic one. He recognizes his abominable sins and accepts his destiny. But again, his emphasis is on his virtuous, affectionate nature, on the simple need he had for sympathy, happiness, and enjoyment. Over and over again he blames his transformation from a benevolent being into a murderer on humanity's lack of compassion. Their incapacity to love him for "the excellent qualities" he possesses degraded him into "the meanest animal." Everybody's suffering pales when compared to his absolute misery. His sins, the Monster insists, are indeed despicable but neither is he responsible for them nor could have he done anything to "disobey" a force greater than his will. "I was the slave, not the master," the Monster sarcastically concludes. The Monster ends by directly accusing Walton of prejudice and injustice, followed by a pathetic promise to commit suicide.

Walton remains speechless, totally paralyzed by the Monster's amazing *tour de force*. He can do nothing but let the Monster retire from the cabin as a great actor would leave the scene after a electrifying monologue that leaves the audience in awe. Readers are probably equally dazzled by this superb performance and, in the end, may side with the Monster. It is easy in the presence of such a magnificent moment to forget that the one who uttered these splendid words was, in fact, a murderer. His first victim was a child, and this is precisely the one victim that he (conveniently) forgets to mention in his enumeration of victims from the first part of his speech.

Despite his hideousness, the Monster is also sublime and magnificent. And when this magnificence reminds us of our greatest, most ambitious dreams, we tend to forget the nightmares (both moral and spiritual) that such Promethean dreams might generate. Had Victor or Walton killed the Monster, they would have killed the dream. Or that is exactly what they are: They are this very dream. Destroying the Monster, they would have destroyed themselves. And they are not alone. Mary

Shelley herself remains equally impotent. The answer to her disturbing question from the Introduction, "How I, then a young girl, came to think of and to dilate upon so very hideous an idea?" remains equally lost in "darkness and distance." Before Freud and psychoanalysis, a very young girl wrote a book about the monsters born in the shadow of our dreams. Thirteen years later, she returned to this book and revised it substantially, but this time, too, she let the Monster live. After all, Mary Shelley told the truth at the end of her Introduction: She did not change the story.

The Monster guards Victor's corpse.
Everett Collection

Notes

CLIFFSCOMPLETE REVIEW

Use this CliffsComplete Review to gauge what you've learned and to build confidence in y our under-standing of the original text. After you work through the review questions and the suggested activities, you're well on your way to understanding and appre-ciating the work of Mary Shelley.

IDENTIFY THE QUOTATION

Identify the following quotations by answering these questions:

* Who is the speaker of the quote?

* What does it reveal about the speaker's character?

* What does it tell us about other characters within the novel?

* Where does it occur within the novel?

* What does it show about the themes of the novel?

* What significant imagery do you see in the quote, and how do these images r elate to the o verall imagery of the novel?

1. I shall satiate my ardent curiosity with the sight of a part of the world never before visited, and may tread a land never before imprinted by the foot of man.

2. I was easily led b y my sympathy which he evinced, to use the language of my hear t, to give utterance to the burning ar dour of my soul; and to say , with all the fer vour that warmed me, how gladly I would sacrifice my fortune, my existence, my every hope, to the furtherance of my enterprise. One man's life or death were but a small price to pay for the acquirement of the knowledge which I sought, for the dominion I should acquir e and trans-mit over the elemental foes of our race.

3. While my companion contemplated with a serious and satisfied spirit the magnificent appearances of things, I delighted in investi-gating their causes. The world was to me a secret which I desir ed to divine. C uriosity, earnest research to learn the hidden laws of nature, gladness akin to rapture, as they were unfolded to me, ar e among the earliest sensa-tions I can remember.

4. But these philosophers, whose hands seem only made to dabble in dir t, and their eyes to pore over the microscope or crucible, have indeed performed miracles. They penetrate into the recesses of nature, and show how she works in her hiding places. They ascend into the heav-ens; they have discovered how the blood cir-culates, and the nature of the air we breathe. They have acquired new and almost unlimited powers; they can command the thunders of heaven, mimic the earthquake, and even mock the invisible world with its own shadows.

5. Little alteration, except the growth of our dear children, has taken place since you left us. The blue lake, and sno w-clad mountains—they never change; and I think our placid home and our contented hearts are regulated by the same immutable laws. My trifling occupations take up my time and amuse me, and I am rewarded for any exertions by seeing none but happy, kind faces around me.

6. I ought to be thy Adam, but I am rather the fallen angel, whom thou drivest from joy for no misdeed. Everywhere I see bliss, from which I alone am irrevocably excluded. I was benev-olent and good; misery made me a fiend. Make me happy, and I shall again be virtuous.

7. But where were my friends and r elations? No father had watched my infant days, no mother had blessed me with smiles and car esses; or if they had, all my past life was no w a blot, a blind vacancy in which I distinguished noth-ing. From my earliest remembrance I had been as I then was in height and pr oportion. I had never yet seen a being resembling me, or who claimed any intercourse with me. What was I?

8. Slave, I before reasoned with you, but you have proved yourself unworthy of my condescension. R emember that I hav e po wers; y ou believe yourself miserable, but I can make you so wretched that the light of the day will be hateful to you. You are my creator, but I am your master;—obey.

9. Think not Walton, that in the last moments of my existence I feel the burning hatr ed, and ardent desire of revenge, I once expressed, but I feel myself justified in desiring the death of my adversary. During these last days I hav e been occupied in examining my past conduct; nor do I find it blameable. I n a fit of enthusiastic madness I created a rational creature, and was bound towards him, to assure, as far as was in my po wer, his happiness and w ell-being. This was my duty; but ther e was another still paramount to that. M y duties to wards the beings of my own species had greater claims to my attention, because they included a gr eater proportion of happiness or misery.

10. But it is tr ue that I am a wr etch. I have murdered the lovely and the helpless; I have strangled the innocent as they slept, and grasped to death his throat who never injured me or any other living thing. I hav e devoted my creator, the select specimen of all that is worthy of love and admiration among men, to misery; I have pursued him even to that irremediable ruin. There he lies, white and cold in death. You hate me; but y our abhorrence cannot equal that with which I regard myself.

TRUE / FALSE

1. T F Walton's father wanted his son to embark in a seafaring life.

2. T F Beaufort was a humble man.

3. T F As children, Elizabeth reads poetry and discovers the beauties of nature, whereas Victor becomes more and more interested in the hidden secrets of nature.

4. T F At the University in Ingolstadt, Victor becomes M. Krempe's disciple.

5. T F Inspired by M. Waldman's speech, Victor dedicates himself to the study of chemistry, which leads to the discovery of the secret of life and the creation of a rational being.

6. T F Horrified by his own creation, Victor gives his M onster a name, but he immediately abandons him and returns to Geneva.

7. T F Clerval comes to I ngolstadt to study Oriental languages.

8. T F Justine is Elizabeth's cousin.

9. T F The Monster's first victim is William.

10. T F At the trial, Justine confesses that she has stolen the miniatur e of Car oline Beaufort.

11. T F The first conversation between Victor and the Monster takes place on the top of Mont Blanc.

12. T F In his first conversation with Victor, the Monster compares himself with both Adam and Satan from Milton's *Paradise Lost*.

13. T F Safie is De Lacey's daughter.

14. T F The Monster learns to speak German by listening to F elix r eading fr om Plutarch's *Lives*.

15. T F Without hesitation, Victor agrees to fulfill the Monster's request and create a female companion for him.

16. T F Victor decides to destr oy the almost finished female monster after the Monster kills Clerval.

17. T F After Victor's release from prison, he and his father travel to Paris, where Victor enjo ys the amusements of the Parisian life and completely r ecovers from his depression.

18. T F After the Monster murders Elizabeth on her wedding-night, Victor follows him into the woods and then shoots and injures him.

19. T F On his deathbed, Victor asks Walton to take upon himself the task of destroying the Monster.

20. T F After Victor's death, the Monster promises Walton to disappear in the uninhibited territories of South America.

MULTIPLE CHOICE

1. How old is Walton at the beginning of the story?
   a. 28
   b. 34
   c. 21
   d. 40

2. What is the name of Walton's sister?
   a. Caroline Beaufort
   b. Elizabeth Saville
   c. Margaret Lavenza
   d. Margaret Saville

3. Why doesn't the Russian sailor marry the woman he loves?
   a. He is poor and cannot afford to marry a rich lady.
   b. Her father wants her to marry another man.
   c. She is in love with another man.
   d. She does not want to marry a sailor.

4. Why does Victor tell Walton his story?
   a. He wants Walton to write and publish his unusual story in England.
   b. He recognizes that he shares with Walton the same fascination with forbidden knowledge.
   c. He considers Walton like a brother.
   d. He wants Walton to pursue the Monster and punish him.

5. What introduces Victor to the study of electricity and galvanism?
   a. A discussion with his father
   b. His readings of Cornelius Agrippa, Albert Magnus, and Paracelsus' theories
   c. A conversation with Clerval
   d. A violent thunderstorm and then a conversation with a famous researcher

6. What is the cause of the death of Victor's mother?
   a. She is too debilitated by the years of poverty and hard work following her father's financial ruin.
   b. She dies giving birth to William, her youngest son.
   c. She dies of scarlet fever.
   d. She is nursing Justine, the family's servant, and catches a highly contagious disease.

7. Where does Victor go to school?
   a. Switzerland
   b. England
   c. France
   d. Germany

8. How many brothers does Victor have?
   a. One
   b. Two
   c. Three
   d. None of the above

9. What causes Victor to change his negative opinions toward modern chemists?
   a. M. Krempe shows enthusiasm for Victor's new program of studies.
   b. M. Waldman lectures on the state of modern science.
   c. Like old masters of science, modern chemists search for the elixir of life.
   d. At Ingolstadt, Victor meets students who introduce him to the extraordinary developments achieved by modern chemists.

10. When and where does Victor create the Monster?
    a. At the end of the summer in Geneva
    b. On a remote island in Scotland
    c. At Ingolstadt in November
    d. In England during his spring break from Ingolstadt

11. What book does Felix use to teach Safie French?
    a. Milton's *Paradise Lost*
    b. Goethe's *Sorrows of Werter*
    c. Volney's *Ruins of Empires*
    d. Plutarch's *Lives*

12. Who are the Monster's first two victims?
    a. Father De Lacey and William
    b. William and a little girl in the forest
    c. William and Justine
    d. William and Felix

13. Why does Victor destroy the nearly finished female monster?
    a. He cannot find enough parts to finish the project.
    b. Clerval returns unexpectedly from Scotland, and Victor does not have enough time to finish.
    c. Victor imagines the monster and his mate producing a race of monsters.
    d. Victor receives a letter from Elizabeth asking him to return immediately to Geneva.

14. Who summons Victor's father from Switzerland to visit Victor in prison?
    a. A nurse who is taking care of Victor while he is sick
    b. Mr. Kirwin, an old and benevolent magistrate
    c. Daniel Nugent, a fisherman who appears as a witness
    d. Elizabeth

15. Why does Victor's father die?
    a. The Monster kills him.
    b. He dies of happiness after the wedding of Victor and Elizabeth.
    c. He dies of grief.
    d. He dies of old age.

16. Where does Victor follow the Monster?
    a. On a deserted island in Scotland
    b. Through Europe
    c. Into Russia and the polar regions
    d. None of the above

17. Why do Walton's sailors revolt?
    a. They are unhappy seeing Walton spending so much time with Victor Frankenstein.
    b. They are infuriated by Victor's speech.
    c. They are tired and want to turn back home.
    d. They profoundly dislike Walton.

ACTIVITIES

1. Read fragments from Mary Shelley's journals and letters (the introduction to the three volumes of letters is an excellent guide) and consult at least three reliable Internet sources. Then prepare minibiographies of Mary Shelley's life and work, paying attention to the contexts that influenced her private and public life as a woman and as a writer.

2. As a continuation of the previous activity, research the situation of women during the early 19th century, expectations for women in the public and private sphere, and their rights and

obligation. Then compare Mary Shelley's attitudes to these ideals and define her personality and her position in the light of this comparison.

3. Mary Shelley's novel provides an important commentary on some important issues that preoccupied the Romantic artists, issues such as imagination, nature, and creativity. Research the general characteristics of Romanticism and write an essay on the differences between Mary Shelley's and other Romantic writers' conceptions regarding imagination and nature.

4. Read Coleridge's poem " The Rime of the Ancient Mariner" and discuss the parallels between the Mariner's story and the story of Victor Frankenstein.

5. Imagine that you are Mary Shelley's friend. Write her a letter immediately after the publication of the novel, addressing specific issues that are of interest to you (education, the relationship between children and parents, etc.)

6. Write a stage adaptation for the most important scenes in the novel, paying attention to stage directions, costumes, lighting, etc.

7. Watch different films adaptations on Frankenstein and then write on specific similarities and differences in characters, setting, and plot between the novel and one or more of these adaptations. Remember that novels and films are two very different mediums, requiring different techniques and working with different limitations and that each art form should be considered in its own terms. Write reviews on how these cinematic productions altered, enriched, complicated, or oversimplified the novel.

8. *Frankenstein* opens with Robert Walton's letter to his sister Margaret from St. Petersburgh, Russia, explaining his intentions to explore the Arctic regions. These letters reveal Walton's obsessive desire to discover an utopian tropical territory at the very center of the pole and, at the same time, introduce almost all major themes of the novel. Based on these letters ask students to imagine Margaret Saville's answers to her brother's letters.

ANSWERS
Identify the Quotation

1. Walton writes these words in his first letter to his sister, Margaret, on December 11, from St. Petersburgh, Russia. He reflects on the events that fueled his dream of traveling to the North Pole to discover a shorter passage to the North Pacific Ocean. He firmly believes that he will find a tropical paradise at the center of the pole, and he wants to be the first to discover it. His words reveal an obsessively ambitious character and a curiosity that exceeds a normal desire for the acquisition of knowledge. This section introduces the novel's main theme: the desire to transgress human limitations.

2. This fragment is from Walton's fourth letter to Margaret recounting his encounter with Victor Frankenstein, the man Walton and his crew recover from the ocean. Walton's instant sympathy for the stranger enables him to talk freely about his Promethean dream. Walton's words divulge the magnitude of his ambition and his dangerous enthusiasm. He insists that no sacrifice is too much when the possibility of regaining Eden is at stake. The passage introduces another important theme—sympathetic affinity between people that generates stronger bonds than any other relationship.

3. Victor uses these words in Chapter 2. They describe the differences between Elizabeth Lavenza (the orphan adopted by the Frankensteins) and Victor regarding their interests and intellectual inclinations as children. According to Victor's description, Elizabeth appears as superficial and childish, whereas Victor presents himself as a focused, determined young man, whose singular aspiration is to discover the final cause of all things. Victor's narcissism and arrogance are clearly disclosed in this fragment.

4. M. Waldman, a chemistry professor at the University of Ingolstadt and Victor's future mentor, uses these words in Chapter 3. They are part of a modern chemistry lecture that Victor Frankenstein attends in his early days as a student. M. Waldman's entire lecture, particularly these words, reveal a philosophy of science based on the idea that the role of the scientist is to aggressively control and manipulate nature. Victor's aggressively inclined nature and unbalanced ambition unreservedly embraces this Promethean perspective. These words and Victor's reaction to them critically impact the progress of the action and the evolution of Victor's character.

5. Elizabeth Lavenza writes these words in her first letter to Victor in Chapter 6. In contrast with the general optimistic tone of her letter and with Elizabeth's seemingly cheerful, vivacious nature, these words advance a surprisingly pessimistic perspective on human existence. Elizabeth affirms that human destiny is controlled by indifferent forces and that rigid, implacable laws govern man and his world. Her attitude coincides with Victor Frankenstein's suspicion that an inexorable destiny also determined his entire life. Mary Shelley expresses through these two characters her own growing pessimism after 1825.

6. In Chapter 10, the Monster addresses these words to Victor during their first real dialogue after Victor's abandonment of his creature. In his speech, the Monster recapitulates his evolution and sufferings and compares himself with Adam, the first man, as well as with Satan, the fallen angel. Although the Monster links himself to Milton's characters from *Paradise Lost*, he is, in fact, fully aware that he differs essentially from both Adam and Satan. Unlike Adam, he was not made in his creator's image, and his creator never protected him. Whereas Satan has a community of devils around him

to encourage and support him, the Monster is all alone in the world. The identification with Milton's characters is a pivotal metaphor in *Frankenstein*. Victor also appears as an Adam-and-Satan figure in the novel, which supports the theory of him and the Monster as doubles.

7. These are the Monster's words at the end of Chapter 13. They reveal the Monster's crisis of identity after listening to Felix's readings from Volney's *Ruins of Empires*. His newly acquired knowledge regarding the origins of humanity, social relations, and gender differences make him reflect on his own origin, condition, and identity. For the first time, the Monster realizes the meaning of being born without a history, being abandoned, and being deprived of a loving family. A sense of absolute dejection accompanies the Monster's reflections. This passage thus establishes the connection between knowledge and suffering as one of the novel's major themes.

8. The Monster uses these violent words in Chapter 22. After Victor decides to destroy the promised female monster, thus annihilating his creature's only hope for a mate and companionship, the Monster visits him at home and promises vengeance. This reversal of roles, casting Victor and his creature alternatively in the role of the master and slave, makes the distinction between them difficult.

9. These are Victor's testamentary words in Chapter 24. Victor examines his actions and conduct and finds nothing objectionable or reprehensible in his attitude or judgment. Therefore, he remains convinced that his actions, as well as his hatred for the Monster and desire for revenge, are perfectly justifiable. The passage indicates that Victor Frankenstein learned nothing from his experiences, sufferings, and failures. There is no catharsis at the end of his tragic story. His words before death reaffirm his Prometheanism and attest to his

inability to accept responsibility or to acquire self-knowledge.

10. These words constitute the Monster's unexpected confession in the final chapter of the book. Unlike Victor, who dies without understanding his role in the tragedy generated by his irresponsible and selfish actions, the Monster admits responsibility to his hideous crimes and repents. He proves that, despite his deformities, he is not morally monstrous.

True/ False

(1) F (2) F (3) T (4) F (5) T (6) F (7) T (8) F (9) T (10) F (11) T (12) T (13) F (14) F (15) F (16) F (17) F (18) F (19) T (20) F

Multiple Choice

(1) a. (2) d. (3) c. (4) b . (5) d. (6) c. (7) d. (8) b. (9) b . (10) c. (11) c. (12) c. (13) c. (14) b. (15) c. (16) c. (17) c.

CLIFFSCOMPLETE RESOURCE CENTER

The learning doesn't need to stop here. CliffsComplete Resource Center shows you the best of the best: great links to information in print, on film, and online. And the following sources aren't all the great resources available to you; visit www.cliffsnotes.com for tips on reading literature, writing papers, giving presentations, locating other resources, and testing your knowledge.

BOOKS AND ARTICLES

Frankenstein. 1818. Ed. Marilyn Butler. Oxford: Oxford University Press, 1994.

Butler's introduction examines the contexts that influenced Mary Shelley's novel. She suggests that the contemporary dispute between two famous biologists, Lawrence and Abernethy, constitutes the model used by Mary Shelley in her use of science in the novel. These scientists represent two different perspectives in understanding and describing life— the vitalist principle and the mechanical principle.

Frankenstein. 1818. Eds. D.L. Macdonald and Kathleen Scherf. Peterborough: Broadview Press, 1994.

This edition contains an introduction, the 1818 text, seven appendices, and a list of recommended readings. Particularly useful is Appendix F, which lists the revisions in the 1831 edition. Also useful is Appendix D, which provides excerpts from contemporary reviews of *Frankenstein*.

Frankenstein. 1818. Ed. J. Paul Hunter. A Norton Critical edition. New York and London: W.W. Norton & Company, 1996.

The edition includes the original text, primary contextual materials, nineteenth century reviews on *Frankenstein*, and a section of modern critical essays. Hunter's introduction and selection of texts provide a useful overture to readers with little experience in Mary Shelley's novel and in Romanticism in general.

Frankenstein. 1831. Ed. M.K. Joseph. Oxford: Oxford University Press, 1980.

The introduction discusses the Romantic Promethean myth and its association with science and with the theme of the double in the novel. Joseph argues that by connecting Prometheus with a scientist, Mary Shelley completely changes the implications of Prometheus' presence in the Romantic mythology. Always a favorite metaphor of the Romantic artist, Prometheus becomes, in Mary Shelley's novel, a metaphor for the usurping creator.

Dunn, Jane. *Moon in Eclipse: A Life of Mary Shelley*. London: Weidenfeld, 1978

A decent biography of Mary Shelley, with occasional, minor inaccuracies.

Spark, Muriel. *Mary Shelley*. New York: Dutton, 1987.

A revised version of *Child of Light* (1951), Muriel's biography presents Mary Shelley as an author in her own right who deserves attention for her splendid literary achievements. Readable and captivating, this biography represents a valuable and adequate resource for any student who wants to understand how Mary Shelley's life shaped and informed her work.

Nitchie, Elizabeth. *Mary Shelley: Author of Frankenstein*. New Brunswick: Rutgers UP, 1953

Although an early biographical and critical study of Mary Shelley's life and work, Nitchie's book is still useful. Particularly effective are the readings of Shelley's fiction written after *Frankenstein*.

The Letters of Mary Wollstonecraft Shelley. Ed. Betty T. Bennett. 3 vols. Baltimore: Johns Hopkins University Press, 1980.

A splendid edition of Mary Shelley's 1,300 letters published between 1814 and 1850. The letters are an important document in understanding not only Mary Shelley's life but also her attitudes toward family and friends as well as political and literary events of the time. The letters reflect Mary Shelley's daily routines, her relationship with Percy and her children, and her passions and aspirations. Particularly interesting are her observations from the early letters revealing concerns for her education. In the letters following her husband's death, Mary Shelley concentrates on her friendships with such writers as Washington Irving and George Eliot.

The Journals of Mary Shelley. Eds. Paula Feldman and Diana Scott-Kilvert. Oxford: Clarendon Press, 1987.

A particularly valuable resource for students and scholars interested in contemporary details, this collection contains Mary Shelley's notebooks between 1814 and 1844. Although the journals provide a wealth of interesting information on Mary Shelley's relationship with Percy, Godwin, and other intellectuals of her time and on her evolving personality, they do not offer any insight into her work as a writer and never reflect on her novels.

Behrendt, Stephen. "Mary Shelley, *Frankenstein*, and the Woman Writer's Fate." *Romantic Women Writers: Voices and Countervoices*. London and Hanover: University Press of New England, 1995.

An excellent study discussing the connections between Victor Frankenstein, the Monster, and Mary Shelley's concerns regarding her public role as a writer. In male-dominated cultures, Behrendt maintains that women are constantly reminded of their public and private roles and discouraged from writing or participating in any artistic expression not characteristically feminine. Victor Frankenstein's difficulties and the Monster's precarious existence reflect Mary Shelley's fear of authorship and say something essentially important about the condition of the woman writer.

Gilbert, Sandra M., and Susan Gubar. "Mary Shelley's Monstrous Eve." *The Madwoman in the Attic: The Woman Writer and the Nineteenth-Century Literary Imagination*. New Haven: Yale UP, 1979.

The core of the argument is that the Monster is really "a female in disguise," which translates, the authors argue, into Mary Shelley's acceptance of female monstrosity. Instead of challenging Milton's attitude toward women and denouncing a tradition that sees women as vile and degraded creatures, Mary Shelley seems to agree to women's moral deformity. The authors conclude that the Monster is as "nameless as a woman is in patriarchal society, as nameless as unmarried, illegitimately pregnant Mary Wollstonecraft Godwin may have felt herself to be at the time she wrote *Frankenstein*."

Johnson, Barbara. "My Monster/My Self." *Diacritics* 12 (1982): 2-10.

An excellent analysis addressing the connections between Mary Shelley's 1831 Introduction and some major themes of the novel. The author examines the intersections of authorship, motherhood, and autobiographical writing. Victor's creation of the Monster, Johnson maintains, parallels Mary Shelley's creation of her novel. Consequently, *Frankenstein* can be read as the story of writing *Frankenstein*.

Lavine, George, and U.C. Knoepflmacher, Eds. *The Endurance of Frankenstein: Essays in Mary Shelley's Novel*. Berkeley: University of California P, 1979.

A valuable collection of essays addressing the novel's scientific, biographical, cultural, and literary contexts. George Lavine's excellent study, "The Ambiguous Heritage of *Frankenstein*," outlines some major themes of the novel and the various traditions that informed them. Kate Ellis's essay, "Monsters in the Garden: Mary Shelley and the Bourgeois Family," is a productive discussion of the sex roles in *Frankenstein*. Dale Scott's essay, "Vital Artifice: Mary, Percy, and the Psychopolitical Integrity of *Frankenstein*," argues that both Victor's education and the Monster's revenge are modeled on differ ent aspects of Percy Shelley's personal, intellectual, and political life.

Mellor, Anne K. *Mary Shelley: Her Life, Her Fiction, Her Monsters.* New York: Methuen, 1988.

Anne Mellor's impressive study examines Mary Shelley's life and fiction, and she argues that a common theme for both is M ary's search for a lo ving family, for a sympathetic center in her life and in the life of her characters. The chapters dedicated to *Frankenstein* look at the novel from several perspectives—feminist, biographical, philosophical, historical, psy chological, and so on—analyzing the implications of this essential failure of the family.

Small, Christopher. *Ariel Like a Harpy: Shelley, Mary, and Frankenstein.* London: Gollancz, 1972

A book dev oted to the Ariel-P ercy / S helley-Caliban relationship, which he believes Mary Shelley exploits in *Frankenstein*.

Poovey, M ary. *The Proper Lady and the Woman Writer: Ideology as Style in the Works of Mary Wollstonecraft, Mary Shelley, and Jane Austen.* Chicago: University of Chicago P, 1984.

A sophisticated analysis of Mary Shelley's social, psychological, and linguistic connections with the eighteenth and nineteenth century concept of the proper lady, which essentially demands that women conform to their assigned roles as mothers, wives, supporters, and comfor ters of men. Women who want to pursue a car eer in pr ofessional writing, Poovey explains, need to engage in a number of strategies that can facilitate the expression of their creative self within a society that generally considers artistic ambitions improper and indecorous.

Brennan, Matthew C. "The Landscape of G rief in Mary S helley's *Frankenstein.* " *Studies in the Humanities* 15:1 (1989): 33-44

Brennan asserts that, like Victor Frankenstein, Mary Shelley is devastated by the loss of her mother and her nurturing presence. In order to escape this consciousness of grief , M ary S helley and Victor Frankenstein turn to the sublime. I n the majestic landscape of the Alps, where Victor hopes to find comfort and relief from sorrow, and wants to symbolically r eunite with his mother , the M onster appears as a reminder of his inescapable suffering. Mary Shelley neutralizes her desire for regression by producing her narrative.

Mary Shelley in Her Time. Eds. Betty Bennett and Stuart Curran. Baltimore: Johns Hopkins UP, 2000.

The essays in this collection offer an ex cellent discussion of various contexts that influenced the work of Mary Shelley, a writer who par ticipated in England's literar y life at a time of pr ofound transformations in all fields. The essays discuss her novels, her editing work, her politics, and her development as a female writer.

INTERNET

"Mary Wollstonecraft and M ary Shelley: Writing Lives."
www.ucalgary.ca/UofC/Others/CIH/WritingLives/index.html

This research network centers on Mary Shelley's relationship with her mother, Mary Wollstonecraft. Papers and commentaries address different aspects of these two writers' works, their attitudes toward writing, and their life as women and as writers at a time of significant changes in England. This network has an excellent Internet Resources page and links to Romantic resources (such as Romantic Circle and Women R omantic-era Writers), listser vs (Wollstonecraft Listserv, NASSR-L), conferences, and online journals (including *Keats-Shelley Journal* and *Romanticism on the Net*). The site is sponsored by the Calgary Institute for the Humanities and is financially supported by various organizations, language departments, and study groups.

"My Hideous Progeny: Mary Shelley's Frankenstein."
http://home-l.worldonline.nl/~hamberg/home2.html

The site consists of sev eral pages dev oted to Mary Shelley's life, family, friends, and novels. The text of *Frankenstein* is available in HTML format. The site also include links to other sites dealing with Romantic and G othic literatur e, M ary S helley's famous relatives (Wollstonecraft, Godwin, and Percy Shelley), and the authors of wor ks that are invoked in *Frankenstein* (Byron, Albertus Magnus, Milton, Wordsworth, and so on).

"Mary Shelley's *Frankenstein* 1816."
www.students.dsu.edu/bushd/frankweb.html

This site was dev eloped to help students and scholars of Romanticism, Gothicism, Science Fiction, or other academic genres work with Mary Shelley's novel. The site includes links to online versions of *Frankenstein*, movie reviews, and academic papers. It also offers pages dedicated to the education of Victor and the Monster, as well as pages containing information on Albertus Magnus, Cornelius Agrippa, and Paracelsus.

"*Frankenstein*: Penetrating the Secrets of Nature."
www.nlm.nih.gov/hmd/frankenstein/frankhome.html

The National Library of Medicine's exhibition on the *Frankenstein* theme is available here. The exhibition considers contemporary scientific connections between *Frankenstein* and popular culture, and different perspectives on the ethical aspects of science.

"Mary Wollstonecraft S helley: Chr onology and Resources Site."
www.english.udel.edu/swilson/mws/about.html

This site offers a chronology of Mary Shelley's life and work, contemporary reviews of her novels, and r eviews of the stage adaptations inspir ed b y *Frankenstein*. Created by Shanon Lawson at the University of Delaware, this page provides excellent links with other pages.

"Mary Wollstonecraft Godwin Shelley."
http://virtual.park.uga.edu/~232/mws.html

This site contains Nelson Hilton's reading notes and excerpts from Mary Shelley's *Journals* and *Letters*, from G odwin's *Political Justice*, and fr om Wollstonecraft's *Vindication of the Rights of Woman*. It also includes a list of the novel's themes.

"Romantic Chronology."
http://english.ucsb.edu:591/rchrono_default.html

This site organizes information by date and provides hypertextual highlights for additional information on particular events, authors, works, topics, and so on. This model allows users to customize their search according to their interests.

"North American S ociety for the S tudy of Romanticism."
NASSR-L@wvnvm.wvnet.edu

Apart from the Web, NASSR offers an ongoing mailing list regarding the Romantic period. To subscribe, contact D avid Stewart at dcstewa@wvnnvm.wvnet.edu.

To subscribe to a mailing list concerning M ary Wollstonecraft, send an e-mail to mailbase@mailbase.ac.uk

FILMS

Frankenstein. Directed by Searle Dawley. Performed by Charles Ogle. 1910.

Produced by Thomas A. Edison and considered lost for more than 60 years, this approximately ten-minute silent film is the first pr oduction based on the plot of Mary Shelley's novel. Charles Ogle's performance received excellent reviews. The film is not available for public viewing.

Frankenstein. Directed by James Whale. Performed by Boris Karloff, Colin Clive, Valerie Hobson, and Elsa Lanchester. Universal, 1931. 71 min.

This is the first sound version of *Frankenstein* directed by the British-born James Whale for Universal Pictures. The script is not based on Mary Shelley's original but on a v ersion of Peggy Webling's London stage adaptation of the no vel. Karloff is effective and convincing, although he is not allowed to utter a single word. Equally effective is Colin Clive in the r ole of H enry Frankenstein (Victor in the novel), the obsessed scientist who isolates himself in a ruined castle to construct a human being. Unlike Victor, Henry Frankenstein has an assistant, Fritz, played by Dwight Frye.

The Bride of Frankenstein. Directed by James Whale. Screenplay b y William H urlbut and J ohn Balderston. Performed by Boris Karloff, Colin Clive, Valerie Hobson, and Elsa Lanchester. Universal, 1935. 80 min.

A typical Gothic film with a dark, mysterious atmosphere. The most intriguing aspect of this production is Elsa Lanchester's double role. In the opening scene, she plays M ary S helley, the charming author of the novel, who tells Byron and Percy Shelley that her story from the original 1931 film did not, in fact, end. Consequently, a sequel of the story begins with the Monster's escape from the burning windmill. A t the end of the mo vie, Lanchester reappears as the bride of the Monster in a memorable interpretation. Although the film suffers from excess and numerous additions that complicate the plot unnecessarily, the performances are remarkable and Frank Waxman's music superb.

Young Frankenstein. Directed by Mel Brooks. Performed by Gene Wilder, Peter Boyle, Madeline Kahn, Cloris Leachman, and Marty Feldman. Fox, 1974.

The film was nominated for O scars in 1975 (Best Sound and B est Writing categories). *Young Frankenstein* is a satire of the 1930s F rankenstein movies in which Frederick Frankenstein, the great-great-grandson of the original Doctor Frankenstein, who has tried hard to escape his name's notoriety, travels to Transylvania to settle his grandfather 's estate. He discovers his grandfather's laboratory, and assisted by Igor and Inga, he creates his own Monster. The movie has succulent humor, is intelligent and wonderfully entertaining

Mary Shelley's Frankenstein. Directed by Kenneth Branagh. Performed by B ranagh, R obert De Niro, H elena Bonham Car ter, Tom H ulce, Cherie Lunghi, Celia Imrie, Ian Holm. 1994.

The virtue (indeed, a major one) of this film consists in giving the monster a v oice, something completely ignor ed by pr evious cinematic tr eatments. However, despite this major improvement

and the beautiful colors, evocative music, enormous energy, and magnificent pictures of the laboratory, Branagh's version represents a flagrant distortion of Mary Shelley's novel. Probably nothing is more questionable in Branagh's treatment of the book than the hideous reanimation of Elizabeth, which, though intriguing in its suggestions, disregards one of Mary Shelley's main themes—V ictor's impossible r elationship with Elizabeth and men's difficult relationship with women in general. S tudents frequently claim that B ranagh's cinematic interpr etations of complex literary works made such a powerful impression on them that, after the film, they became interested in the book themselves. Although this fact is in many ways problematic, students still like to read good books, which is wonderful news indeed.

Frankenstein. Directed by David Wickes. Performed by Patrick Bergin, Randy Quaid, John Mills, Fiona Gilles, Lambert Wilson, Roger Bizley, Jacinta Mulcahy. 1993.

This almost 120-minute adaptation of *Frankenstein* is a TV production that pr esents a monster (Randy Quaid) assembled not from various parts but cloned fr om Victor himself. This interpr etation, echoing *Jeckyll and Hyde,* has interesting implications for the theme of the double that so many critics identified in the book. The performances of Begin and Quaid are powerful and provocative. Like all other film versions, this adaptation erroneously presents Victor as a doctor rather than a student, as M ary Shelley portrays him.

Frankenstein

CLIFFSCOMPLETE READING GROUP DISCUSSION GUIDE

Use the following questions and topics to enhance your reading group discussions. The discussion can help get y ou thinking—and hopefully talking—about Frankenstein in a whole new way!

Discussion Questions

1. Discuss the imagery of *light* in the novel, paying attention to the implications that the use of this image has for differ ent characters. For instance, what is the significance of Walton's search of "the country of eternal light"?

2. Compare and contrast the women of the novel. Do you see significant differences between Elizabeth and Safie? Between Safie and Agatha? How does Elizabeth differ from Caroline? How is she similar to Car oline? What do Caroline, Elizabeth, and Justine have in common? What kind of mother is Mrs. M oritz compared to Caroline Beaufort Frankenstein?

3. Compare and contrast the fathers in the novel. Are there differences between Mr. Clerval and Alphonse Frankenstein regarding education? What similarities and what differences do you see between Beaufort, Caroline's father, and Alphonse F rankenstein? H ow do the other fathers in the no vel differ fr om Father D e Lacey? What do you think Mary Shelley is saying through the character of Safie's father? Why are ther e mor e fathers than mothers in the novel? Which one, if any, is the ideal father?

4. Discuss the themes of *friendship* and *education* in the no vel. H ow ar e these two themes related? What do they reveal about different characters? Can you identify how these two themes ar e used to sho w the differ ences between men and women? Also, why is the Monster mor e violent as he becomes mor e

educated? Is there a relationship between education and the concept of *sympathy*?

5. What function does the De Lacey family serve in the narrative?

6. Identify instances of the sublime in the novel. Are, for instance, the North Pole, Mont Blanc, the Alps, and the O rkney I slands sublime? Why or why not? What is the function of the sublime in the novel?

7. The M onster claims that the book that impressed him the most was Milton's *Paradise Lost*, and in his first conversation with Victor he identifies with both A dam and S atan. Whom does the Monster identify with most? In y our opinion, is the M onster mor e like Adam or like Satan?

8. Discuss the theme of the Promethean scientist in the novel. What do the characters of Victor Frankenstein and R obert Walton o we to Prometheus in his double role of fire-bringer and creator of humanity? Does Mary Shelly share other Romantic poets' enthusiasm for Prometheus and Satan, the divine rebels? How would you characterize her attitude to ward Promethean ambition?

9. What is Victor's relationship with women? Do his remarks to or about Elizabeth reveal any tension in their r elationship? What are the implications of his considering Elizabeth his "gift" and his "possession"? Why does he postpone the marriage? What are Victor's real reasons for stopping the cr eation of a female companion for the Monster? Why doesn't he come forward to defend Justine?

10. What do readers and Margaret Saville have in common? What is a good reader as defined in the novel?

Index

continued

continued

Y

CliffsNotes™

CLIFFSCOMPLETE
Hamlet
Julius Caesar
King Henry IV, Part I
King Lear
Macbeth
The Merchant of Venice
Othello
Romeo and Juliet
The Tempest
Twelfth Night

Look for Other Series in the CliffsNotes Family

LITERATURE NOTES
Absalom, Absalom!
The Aeneid
Agamemnon
Alice in Wonderland
All the King's Men
All the Pretty Horses
All Quiet on Western Front
All's Well & Merry Wives
American Poets of the
   20th Century
American Tragedy
Animal Farm
Anna Karenina
Anthem
Antony and Cleopatra
Aristotle's Ethics
As I Lay Dying
The Assistant
As You Like It
Atlas Shrugged
Autobiography of Ben Franklin
Autobiography of Malcolm X
The Awakening
Babbit
Bartleby & Benito Cereno
The Bean Trees
The Bear
The Bell Jar
Beloved
Beowulf
Billy Budd & Typee
Black Boy
Black Like Me

Bleak House
Bless Me, Ultima
The Bluest Eye & Sula
Brave New World
Brothers Karamazov
Call of Wild & White Fang
Candide
The Canterbury Tales
Catch-22
Catcher in the Rye
The Chosen
Cliffs Notes on the Bible
The Color Purple
Comedy of Errors...
Connecticut Yankee
The Contender
The Count of Monte Cristo
Crime and Punishment
The Crucible
Cry, the Beloved Country
Cyrano de Bergerac
Daisy Miller & Turn...Screw
David Copperfield
Death of a Salesman
The Deerslayer
Diary of Anne Frank
Divine Comedy-I. Inferno
Divine Comedy-II. Purgatorio
Divine Comedy-III. Paradiso
Doctor Faustus
Dr. Jekyll and Mr. Hyde
Don Juan
Don Quixote
Dracula
Emerson's Essays
Emily Dickinson Poems
Emma
Ethan Frome
Euripides' Electra & Medea
The Faerie Queene
Fahrenheit 451
Far from Madding Crowd
A Farewell to Arms
Farewell to Manzanar
Fathers and Sons
Faulkner's Short Stories
Faust Pt. I & Pt. II
The Federalist
Flowers for Algernon
For Whom the Bell Tolls
The Fountainhead
Frankenstein
The French Lieutenant's Woman
The Giver
Glass Menagerie & Streetcar
Go Down, Moses

The Good Earth
Grapes of Wrath
Great Expectations
The Great Gatsby
Greek Classics
Gulliver's Travels
Hamlet
The Handmaid's Tale
Hard Times
Heart of Darkness & Secret Sharer
Hemingway's Short Stories
Henry IV Part 1
Henry IV Part 2
Henry V
House Made of Dawn
The House of the Seven Gables
Huckleberry Finn
I Know Why the Caged Bird Sings
Ibsen's Plays I
Ibsen's Plays II
The Idiot
Idylls of the King
The Iliad
Incidents in the Life of a Slave Girl
Inherit the Wind
Invisible Man
Ivanhoe
Jane Eyre
Joseph Andrews
The Joy Luck Club
Jude the Obscure
Julius Caesar
The Jungle
Kafka's Short Stories
Keats & Shelley
The Killer Angels
King Lear
The Kitchen God's Wife
The Last of the Mohicans
Le Morte Darthur
Leaves of Grass
Les Miserables
A Lesson Before Dying
Light in August
The Light in the Forest
Lord Jim
Lord of the Flies
Lord of the Rings
Lost Horizon
Lysistrata & Other Comedies
Macbeth
Madame Bovary
Main Street
The Mayor of Casterbridge
Measure for Measure
The Merchant of Venice

Middlemarch
A Midsummer-Night's Dream
The Mill on the Floss
Moby-Dick
Moll Flanders
Mrs. Dalloway
Much Ado About Nothing
My Ántonia
Mythology
Narr. ...Frederick Douglass
Native Son
New Testament
Night
1984
Notes from Underground
The Odyssey
Oedipus Trilogy
Of Human Bondage
Of Mice and Men
The Old Man and the Sea
Old Testament
Oliver Twist
The Once and Future King
One Day in the Life of
   Ivan Denisovich
One Flew Over Cuckoo's Nest
100 Years of Solitude
O'Neill's Plays
Othello
Our Town
The Outsiders
The Ox-Bow Incident
Paradise Lost
A Passage to India
The Pearl
The Pickwick Papers
The Picture of Dorian Gray
Pilgrim's Progress
The Plague
Plato's Euthyphro...
Plato's The Republic
Poe's Short Stories
A Portrait of the Artist...
The Portrait of a Lady
The Power and the Glory
Pride and Prejudice
The Prince
The Prince and the Pauper
A Raisin in the Sun
The Red Badge of Courage
The Red Pony
The Return of the Native
Richard II
Richard III
The Rise of Silas Lapham
Robinson Crusoe

Lightning Source UK Ltd.
Milton Keynes UK
18 November 2010

163033UK00002B/1/P